The Common Enemy

PAUL GITSHAM

ONE PLACE. MANY STORIES

This novel is entirely a work of fiction. The names, characters
and incidents portrayed in it are the work of the author's
imagination. Any resemblance to actual persons, living or
dead, events or localities is entirely coincidental.

HQ
An imprint of HarperCollins*Publishers* Ltd
1 London Bridge Street
London SE1 9GF

This paperback edition 2018

First published in Great Britain by
HQ, an imprint of HarperCollins*Publishers* Ltd 2018

Copyright © Paul Gitsham 2018

Paul Gitsham asserts the moral right to be
identified as the author of this work.
A catalogue record for this book is
available from the British Library.

ISBN: 9780008310165

MIX
Paper from
responsible sources
FSC™ **FSC® C007454**
www.fsc.org

This book is produced from independently certified FSC™ paper
to ensure responsible forest management.

For more information visit: www.harpercollins.co.uk/green

Typeset by Palimpsest Book Production Ltd, Falkirk, Stirlingshire
Printed and bound in Great Britain by
CPI Group (UK) Ltd, Croydon, CR0 4YY

All rights reserved. No part of this publication may be reproduced,
stored in a retrieval system, or transmitted, in any form or by any means,
electronic, mechanical, photocopying, recording or otherwise,
without the prior permission of the publishers.

This book is sold subject to the condition that it shall not, by way of trade
or otherwise, be lent, re-sold, hired out or otherwise circulated without
the publisher's prior consent in any form of binding or cover other than
that in which it is published and without a similar condition including this
condition being imposed on the subsequent purchaser.

Also by Paul Gitsham, featuring DCI Warren Jones

PAUL GITSHAM started his career as a biologist, working in such exotic locales as Manchester and Toronto. After stints as the world's most over-qualified receptionist and a spell making sure that international terrorists and other ne'er do wells hadn't opened a Junior Savings Account at a major UK bank (a job even less exciting than being a receptionist) he retrained as a Science teacher. He now spends his time passing on his bad habits and sloppy lab-skills to the next generation of enquiring minds.

Paul has always wanted to be a writer and his final report on leaving primary school predicted he'd be the next Roald Dahl! For the sake of balance it should be pointed out that it also said 'he'll never get anywhere in life if his handwriting doesn't improve'. Over twenty-five years later and his handwriting is worse than ever but millions of children around the world love him.*

You can learn more about Paul's writing at www.paulgitsham. com or www.facebook.com/dcijones

*This is a lie, just ask any of the pupils he has taught.

Also by Paul Gitsham, featuring DCI Warren Jones:

The Last Straw
No Smoke Without Fire
Blood is Thicker than Water (A DCI Warren Jones novella)
Silent as the Grave
A Case Gone Cold (A DCI Warren Jones novella)

To Cheryl – with me every step of the way!

Saturday 19th July

Prologue

Waste containers with sliding lids made the narrow alleyway even harder to navigate. Tommy Meegan bent over, hands on knees, breathing heavily. Behind him he could hear the sounds of fighting continuing. He smiled, baring his teeth, his blood singing from the adrenaline surging around his body.

It had gone better than he could have hoped for. He'd seen crews from the BBC, Sky News and ITN, all perfectly poised to capture the action when it finally kicked off.

Untucking his T-shirt, he bunched it up and used the front to wipe the sweat from his shaved head, leaving a red smear on the white of the St George's flag. He reached up, wincing as his fingers found the cut above his temple. He hoped the TV cameras had caught that. He had no idea what it was that had actually struck him, just that it had come from the crowd of anti-fascists loosely corralled behind the cordon of under-prepared riot police.

Already he was planning the evening's tweets and a press release for the website. A two-pronged strategy, he decided: they'd pin the attack on the Muslims and claim that the police hadn't done enough to protect their right to free speech.

He touched his head again, another idea forming. The cut was still bleeding, but it was little more than a nick. He'd need to do something about that. If he was going to garner any sympathy on the evening news he'd need some real war wounds.

He squinted at his watch; he was actually a few minutes early. It had been touch and go with the timing after the police had kept them on the bus. He'd been worried that he'd get to the alleyway too late. Fortunately, the protestors had finally broken through the police line and the party members had scattered every which way.

He'd found himself running alongside Bellies Brandon and been concerned that he wouldn't be able to find his way to his rendezvous unseen; his contact had made it very clear that he was to come alone. Fortunately, the fat bastard was so unfit Tommy had soon left him behind.

A whoop of sirens in the distance finally signalled the arrival of more riot police. Tommy smiled again. Assuming that all had gone to plan and everyone had done as they were told, all the party members should have left the scene long ago. The only fighting should be between the Muslim-lovers and the police. Even the left-wing, mainstream media couldn't bury that.

The alleyway remained silent. He pulled the battered Nokia from his back pocket – no new messages. He'd made certain to empty the inbox; he didn't want to make things too easy for the pigs if he got arrested.

The lack of any communications irritated him and worried him in equal measure. The promised reinforcements hadn't transpired, meaning he'd had to scrap some of his speech. And what if his contact had changed their meeting point or the time of their rendez-vous? He wished he had his smartphone with him so he could access his email or Facebook, but everyone knew that the little devices would betray you in a million different ways if they fell into the wrong hands. He'd have to trust that any changes to their plans would be sent the old-fashioned way, by text or phone call.

He wiped the back of his hand across his mouth, the adrenaline had made it dry. As excited as he was about the meeting, he hoped it wouldn't drag on. The beers on the coach that morning seemed a long time ago and he'd worked up a thirst. The landlord of The Feathers was an old mate, sympathetic to the cause. He'd treat them right until the bus arrived to take them home.

The sound of a boot scraping the tarmac behind him caused him to spin quickly, bringing his hand up into a boxer's stance. He squinted at the newcomer.

'Why are you dressed like that?' Tommy asked. 'What's that in your hand?'

Sunday 20th July

Chapter 1

'Tommy Meegan, leader of the British Allegiance Party, found stabbed in the alleyway between the Fry and Tuck chip shop and the Sparkles nail bar.'

DCI Warren Jones pointed to the mugshot glaring across the crowded briefing room. The face was that of a shaven-headed, middle-aged white man sporting a few days of dirty yellow stubble. The man's file on the Police National Computer didn't detail if the missing front tooth was a casualty of the same incident that that had left a three-inch scar on his cheek or the same fight that had re-shaped his nose. The headshot extended to shoulder level, showing the top of a Union flag tattoo poking out of his T-shirt.

The 8 a.m. briefing was even more crowded than usual, with many of the evening shift still in attendance. The update was the third that Warren had given in the past twelve hours. The snatched sleep between two and five had been supplemented by several cups of strong coffee, but his brain was starting to feel mushy.

He glanced at the front row, then wished he hadn't. Ordinarily the only uniform visible in Middlesbury CID belonged to his immediate superior, Detective Superintendent John Grayson, and even he reserved his dress jacket and flat cap for formal events such as press conferences and visits by senior brass. Assistant Chief Constable Mohammed Naseem certainly qualified as senior brass, as did the two chief superintendents, tablet computers resting on their laps.

Warren took a sip of water and continued.

'Mr Meegan spent thirty-nine years on this planet, with a total of eleven residing at Her Majesty's pleasure for football hooliganism and racially aggravated assault. For the past three years he has been chief spokesperson for the British Allegiance Party. I'll not go into too much background detail about that for the moment, I'll leave that to Inspector Theodore Garfield of the Hate Crime Intelligence Unit.'

Warren switched slides, immediately noticing a small typo on the second line of the timeline. He cringed inside, hoping nobody else saw it – or if they did, that they were generous enough to see it in the context of almost twenty-four hours on shift.

'These are the facts as we know them.

'At midday yesterday morning a coach containing forty-three supporters of the British Allegiance Party, including Meegan, his younger brother, Jimmy, and other senior members, arrived in Middlesbury after setting out from Romford, Essex. As you are no doubt aware, they were due to hold a protest and march against the proposed Middlesbury Mosque and Community Centre, referred to by some as a "super mosque".'

Warren switched briefly to a photograph of twenty or so men posing in front of a single-decker coach, like a touring pub football team. All were white, most with shaven heads, and they sported a remarkable collection of tattoos between them. All wore England football shirts or T-shirts with the stylised version of the Union flag that had been filling the rolling news channels for the past few hours. If nothing else, the British Allegiance Party had brand recognition now.

'They tweeted this along with the hashtag #NoSuperMosque on several of their social media accounts.' Warren used the laser pointer to circle a face in the centre. 'There's Tommy holding the banner with Jimmy, his brother next to him. These are the less camera-shy members; there are a similar number out of shot.'

He flicked back to the timeline. 'They were met on arrival by riot control police and led to the agreed rally point. As I am sure you already know, their plans to march down Sparrow Hawk Road, where the current Middlesbury Islamic Centre is located, were blocked by the city council, so they agreed to a symbolic march to the council offices before holding a rally then dispersing. As I'm sure you also already know, the Islamic Centre caught fire yesterday afternoon at the same time that the BAP were holding their rally. I don't believe in coincidences and so DI Sutton will be running a separate but linked investigation that he'll brief you on after this one is concluded.'

Warren took another sip of water.

'The demonstration was supposed to start at midday but was delayed after there were problems clearing the route of protestors.' Warren moved on quickly. The blame game for what happened later had already started and he wanted nothing to do with it. As far as he was concerned Tommy Meegan's murder, and the fire, were where the responsibility of CID started and ended.

'Eventually they made it to the front of the council building where they set up their stall.' Another photograph, this time the image was time-stamped and had the constabulary's logo in the corner. 'As you can see, a number of those present, including Tommy Meegan and his brother, addressed their supporters with loudhailers.' Another photograph, taken at a wider angle, showed the gathering encircled by a ring of fluorescent-jacketed officers, arms linked against a much larger crowd of protestors.

'As you know, there was a vigorous counter-protest held by a wide range of anti-fascist and anti-racism groups.' Vigorous was an understatement. 'Unfortunately, protestors managed to breach the police line and confronted the BAP supporters directly.' The next photograph was taken from a helmet-mounted camera.

11

'This is the last photo we currently have of Tommy Meegan before he disappeared and his body was found.'

The image was blurry, but showed the man brawling with a masked protestor. His face was split by a huge toothy grin and despite the cut on his forehead, it was obvious that the former football hooligan was loving every second of the confrontation. The time stamp read 14:36:11.

'As you can imagine, the scene was pretty chaotic and it was some hours before order was restored. Eight BAP supporters and seventeen protestors were arrested at the scene, with the rest disappearing into the surrounding streets.

'It looks as though there was some contingency planning on the part of the BAP as they eventually regrouped at The Feathers pub.' The bar was a dive frequented by the sort of clientele that would welcome members of the BAP with open arms.

'When did they realise Tommy Meegan was missing?'

As usual it was Detective Sergeant David Hutchinson who asked the first question.

'Apparently his brother tried to ring him at about 4 p.m., but the phone went straight to voicemail. He wasn't worried at first, he figured he was either in custody or taking cover somewhere. He and a couple of others rang him again between four and five and eventually assumed that he had been arrested. They already knew that at least some of their friends were in the back of a police van.'

'So nobody raised the alarm?'

'No, although I don't think that's too surprising. I doubt their first instinct would be to call the police. Besides which, they were enjoying the hospitality of The Feathers. They weren't planning on going anywhere for a few hours.'

'When was the body found?'

'The switchboard received a call at 6.31 from the owner of the chip shop to the left of the alleyway. They'd closed for a few hours when the trouble kicked off and were putting the bins out prior to reopening when they found him.'

Warren changed slide to one showing a wide angle shot of a narrow gap between a fish and chip shop and a nail and hair bar. Large waste bins took up three quarters of the width, leaving barely enough room for a large man to squeeze past. Blue and white crime scene tape demarked the entrance. A large pool of dark red blood was clearly visible.

'So we have a gap of almost four hours between the last known photograph of him and his body being discovered. Do we have a time of death yet?' This time it was Detective Constable Gary Hastings who asked the question. The young officer was currently applying for promotion to sergeant and was no doubt desperate to ask a question in the presence of senior officers. Unfortunately, he was standing at the back and nobody bothered to turn around to see who had spoken.

'I'm afraid the weather was so warm that his core temperature had yet to fall by a significant amount, DC Hastings. The pathologist may be a bit more helpful after the post-mortem is completed, but I doubt we'll narrow the window of opportunity very much.'

Even if ACC Naseem didn't know Hastings' face, Warren could at least name-drop the young officer.

'What about cause of death?' asked DC Karen Hardwick.

'Preliminary finding is stabbing; you can see how much blood was lost. He has some other superficial cuts and bruises that may have arisen during the riot. Again, the PM will tell us more.'

'What about CCTV?' DSI Grayson was the questioner now.

'We've pulled the footage from all of the cameras on the high street and all the businesses in the vicinity, but, as you can see, there are significant blind spots.'

A simple, top-down line drawing of the alleyway and the surrounding street replaced the photograph. The locations of fixed cameras were marked, along with arcs showing their fields of view.

'Unfortunately, there was only one camera covering the

opening of the alleyway and none at the rear. Irritatingly that camera was broken a couple of days ago and hadn't been repaired.'

ACC Naseem shifted slightly in his chair. 'Premeditation?'

'A good question, sir. It was taken out by a brick on Thursday night. Since there were no break-ins or crimes reported in the area, it was logged as petty vandalism and no one attended.'

'I hope that oversight has been addressed, DCI Jones.'

Warren let the implied rebuke slide; pointing out that the unit's strategic priorities placed low-level criminal damage well down the list would have been unwise, given that several of the people responsible for deciding those priorities were seated in the room.

'Yes, sir. We're looking at other cameras in the vicinity from that time period to see if we can identify the culprit.'

'What is the status of the crime scene?'

'The crime scene investigators are still there, doing a fingertip search for the murder weapon. We've blocked off most of the town centre because we aren't sure what route Mr Meegan took to the alleyway. Sunday trading laws mean we have the area to ourselves for another couple of hours, but I'll need authorisation to keep the area closed much longer.'

Naseem nodded to Grayson.

Warren clicked to the blank slide that signalled the end of the presentation.

'It's going to be a big investigation, people. We have a team from HQ down in Welwyn Garden City joining us later to boost our numbers. In addition, the fire that broke out at the Islamic Centre at about the same time has been confirmed as suspicious. It looks as if it might also be upgraded to homicide if two victims sheltering in the centre when it caught fire don't pull through.'

'How likely do you think it is that the fire was linked with Tommy Meegan's murder?' asked the Superintendent sitting to the left of ACC Naseem. 'Could it have been tit-for-tat?'

'Based on the timings, it looks as though a direct retaliation either way is unlikely, ma'am. However I believe that some sort of link is likely.'

'Thank you, DCI Jones.' Naseem stood up and turned to address the assembled officers.

'As you all know, it takes a lot to get me out of my office.' A few polite chuckles passed around the room. 'Unfortunately, this is going to be a big deal. I think we can all agree that the death of Tommy Meegan is no great loss to humanity, but his murder is going to cause us significant problems going forwards. Middlesbury's a small town, with pretty good community relations for the most part, but this could cause all manner of trouble. You don't need me to tell you that what is likely to happen if it transpires that the fire at the Islamic Centre and the protest march are linked. You also don't need me to tell you that yesterday's counter-protest policing didn't go to plan. Clearly, not enough resources were deployed. The decision was then made to reassign other resources, leaving the Islamic Centre vulnerable.

'The press are all over us. We'll be announcing a review in due course but in the meantime I want to make it absolutely clear that all communication with the media goes through the press office.' He fixed the room with a glare. 'Anybody caught going off-message with members of the fourth estate will be in my office explaining themselves. That includes social media. Keep your mouths shut and stick to posting pictures of kittens on Facebook.'

A mutter of assent rippled around the room. Warren hoped the rebuke would have effect, these days one ill-thought tweet could go viral and end a career.

With that, Naseem retook his seat and the next speaker stood up.

'Morning, everybody, I'm Theo Garfield from Hertfordshire Constabulary's Hate Crime Intelligence Unit. I liaise with the National Crime Agency and other groups such as the Football

Intelligence Unit and the Social Media Intelligence Unit. I'm here to make sure that you have all the information you need about the late Mr Meegan and his band of merry men and to place some of yesterday afternoon's events into context for you.'

Theo Garfield was a whip-thin man with a shaved head and dark olive complexion. His accent remained resolutely Merseyside, although it was clear that he had been living in the south for some years. He too was armed with a PowerPoint presentation, although his was a lot slicker than Warren's.

'As you are aware, Mr Meegan was the spokesperson for the British Allegiance Party, or BAP as it is commonly known; apparently all the good names were taken.' Garfield smiled briefly. 'They tried a couple of other three letter acronyms, but were threatened with legal action if they didn't stop using them. Not that their current name is without its problems Allegiance is a difficult word to spell and so Unite Against Fascism have bought the web domain names with the most common misspellings and redirect lost visitors to their own site.'

Laughter rippled around the room.

'BAP are a motley bunch. As always with these organisations, the hardcore wouldn't fill more than a minibus, but they can muster a coachload for special occasions, and their numbers appear to be increasing. Pretty much everyone who turned up yesterday was already in our files. Almost everyone on that bus has at least one conviction for violent assault.'

The slide changed to a photograph of Tommy Meegan and his brother in a pub, arm-in-arm, wearing England football shirts and holding half-empty pint glasses aloft.

'This was taken a few years ago, probably during the 2012 European Championships – we know it's not this year's World Cup because they are celebrating a win.' This prompted more laughter. 'The driving force behind the party are the two brothers, Tommy and younger brother Jimmy. Local boys, they went to school in Middlesbury before they moved down to

Essex. This weekend was supposed to be a bit of a homecoming for them.

'Tommy has multiple arrests for racially aggravated assault, but he's an absolute charmer compared to Jimmy who has spent more time since his eighteenth birthday inside than out. Like father, like son. Football hooliganism, racially aggravated assault, beating up homosexuals… you name it, he's been done for it and there's almost certainly a whole lot more besides.'

The slide switched to a photograph of an older man. Even without the bent features of his two sons, the family resemblance was immediately clear. 'Meet the late, unlamented Ray Meegan. A veteran of the Seventies' and Eighties' hooligan scene he also did time for armed robbery. In fact, he was wanted in connection with an attack on a post office when he dropped dead of a heart attack seven years ago.'

He smiled. 'The family tried to talk down the far-right connections and play the victim when the local paper interviewed them after anti-fascist protestors gatecrashed the funeral, but a half-page photograph of the coffin in the background draped in swastika-shaped wreaths kind of scuppered that.'

Garfield was an engaging speaker and the team were enjoying the break from the typical dry presentations, however Warren got the impression that if he let him, the man would chatter on all day.

'You said that we know who the hardcore of the party are?'

'Yeah. The party has only existed in its current form for about five years and most of its founding members came from other organisations that we were tracking. Ideologically it is not a political party and is unashamedly racist. The far-right scene has been undergoing serious ructions in the past decade or so with many of the slightly more moderate believers joining quasi-political parties such as the BNP, the EDL or, more recently, UKIP.

'BAP on the other hand claims to have no belief or faith in the democratic process and draws support from the real nasty

17

end of the political spectrum, including former members of Combat 18 and the National Front. They are openly affiliated to some of the European neo-Nazi parties, such as the Austrian Freedom Party and populist anti-Islamist movements, such as Pegida.

'Yesterday's march was their biggest event to date. Apart from a few so-called "direct action" events, most of their presence is internet-based.'

Garfield switched slides. 'They may be uneducated thugs for the most part, but somebody in the party has clearly been on a few social media training courses. Their website is pretty slick, but their main strength lies in their use of Twitter, Facebook, Instagram and the like.

'The big social media firms remove some of their more racially charged and offensive posts, but for the most part they stick within the rules. Perhaps more insidious are their subtler campaigns. This is typical…' He clicked to another slide, a picture of a homeless person and a banner urging viewers to 'share if you think it's a disgrace that former soldiers starve whilst immigrants get free housing'. Warren recognised the image from his own Facebook feed. He'd deleted it without sharing.

'They have several dozen known accounts, some with openly provocative names such as "Keep Britain British" and others with more innocuous titles such as "Proud to be British", sharing harmless patriotic fare. The First World War commemorations have been a real party for them, with lots of pictures of poppies and young Tommies. We're expecting a major offensive in the run-up to Remembrance Sunday with attempts to hijack the poppy appeal.'

'Why? Surely most of the people sharing these posts have no idea who's behind them and would be appalled if they knew?' The tone of the questioner, sat somewhere towards the back, suggested that they may be reconsidering some of the pages that they had personally liked or shared.

Garfield gave a shrug, 'Nobody's really sure. Some of it's plainly propaganda and the number of shares – which is in the tens of thousands for some of these posts – probably helps them claim to be on the side of the "silent majority". We think it might also be a form of market research, using the number of likes, shares and retweets as a means of gauging popularity for different causes. They might also get a bit of click-through revenue from people visiting their websites. As to its effectiveness in terms of active members, it's hard to tell. They operate a lot of sock puppets – fake accounts – so it appears as if they have more supporters than they actually do.'

Warren cleared his throat slightly, he didn't want to end up spending all morning discussing the far-right's social media strategy.

Taking his cue, Garfield switched to the next slide.

'On the opposite side of the argument to the BAP, we have the counter-protestors. It's early days, but part of my team is also trying to identify as many of them as possible. Somebody killed Tommy Meegan and it's as good a place to start as any. There were a lot more there than we expected, so we'll have our work cut out for us.'

That was something of an understatement. From what Warren had gleaned so far, the number of BAP supporters was as predicted, but the counter-protest was significantly larger than anticipated. It had been sheer weight of numbers that had caused the lines to collapse and it was little more than good luck that more people hadn't been injured or even killed.

'We're compiling a list and scrutinising CCTV for known faces, but we know that a lot of attendees were either concerned locals, or not known to us. We have a couple of super-recognisers helping us, but the seasoned veterans were wearing masks or had their faces and tattoos covered. Aside from the usual agitators there were also protestors from more mainstream leftist groups, people showing solidarity with the local Muslim community, and lots of students, none of whom are likely to be in our files.'

'Any indicators from social media about who may have wanted to kill Meegan?' asked Warren.

'It's hard to tell. BAP members, particularly the Meegans, get so many death threats posted on their blogs, Facebook pages and Twitter feeds they hardly bother to block them anymore. Where possible, we're identifying and cross-referencing accounts with the list of attendees, but it's slow going.'

Warren thanked him, feeling slightly dejected. The power of the internet had transformed policing in recent years, with many officers like Mags Richardson in his own unit becoming experts in its use. However, that power was also its downfall. The chances were good that buried amongst the vast amounts of data being collected were hints to the identity of Tommy Meegan's killer. But finding those clues could take months or even years of sifting. Quite aside from the huge budget implications, Warren didn't have months or years. The local and national media were already reporting a spike in inflammatory social media posts, from the far-right, the Muslim community and anti-racism campaigners. Even if Warren and his team had yet to find a direct link between the fire and the protest march and its aftermath, the public at large were already conflating the two events. Unless something was done soon Middlesbury was facing a bloodbath.

Chapter 2

After the briefing, Warren was summoned to DSI Grayson's office. The privacy blinds were drawn on the door, so he had no idea who or what was awaiting him when he entered.

'Sirs,' Warren greeted the seated officers. There were no spare chairs, so Warren found himself standing like a naughty schoolboy.

'Coffee?'

That was a good sign, the Assistant Chief Constable didn't offer you some of John Grayson's finest roast if you were in trouble.

'That'd be lovely, sir.'

As one of the ACC's assistants poured Warren a cup, he got down to business.

'Let's be blunt, Warren. Yesterday was a colossal cock-up on several levels, not least the murder of Tommy Meegan. We massively underestimated the number of counter-protestors and had to pull in reinforcements from across the region. The riot was bad enough, but a politically charged murder and an arson attack on a vulnerable target that we should have been protecting… we dropped the ball big-time.'

Warren stole a glance at DSI Grayson, who looked grim. The problem had landed squarely in his lap – which by extension meant Warren's. The subtext was clear. Hertfordshire Constabulary was already looking foolish; now it was time to clean up the mess, and do it quickly. The grapevine was already buzzing with speculation that the officer in charge was likely to fall on her sword. Would the same be expected of Grayson – even Warren – if he failed to deliver?

'Monitoring from the Social Media Intelligence Unit indicated tensions were already running high before the march, and now the far-right have gone ballistic,' continued Naseem. 'They're already deciding how to capitalise on yesterday's events. These buggers couldn't decide on the colour of the sky normally, they hate each other almost as much as they hate non-whites and homosexuals, but yesterday's killing is uniting them. The same goes for a lot of the anti-fascist organisations; we're already seeing calls for mass protests if we don't start making arrests over the Islamic Centre fire soon. More than a few keyboard warriors have said that what happened to Tommy Meegan was long overdue and have started naming other far-right activists as potential targets.'

The room settled into a leaden silence; eventually Garfield spoke up.

'This time of year is full of significant dates for the far-right. They were originally planning on marching on the seventh of July, the anniversary of the London bombings. I guess they figured they could try and make a link between the proposed new mosque and Islamic extremism. We blocked that as too provocative. Then they tried to march on the first of August. Obviously we're wise to that and said no.'

Warren evidently didn't hide his ignorance fully.

'The first of August, written 1/8 represents the initials of Adolph Hitler. It's where Combat 18 get their name from.'

'I see.'

'So they suggested the next day. We almost let them have it, until we ran it through the computer – the eightieth anniversary

22

of Hitler's rise to Fuhrer. Finally, we settled on Saturday the nineteenth of July as comparatively harmless.'

'OK.'

Warren didn't quite see what they were so concerned about, surely the issue had been fixed?

'The problem is that whilst we could stop a march through town on the grounds that it was likely to cause a breach of the peace, they're already calling for his funeral to be held on August the first.'

'Shit.'

'Exactly. It'll be a magnet for every right-winger in Europe. He's already being eulogised as some sort of bloody martyr.'

'Can we block the funeral?'

ACC Naseem snorted. 'That'd be political dynamite. Can you imagine the reaction – "Police block grieving family's funeral"? No, that's a decision well above the pay grade of anyone in this room.'

'Home Secretary?' asked Grayson

'You'd think, but we're less than a year away from a general election, I wouldn't bet on a speedy decision. Nevertheless, Mrs May has let it be known that she is following events closely.'

Warren's head spun. He'd known the repercussions of the previous day's murder were likely to be significant but he'd had no idea what was at stake. And he really wasn't happy about the Home Secretary taking an interest. That sort of interest could end an officer's career pretty quickly.

'So where does that leave us?'

'We need to know who was responsible for the murder as soon as possible to manage the fallout. If it was one of the protestors, it'll be bad enough. If it turns out it was a member of the local Muslim community seizing an opportunity, the consequences don't bear thinking about.' He paused. 'Without wanting to pre-empt DI Sutton's briefing, are we treating the fire as arson?'

'From witness reports, it's looking that way.'

'Great, that's all we need.'

Naseem removed his glasses and rubbed the bridge of his nose. Warren watched him carefully over the top of his coffee cup.

At first glance it seemed strange that a small, first-response unit like Middlesbury would be taking the lead in such a politically sensitive operation, but it didn't surprise him. Ostensibly, Middlesbury was most suited to coordinate investigations on its own turf; the CID unit's intimate local knowledge made it ideal for dealing with crimes taking place at this end of the county, miles away from the Major Crime Unit's headquarters in Welwyn Garden City. But there was more to it. Yet more cutbacks to the policing budget were making Middlesbury CID's special status harder and harder to justify. A successful resolution to such a big, high-profile case would do wonders for the unit's long-term future. The question was, were they being given an opportunity to prove themselves or handed enough rope to hang themselves?

Naseem's face was unreadable. Beside him, Grayson looked similarly impassive, but his knuckles were slightly white as they gripped his coffee mug. Naseem turned to Grayson. 'Blank cheque, John.' His mouth twisted in disgust. 'This needs sorting in the next ten days or we're looking at the Brixton riots all over again.'

So there it was: make or break time for Middlesbury CID – and the career of John Grayson. Solve the murder quickly and efficiently and Grayson was one step closer to his next promotion; mess it up and it was the end of Middlesbury CID's independence and perhaps John Grayson. And, quite possibly, Warren Jones.

Chapter 3

DI Tony Sutton dropped wearily into the comfy chair opposite Warren's desk.

'The fire at the Islamic Centre is almost certainly arson; I'll be meeting the fire investigators later today.'

'Is there a final casualty count?'

'There were about thirty in the centre at the time, almost all women and children or older folk. They managed to get upstairs, where the fire service rescued them. A total of eight were treated for smoke inhalation, with two remaining in hospital. An eighty-nine-year-old woman already in poor health is in intensive care alongside a three-year-old boy.

'Fortunately, lunchtime prayers had finished a couple of hours before and it wasn't a Friday. Karen and I will be visiting the imam in charge later, but he's already said that ironically they were in there because of the trouble brewing in town. The centre has invested heavily in security in recent years.'

'Speaking of security, do we have any CCTV?'

Sutton smiled humourlessly. 'It's funny you should ask that. The CCTV at the front of the building wasn't working.'

Warren sat up slightly straighter. 'Really? Can I guess what happened?'

'Be my guest.'

'It was broken by a brick on Thursday evening.'

'Half right, Wednesday evening.'

* * *

Tommy Meegan's body had been found almost eighteen hours ago, but this was Warren's first opportunity to visit the crime scene. Even in a small, specialist CID unit like Middlesbury, with its unique role as a first responder to local crimes, most of the legwork was performed by those with the rank of Inspector or below. Warren's immediate superior, DSI Grayson, seemed to only leave his office to play golf or schmooze with the senior ranks at the force's headquarters in Welwyn Garden City.

At Warren's last appraisal, it had been suggested that he needed to practise delegating more. His wife, Susan, had certainly been pleased; Warren's first few cases at Middlesbury had placed him – and his loved ones – directly in the firing line and she had questioned on more than one occasion why he needed to be so hands-on.

The problem was that Warren missed the excitement that came with solving a case. When he'd moved to Middlesbury three years previously, it had been to further his career. There were precious few DCI opportunities on the horizon in the West Midlands Police and the sudden vacancy at Middlesbury had seemed too good to be true. He'd applied and then accepted the post immediately.

The unit's unusual position would provide Warren with a perfect mix of both smaller, community-style policing and management, with the safety net of a senior officer directly above him. A couple of years in that sort of environment and he would be ready to move on.

It hadn't quite worked that way. Even assuming he hadn't permanently blotted his copybook after the Delmarno case two years ago, he'd realised that he liked Middlesbury. His predecessor, Gavin Sheehy, had once described leading the unit as the best job he'd ever had. Warren had disagreed with Sheehy over much – but he was being won over on that score.

It had been made clear that solving the death of Tommy Meegan was to be Warren's number one priority and he had interpreted that to mean 'leave the office and get your hands dirty'.

But not literally. The body might have been removed, but the alleyway was still an active crime scene and Warren wasn't getting a close look without appropriate precautions. The CSIs were still looking for trace evidence and so gloves and booties weren't enough, particularly when TV camera crews with zoom lenses were in attendance. The last thing they needed was for some defence solicitor to claim evidence gathering procedures weren't properly followed and use TV footage to demand that key exhibits be declared inadmissible.

The plastic-coated paper suits were far from ideal attire on a hot July day. The face mask trapped the heat from his breath and within moments he was licking sweat off his top lip. Suddenly his air-conditioned office seemed a lot more attractive…

Stepping out from the police van that he'd changed in, Warren glanced towards the gathered news crews. Thankfully, nobody seemed to have registered his presence. Warren was hardly a celebrity but a few of the local hacks would recognise him and he had no particular desire to have his face splashed all over the *Middlesbury Reporter*'s online edition, with the attendant excuse to rehash old stories from years ago. Perhaps the face mask had its uses after all.

'DCI Jones, what brings you out here on such a fine day?'

As always, the jollity of Crime Scene Manager Andy Harrison conflicted with the sombre nature of his job. But given what he saw on a daily basis, Warren figured it was probably a survival mechanism. Naturally, the burly Yorkshireman didn't offer to shake his hand.

'I'm here to make sure you aren't cutting any corners, Andy.'

To Warren's surprise, the man's eyes – the only part of him visible above his mask – narrowed slightly.

'It's not us who's cutting corners, sir.'

Warren paused before realising what the man was referring to.

'DetectIt Forensic Services?'

'I caught one of them using a box of out-of-date saline swabs to take blood samples from the patch next to the body.'

'How can a saline swab be out-of-date?'

'That's exactly what he said. And of course he's right, but any defence counsel worth his salt would move to have that evidence ruled inadmissible.'

Warren shuddered. 'What happened?'

'Fortunately, the victim bled like a stuck pig so there was plenty of blood to go around and the lad hadn't started taking samples from some of the tiny specks we found further up the alleyway. I got him to fetch a fresh box and retake the swab.'

'Shit.' Warren lowered his voice. 'Is this going to be a problem, Andy?'

The veteran CSI sighed. 'At the scene I can keep an eye on the newbies and we're whipping them into shape, but God only knows what happens when the samples go off to the lab. The Forensic Science Service might not have been perfect, but at least we knew who was doing the testing. Some of these new private companies didn't even exist eighteen months ago. Their only qualification seems to be that they're cheap.'

Warren felt a tightening in his gut. The thought that such a high-stakes case could be scuppered by a cut-rate CSI with a box of out-of-date swabs wasn't worth contemplating.

'Thanks for the heads up, Andy. In the meantime, talk me through what you've got.'

'The victim was probably standing close to those bins when he was stabbed. There's some spatter consistent with arterial spurt and from the blade when it was pulled out.' He picked up a tablet computer with a removable plastic coating and started scrolling through images on its screen.

'See this picture of that bin over there? The angle of the droplets suggests they were probably flicked off the tip of the blade when it was withdrawn. The droplets then continue in that direction—' he pointed down the alleyway in the opposite direction to the shop front, where a series of numbered markers had been placed on the tarmac '—with a pattern consistent with dripping—' he turned a half-circle on the spot, gesturing back towards the main road '—and our victim appears to have crawled in that direction, presumably away from his attacker. He didn't get far; that big patch of blood behind that bin is where we found the body.'

The blood smears were no more than three metres in length and thick. Warren pictured the victim dragging himself away from the person who'd just stabbed him. Another few metres and he'd have been visible to passers-by in the high street. Could he have survived if somebody had found him and called for help? Without realising, he'd asked the question out loud.

'That's the sort of question that can only be answered by a pathologist, sir. But if I had to speculate… it's doubtful. I think it's a miracle he got as far as he did.'

Warren felt a brief flash of sympathy. Tommy Meegan had been a deeply unpleasant individual, but in those last few moments he was nothing more than a human being facing death – and probably terrified. Did he feel any remorse for the life he'd led? Warren shook off the feeling and turned to point back at the waste container with the blood spatter.

'Is that where you think the murder weapon is?'

Harrison nodded. 'We've finished sweeping the area around it for trace and we're about to get in and start looking for it. Unfortunately, somebody from the nail bar dumped a load of rubbish in there shortly before the owners of the chippy discovered the victim behind their own bin. If the weapon was dumped in there it will be buried under half a ton of hair clippings and fake nails.'

Warren sighed.

'Great, that screws the hair and fibre analysis.'

Visiting the scene probably hadn't told him anything that he didn't already know, and the high-resolution photographs that Harrison promised to send him would tell him far more than his eyes ever could, but it gave him a sense of what had taken place.

'What about clothing?'

'It was an arterial cut and he would have been pumping blood under high pressure, so I doubt the killer got away without at least some transfer. We'll be looking for any discarded clothing. Failing that, find me a suspect and give me access to his laundry bin and shoe collection. We'll find something.'

Chapter 4

Imam Danyal Mehmud's eyes were bloodshot and the shaking of his hands attested to the adrenaline he was running on. Karen Hardwick and Tony Sutton were seated in the imam's living room, two streets over from the remains of the community centre. The air in the street still smelled of smoke. The house was a two-bedroom affair with a modest front room whose walls were covered in a mixture of family pictures and framed scripture.

'Is that the *Frozen* fan?' Sutton nodded towards a picture of a smiling infant in a light summer dress. She hadn't been smiling ten minutes ago when her father had switched the cartoon off and sent her upstairs so they could speak in peace.

'Yes, that's Fatima. If I hear "Let it Go" one more time... she's obsessed.'

'My niece is about the same age,' said Hardwick. 'At least choosing a birthday present was easy this year.' She paused. 'Is the little boy in the picture with her the other victim, Abbas?' Both children were dark-haired, with light brown skin and faces smeared with ice cream.

'Yes, they're cousins. My sister's little boy. They're almost exactly the same age.'

'So that means Mrs Fahmida must be your grandmother?'

31

Mehmud nodded sadly.

'I'm very sorry, I had no idea.'

The man in front of them was in his late thirties, wearing a white dishdasha over his jeans and trainers. By all accounts he'd been awake for pretty much the entire past twenty-four hours, comforting his congregation and, Sutton now realised, dealing with his own shock and grief. He was clearly running on adrenaline and little else, given that he was still fasting during daylight hours to mark the Muslim holy month of Ramadan.

'Have you heard anything more from the hospital?' asked Hardwick.

Mehmud shrugged helplessly. 'Nani is in intensive care. They aren't very hopeful. Abbas is poorly but stable. We are praying for his recovery, *inshallah*.'

Mehmud stood up suddenly as if filled with an energy he didn't know what to do with.

'I haven't told Fatima anything yet. I'll wait to see what happens in the next twenty-four hours or so. If he… well, she'll be devastated. My sister and I are very close and Fatima and Abbas are like brother and sister.'

'I realise that it's been a trying time but could you take me through what happened that day,' asked Sutton after a respectful pause.

'We knew all about the BAP march of course, but I'd tried to persuade people to keep their heads down and not get involved.' Mehmud shrugged. 'Not everyone listened. We found out that the BAP were due to arrive about midday. It was easy enough to find their plans on the internet. We'd spoken about it the day before at Friday prayers. We had a higher than usual attendance; there were some brothers and sisters that I didn't recognise.'

'People from outside Middlesbury?' asked Hardwick.

'I think so. Not many, but I got the feeling that they weren't there by chance.'

'You think they'd arrived specifically to join the counter-protest?'

'Yes. I tried to counsel against it – the last thing we as a community need is to be involved in violence, especially with the planning hearing for the mosque and community centre coming soon.'

'So what happened on Saturday?'

'There was an informal gathering here after dawn prayers. Some of the more *fiery* members of the congregation wanted to take part in the protest marches. A few went off to join in, but most stuck around until midday prayers.'

'What happened then?'

'A few more went to the protest and about half went back to lock up their shops and businesses. In the end there were about thirty, mostly women and children, who chose to stay here. I decided to lead by example and stick around.'

'Why did they stay?' asked Hardwick.

'They were scared. There were all sorts of rumours on the internet about Muslims being targeted on the street or having their houses vandalised. All nonsense, of course, but I decided that anybody who wanted to remain was welcome.'

He closed his eyes briefly. 'They should have been safe here. We locked the doors and there was a police car outside.' His voice cracked and his bottom lip started to tremble. 'But they weren't, were they? We were trapped like rats.'

'Tell us what happened inside the centre.'

'It was pretty tense. As the protests got more violent the BBC started to cover it and there was loads of activity on Twitter. We moved the older children upstairs with some toys and the rest of us stayed downstairs to watch the telly.' His voice hardened, and for the first time an edge of anger crept into his tone. 'We still thought we were safe. There was a police car up the street, and all of the action was happening in the town centre. Nobody told us the police car had…' He stopped, unable to continue the sentence.

'We haven't been able to get inside the centre yet,' said Sutton, 'so you'll have to help us with the layout. Where were you watching TV?'

'In the kitchen area, out the back. As you enter through the front door there are shelves for footwear and some sinks for ablutions, straight on is the kitchen, to the left the musallah, the prayer hall.'

'And where are the stairs?'

'To the right of the entrance.'

'And what do you have upstairs?'

'There are several rooms. The largest is a function room, then there is a storeroom, some bathrooms and another couple of rooms that we use for wedding guests to get changed etc.'

'Did you know everybody?' asked Hardwick.

'Yes, the visitors had all gone off to the march.'

'Did you see anybody strange hanging around outside?'

'There were a few brothers outside, but they left eventually.'

'What do you mean by brothers?' questioned Sutton.

'Other Muslims.'

'How did you know they were Muslims if you didn't know them?'

Mehmud blinked. 'Well, they were dressed in *thawb* with full beards and well, you know, they were Asian.'

Sutton decided to move on.

'When did you realise the building was on fire?'

'About two-thirty we heard breaking glass out the front. I told everyone to head into the musallah, since it doesn't have any windows. However, as we went into the hallway, we saw that the area in front of the door was on fire. I told the women to go through the kitchen and leave through the back door, whilst me and the men ran to get the children.'

The man's eyes took on a faraway cast.

'The mats in front of the stairs were starting to catch, so I sent the rest of the men upstairs whilst I tried to put the blaze out with a fire extinguisher. And then my wife came back through to tell me that the back door wouldn't open.'

He closed his eyes briefly and his voice dropped to a whisper.

'I didn't know what to do. We couldn't stay downstairs and I couldn't put the fire out. So I sent them all upstairs to join the others. We'd called the fire brigade and I figured they'd be able to rescue us from the top floor more easily.' His voice broke slightly. 'The smell was horrible. Some of the shoes had caught fire and there was thick black smoke everywhere. Nani couldn't get up the stairs unaided though, she's almost ninety, I had to carry her. By the time we got to the top floor she'd passed out and Abbas was having an asthma attack.'

He looked imploringly at Sutton. 'Did I do the right thing? Perhaps I should have gone and tried to force the back door open instead. Then she could have got out. But if I'd done that, maybe we'd have ended up trapped downstairs.'

'I don't know,' said Sutton softly, 'but I do know that your quick thinking made a big difference. You bought everyone valuable minutes for the fire service to arrive.'

It was the best he could offer.

Mehmud smiled his thanks.

'Before we go any further, do you have any thoughts about who might be responsible?'

For the first time since they'd arrived, the man's politeness slipped.

'Bloody obvious, isn't it? A coach-load of fascists and Islamophobes turn up in the town centre and distract the police, then we get torched. It doesn't take a rocket scientist.'

'We're keeping an open mind at the moment,' said Sutton, cautiously.

Mehmud took a deep breath. 'Of course, you're right. I apologise.'

'Have you had any other incidents recently?' Hardwick took over.

Mehmud shrugged helplessly. 'Some graffiti appeared a couple of nights ago. I didn't have any paint to cover it up. Before that, nothing really. We get on pretty well with the neighbours. I know that some of my brothers and sisters have been insulted in the street, especially if they are wearing the veil, but Middlesbury is a lot better than some places. The community centre hasn't been attacked in years, not since nine-eleven or the London bombings.'

Sutton looked at his notes. 'Can you remember what night the graffiti appeared?'

He thought for a moment. 'Wednesday night or Thursday morning, I think. We hosted a meal after sundown to celebrate breaking the day's fast. I locked up about midnight and there was nothing on the wall then.'

The same night the CCTV cameras had been vandalised.

Chapter 5

Visiting the newly bereaved was something that Warren never found easy. Today promised to be even trickier than usual.

To the casual observer, Middlesbury was a quiet, prosperous market town, populated by well-to-do professionals attracted by its semi-rural location, close proximity to Cambridge and Stevenage, and trains that could get you to central London in less than an hour.

All that was true – the house prices certainly favoured the upper-middle classes – but you only had to scratch the surface of anywhere to see its true character. A closer look showed the town's real inhabitants, its beating heart.

Just under half of Middlesbury's inhabitants earned less than the median adult wage for the UK. The proportion of residents claiming out-of-work or disability benefits were broadly in line with the regional average and the number of households requiring housing benefit was typical for a town of its size. But as is often the case, such raw statistics obscured the real story.

Three-quarters of Middlesbury's poorest households lived in a single area, known locally as the Chequers estate – the six tower blocks being named after Prime Ministers from the first half of the twentieth century.

The name was the grandest thing about Churchill Towers, the ten-storey block that Mary Meegan lived at the top of. Had it not been for the two uniformed officers standing conspicuously at the entrance to the building, Warren would have thought twice about leaving his car unattended in the only parking bay not occupied by either a police car or dumped furniture.

Warren peered up at the balconies jutting out of the side of the building. Some had washing on clothes horses, a few had pot plants. Most had people staring at him.

'Fuck the pigs!' spray-painted across the doors completed the montage.

'Ever get the feeling we aren't welcome here?' muttered Gary Hastings as he joined Warren.

The call button for the lift remained unlit and it was only the loud clanking and whining from the mechanism that reassured Warren that the stairs wouldn't be necessary. He almost wished he'd opted for the exercise when the elevator finally arrived. A potent smell of urine, stale beer and cigarette smoke – somebody had tried to burn the no smoking sticker – engulfed the two men as they climbed into the empty lift. Hastings beat him to the number ten button. Turning so that he could face the doors, Warren felt the soles of his shoes sticking to the linoleum flooring.

'Do you think that's dog?' asked Hastings, his face an even sicklier colour under the harsh fluorescent lighting. Warren eyed the sticky brown mess at the edge of the lift. 'I hope so.'

Apartment ten-fourteen was a dozen steps down the corridor. The uniformed police officer standing outside greeted Warren and Hastings politely, before ringing the doorbell and stepping to one side.

Warren didn't know what to expect when the door opened into the two-bedroom flat that Mary Meegan, her husband and their two boys had lived in since the late Seventies. Before he'd arrived, Warren had been prepared for everything from Nazi memorabilia and a swastika carpet to snarling Rottweilers and

St George's flag wallpaper. Then upon arrival at the tower block he'd feared he'd be stepping into a dwelling from one of those dreadful 'how clean is your home' filler programmes that Channel Four seemed so fond of.

He wasn't expecting tasteful floral-patterned wallpaper, deep, shag pile carpet and shelves of carefully chosen miniature porcelain figurines. The leather couch was plainly well used, but the polished wooden arms were evidence that the glass drinks coasters weren't just because Mrs Meegan had visitors. The building around her might be filthy and neglected but she clearly had her standards.

Mary Meegan was a smoker – that much was evident from the thick crevices that lined her face and the staining of her teeth. Nevertheless, the room smelt of air-freshener and furniture polish. A faint breeze carried the smell of cigarette smoke from the open balcony, where Mrs Meegan no doubt partook of her habit and banished similarly addicted visitors.

Through the window, Warren could see the backs of two men seated at a metal table, flanked by large earthenware flower pots containing lovingly maintained bonsai trees. Both had shaven heads. Both of them, he'd want to speak to.

'Mary, this is Detective Chief Inspector Jones.' The Family Liaison Officer was a young man with sympathetic eyes.

Mary Meegan turned her head slowly, almost dreamily. The FLO flicked his eyes towards the breakfast counter, where a bottle of whisky sat, half empty.

'Hello, Mrs Meegan. I'm DCI Jones and this is my colleague Detective Constable Hastings, we're part of the team that are investigating the death of your son. We're very sorry for your loss.'

'Bollocks.'

The speaker had emerged from a doorway that Warren assumed led to the bathroom.

Even without seeing the mugshots that morning, it was clear that this was the brother of the murdered man. Dressed in a white England football shirt and black tracksuit bottoms, he did nothing to hide the tattoos crawling up the side of his neck and covering his sinewy forearms. He stepped forward and Warren caught the whiff of cigarettes and whisky on his breath. He forced himself not to recoil.

'Jimmy Meegan, I presume?'

The man ignored him.

'Why are you around here, harassing my mum? You should be out there on the streets arresting the bloke that killed my brother.'

It wasn't exactly how Warren had planned to open the questioning, but he decided that since Meegan had brought it up, he may as well go with the flow.

'That's what we are intending to do. Perhaps you could help us with that. Do you have any suggestions about who may be responsible?'

Meegan stepped even closer.

'Take your pick, there's fucking hordes of them.'

Warren had to ask, but he already knew what the answer was going to be.

'The fucking Pakis. The Muslims, the Sikhs, the Jews, the place is full of them. Half the bastards live in this building. Go out there and start arresting them, you'll find who did it quick enough. Fingerprint them all and you'll probably solve most of the unsolved crimes in town.'

Out of the corner of his eye, he could see Hastings trying to keep a blank face. The Family Liaison Officer looked bored; no doubt he'd been hearing this all morning. Unfortunately, Jimmy Meegan was only just getting started.

Warren had dealt with racists a lot over his career. You didn't spend your early uniform years in such racially diverse cities as Coventry and Birmingham without encountering your fair share of bigots, from all communities. Sometimes it could be dealt with as a public order offence; a verbal warning about use of abusive and racially charged language would usually quieten most of the people he encountered. If that didn't work, and especially if alcohol was involved, handcuffs and the back of a police van would at least remove them from the scene and ultimately make them the custody sergeant's problem.

In circumstances such as this, the heavy-handed approach wasn't really appropriate. Warren recognised that Jimmy Meegan was grieving the death of his big brother. Furthermore, the dilated pupils, reddening of the nostrils, and the obsessive scratching of his left forearm suggested that a presumptive cocaine test on the traces of powder on the man's top lip would come back positive.

Warren chose his next words carefully, but before he could mouth them he was interrupted by an unexpected source.

'I've told you not to use that language in this house.'

Mary Meegan's voice was rough, but had the edge of one used to being obeyed. Jimmy Meegan's eyes flicked towards his mother. For a moment he looked as though he was going to protest, before he shrugged and stalked across the room to one of the armchairs, where he grabbed a grey hoodie.

'You know I'm right,' he muttered. 'Pigs don't care about us. They don't care who killed Tommy. We're an endangered species in our own country.' He sounded as if he was about to start again, but his mother silenced him with a glare.

'Boys, we're going to the pub.'

Ideally, Warren would have liked to interview them there and then, but he could see that Jimmy Meegan was not going to be any help and he decided he'd rather have him and his two cronies out of the way for the time being.

'Jimmy, I'd like to talk to you later. Do you have a number I can contact you on?'

Warren tried to make his tone as conciliatory as possible.

'He'll be here,' said Mary Meegan.

'And what about you gentlemen? I'm sure you have plenty of information you'd like to share.'

The two men entering the apartment from the balcony obviously shopped at the same clothing outlet as Jimmy Meegan, and shared his tastes in hair styling and body art. But that was where the similarities ended. The first of the men was hugely obese, his enormous belly straining through the T-shirt. His florid, sweat-spotted face and wheezing made Warren mentally bump him to the top of the interview list, if only so they could speak to him before he dropped dead of a massive coronary. He walked past Warren and Hastings without even looking at them.

His companion was exactly the opposite, the man looked almost emaciated. A gold earring in his right earlobe matched his right incisor, which flashed as he sneered at Warren. 'I'll make sure my assistant contacts your office to compare diaries.'

Warren resisted the urge to respond in kind. It didn't really matter if they refused to give their addresses, he recognised both men from the briefing notes he had read that morning. Harry 'Bellies' Brandon and Marcus 'Goldie' Davenport were well known and could easily be picked up for questioning back in Romford if necessary.

The police officers waited until the three thugs swaggered out the door, before turning back to Mary Meegan.

'As I was saying, Mrs Meegan, I'm very sorry for your loss and I promise you that my colleagues and I are doing everything we can to catch your son's killer.'

The older woman stared at the floor for a few moments without saying anything and Warren debated whether or not he needed to repeat himself. Perhaps a little louder – he'd just noticed the discreet hearing aid.

'Sit down and take the weight off. Can I get you boys a cup of tea?'

She started to get up. Warren blinked in surprise; he hadn't expected this. Before he could respond, the Family Liaison Officer spoke up.

'I'll get it, Mary.'

As the officer busied himself in the kitchen, Warren mentally changed tack. He'd been anticipating a hostile reception from Mrs Meegan – a woman who it was reported had experienced more than her fair share of run-ins with the police, albeit indirectly through her late husband and wayward sons. An offer of a sit down and a cup of tea was the last thing he'd expected.

'You know, they aren't bad boys. Not really.' The old woman's voice was gravelly and slightly wistful, but it had lost its dreamy quality. Warren detected no slurring and he suspected that whilst Mary Meegan may have had a glass of whisky to settle her nerves, most of the bottle had been consumed by her visitors.

She indicated towards a picture on the wall. 'It was him that made them the way they are.' The photograph of Ray Meegan enjoyed a prominent place above the three-bar electric fire. On the mantelpiece, flanked by yet more porcelain statuettes, a colour wedding photograph showed far younger versions of the man in the portrait and somebody immediately recognisable as Mary Meegan. Whilst Ray Meegan was never what you would call handsome, something that his lank moustache and purple velvet suit hardly helped, Mary Meegan had been a real head-turner back then. Even her thick-rimmed NHS glasses could do little to hide her pretty features; in the same way that the large bouquet of flowers barely concealed her large bump. A shotgun wedding, it would seem.

'I knew he liked a drink with the boys when he went to the football on a Saturday, but it wasn't until he was arrested that I realised the truth, silly bastard.' She shook her head. 'The first time, it was for knocking a policeman's helmet off. He thought it was all a bit of a laugh. A night in the cells and that was it.'

She sighed. 'Or so I thought. The next time he got arrested, it was more serious. He glassed someone in the pub. He claimed it was self-defence. He and his mates were celebrating a win when the losers attacked them.'

Now her expression turned to derision. 'I took his word, if you can believe that?

'I went to court expecting him to get off, but the prosecution produced a dozen witnesses, some of them supporting his own team, who claimed that Ray and his mates started the fight. That they'd spotted the two lads on their own and started calling them names. One of the lads was Asian and he reckoned Ray called him a "Paki" and told him to go home. Nobody else heard that, so the magistrate dropped the racially aggravated bit, but he still got six weeks for assault.'

Warren had only skimmed the file on Ray Meegan, since he was more interested in his son, but his gut told him that Mary Meegan had things to say worth listening to.

'When he came out, he claimed he was done with the football and the violence, but it didn't last. He used to be a taxi driver, but the council were tightening the rules and didn't think he was suitable. He drove minicabs for a while, but there were too many foreigners prepared to work for peanuts and he couldn't earn enough to put food on the table.'

Warren could see where the story was going now.

'I guess it colours your view of folks when you think they're out there taking your job. It certainly did for my Ray.'

She sniffed. 'By the time the boys were at secondary school a load of immigrants had turned up to work on the building sites. My Ray kept on applying – he was a big bloke and not scared of a hard day's work – but they turned him down. Reckoned he was too expensive. The Asians would do it cheaper.'

She sniffed again. 'At least that's what he said. I reckon it was because he had a criminal record. Besides, these young lads were half his age and twice as fit. Still, he blamed it all on the Indians or the Pakistanis. He used to talk about it all the time at the dinner table. I told him not to use the P word in front of the boys, but he ignored me.

'And then he started taking the boys to the football. I didn't want him to, but he promised me he'd keep away from any trouble and said that he wouldn't be a real dad if he didn't take the boys to the footie. For some of his mates Saturday at the match followed by the chippie was the only time they spent with their kids. I was just glad that we weren't like that.'

She paused again, taking a mouthful of her tea, grimacing at the cold temperature.

'Let me get you a top-up, Mrs Meegan,' interjected Hastings.

She smiled at him and handed him her teacup, which he carried back to the kitchen.

'Do you think their father's employment situation helped form the boys' political views?' Warren asked carefully.

Mary Meegan laughed throatily. 'By "forming their political views", do you mean "is that why they are nasty racists?"' She answered her own question. "Course it is. I believed Ray when he said he was keeping the boys away from any trouble at the football, but you tell me where the hell a nine-year-old learns to throw a banana at the TV when a black player comes on the pitch? I threatened to tan Tommy's backside if he ever used that language again, but Ray laughed and said it was just a bit of fun.'

Mary Meegan slumped into her seat, as if the wind had been let out of her, and for the first time Warren saw the pain in her eyes.

'Mrs Meegan, do you have any idea who might have attacked your son?'

Warren wasn't expecting any great insights, but Mary Meegan was a lot more clued-in than she might at first seem.

'It's like Jimmy said – take your pick. They think I'm a fool, that I don't know what they get up to. Until today they'd never really made the news and I don't think they had any idea how much I know about them.' She smiled sadly. 'I don't exactly bring it up over Sunday lunch – not that I ever see them for Sunday lunch these days.' The smile disappeared and her bottom lip trembled. 'I just want my boys with me. The way it used to be.'

She cleared her throat loudly and fished a handkerchief from out of her sleeve. Warren picked up his own teacup and joined Hastings and the Family Liaison Officer in the kitchenette. Mary Meegan was a proud woman and would want a few moments to compose herself. By the time they returned a minute later, it was as if nothing had happened. She took the fresh cup of tea from Hastings with a grateful smile.

She pointed at the laptop on the dining table.

'They think I just use that for online shopping. It was an old one that Tommy gave me. But there's a silver surfer club at the library. One of the boys that helps out upgraded it. Now I can use it for looking at Facebook and surfing the web.' Her face darkened. 'I'm not an idiot. I know exactly what they're involved in. I even follow them on Twitter. I see what people post on there. The language they use... the threats...' Again, her bottom lip trembled. 'They used to try and hide it from me – still scared of their old mum,' she barked. 'But by the time they'd both been to prison it was obvious. They started showing off their tattoos, horrible things.' She shuddered. 'It's as if they want to be unemployed. They're supposed to be painters and decorators, but who'd let someone looking like that into their house?'

'So they aren't working?'

'Not really. Tommy moved down to Romford about five years ago, the last time he was released. He said it was to set up as a decorator – he completed a City and Guilds in prison – as a mate had some work on. But I'm not daft. That part of Essex is full of right-wingers. Jimmy joined him three years ago when he got out and they were supposed to set up a business together.'

'But they didn't?'

'I think they tried, but they can't get any work. Of course, they blame the immigrants. They reckon there are too many Poles down there.' She shrugged. 'Maybe they're right. But who would you rather invite into your house? A nice young Polish fellow who turns up on time with a smile, or some scruffy English bloke who turns up late covered in tattoos with a mouthful of foul language?'

'And so they hooked up with the local far-right?'

'Yeah, although they never use that term. They call themselves "patriots".'

'Before today, when was the last time you saw your sons?'

Again, her bottom lip trembled. 'It's been a while. Months.'

'So they don't visit Middlesbury very often?'

She shrugged. 'I think they still have friends up here. Tommy used to see a girl over in Attlee Place, but they split up ages ago.' The ghost of a smile passed across her face. 'She's seeing a black fella now – got a lovely little boy. I thought it best not to say anything.'

Warren returned the smile. Despite everything, he was warming to Mary Meegan, and he felt more than a little sorry for her. It wasn't hard to imagine the life she'd found herself trapped in. A man like Ray Meegan couldn't have been easy to live with. Had she been the victim of domestic abuse? He doubted she'd admit it even now. And she'd had two boys with the man; boys that she loved and feared in equal measures. Boys that she'd tried in vain to steer away from the life their father had chosen.

It was easy to blame the parents in such circumstances, but was that always fair? Not for the first time, Warren found himself wondering what he'd do in her place. He doubted Ray Meegan was the sort of man who'd let her run off with his kids, and he couldn't imagine Mary Meegan leaving without them. Having children seemed the easiest decision in the world, but was it always the right choice?

Suddenly, she grabbed Warren's hand.

'Please find the man who killed my boy. I know he wasn't a nice man, but he didn't deserve that. And now he's gone I'm afraid of what will happen.'

'Do you feel you're in danger, Mrs Meegan?' asked Warren.

'Not me, Jimmy. Despite it all, Tommy was a good influence on him. Jimmy's easily led and… he can get himself into trouble. Tommy used to hold him back.'

Warren had read Jimmy Meegan's file. If that was how he behaved when his older brother restrained him, he dreaded to think what the man would do now that he was gone.

47

Chapter 6

Tony Sutton hated fires. Fortunately, there were no bodies, nevertheless the scene conjured up old memories that he'd rather not dwell on.

The Islamic Centre was a converted residential property, and luckily for the neighbours was detached. The blaze had done significant damage to the downstairs, with the windows on the ground floor broken, the frames blackened. The smoke that smudged the centre's sign hadn't obliterated the racist graffiti scrawled across it. The front door hung off its hinges where the fire service had smashed it open to tackle the blaze behind. It too had graffiti, along with a couple of crudely drawn swastikas for good measure. A white-suited CSI was taking a swab from the paint in the hope that they could match it to any aerosol cans recovered from a suspect.

Hardwick resisted the urge to hold her nose; the smell of scorched plastic was making her feel nauseous.

'Imam Mehmud seemed pretty worried about the long-term fallout,' she commented.

Sutton agreed. 'It doesn't look good. When you were in the bathroom, he told me he's concerned about strangers turning up and using the fire as an excuse to make a point. There are some pretty angry social media posts in amongst the calls for solidarity and prayers for the victims. He's pretty young and I don't know if he wields enough authority to stop troublemakers.'

'What about the stabbing? What if it turns out to be a member of his congregation?'

'I don't know. I'm trying not to think about it.'

'Well we haven't exactly covered ourselves in glory either. I can't believe they pulled those two officers off guard duty, they left the place completely unprotected. No wonder everyone is so angry. What do you think will happen to Superintendent Walsh?'

Sutton shrugged; he only knew the Gold Commander for Saturday's operation in passing, but by all accounts she was a good officer.

'Let's not judge. It sounds as though she faced an impossible choice. I don't think anybody was expecting that many protestors; she needed every warm body at her disposal in the centre policing the riot.'

'Do you think the arson was planned, or just an opportunist? Could they have known that the patrol car would be pulled away?'

'That's what we need to find out,' replied Sutton.

'I don't know what would be worse,' said Hardwick quietly.

The two officers' reverie was broken by the appearance of Chief Fire Officer Matt Brown, one of the county's fire investigators. Sutton stuck a hand out and greeted a trim-looking man with steel-grey hair and thick crow's feet that spoke of a lifetime squinting against smoke or bright light. Black smudges on his overalls confirmed that he was a hands-on investigator.

'Walk me through it, CFO Brown,' Sutton instructed after he'd introduced Hardwick.

'Nine-nine-nine received a mobile phone call from somebody trapped on the top floor at 14.28. They called the volunteer appliance, but the roadblocks slowed things down and it took nearly eight minutes to assemble and another six to get to the scene. They only beat the crew from Cambridge by about two minutes. By that time the fire had taken hold of the whole ground floor.'

Brown pointed up. 'Fortunately, everybody inside had managed to make it upstairs and was accounted for and we were able to start bringing them out by ladder.'

'How did it start, you suggested arson?'

'No question in my mind.' He handed over a couple of hard hats and motioned for the two officers to follow him as he started up the front path.

'Watch your step,' instructed Brown as they stepped over the threshold.

The floorboards were warped and split and a pool of melted plastic had oozed across the floor.

'The fire started here after somebody poured an accelerant, probably petrol, through the letter box. There was a plastic welcome mat that worshippers used to wipe their feet on here and as you can imagine that went up a treat.'

Brown pointed up the wall, where black smoke stains were visible.

'Lots of soot and smoke damage, but the main structure remains sound.'

Straight ahead, the entrance to the prayer hall was visible. Stacks of rolled prayer mats still dripped water from the fire-fighters' ultimately successful bid to stop the fire spreading further. To the right, a set of stairs led upwards. Black soot smeared the walls all the way up to a small landing halfway up that allowed the steps to turn through ninety degrees.

Either side of the entrance were open shelving units, with the remains of what looked like shoes, a number of pairs clearly children's, the brightly coloured plastic burnt and twisted from the heat.

'It's early days, but as far as we can tell, there is no accelerant on the shoes.'

'Meaning what?' asked Hardwick.

'It suggests that the person didn't spray it through the letter box from a squirty bottle, but poured it from a canister. The doormat caught alight, which then spread and the shoes caught fire afterwards.'

Sutton scowled. If and when they caught the culprit, he could envisage a canny defence lawyer trying to use that as some sort of mitigation.

'The fumes from these different materials are pretty nasty and would have filled the downstairs quite quickly.' Brown pointed at the dark smoke stains travelling up the staircase. 'Hot air rises, so we'd ordinarily recommend getting low, however in this case, going upstairs probably bought them some time as it took a little longer for the smoke to fill the landing and double back on itself.'

Sutton made a mental note to reassure Imam Mehmud that his decision to head upstairs had been the correct one.

'What about the rear entrance?'

'Come and see for yourself.' Again, Brown led the way.

'That metal wheeled bin was in front of the door to stop anyone getting out, so you can definitely add attempted murder to the charge sheet as well.'

The container was a large, heavy, dented affair with a lid, a design long since supplanted by plastic recycle bins. Sutton supposed it must have been an old one that the centre used if they filled the newer ones.

He squatted down and looked beneath. The wheels were rusted and at least one looked as though it would fall off if the bin was lifted.

'We'll get scenes of crime to take a closer look, but I doubt this has been wheeled anywhere for years.' He pointed to white score marks leading back to a slightly darker patch of tarmac in front of the fence about three metres away. 'I'll bet it was dragged over.'

'So no chance of it being an accident, then.' Hardwick looked at her notes and then back at the door. 'Imam Mehmud said that they rarely opened the back door and it hasn't got a window so it's unlikely anyone noticed when the bin was moved.'

Back on the street, Hardwick and Sutton were met by DS Hutchinson and a team of constables ready to start house-to-house inquiries.

Sutton consulted his notebook. 'OK. According to the log, there was a patrol car with two uniforms sitting here as a visible deterrent until about 14.02 when they were called to the town centre to deal with the riot.

'That leaves a twenty-six-minute window during which the arsonist or arsonists set the fire.' He gestured at the street. 'The street is a mixture of student and non-student properties and there was a fair-sized crowd of rubberneckers by the time the fire brigade turned up. Some of the morbid bastards were even filming it on their mobile phones. Let's see if anybody saw anything suspicious; strangers hanging around, cars they didn't recognise, people pouring petrol through the letter box, that sort of thing. I'd also like to know if there were any issues before Saturday. What were relations like with the neighbours?

'Can anyone pin down when that charming graffiti appeared? We think it was late Wednesday night or early Thursday morning. Did anyone hear the bin being dragged? I imagine it wasn't quiet. What about the CCTV camera? It was broken in the early hours of Thursday morning.'

As they headed back to the car, Sutton looked over at his younger colleague.

'You were very quiet back there, Karen.' Sutton had noticed her pale complexion.

'I'm still a bit under the weather.'

'That bug you caught on holiday still bothering you?'

'It's been over a month now. Every time I think I'm getting over it, it starts again.'

'What did the doctor say?'

'I haven't seen him yet, I can't get a bloody appointment.'

'How's Gary?'

'Fit as a butcher's dog, the lucky bugger. He was sick first. By the time he'd finished puking, I was just starting. He was done in twenty-four hours, but it took me nearly three days to get over the first bout.'

'And you're certain it's the food poisoning coming back?'

'Not one hundred per cent, but the doctor that treated me in France reckoned it was a viral infection, and warned me it might.'

'You'd think they'd be able to make an omelette properly in Paris.'

'I guess not.'

53

Chapter 7

'Single stab wound to the chest. Almost certainly a knife or bladed implement. Curved blade, no serration.'

Professor Ryan Jordan's accent was still predominantly American, but decades living in England – married to an Englishwoman – had left their mark.

'What can you tell about the attack?' Warren had the phone on speaker so he could look at the emailed files Jordan had sent him without getting a crick in his neck.

'It pierced his left lung, catching a rib on the way in. It didn't reach the heart, but it nicked an intercostal artery. The knife was pulled out without twisting. He'd have bled out in less than a minute. From the shape of the pool of blood under the body and the lengthy smear, I'd say he expired where he finally collapsed. I see no evidence that his body was moved post-mortem.'

'What about his killer. Any ideas?'

'From the angle and position of entry, I would guess someone of a similar height, probably standing face-on.'

'So his attacker would have been covered in blood?'

'No question. Even if he jumped back, I'd say he'd have got a good spattering.'

Warren really hoped Andy Harrison and his team found the

killer's clothing, only a tiny speck of blood would be needed to tie it to the scene.

'Anything else you can tell me about the weapon?'

'Not a lot, but I've photographed the marks on the rib, so I should be able to match any suspect blade.'

'What else have you found? Any defensive wounds?'

'Inconclusive. He had a number of pre-mortem injuries. A cut on his scalp was clearly inflicted sometime earlier, it had already started to bruise. His knuckles also had contusions consistent with fighting, but again they were probably picked up a few minutes before he was killed. Unless there was a pause of several minutes between him meeting his attacker and the final wound, I'd say the injuries occurred during the ruckus in the square. I've scraped under his fingernails just in case.'

Warren thanked him and hung up. The first twenty-four hours of any investigation were crucial. The clock started ticking the moment a crime was committed, as evidence disappeared, memories began to fade and killers continued to cover their tracks. It had been a promising start and a couple more hours remained. He just hoped they could maintain this momentum over the coming hours and days.

Chapter 8

Arranging a preliminary interview for all those present at the previous day's riot was no trivial task. Many of the members of the British Allegiance Party were from East London, or further afield, and those who had managed not to get arrested had returned on the coach late Saturday night. To help process them more easily, Welwyn had sent a minibus full of officers clockwise around the M25 and taken advantage of the generosity of the Metropolitan Police in securing the use of some interview suites. The news of their leader's murder had shocked most of the BAP members into docility and, to everyone's surprise, all of those invited to give a statement had meekly turned up first thing on Sunday morning. Anybody with something interesting to say would be interviewed more formally, under caution if necessary, at a later date. Establishing alibis prior to the fire breaking out as well as in the last minutes before Tommy Meegan's demise were equally important at the moment; Warren was acutely aware that a quick arrest over the fire would go at least some way to making good the mistakes made by the police that day.

Tracking down the many counter-protestors was more difficult. Those arrested during the riot had already been processed; a few more would no doubt be identified from CCTV footage and picked up later, but the majority had gone home, scattering to all corners of the UK. The press office had released a public appeal for information, but given who the victim was and many of the protestors' attitudes towards the police, nobody was especially hopeful.

Nevertheless, there were still plenty of witnesses and potential suspects remaining in Middlesbury to interview, and none of them were happy. Some had spent the night in the cells and a couple were even trying to pin the responsibility for their assorted bumps, cuts and bruises on the police. More than a few of the BAP members were calling foul because they had been thoroughly searched as they left the bus whilst the counter-protestors hadn't. Perhaps, more than one had suggested, the knife that killed Tommy Meegan could have been confiscated from the outset and a 'good man' wouldn't be dead.

Many of the counter-protestors arrested at the scene were old hands and knew exactly what to do: namely keep their mouths shut and wait out the custody clock.

That left Tommy Meegan's closest friends. Much to Warren's surprise, Jimmy Meegan, Goldie Davenport and Bellies Brandon had actually stuck around in Middlesbury to be interviewed that afternoon. He suspected the influence of Mary Meegan.

First up was Harry Brandon.

'He was a good lad. He didn't deserve what happened to him.'

'Then help us find who did it and bring them to justice.'

Bellies Brandon was well named. A good few inches under six feet tall, he still weighed well over twenty-five stone. Warren had no idea the kit makers made England football shirts that large; no wonder he'd not been able to keep up with Tommy Meegan when the counter-protestors had broken through the front line and the BAP members had scattered. He was the last person to be seen with Tommy Meegan as the two of them ran off the edge of the CCTV's field of view.

'Why did the two of you decide to run in that direction?'

Brandon shrugged and it was all Warren could do not to stare at the ripples and wobbles that flowed across his huge frame.

'Dunno. It all went to shit when you guys let the Pakis and the Muslim-lovers attack us. Tommy started legging it and I followed him, 'cos he knows Middlesbury.'

Warren had twice reminded Brandon that although the interview was voluntary, he was being recorded and that he might want to consider his choice of language. The sneer on the man's face left him in no doubt that he was choosing his words deliberately.

'Then what happened?'

'We could hear the fighting behind us. Tommy already had a cut on his head after some bastard threw a stone at him, so we just kept on going.'

'I'm assuming the two of you split up before Tommy disappeared. Can you describe what happened then?'

'I had to stop by the edge of the market square at the war memorial – my asthma's been playing up lately – and I let him run on.' Warren let the white lie slide; he couldn't imagine the huge man being able to trot more than a few dozen paces before his massive weight and smoking brought him to a halt.

'Was that the last you saw of Tommy?'

'Yeah, he kept going down the road between the Marks & Spencer and Next.'

The protest had taken place in the market square in front of the town hall. Metal barricades had surrounded the BAP members, as they were addressed by Tommy Meegan with a loudhailer. A ring of police had kept protestors to the eastern end of the square, allowing a clear pathway to the BAP's coach parked at the edge of the bus station.

After passing between the two department stores, Tommy Meegan would have found himself on the much narrower Ackers Street, lined with smaller businesses. Turning north then took the fleeing man up the road, where a left turn led to the alleyway where he finally met his fate.

If he'd continued down that alleyway he'd have exited onto Stafford Road, then entered the maze of back streets leading to The Feathers pub where the marchers had agreed to meet for a celebratory drink.

'Did you see anyone else run in the same direction as Tommy?'

Brandon shook his head. 'Goldie and Jimmy legged it towards BHS but I don't think anyone else went the same way as Tommy.'

The CCTV footage processed so far backed him up; Tommy Meegan was on his own when he left the square.

'Was the meeting at The Feathers planned in advance?'

'Yeah, the landlord's a mate of Tommy and Jimmy's, he used to go to the footie with their old man.'

'You aren't from Middlesbury, so how did you find your way there?'

'When I got me breath back, I went and hid in a beer garden at the top of the square whilst you lot finally arrested those bastards that attacked us. I tried to phone Tommy…' For the first time the large man's façade looked in danger of cracking and he cleared his throat before coughing ostentatiously. 'I tried to phone Tommy, but he didn't pick up. Then I phoned Jimmy and Goldie. Neither of them answered either.'

'So how did you find your way to The Feathers?'

'When they reopened the pub's doors I asked one of the drinkers for directions.'

So far he hadn't given Warren very much in the way of new information.

He decided to change tack.

'I can see that you and Tommy knew each other well. How did you meet him?'

Brandon scowled. 'What's it to you?'

'Look, Harry, my job is to find out who killed your friend. That's all. The more I know about him, the easier it is for me to picture what happened.'

'Bullshit. You don't care about Tommy. We're scum to you.'

He raised a hand. 'Don't try and deny it. In the days before those helmet cameras you lot would try and wind us up and then when we stuck up for ourselves, arrest us.'

Warren said nothing – he'd earned overtime policing such protests back when he was in uniform. The atmosphere had been nasty and brutish. The two sides had hated the police as much as each other, seeing them variously as fascist sympathisers, state-run paramilitaries or members of a big conspiracy to chase indigenous Britons from their historic homeland. Stuck in the middle, arms linked with colleagues to form a human wall, Warren had felt fear. He'd been spat at, hit, and called names he'd had to look up online. Once somebody had even thrown a cup of urine over him.

It didn't matter which direction he was facing; the hatred was like a physical force. And you reacted in one of two ways. Either you turned the other cheek and rode it out, or as soon as the opportunity arose, you let go of your comrades, unhooked your baton and waded in. One thing Warren was sure of was that everyone who'd ended up in the back of a police van that day had well and truly earned their seat.

Nevertheless, he needed to win Brandon's trust.

'Look, I'm CID. I don't get involved in that sort of policing. I solve murders. I don't care what people are supposed to have done. A murder victim is just that, a victim and they deserve justice as much as anyone.'

Brandon looked down at the table for a long moment, before finally meeting Warren's eyes.

'I guess I've known him getting on for ten years now. At first it was just to say "hello". He'd travel down to Essex if there was a meeting on. Then he went away for a bit—' he meant prison '—and when he came back he moved down to Romford. We're about a mile apart. I'm a painter and decorator and Tommy needed some work and a place to stay, so we teamed up. I guess that was about five years ago.'

'You lived together?'

Brandon scowled. 'Not like that. He kipped on my couch for a couple of months until he found a flat.'

'Of course, I didn't think otherwise.'

Brandon grunted.

'After he moved out, did the two of you stay good mates?'

'Yeah, he repaid the favour a few months ago when me and the missus went through a rough patch.' His voice cracked slightly. 'He was an untidy bastard, but it's times like that you find out who your mates are.' He paused. 'He wouldn't even take any rent.'

'But you aren't living with him now?'

'No, I got myself a bedsit.'

'Did you still see each other outside work?'

'Yeah, we both like a bit of golf and we used to go and play on a Sunday afternoon.' He smiled slightly. 'He was crap.'

'What about Jimmy?'

Brandon snorted.

'You'd never get Jimmy on the golf course, far more likely to find him in a wine bar with Goldie. Me and Tommy used to take the piss out of him. He had the cleanest overalls you ever saw. God knows what he used to wash them with. I swear, if he wasn't always on the pull, I'd think he was batting for the other side.'

'So he used to work with you guys as well?'

'Yeah, me, Tommy, him and Goldie.'

'I'm surprised you managed to find enough work, what with all the Poles.'

If Brandon realised he was being provoked, he didn't seem bothered.

'Yeah, fucking Europe. Sooner we're out and can send them all packing the better. How is a man supposed to put bread on the table when he has to compete with that? They use cheap materials, charge half as much and don't pay fuck all in tax. Half of them just want to use the NHS. There are plenty of good, honest British tradesmen out there, why do we need to bring in foreigners?'

Warren was beginning to wish he hadn't broached the subject, but he needed to get Brandon worked up.

'But you weren't up here for work?'

''Course not.' Brandon looked at him scornfully and Warren worried his deliberately clumsy questioning had been too obvious. 'You know why we're up here. To stop that fucking super mosque.'

'But what's so special about Middlesbury? You didn't march on Dudley or Newham.'

'Some of us did. But Middlesbury is personal to Tommy and Jimmy. They grew up here. Their old lady still has to live here. You've seen the town, it's like fucking Islamabad.' He leant forward, warming to his topic. 'You mark my words, it's a slippery slope. Before you know it the local schools will be serving halal food and teaching the boys and girls in separate classrooms so they don't offend the Muslims. And what will they be teaching? They'll be learning the Koran by heart and listening to preachers telling them to destroy the West and earn their seventy-two virgins by blowing themselves up on the underground.'

Brandon was now in full flow and Warren found himself watching with a disturbed fascination. How much did he actually believe and how much was just hyperbole spouted to justify his unabashed racism?

'Fancy a pint on a Friday night? Forget it, before you know it they'll be demanding pubs shut down. It'll be like Iran. Islam will be the biggest religion in the UK within twenty years the rate we're letting them into the country. They're breeding like fucking rabbits and converting people left, right and centre. And what do we do about it? We build more mosques and give them free houses and let them use the NHS without paying.' Brandon leant forward.

'You and me are an endangered species, pal. Look around you. Middlesbury is supposed to be at the heart of England. If anywhere in this country should be full of white people it's here, but it's not. It'll be as bad as Birmingham or Bradford before you know it.'

The man's face was bright red and he used the edge of his shirt to wipe the sweat from his forehead.

'Help me out here, Harry. Who killed Tommy? Point me towards them.'

Brandon slumped back in his chair, the plastic creaking alarmingly.

'I don't know. Take your pick. It could have been one of the Muslims or it could have been one of those Muslim-lovers throwing stones and making death threats on Facebook.' He smirked. 'Hell, it could even have been a bunch of Polish painters trying to wipe out the competition.'

Chapter 9

Marcus 'Goldie' Davenport, was another person whose nickname was both unimaginative and descriptive. In addition to his gold earring and incisor, he also sported several gold sovereign rings. Like his friend, Bellies Brandon, he too wore an England shirt, although it was probably one-third the size.

'Can we be quick about this? I need to get back home to feed the cat.'

Davenport's face was inscrutable and Warren couldn't tell if he was being serious or facetious.

'It'll take as long as it takes, Mr Davenport. After all, we don't want to miss something that could let your friend's killer go free.'

Davenport sighed his acquiescence.

Much of his story matched that of Bellies Brandon, so Warren focused on the small details. Davenport enjoyed the audience.

'I'm a pacifist, me. I wasn't going to get involved in any violence. I was just there to exercise my freedom of speech. So when the police let the protestors attack us, I left quickly.'

'Where did you go when you left the square?'

'Me and Jimmy headed past the war memorial then towards BHS.'

'Did you go into the shop?'

'Nah, 'course not. They'd pulled the shutters down, probably to stop the muzzers and the soap-dodgers from nicking stuff, you know what they're like.'

'So where did you go?'

'Down the alleyway and onto the street behind.'

'Did Tommy and Mr Brandon follow you?'

'No, we split up at the war memorial. Bellies is too fat to run, so Tommy left him and headed towards Marks & Spencer.'

'Do you know where he went after that?'

'I reckon he probably cut through into the backstreet, but we were ahead of him and didn't see him again.'

'And that was definitely the last time you saw him?'

'I just said that, didn't I?'

'OK. Did you see anybody else in the street or around the area?'

'Nobody.'

'Where did you go after you cut past Marks & Spencer?'

'BHS,' Davenport corrected.

Warren acknowledged the correction.

'We went through another alleyway next to a key-cutter's and then headed towards the pub.'

'Which pub was that?'

'The Feathers.'

'And you went straight there.'

'Yeah, pretty much. Jimmy led the way, he knows the area.'

'Do you know roughly what time you arrived?'

'No, I wasn't wearing a watch.'

'Were you the first to arrive or were there others there already?'

'We were pretty much the first.'

'Do you know when everyone else arrived? Was anybody late?'

'Most everybody else arrived at the same time. Bellies got lost and came in last.'

'How long did you stay for?'

'We were supposed to be there until about nine, then catch

the coach back home. The beer was flowing and they'd laid on food. It was the shittiest chicken Kiev I've ever eaten, even Bellies didn't finish it.'

Warren looked over his notes. Despite his attitude, the man had been helpful. A picture of Tommy Meegan's movements in the hours before his death was being built, but it was slow going. Large gaps remained and they had yet to identify any concrete suspects.

With that, he turned off the tape recorder and thanked Davenport for his time. The man merely grinned.

Chapter 10

Up close the similarities between Jimmy Meegan and his brother were even more striking. It was strange what death did to a person; if anything, Tommy looked younger.

Warren scrutinised the man sitting opposite him. His eyes were still bloodshot and the edges of his nostrils inflamed, but his pupils weren't dilated and the nervous energy that he'd radiated that morning was gone. It would seem that he wasn't high on cocaine at the moment; leaving him until last had probably been the right decision.

What remained was the anger; it seemed to infuse the very air.

Warren decided not to repeat his condolences. They'd been thrown back in his face that morning and he saw no reason to start the interview on a negative note. It was likely to go sour all on its own.

From the outset, Meegan made it clear that he regarded the interview as a waste of time, and that he thought Warren was only going through the motions.

'Why don't you tell me who you think killed him?'

Warren knew exactly where this would go, but he might as well get it out of the way now.

'Take your pick. Look at anybody who was behind that pathetic line of nancy boys you sent to protect our right to free speech.'

'There were a lot of people there, Mr Meegan, was there anyone that you recognised that may have been involved? Perhaps we could review some of the CCTV footage.'

'Are you taking the piss? None of those fucking cowards were man enough to show their faces.' He pointed a finger at Warren. 'I tell you what you lot need to do, you need to arrest anybody that turns up at these things with their face hidden. What have they got to hide?' He turned the finger back towards himself. 'I'm fucking proud of what I am. You won't ever catch me wearing a mask.

'It's like those burqas. We don't let people wear helmets when they go into the garage or the bank, we should make them take off their masks. Who in their right mind lets someone dressed like a fucking ninja go into a shop?' He suddenly giggled. 'Maybe we should get Bruce Lee to sort them out.' The laughter disappeared as quickly as it had appeared.

'If their women want to dress like that at home, that's their business, but they shouldn't be allowed on the public streets.' He blinked and paused as if he'd forgotten his train of thought, before brightening again.

'Anyhow, the same should go for those fucking terrorist-lovers at the march, with their ski masks. Traitors to their race they are. They should show some pride in their white skin.' He looked towards the CCTV camera in the corner of the room. 'Fucking White Pride,' he shouted.

Warren paused for a beat. It was clear that Meegan was a regular drug abuser and it was taking its toll on his mental stability. He wondered what he'd get out of the man.

Finally, Meegan's face took on the sullen tone of a teenager. As exasperating as it was, Warren forced himself to remember that the man had just lost his older brother.

'Look, Jimmy, help me put together a timeline here. Let's figure out your brother's last moves and then we can work out what happened and bring whoever killed him to justice.' He locked eyes with Meegan. 'I know you don't believe me but I promise you I do want to find your brother's killer. I'm a CID officer, working the murder squad. Your brother was a victim and I will find justice for him.'

The silence stretched between them. Would the rhetoric persuade Meegan to cooperate or would it push him further away?

Eventually, he nodded.

'Take me through the day as it happened.'

The story was essentially the same as that told before, with the BAP scattering after the police line was breached, Jimmy Meegan and Goldie Davenport going one direction and Tommy Meegan and Bellies Brandon the other, before they too split.

Warren was suddenly struck with the thought that perhaps if Tommy hadn't abandoned his friend, he wouldn't have been in the alleyway on his own... karma?

'So you and Mr Davenport must have emerged onto Ackers Street at about the same time as Tommy?'

'No, we had a bit of a head start.'

'And you didn't see Tommy come out?'

For the first time since the interview had started, Warren saw something other than anger and contempt in his eyes.

'Yeah. I never saw him again.' He put his head in his hands, hiding his face. Warren waited patiently. He knew better than to offer the man tissues or even acknowledge his distress.

Finally, with a loud sniff, Meegan straightened.

'Did you see any other possible witnesses along the way?'

Meegan started to shake his head, before suddenly pausing. 'Hang on, we wasn't the only ones in Stafford Road.'

Warren raised an eyebrow.

'Yeah, I remember now. There was some bloke hanging around the back of the shop next to the key-cutter's.'

'The Starbucks?'

'Yeah, must have been.'

Warren made a note to prioritise any CCTV from the rear of the coffee shop and other businesses along Stafford Road.

'Can you describe this person.'

'Skinny, Asian, wearing a black turban.' Meegan's eyes flashed dangerously. 'There's your suspect, DCI Jones. Round up all the Pakis, you'll solve it before sundown.'

Warren ignored the man's language.

'Can you remember anything else about him?'

Meegan thought for a moment, before shaking his head.

'OK, let's go back to The Feathers, just so I have the complete timeline sorted. When did you arrive?'

Meegan shrugged. 'Dunno, I didn't check the time.'

'Was the pub empty or were there others already present?'

'We were pretty much first.'

'And did the rest of your friends arrive soon after?'

'Yeah, most of them.' He grinned. 'A few got a bit lost on the way, but they made it there eventually with the help of a few friendly natives.'

According to the switchboard at least a half-dozen callers had complained about intimidation and foul language as the BAP supporters made their way to their rendezvous point. However, that had been the least of the police's worries by that time, with riot control officers still arresting those protestors who had yet to disperse peacefully and, on the other side of town, uniformed officers hastily dismantling roadblocks to make way for fire engines rushing towards the Islamic Centre.

'Why The Feathers?'

'Why not? It's a free country. Besides, I have a thing for over-cooked chicken Kiev.'

'Did anyone not make it to The Feathers on time?'

'Bellies, but he got there in the end.'

Warren paused for a moment.

'When did you realise your brother was missing?'

'I figured Bellies was late 'cos he'd gone back to find him. When Bellies said he hadn't seen him, I tried to phone him, but he didn't pick up.'

'What time would you say that was?'

'Probably about four.'

'So what then? Weren't you worried?'

Meegan shrugged. 'Not really. He's a big boy. I figured he'd either decided to lie low somewhere or he'd been nicked.'

'And so you kept on drinking?'

'Thirsty work.' Meegan looked away. Was that a hint of shame?

'Some of the lads kept on calling him,' he continued, 'but it kept on going to voicemail. By about five-thirty we reckoned he'd been nabbed and we'd hear from him later.'

'When did you hear about your brother's death?'

Meegan looked down at the table again, and Warren worried that he wasn't going to answer. Eventually, he started to speak, his voice soft.

'About eight o'clock, four coppers came into the bar. We assumed they were there to escort us out.' He smiled humourlessly. 'Perhaps give us a bit more aggro before we left. We'd already given up on Tommy, the coach was waiting to take us home. I'd left a message telling him to call me when the pigs let him go and that he'd have to crash at Mum's if they didn't keep him overnight.'

He paused as he remembered.

'They knew exactly who they were looking for. They came straight for me.'

For the first time since the interview had begun, Meegan paused and reached for the polystyrene water cup.

'They asked if I had seen Tommy. I said no, obviously.'

Whether he meant that obviously he hadn't seen his brother, or that he'd have denied seeing him even if he was sitting next to him, just because, Warren was unsure.

'They asked for a private word and I said that anything they had to say to me, they could say in front of my esteemed colleagues.'

He took another sip of water.

'And then they told me.'

Chapter 11

'Well, that was enlightening.' Warren sat opposite Theo Garfield, who'd been watching the interviews via CCTV. He felt exhausted. He'd had no idea how hard it would be to maintain his professional detachment, or to empathise with the victim. He said as much.

Garfield grimaced. 'Par for the course, Warren, I'm afraid. I'd offer to help, but none of them know me and I need to keep it that way. You get used to the language eventually. They're just words.' He leant back against the wall. 'It's the hatred I struggle with. I really do think that there is something fundamentally wrong with these guys. They *need* that hate. There has to be something for them to direct their anger towards, it's cathartic. If they didn't have a target, they'd explode.'

Warren looked at him thoughtfully. 'So you think the racism and bigotry is secondary to their need to let out their frustrations?'

Garfield shrugged. 'I really don't know. I'm not a psychologist, but I reckon they've some sort of innate tribalism. If you brought them up from birth in an environment where they never met others with different-coloured skin or from a different culture, they'd divide the world by eye colour. I don't think it's a coincidence that these guys are fanatical football supporters. Often they don't even support their local team; they almost arbitrarily pick a team who they have no personal connection with and take part in the most extreme violence in the name of that club, literally risking life and limb. It makes no rational sense.'

Warren sighed. 'These guys aren't the biggest arseholes I've ever interviewed, but they're close. Still, I got a few leads and their stories pretty much match, so either they were in it all together or they're telling the truth. What about you? Anything useful?'

Garfield shrugged again. 'I think it was interesting that they largely only had a go at Muslims. These guys are full-spectrum far-right, they usually bring in Jews, blacks, Asians and homosexuals whilst they're at it.'

He scratched his chin. 'It confirms something I've suspected for a while. Ever since Tommy Meegan took over the BAP, we've seen a ratchetting up of the anti-Muslim rhetoric, at the expense of some of the other crap. That might just be because of recent events; Islamic State, Boko Haram and Al Quaeda are stealing all the headlines lately.' He shifted his stance. 'The thing is, forget idiots like Bellies Brandon and Goldie Davenport, they're just foot soldiers who couldn't find their arse with both hands. The brains are people like Tommy Meegan. He definitely wasn't an idiot. He knew the way the wind was blowing.

'Old school racism against blacks or other minorities just because they look or speak differently hasn't completely died out, but it's generally social suicide if you express it publicly. When was the last time you saw anyone admit to owning a Bernard Manning DVD? Overt homophobia is also a no-no. Plenty of prejudice still exists, but opponents of gay marriage are seen as out of touch and embarrassing in this country; if the thought of gay sex is icky to you, you keep it to yourself. You can't even criticise Israel without making it clear that you aren't an anti-Semite first.

'We've seen it in the evolution of organisations like the BNP; out go the jackboots and the Combat 18 jackets, in come the sharp suits and the election manifestos. Until UKIP started stealing their thunder, they even had some success. Nick Griffin was invited on the BBC's *Question Time*, remember – mind you, he got such a spanking, it probably did him more harm than good.'

'And you think the BAP are going that way?'

'Well, quite the opposite, we thought. The BAP were supposedly one of a number of ragtag groups formed out of the old guard who didn't want to go down the political route. They were proud of who they were. I have to confess, our intelligence on them was pretty slim until recently, much of the information we had on the key players came from their previous associations with more established groups, or through other sources such as criminal records.'

'So what changed?'

'The rhetoric on social media, primarily. We were already watching Islamophobic groups, such as Britain First, and when we saw the BAP starting to share followers and content, we started to pay attention.

'At first, we saw them as a bit of a joke. The usual muddled neo-Nazi rhetoric, wrapped up with so-called British patriotism – a ridiculous contradiction if you think about it too hard, citing Winston Churchill in one breath and praising everything he stood against in the next. Their philosophy varied depending on who was in charge of their Facebook page that day. But when Tommy Meegan became their de facto leader, that all changed.

'Tommy recognised that Islam is fair game nowadays and he started playing on those fears, whilst also moderating their public image. He understood that it's about far more than how many troglodytes you can pack in a coach and drive to a rally. It's about how many retweets or likes you get on social media.

'Protests against so-called super mosques are just a bone to keep the hardcore onside and stop them pissing off to join some-body else. Tommy Meegan knew that he'd never effect social change that way. But a leopard doesn't change its spots and he and his brother were nasty, violent pieces of work. Wherever the hell he is now, I'll bet Tommy Meegan is loving every minute of this; his death could lead to the sort of race war he could only dream of in his lifetime.'

Warren needed to change the subject.

'So how did you get into this game?'

Garfield pointed to himself.

'Well, when you're the colour I am, growing up in Liverpool in the Seventies and Eighties, racial politics is hardly something that passes you by.' He held out his hand. 'This sexy brown is the result of a white mum and a black dad.

'Now I know what you're thinking: I was brought up by a single mum on a housing estate in Toxteth with no opportunities and no job prospects until I decided to turn my back on a life of crime and either enlist in the army or join the police.'

Warren said nothing; he'd not really given it much thought, but it was obvious Garfield enjoyed telling the story.

'Actually, it was far worse than that. I was born into a loving family in the Wirral – that's the posh end of Liverpool – you know, indoor toilets and electric lighting,' Warren smiled; he'd heard the exact same joke told about parts of Coventry many times. 'My father was second-generation Jamaican and only retired as a consultant gynaecologist last year. He was the most well-spoken man in the street. My mother is still an education officer for the council and I've never heard them exchange an angry word. They sent me to the best school in the area and I went to university in Manchester and got a first in History.'

'Oh.' Warren wasn't entirely sure where this was going.

'Mum and Dad did their best to shield me from everything of course, but they couldn't be there in the playground at school, or on the bus on the way home. It got a bit better when

I joined the local sixth-form college; I wasn't the only mixed-race kid anymore and most of the real racists never made it that far.

'By the time I went to university, I figured the worst of it was over.' He snorted. 'The first time somebody threw a stone at me and shouted at me to "fuck off home", I pledged not to wear my Liverpool shirt in Manchester again. The second time I heard it, I wasn't wearing my shirt and the penny dropped.

'I phoned my parents and asked right out how bad the racism had really been when I was a kid. I was shocked by their response. Dad had always said he didn't like golf, so he didn't play with the other consultants. In reality, he was never invited. When he took over the running of some clinics, about a dozen patients asked to be transferred, claiming that they weren't comfortable being examined by a man. Dad's predecessor had been an old, white guy.

'I remember our car was always being vandalised. My parents shrugged it off; car crime in Liverpool was an epidemic. I don't know if I was naive or in denial but I never twigged that ours was the only car in the street that was attacked, and that we were the only non-white family.

'Nobody was ever racist to Mum's face, but when I was born she was the only mother in her birthing group who didn't stay in contact with the rest. At playschool, I was never invited to birthday parties.'

'So when did you join the police?'

'After university. I'd joined a couple of protest groups but we never really felt we were achieving anything. Some of my mates wanted to go down the direct-action route – getting stuck in against the BNP – but it didn't seem the right approach.

'Then one day we had a talk from a police commander in charge of race relations. Until then, I'd kind of gone along with the idea that the police were almost as bad as the far-right. Full of old-school bigots at the very least willing to turn a blind eye.

The Stephen Lawrence inquiry was just wrapping up and the police were being branded as institutionally racist.

'But I had trouble squaring what I was hearing from this police officer with what I was hearing on the news, and what I was being told by the people I was going on marches with. So in the end I attended one of the force's recruitment days and decided that whilst the police were far from perfect, it was better to be inside the tent pissing out than outside the tent pissing in.'

'So how did you end up down here?'

'Career advancement. I was stuck on sergeant up in Liverpool with no vacancies on the horizon, whilst Hertfordshire was building up its Hate Crime Intelligence Unit. My missus is a schoolteacher and had no particular ties to Liverpool, so we decided to move south.'

The tale sounded familiar to Warren and he said so.

Garfield raised his mug and clinked it with Warren's. 'Here's to Hertfordshire Constabulary and understanding wives!'

Chapter 12

Warren's conversation with Garfield had given him much to think about. The man's hypothesis about the BAP's motivations was intriguing. He looked at his watch. It was already after 9 p.m. The first twenty-four hours were over. Every fibre in his body wanted to go to bed, but he decided to speak to the team one last time before he left. It was a bad habit and his wife would tell him off – that was what email was for, she always said – but experience told him that small, important details that might come out in conversation may not be recorded in an email.

Heading back upstairs, he entered the section of the building allotted to CID. It might have been late on a Sunday evening, but the office was still packed.

Dusk at this time of year was perfectly timed for the candles outside the Islamic Centre to appear on the late-night news. Earlier in the evening Tony Sutton had tuned the wall-mounted screen at the back of the office to BBC News with the sound turned low. Now he turned it up, switching off the garbled automatic subtitles.

The crowd featured in the panning shot had been gathering all afternoon, the pile of flowers and soft toys growing taller by the hour. Numbers had swelled after lunchtime prayers as minibuses from other towns brought in more Muslims to pay their respects. They were soon joined by several dozen members of a local church and a nearby Hindu temple showing solidarity with their Muslim neighbours. By mid-afternoon there were at least three hundred people gathered, the crowd representing a mixture of Muslims and non-Muslims, residents of Middlesbury and those who had travelled from outside. Many carried placards bearing the Twitter hashtag #Justice4Muslims.

'I don't know whether to be pleased at the show of unity across so many faith communities or dismayed by the fact that they seem to be united against the police,' Grayson had muttered before stomping back to his office.

The centre was still an active crime scene and surrounded by tape, however the dozen or so officers policing the crowds that had gathered for the candle-lit vigil were trying to be as unobtrusive as possible. It wasn't working.

'Where were you when those animals torched the place?' yelled a bearded young man into the face of one of the officers standing in front of the entrance to the community centre's driveway. To her credit, she didn't so much as flinch. The man was showboating for the TV cameras, who duly obliged by zooming in.

'Emotions are running high outside Middlebury Islamic Centre, the scene of yesterday's arson attack that injured eight and left an eighty-nine-year-old and her three-year-old great-grandson fighting for their lives in hospital,' intoned a grave-looking reporter.

'Crowds have been gathering all day to pay their respects and send their prayers and best wishes to those hurt in the attack. Middlesbury's close-knit Muslim community are understandably upset and worried by yesterday's attack but some are also concerned by the wider implications. Imam Danyal Mehmud leads prayers at the community centre.' The camera panned back slightly, revealing the young imam. He looked sick.

'Can you describe how residents are feeling at the moment?'

'Umm, obviously we are shocked and saddened, and we pray for the recovery of those injured yesterday.'

'What are your thoughts on calls for the officer in-charge of yesterday's operation to be suspended? Should there be an inquiry into the decision to remove the guard from the Islamic Centre in favour of policing the town centre?'

Mehmud licked his lips, trying to find appropriately diplomatic language.

'Ask the police why they are spending so much money protecting white fascists marching through our town centre and won't lift a finger to help innocent Muslims?' The young man with the beard had somehow pushed his way in front of the camera again.

The camera-operator nimbly twisted to keep Imam Mehmud in shot whilst blocking the intruder.

'Obviously, we welcome any inquiry into the events of yesterday...' started Mehmud.

'It'll be a whitewash,' interrupted the man with beard again. 'The police don't care about Muslims. They never have done. They may as well have given a box of matches to those fascist scum.'

'It should be pointed out that a spokesperson for the British Allegiance Party has categorically denied any involvement in yesterday's arson attack,' the journalist interjected hastily.

'Well, they would, wouldn't they?' The unknown bearded man was now centre shot again and it was clear that the reporter had been told to go with him.

Sensing he now had an audience, the man puffed his chest out.

'The government and the police are quick enough to close down so-called hate preachers but won't touch groups like the BAP who call for Muslims to be locked up or deported and set fire to their mosques or put bricks through their shop windows.'

Again the reporter interrupted swiftly with, 'A charge which the BAP deny.' Her expression froze for a moment, evidently listening to a disembodied producer instructing her to move away from the angry young man before he said something even more defamatory.

'I believe we can go over to our correspondent Steven, who has been joined by Councillor Lavindeep Kaur.'

The camera cut, but not before the bearded man flashed a handwritten placard bearing '#Justice4Muslims' and started shouting about the 'fascist police'.

The abrupt change was dealt with smoothly by the experienced correspondent, who wasted no time introducing Councillor Kaur. The councillor expressed her sympathy and support for the victims of the fire and drew attention to the wide variety of people, across all sections of society, who were condemning the violence both in person and online.

'Do you agree with calls for the suspension of the officer in charge of yesterday's policing operation, and calls for an independent inquiry?'

Kaur adopted a concerned look. A middle-aged Sikh woman with jet-black hair, she wore a smart black trouser suit, a pale blue scarf her only splash of colour.

'Far be it for me to suggest how the police should deal with internal disciplinary matters such as these. However, I think the people of Middlesbury – indeed Hertfordshire as a whole – have a right to ask questions about the decisions made yesterday. Decisions that led to an obviously vulnerable target being left unprotected and which ultimately resulted in an innocent toddler and his great-grandmother being seriously injured. The officers in charge of those operational decisions must be prepared to justify them.'

'Sounds like a bloody lynch mob,' grumbled Sutton quietly.

On screen the original reporter had ditched the vocal bearded man and found somebody else to interview.

'Since when have the BBC interviewed masked protestors?'

asked Sutton, aghast. 'And what about Danyal Mehmud? He barely got a word in edgeways.'

Glimpses of the interviewee beneath her black face mask, bandana and oversized sunglasses suggested a blonde woman of indeterminate age. Her baggy long-sleeved shirt, devoid of any identifying logos, successfully concealed her figure and comparison against the interviewer suggested unexceptional height and build.

'I'm joined by Kay – not her real name – who claims to have been part of the group of counter-protestors involved in yesterday's demonstration. My first question is why we should listen to you when you are not prepared to reveal your face?'

The protestor's polished response suggested the question had been anticipated.

'Unfortunately, we have no choice. We supposedly live in a free and democratic society, but the state routinely tracks and follows those of us who wish to protest peacefully and exercise our right to free speech.' The protestor's accent gave Warren no clues about her upbringing, although he freely admitted to still struggling with accents outside the West Midlands where he'd spent his formative years.

'Members of the British Allegiance Party who marched yesterday say the same thing, but they are willing to show their faces. Why should you be treated any differently?'

'We are forced to wear face masks to protect ourselves from reprisals, both from the fascists and the authorities. As we saw yesterday, the police are willing to use excessive force on peaceful counter-protestors to allow the BAP to express their hateful views.'

'Views that are protected by the same right to free speech that you yourself cite.'

'Hate speech should not be protected speech. In fact, we have lawyers studying transcripts of the BAP's address with a view to demanding a prosecution on the grounds of inciting racial hatred.'

'Much has been made of the police discontinuing the patrol

outside the Islamic Centre and how that may have left it open to attack. Could you tell us some of the views that you are hearing about that decision?'

The masked protester straightened her shoulders slightly.

'Many of us think it is symptomatic of the institutionalised racism that still exists within the police and their widely held view that the concerns and well-being of minorities are less important than those of others.'

There were ripples of disgust from the officers watching the TV. Fortunately, the reporter was too professional to let the slur go entirely unchallenged.

'That's a rather sweeping statement.'

'Kay' shrugged.

'How do you answer charges that the actions of the protestors in breaking through the police line meant that the officer-in-charge had no choice but to call in as many reinforcements as possible?'

Again 'Kay' shrugged. 'Yet more evidence that the police's priorities on Saturday were wrong.'

'Are you suggesting that the police should have allowed protestors to assault the marchers? After all, there is clear footage of protestors throwing stones and bottles at both the police and the BAP.'

'Kay' paused, realising the dangerous waters she suddenly found herself in.

'At last some balanced journalism,' somebody muttered from the back of the office.

'No, what I meant was the police had clearly under-resourced yesterday's operation, even though it was obvious that there was potential for significant trouble...'

'Caused in part by the actions of some of the counter-protestors,' interjected the reporter.

'... caused by the police not taking seriously the concerns of local residents – from all sections of the community – who have repeatedly said that they did not want fascists marching through their town.' She paused for breath.

'If the officer in charge of the operation and his or her superiors had taken the threat posed by the BAP to minorities seriously, they would have deployed enough officers to not only adequately police the march but to protect the targets of this group's hatred. Not just the Islamic Centre but the synagogue, the Afro-Caribbean centre, meeting halls for the Sikh and Hindu communities and pubs and bars associated with the LGBT community among others.'

'Anywhere else you'd like us to stand outside?' grumbled the voice from the back again. Warren decided not to turn around but made a note to address the discontent later.

'That would be an expensive operation at a time when police budgets are under increasing pressure,' noted the reporter.

'You can't put a price on people's lives,' the protestor responded primly. 'I'm sure that with enough motivation Hertfordshire Constabulary could have policed the event proportionately and cost-effectively.'

'But doesn't that require the cooperation of all parties involved?'

'Of course. We made it clear that we would be counter-protesting at the march; yesterday was entirely predictable.'

'But was it? According to sources involved in yesterday's counter-protest, steps were made to conceal the true numbers of protestors planning on turning up to the march.'

For the first time, 'Kay' seemed to be lost for words.

'According to an email seen by the BBC, organisers were told to "keep it quiet" and "not let the pigs get a handle on numbers". In fact, they were deliberately told to "go old school and keep clear of social media" and make arrangements by word-of-mouth.'

'Hah! Burned!' came the voice from the back.

Suddenly on the back foot, 'Kay' mumbled something about not having seen the email and being unable to comment. The journalist let her stew for a moment before thanking her for her time and returning to the studio.

'Could have gone worse, I suppose,' said Sutton.

'Well, at least we're trending on Twitter,' said Gary Hastings, holding up his smartphone.

'Is that a good thing?' asked Warren.

Hastings scrolled for a few seconds and winced.

'No, not really.'

'Well, let's leave Twitter to sort itself out.' Warren raised his voice slightly, and pointedly addressed the back of the room. 'I shall repeat the Assistant Chief Constable's instruction, "stay off social media".'

A few muttered assents, including from the back corner, were enough to satisfy him.

A brief circuit of the room revealed nothing urgent that couldn't wait until the following morning and so Warren decided to check his email for anything pressing and finally head home.

The blinking red light on his telephone console told him that he had a voicemail waiting for him.

'DCI Jones, it's Andy Harrison here. Check your email, we've found the murder weapon. I've taken a photo and sent it to you.' The man's voice sounded more serious than Warren could ever remember. 'If it's what I think it is, the shit's about to hit the fan big time.'

Warren's gut tightened as he typed his username and password into his computer then clicked straight to the message from Harrison, with its attached image.

Warren felt as if he'd been punched.

Middlesbury was going to burn.

Monday 21st July

Chapter 13

'It's a Kirpan. A ceremonial knife worn by baptised Sikhs.'

A groan rose from the officers assembled for the 8 a.m. briefing.

'SOCO have already done a presumptive blood test on the stains on the blade and it's come up positive. We'll need a DNA match obviously, and Professor Jordan will be checking it's consistent with the wound, but I wouldn't want to bet against it.'

The knife on the screen had a wicked-looking curved blade made from stainless steel. A blade covered in blood. The handle was made of brass with elaborate engravings in Indian script.

'They're using acrylate to pull some partial prints off the handle. Hopefully there will be enough reference points for a positive match. They also found a dark blue nylon fibre caught on the edge of the blade. It doesn't match anything on the victim and they're trying to exclude contamination from the bin.'

DSI Grayson cleared his throat, taking over from Warren.

'Confirmation that the leader of the BAP was murdered by an individual from one of our minority communities has the potential to spark rioting or even worse.'

'I thought the BAP were marching against the new super mosque?' said a middle-aged sergeant on loan from Welwyn. 'What would one of them be doing with a Sikh knife?'

'The BAP are a threat to anyone who doesn't fit their notion of what modern Britain should consist of,' answered Warren, uncomfortable with the man's usage of the tabloid term 'super mosque'. 'There were counter-protestors from lots of different sections of the community.'

Grayson took over again. 'We can all imagine the significance of this find – and the need for discretion.'

He looked around the room, making eye contact with everybody present. 'I shall repeat what ACC Naseem said yesterday: there will be no contact with the press or the general public without my direct say-so. Any queries are to be directed specifically to the press office. Have I made myself clear?'

There were nods all around the table.

* * *

'This is bad news, Warren.' The two men were sitting in Grayson's office. 'You were in that meeting yesterday. That was a clear warning about the future of Middlesbury CID if we don't solve this quickly. It's personal for all of us.'

Warren remained silent. He'd worked for Grayson for three years, and whilst the two men were hardly close, he could see that the older man needed to get something off his chest.

Grayson stood up, and walked to the window, staring out onto the car park below.

'Tommy Meegan was an arsehole. Part of me is relieved that he's dead. But the fallout from this could be devastating.' The man's shoulders bunched as he gripped the window ledge.

'If it turns out that he was killed by a minority, then it's playing right into the far-right's hands. Some of these bastards still want a race war, and now they're the victims. With the power of social media behind them this could give them exactly what they want.'

He turned and Warren saw a rare crack in the man's usual composure.

'The Stephen Lawrence murder was a turning point in this country, I truly believe that. Not just the institutionalised racism charges, Lord knows the police have got a lot more work to do on that score, but for the public's perception of what it can be like to be black in this country. That poor boy was simply waiting for a bus and those animals killed him, just because they could. It shocked our society, Warren, and made people start to see these racist thugs for what they are. The legacy of that killing was to expose the nasty, filthy underbelly that still exists in some quarters.

'It's why the BAP have been looking for new targets. We know that every time some so-called Islamist extremist commits an act of terror, the number of attacks on Muslims jumps. If the murder weapon does turn out to be a Kirpan, it'll be open season on our Sikh community also, and anyone else with brown skin and a beard. Will we see a surge in popularity for groups like the BAP?'

'I'm also worried about copycat killings,' said Warren. 'What if we see a rise in vigilante justice? At the moment, the anti-fascist crowd limit themselves to counter-protests; what if the murder of Tommy Meegan is just the first?'

Grayson was silent. When he eventually spoke again, his voice was quiet. 'This goes no further than this room, you understand?'

'Of course.'

'ACC Naseem has asked for a report into the likelihood that this might be the start of concerted action against individual members of the far-right. There are those within the anti-fascist community who publicly state that the laws regarding hate speech and racially motivated violence do not go far enough, and that the police do not have the resources – or the motivation – to deal with the problem. Until last week, the feeling was that these people were all mouth and trousers, but now we're starting to wonder if there might be real intent behind the computer screens.'

'Shit,' breathed Warren. 'That's all we need, vigilantes taking the law into their own hands.'

The situation was worse than he'd feared; where would it end? Far-right extremists and overzealous anti-fascists attacking and killing one another would be bad enough, but what about the general public? What about those innocents in the wrong place at the wrong time? Could the hatred between these groups really undo all the progress made since the Eighties?

Warren vividly remembered the Bradford riots in 2001. On the face of it, modern day Middlesbury was as far removed from the Bradford of a decade and a half previously as one could imagine. But society had changed enormously in that time, not least with the rise of social media. Could Middlesbury really be at the epicentre of a new explosion of violence? The fact that senior officers had gone as far as commissioning a study into the likelihood of such a scenario, told Warren that it was more than idle speculation; no wonder he had been sworn to secrecy. If the media got wind that such a report was being prepared, the headlines would be explosive.

'Maybe I'm overreacting,' said Grayson. 'Maybe the progress made since Stephen Lawrence was killed is too great to be derailed by this one act, but I don't mind telling you, I'm scared, Warren. For Middlesbury and for Britain as a whole. And for my kids.'

Grayson picked up the photograph that sat on his desk.

'You know my family, Warren. You know it's personal to me. When our boys started going out in the evening, Refilwe and I would lie awake until we heard them come in. They're only a quarter black, but you can see it in their features. It would certainly be enough for those bastards to take exception to. We tried to play it down of course, but we still had to talk to them about it: keep an eye out for trouble, don't react to provocation, and if in doubt run.' He smiled grimly. 'All things that my wife is singularly bad at. Touch wood, nothing's ever happened and we stopped worrying about it so much once they went to university. Things have moved on, we told ourselves. But now...'

Warren wasn't really sure what to say. What could he say?

'Catch whoever did this, Warren. And do it quickly. The sooner we get a handle on this, the sooner we can start repairing the damage and perhaps we can avoid disaster for Middlesbury.'

Chapter 14

Warren sat in his office, filled with a nervous energy only partly attributable to caffeine. Despite not arriving home until 11 p.m. the night before, after over twenty-four hours with barely any sleep, he'd been unable to rest, the image of the Kirpan burned into his retinas. Eventually he'd given up and headed back into the office. Susan had barely turned over. Forcing himself to eat some toast, he noticed that the kitchen still smelled of the reheated meal he'd eaten alone the previous night. He'd have to make it up to her; they should be spending more time together these days, not less.

He drummed his fingers on the table. He should stay here to coordinate the various strands of the investigation. He was a DCI after all; visiting suspects and crime scenes was a job best suited to more junior ranks. But his meeting with Grayson had left him with the urge to get out, to do some real policing.

He looked through the window at the job board. Tony Sutton and Karen Hardwick were assigned to the arson at the Islamic Centre, with David Hutchinson coordinating house-to-house inquiries. Gary Hastings and one of the detectives on loan from Welwyn were out double-checking the stories told yesterday. DS Mags Richardson was liaising with the force's video surveillance unit down in Welwyn. Allowing for annual leave, that accounted for almost all of Warren's usual team. He picked up his desk phone to dial headquarters and arrange for some bodies to interview Tommy Meegan's significant other and take a look inside his flat.

Theo Garfield walked past the window. The man had arrived first thing that morning on the train for a meeting with Grayson and was now hot-desking in the corner of the office. He looked as impatient as Warren.

A quiet ping announced the arrival of an email. 'Quarterly budget projections' teased the header. Warren replaced the handset and grabbed his jacket.

'Fancy a road trip, Theo?'

'Thought you'd never ask.'

* * *

Micky Drake was well known to Middlesbury Police, as was his establishment, The Feathers pub. Nevertheless, Drake didn't have a criminal record and he was just good enough at keeping the behaviour of his clientele in check to retain his licence and keep his premises open.

Hastings and Moray Ruskin, an eager young probationary DC from Welwyn, had left their unmarked patrol car in the car park. Both wore their ties loosened in deference to the warm weather. Nevertheless, they were met with a chorus of pig noises as they shouldered their way through the crowd of smokers by the front door.

Ignoring them, they entered the bar. Dimly lit, it took a few seconds for their eyes to adjust. A couple of early morning drinkers got up and pushed past them, leaving their half-finished pints behind. Hastings suspected they probably had something weighing on their conscience.

There was no mistaking Drake. His shaved head sat directly

atop his shoulders, with no visible evidence of a neck. As if to stand out from his customers, rather than the ubiquitous England football shirt, he wore a Six Nations England rugby shirt.

Hastings glanced over at his companion; ordinarily he might think twice about bringing such an inexperienced colleague to this environment. But Moray Ruskin was six feet five inches tall and weighed over eighteen stone, none of it excess fat. He could handle a bit of verbal abuse over his Scottish accent.

Drake leant over the bar and leered at Hastings.

'How may I be of assistance, officers?'

Hastings resisted the urge to ask for a bottle of Cobra; somehow, he doubted they served the popular Indian lager

'May we have a word in private, Mr Drake?'

He looked at the two officers hard, before lifting the serving hatch and motioning them to follow.

'Jaz, I'm taking a break,' he called out.

The back of the pub was narrow, a state of affairs not helped by a ceiling-high stack of boxes containing bar snacks. To the left of the entrance a flight of stairs presumably led towards the landlord's private accommodation. Following Drake to the right, into his office, Hastings caught a glimpse through beaded curtains of a small, dingy-looking kitchen area. He hoped the food preparation surfaces were cleaner than the carpet sticking to his shoes. The air was so heavy with the smell of air-freshener, Hastings couldn't help wondering what he was covering up.

Drake dropped into a rickety-looking leather office chair; it creaked alarmingly, but didn't collapse under his substantial weight. He waved vaguely across the desk in what Hastings decided to interpret as an invitation to pull over one of the moulded plastic seats.

'Thank you for taking the time to see us, Mr Drake,' Hastings started.

'Don't really have much more to tell you than what I said Saturday night.'

'Nevertheless, it may help us to piece together what happened that afternoon.'

Drake sighed. 'Suppose it's the least I can do for Ray's boy.'

That seemed to be as good a starting point as any, Hastings decided.

'I knew Ray way back when, when we used to do jobs together.' Hastings fought the urge to ask what he meant by 'jobs'.

'We'd go to the footie on a Saturday afternoon, you know to get away from the wives.' He smiled. 'That Mary of his was a cracking bird – he was punching well above his weight – but she can't half nag.'

'And did you get to know his boys then?'

'Yeah. He started bringing them along to the matches when they were nippers. It was a cheap afternoon's entertainment, not like today. When they was old enough, he used to bring them in here for a bag of crisps and a glass of lemonade.' He smirked slightly.

'Did you keep in touch with the boys and their father after they went away?'

'If by "went away", you mean after they got banged up, yeah I did.' He glared fiercely at the two officers. 'It's times like this you find out who your real friends are.'

'What about when Ray died?' It was the first time Ruskin had spoken.

He nodded. 'We held the wake in here. 'Course the boys couldn't come. They got released to attend the funeral but they were sandwiched between two fucking apes from the prison service and the bastards wouldn't let them raise a toast to their old man's memory.' His voiced dropped. 'A fucking disgrace it was. You'd think they'd make an exception.'

Hastings had read the files of both men and was rather glad they hadn't taken any chances. There had been enough concerns about the potential for trouble that the force had decided to spend the best part of five thousand pounds on overtime to keep the peace. That figure would no doubt be dwarfed when Tommy Meegan's final send-off took place next week.

'After Ray passed away, did you keep in touch with the boys?' asked Ruskin.

'Off and on, they don't come back as often as they should. That poor mum of theirs lives all alone in that tower block.'

'But they contacted you Saturday before the rally?'

'Yeah. They just wanted somewhere friendly they could enjoy a quiet pint and unwind after they'd had their say about the super mosque.' The man said it without a hint of irony.

'OK, so tell me about Saturday.'

'The plan was to leave Romford in the morning on a coach, and get to town about midday. Then they was going to have a march, exercise their right to free speech and walk back here for about two or three. They wanted a bit of grub, so I got the kitchen fired up.'

'Who was organising?'

'Tommy, he's the leader.' He paused. 'He was the leader.'

'Did he say how many they were expecting?'

'Tommy said about sixty.' He smiled. 'He always was a bit optimistic. I catered for about forty. The coach was only a fifty-seater. Mind you that big lad Bellies could probably have helped me out if I'd made too much. The bugger's huge.'

'So what time did they all start arriving?'

'Most arrived about three. None of them knew where they were going and they had to ask directions.'

'Were any late?'

'Yeah Bellies waddled in about five minutes after the scrawny one with the gold tooth. Reckon they turned up about half past three, twenty to four.'

'I don't suppose you have any CCTV footage that could help us pin down the times more accurately?'

Drake grinned, revealing a number of missing teeth. 'Sorry, been meaning to get it fixed.'

'When did they realise Tommy was missing?'

He let out a hiss of air.

'To be honest, I don't know. The beer was flowing and they were hungry. They'd probably been here over an hour before I realised I hadn't seen Tommy.'

'What did you do?'

He shrugged. 'Nothing really. The tills were ringing and I was too busy to think about it. I asked Jimmy where he was and he just shrugged. Everybody figured he'd probably been arrested. There was a bit of piss-taking about not dropping the soap in the shower, that sort of thing.'

'OK. Can you take me through the rest of the evening?'

'They were supposed to knock it on the head about eight-ish and get back on the coach. The driver had moved it into the car park and was waiting for them to finish their pints. Then I was going to open the doors again to a few of the regulars, but that never happened.' For the first time the older man looked sad. 'Four of your lot turned up unannounced. I assumed they'd arrived to give the lads a bit of hassle before they went home so I told them to piss off and wait outside unless they had a good reason to come in.

'The lead fellow was all right for a copper. He took me to one side and explained what had happened and asked me to point out Jimmy.' He paused again. 'I knew before he did, the poor sod.'

'What happened next?'

'They took Jimmy out the back, he was in a bit of a state. The big lad and the one with the gold tooth went with him. The rest of the boys were pretty shocked as you can imagine. A few more coppers turned up and asked a few questions, took their names and addresses, that sort of thing.'

'When did they all leave?'

'About eleven. The coach driver was banging on about being over his hours, but everybody wanted to go home.'

'And did they all go?'

'Everyone except Jimmy and his two mates.'

'Mr Brandon and Mr Davenport?'

'If you say so.'

'Bellies and Goldie?'

'Yeah.'

'Where did they go?'

'The police took them to see Mary. To break the news, I guess. Poor bastards; I offered my spare room, but I think they all stayed with her.'

Hastings looked at Ruskin who shook his head. No more questions.

He stood up. 'Well, thank you for your help, Mr Drake.' He didn't offer his hand. Drake's smirk returned.

'My pleasure and come back any time, there's always a warm welcome for proper patriots. Besides I do good food. The chicken Kiev is especially popular.'

Chapter 15

Annabelle Creasy fulfilled several stereotypes. A gravel-voiced forty-something, she'd tried her best to smooth out the wrinkles with what Warren had heard termed an 'Essex facelift' – a painfully tight hair grip that pulled her dyed blonde-hair back, stretching the skin on her forehead and exposing her dark-brown roots. Aside from that, the best one-word description he could think of was 'orange'.

It was strange, Warren mused, the way that despite the steady march of cosmetic science, fake tans seemed to have gone backwards. He was certain that they used to look more natural, as if you'd spent a couple of weeks sunning yourself in the Mediterranean, rather than a month at what Garfield had termed 'Camp Oompah-Loompa'. Warren had to fight hard to keep the rather mean observation out of his mind as he expressed his condolences to the woman sat before him. It was just as well that Garfield had opted to keep a low profile and borrowed the car to go and pick up the keys to Tommy Meegan's flat.

Creasy had barely acknowledged him and Warren felt a twinge of shame at his unkind thoughts. Regardless of what he may think of her political views – and the tattoo on her left bicep gave no doubt about which end of the political spectrum she leant towards – she was still a grieving partner, her eyes bloodshot and her nose reddened.

The mantelpiece was covered in photographs of her and Meegan. In many of them they stood either side of a young boy. Judging from the way that the lad aged, the couple had been together for several years.

'Is that your boy?' asked Warren, deciding to start the conversation on a neutral topic. Typically, when he did this sort of inquiry, the great British tradition of offering a cup of tea could be relied upon to break the ice. Warren knew he would not be getting that sort of hospitality here.

Often a Family Liaison Officer would already be present. By now they would have got to know the bereaved a little and could give him a quick heads up. Creasy had made it clear that an FLO was still a police officer and that they wouldn't be welcome in her house. She'd grudgingly agreed to the presence of a uniform outside to deter any unwanted visitors, such as the press, but she'd not engaged at all with her.

She'd had a couple of visitors – a slightly younger looking woman who'd identified herself as her sister and a much older woman that had claimed to be her mother. They'd both stayed for less than an hour.

Creasy answered his question with a nod.

'Yeah, that's Dale. His old man's got him this weekend.' Her mouth twisted. 'He's heartbroken with what happened to Tommy. I said he should be here, you know, but a court order's a court order.' Her eyes brimmed with tears and Warren felt even more sympathy. He'd scanned her record before arriving and seen that she and her former partner were embroiled in an ongoing custody battle over the young boy. The police had been called on several occasions to deal with incidents concerning the former couple, including criminal damage and assault, hence the record. It was a classic case of a relationship gone sour, with the couple acrimoniously dividing up the spoils – the spoils in this case being a young boy. That perhaps explained why she and Tommy Meegan hadn't lived together. Meegan's own record was hardly going to impress the courts.

'How old is Dale?'

'He's just turned eleven.' She smiled slightly. 'Off to big school in September.' Her smile faded. 'Tommy was going to take him to get his new uniform next week.'

Warren gave her a few moments.

'He wasn't a bad man.' Creasy's voice had become stronger. 'But the press painted him that way. He just wanted to stand up for his country. For all of us.' Her rhetoric was practised, peppered with the same innuendo, hyperbole and half-truths that Warren had been subjected to since the investigation had started. Out of the corner of his eye he could see a picture of young Dale, his light blond hair no doubt shaved to the limit of his school's uniform policy. He wondered what sort of poisons had been pumped into his developing brain by his mother and Meegan. What sort of citizen would he grow up to be? Tommy and Jimmy Meegan were the product of their father's views. What would be the effect of Tommy Meegan's death on the young boy's development? Would the removal of such a toxic role model prevent him from following that same path, or would it reinforce those views? If it transpired that a member of the Sikh community was responsible, rather than the Muslim community, what would the effect be on him? Not good, he suspected. Warren pushed the thought away for the time being and focused on keeping his face neutral.

Creasy finally finished her diatribe, stuttering to a halt and blowing her nose loudly.

'It's my job to find out who killed Tommy, but I need your help. Had Tommy mentioned any threats against him recently? Did he speak about any fears?'

'Check out the BAP's Facebook page or Twitter feed. They received death threats every day.' She scowled. 'We report them, but nobody gives a shit. All the time you read about how trolls are being done for posting vile things on the web or tweeting about how they want to rape or kill feminists—' she sniffed loudly '—but nobody gives a toss when somebody threatens to stab or shoot Tommy and party members. It isn't fashionable. Offend some Muslim on Facebook and you're taken down in hours. Tell a patriot that he'll be killed if he tries to exercise his right to free speech and nobody does anything.'

Warren kept his face neutral. Garfield's observation from the interview with Bellies Brandon rang true. She'd mentioned Muslims repeatedly, but had said little about the other groups traditionally targeted by the far-right.

'We're going through all of Tommy's social media accounts looking for suspects, but we need your help. Did he mention anyone in particular that he was worried about? Did he have any fears about what might happen on Saturday?'

She shrugged. 'No, not really. In fact he seemed really excited about going back to Middlesbury.'

'That was his hometown, I believe.'

'Yeah. He and Jimmy were brought up there. But it was more than that.'

'What do you mean?'

'He said something about it being a turning point for the BAP. That it would secure the party's future.'

'How do you mean?'

'I don't know. He wouldn't say.'

Warren thought about her phrasing. 'Securing the party's future' sounded almost financial. Had the party found some sort of backer? Somebody who was willing to help pay for their activities? According to the coach firm they had hired for the day, it had cost them about six hundred pounds – roughly fifteen pounds each for the forty-odd participants. Usually, they travelled by public transport, which typically cost even more. The majority of the BAP's active supporters were in low-paid jobs or unemployed. If Meegan had secured some sort of sponsorship for his activities, then he would have been understandably excited.

He decided to change the subject slightly.

'The coach they hired still had a few empty seats. Why didn't you go?'

Her eyes flicked away from Warren's.

'I had to look after Dale.'

'I thought he was with his father this weekend?'

Her mouth opened slightly; Warren could see her thinking furiously.

'I was going to have him, but his dad changed his mind at the last minute.'

She was lying. Warren could tell that from her body language, let alone the fact that she'd made it clear just a few moments ago that the relationship between her son and his father was dictated by court order. He doubted she would let her ex-partner change the terms in that manner.

'OK. What about other times? Do you usually go with him? If you don't have Dale.'

Warren already knew the answer to the question. Garfield had told him they had no record of her attending any other rallies.

'No, Tommy says it's no place for a woman.'

Her expression was unreadable. What she said wasn't strictly true. Although Saturday's jaunt had been a definite boys' day out, there was a small core of female party members who often attended protests.

Warren took out his notepad and a pencil.

'We're still struggling to fill in the details of exactly what took place that day. I could use your help.'

He took her silence as acquiescence.

'When did Tommy leave for the protest?'

'He was up about seven-ish, I guess. He left here about eight after a fry-up.' She smiled slightly at the memory. 'He always liked to start the day properly, although I reckon he was mostly just lining his stomach for the journey.'

'Where did he go then?'

'He had to catch the bus to the pub where they were being picked up by the coach. I think he met Bellies on the way.'

'What about his brother or his friend, Mr Davenport? I understand they live quite close.'

Her eyes darkened slightly.

'I don't know.'

'Was everybody getting on the coach at the pub, or were they doing pick-ups?'

She sneered slightly. 'Why are you asking me? You videotaped them and followed them up the motorway.'

'OK, so they left at ten. What time were you expecting him back?'

'I wasn't. He was going to spend the night at his mum's, then catch the train back.'

'Was Jimmy going to stay as well?'

'I guess so.'

Interesting. Annabelle Creasy hadn't expected her boyfriend to return that night, but Mary Meegan had made it sound as if the arrival of Jimmy and his friends had been a complete surprise and a result of his brother's death. Nor had she mentioned that Tommy had been planning on visiting her. The Meegans didn't strike Warren as the sort of family that spontaneously dropped in on each other without warning, confident of a warm welcome.

So what was Tommy planning on doing that night? Was he going to stay with his mother? Or was he going to stay somewhere else?

Chapter 16

Warren emerged from Annabelle Creasy's house having secured a grudging agreement to call him if she thought of anything else significant.

Even in the bright, summer sunshine, the area was grim. Creasy's house, like all those nearby, was at least thirty years older than it should be. The street reminded him of parts of Coventry from his childhood. Supposedly temporary houses had been slung up rapidly in the Fifties, both to replace houses destroyed during the Blitz and to house the wave of immigrants, mainly Irish, who had arrived to rebuild the devastated city. Decades on, the houses were still there, desperately in need of modernisation.

Creasy's street was opposite an overgrown cemetery. This in turn was overlooked by a huge, rusting, defunct gas works. The waist-high brick wall that divided the end of the short row of houses and the main road had been painted white once upon a time, perhaps in an attempt to smarten the area. All it had done was provide a blank canvas for graffiti. Some of the more offensive slogans and images had been crudely whitewashed – they could still be seen under the paint – but whoever was in charge of maintenance had finally given up. The wall was now awash with scrawled tags, the urban equivalent of a dog cocking its leg against a lamppost to mark its territory.

If it hadn't been for the presence of Theo Garfield, Warren wouldn't have been surprised to find his car had been similarly decorated in his absence.

Warren closed the wrought iron gate behind him; a rather pointless gesture given that most of the rotten wooden fence was lying flat across what could have been a flower bed with some care and attention. He was using a tissue to remove some of the rust and peeling paint from his hands as he walked back to the car, when he noticed an older man from the house opposite staring at him.

Short and wiry, he could have been anywhere between fifty and seventy, his paint-splattered vest revealing what Susan called a 'PE teacher's tan'; a dark mahogany brown covering his arms and neck in the shape of a T-shirt, surrounded by pasty white flesh. A roll-up cigarette hung from his bottom lip. Alone amongst the line of houses, his had a freshly creosoted fence, its metal gate a gleaming red. Instead of the cheap, faded, plastic numbers nailed to some of the front doors, his was a hand-painted plaque with what looked like oriental script underneath. Warren wondered if he had taken it upon himself to cover the worst of the graffiti on the end wall rather than waiting for the council to get their act together.

Warren smiled politely as he passed the man.

'Officer.' The man's voice was gravelly.

Warren had given up being surprised at how easily people recognised him as a policeman. This wasn't the sort of area that men in suits and ties tended to frequent, and after what had happened to Annabelle Creasy's partner, it hardly took a master detective to figure out why he was there.

Warren continued walking. Three more paces, he judged. He could see Garfield folding the newspaper he'd been reading – a copy of the *Mirror* he'd bought in a half-hearted attempt to fit in whilst he waited in the car.

'This place is not exactly a bastion of *Guardian* readers, and I'm a Scouser so I'm certainly not reading *The Sun*,' he'd commented with a slight curl of the lip on his return from the newsagent.

'You could always listen to Radio 4,' Warren had offered. 'I hear Germaine Greer's on *Woman's Hour*.'

Three paces exactly.

'Officer?' This time the voice was even quieter and grumbly.

Warren paused and half turned.

The man shuffled from foot to foot, coughed slightly then took another drag of his cigarette.

'I 'spect you're here about what happened?'

Warren appraised the man carefully. In his experience, the merely nosy tended to be more explicit. The man was furtive and unsure; he glanced up and down the empty street.

Warren said nothing. Out of the corner of his eye, he saw that Garfield was now standing by the car door.

A few more seconds passed.

'It's probably nothing…'

* * *

'Well, that puts a different complexion on things,' remarked Warren as they pulled away from the kerb.

Garfield pulled at his lip slightly.

'You think? I'm not sure he's that reliable, and it's just gossip anyway.'

'It needs checking out, because if what Mr Procter says is true, then I'd say we have another potential motive.'

At first Terrence Procter had been unsure of himself. However, after deciding that the two officers should come inside, away from public view, he became more confident.

'I'm not going to lie, I never liked that woman and the people she brought into the area.'

'That woman' was Annabelle Creasy and Terrence Procter had watched with dismay as she'd moved in about eight years previously.

'This place might not be the smartest in Romford, but folks generally got on with each other. I've been here nearly fifty years and we used to fit right in.' He inclined his head towards the mantelpiece, where a black and white picture of a strikingly beautiful Chinese woman took pride of place.

'When Annabelle and her little boy moved in across the way, Kuangyu knocked on the door to say hello. She always did that.' Procter smiled sadly. 'I suppose the tattoos should have given her a warning, but Kuangyu never used to notice that sort of thing.' The smile disappeared. 'I don't know what she said to my wife but she was still in tears when I returned an hour later.' Now the memory was making him angry. 'I wanted to go and have words with her, but Kuangyu wouldn't let me. It was the last thing we ever argued about.'

He cleared this throat.

'Anyway, that was years ago. Kuangyu always told me not to dwell in the past.'

'So what was it you wanted to tell us about?' Warren asked.

'That fella on the news? The one stabbed after that march?'

'Yes, what about him?'

'He was her boyfriend. I recognised his picture.'

Beside him, Garfield shifted in his seat. He'd waited in the car whilst Warren had interviewed Annabelle Creasy, reluctant to reveal himself to such a prominent member of the far-right unnecessarily. However, it seemed curiosity had gotten the better of him when Procter had invited them in. Either that or he'd exhausted the *Mirror*.

Procter picked up on Garfield's impatience.

'Which is why you're here, obviously.'

'Why don't you tell us what you know about Mr Meegan,' invited Warren.

'He was a nasty piece of work; I guess you don't need me to tell you that.'

Warren said nothing.

'You only needed to see the tattoos to know. He didn't live with her – I heard that she was fighting a custody battle over the little 'un and they were worried that it wouldn't look good if a thug like him was living there.' He sighed. 'It's probably too late now. The boy's real dad wasn't ever going to win any prizes for father of the year, like, but he was better than that Meegan and his mates. He tried his best, I heard him telling the lad off for using the P-word, but the kid just laughed. The old man was unemployed and couldn't afford much. Meegan always seemed to bring something around when he visited.'

So far, Procter had simply confirmed what Warren had already guessed.

'His mates weren't much better. They'd come round sometimes too. They used to get the barbecue going in the front garden and hang the speakers out the front windows. It'd be going on until gone midnight, shouting, swearing, racist language. They'd chuck their empties over the wall into other people's gardens.

'The police turned up once. I've no idea if somebody called or they just heard the racket and came to investigate. I thought it was all going to kick off but they eventually went inside the house and turned the music down. The next morning, both her neighbours had swastikas painted on their doors and dog muck smeared on the handles. Nobody ever called the police again.'

Procter had been fiddling with a pack of cigarette papers whilst he spoke. Now he slid one out and produced a packet of rolling tobacco. The familiar action seemed to focus him.

'Sometimes there'd be a dozen or so folks there of a night, all tattooed and wearing England shirts you know, but there were a few who came more often.'

'Could you describe them?' Warren's instincts were telling him that the man's story was edging towards the most important part.

'All had shaved heads obviously. One of them I recognised from the TV, they said he was Tommy's brother, Jimmy or something. Another was absolutely huge; looked like a bloody great tattooed whale. It was him that brought her fence down, when he got pissed and fell on it. The other bloke was the opposite, scrawny with loads of gold chain and a gold tooth.' Procter's mouth twisted. 'I didn't like the look of him much. I saw him the most.'

'He was with Tommy?'

'No. In fact he was usually there when Tommy wasn't, if you catch my drift.'

'Can you remember the last time you saw him?'

'Yeah. He was coming out of there early Saturday morning. I saw him when I went to pick up the papers.'

Chapter 17

'So Goldie Davenport was bumping uglies with Tommy Meegan's missus. It hardly makes him a killer.'

Garfield was playing devil's advocate and Warren appreciated the man's alternative perspective; ordinarily he'd have relied on Tony Sutton to play this role.

'I agree, but folks have certainly killed for less.'

Garfield thought for a few moments.

'Didn't you say that Annabelle Creasy claimed that Tommy Meegan had left her place Saturday morning to go attend the rally?'

'Yes, she said he left at about seven.'

'Well, surely that blows away the theory that she was having an affair with Goldie Davenport? That old boy just said that he saw Goldie leaving Saturday morning, he didn't say that Tommy wasn't with him. Maybe he stayed over so they could get an early start the next morning. Perfectly innocent.' He leered. 'I suppose they could have been having a threesome, but that'd be consensual.'

Warren took his left hand off the steering wheel and used it to count off points.

'Taking them backwards, threesomes are rife with jealousy. Plenty of motivation for murder.'

Garfield inclined his head in acknowledgement.

'Next, Procter didn't say Tommy *was* with him. In fact he was quite clear that he'd seen Goldie leaving on his own on previous occasions, so the implication was clear that he was alone this time—' he raised a hand slightly to stall Garfield's counter-argument '—but you have a point. We'll be sure to clarify in any follow-up interview.

'Look, if Annabelle Creasy was lying about Tommy leaving her house that morning, then we have to ask ourselves why? She could be trying to hide her affair with Goldie from everyone else. Jimmy Meegan is unlikely to take kindly to finding out his brother was being cheated on, so I doubt Goldie Davenport would be happy about his bed-hopping becoming public knowledge.'

Garfield still didn't look convinced. After a few moments silence he spoke up,

'The thing is, I could understand Tommy Meegan killing Goldie. He finds out his mate is shagging his girl, so he kills him in a fit of jealous rage. I could even imagine the two of them getting into a fight and Goldie killing Tommy by accident. That would make sense. But from what I've heard of the crime scene, it doesn't support that sort of confrontation. You're the expert, what do you think?'

Warren pursed his lips. 'It's impossible to say. He had bruises consistent with a fight, but he probably picked them up from the riot. The alleyway was bit of a bloodbath as you can imagine and I've not seen anything consistent with a prolonged struggle, but then nothing rules it out either. I'll let the CSIs process it fully before I draw a firm conclusion.'

'So unlikely to be Goldie then,' Garfield concluded.

Warren shook his head at his colleague's hastily drawn conclusion. He'd forgotten that Garfield wasn't CID; his expertise lay in intelligence gathering, whilst interpreting crime scenes and discerning motives was Warren's bread and butter. He wondered how long it had been since Garfield had flexed those intellectual muscles. He'd have to remember that in future.

'It didn't have to be a hot-blooded fit of jealousy. In fact, I'd argue it almost certainly wasn't; those sorts of murders tend to be solved pretty quickly. I'd say a degree of planning and preparation went into this. If Davenport was the killer, I think it's more likely he wanted to get rid of his love rival and live happily ever after with the lovely Ms Creasy. Not to mention, where would he get a Kirpan? I doubt he had one lying around.'

'From everything you've told me and what I've read about her it seems a bit far-fetched. Some tart the colour of a parking cone with a kid whose old man keeps on trying to get custody; hardly worth the fight, if you ask me.'

Warren bit his tongue; no matter what Garfield thought of the woman and her beliefs and associations – not to mention his own unpleasant experiences in the past – as far as he was concerned, she was grieving and deserving of at least some respect. Had Garfield been in his direct chain of command, he'd have pulled the car over and called him to task over his attitude.

Garfield appeared oblivious to the effect his words were having on his colleague.

'A far-right love triangle. I suppose you could call it a far-right-angled triangle.'

Warren winced. Nevertheless it had reminded him of something that Annabelle Creasy had said.

'It could be more of a love square than a love triangle.'

Garfield raised an eyebrow.

'How so?'

'Regardless of whether Tommy Meegan departed from Annabelle Creasy's house Saturday morning, she wasn't expecting him to return that night. She said that he was going to stay the night with his mother in Middlesbury.'

'So? Makes sense; kill two birds with one stone.'

'Well, not from what we've heard. Mary Meegan said she had

been surprised by the appearance of Jimmy at her door that night. She knew they were in town but wasn't expecting them to drop by; in fact, I got the impression that she rarely saw them these days.'

Garfield thought for a moment.

'So if he wasn't staying at his mum's, where was he planning on staying? Was he going to stay in Middlesbury and come back on the train like Annabelle Creasy said, or was he going to come back here on the coach and then go somewhere else?'

'Maybe he just wanted a quiet night in after all the excitement and didn't fancy going around to his girlfriend's.'

'Nah, not likely. These guys really get off on the violence. If anything he'd have been straight round here to get his end away. I think you're right. There's somebody else.'

'Apparently Annabelle Creasy never goes on the trips, he's told her it's no place for women. I'm not convinced she believes him.'

Garfield was already shaking his head. 'That's bollocks. She's right that she never goes on the trips, but there are about half a dozen wives and girlfriends who do go with them regularly. We call them the WAGs on account of all the tattoos and England shirts.'

'So he liked a bit of time away from his significant other. I think it would be prudent to work out who he's visiting, don't you?'

'I'll have a look at the files.' A sly grin spread across Garfield's face. 'You know a love square is even better than a far-right-angled triangle? A square has *four* right angles.'

'We're here,' announced Warren with relief.

Chapter 18

Garfield and Warren wore protective overshoes and gloves as they opened the door to Tommy Meegan's flat, using a master key from the letting agent.

The flat was a modest affair, typical for this part of East London or Essex. A converted terraced house, it had its own front door leading immediately to a flight of stairs that took visitors up to the main living area, a lounge cum dining room cum kitchenette. A single open doorway led to a small vestibule with doors leading to a hot water boiler and airing cupboard, bathroom and double bedroom.

'I'll check the bedroom, whilst you do the lounge,' suggested Garfield heading towards the back room. Strictly speaking, as Senior Investigating Officer it was Warren's case and he should be giving the orders, but all the way over, Garfield had been itching to get into the flat. Warren knew that quite aside from what they might find about the murder, Garfield was looking forward to the general intelligence he might glean.

'Tell me if you find his laptop,' Warren called through.

'Got it. Turned off under a pile of rather smelly T-shirts.'

'Bag it and log it, I'll get Forensic IT to look at it.'

As Garfield continued rooting through the bedroom, Warren

worked his way around the kitchen, soon finding that Meegan was unlikely to find himself the recipient of any *Good Housekeeping* awards. The smell from the open bin suggested it hadn't been emptied for some time. The sink was filled with several days' worth of dirty dishes. The microwave door was ajar and Warren could see that it was coated with grime. The countertop was pulling double-duty as a desk and a table – it looked as though Meegan preferred to eat standing up, ideally frozen microwave meals. A quick look in the freezer suggested that either Meegan possessed a fine sense of irony or was a culinary ignoramus; amongst the dozen or so ready meals Warren identified delicacies from at least eight different countries.

Next to the dishes was a pile of opened mail. Leafing through it, Warren found a bill from O2 for a mobile phone plan. Just as he'd suspected, the pay-as-you-go brick found at the scene was not his main phone. So where was his regular phone?

'Theo, keep an eye out for another mobile phone, I've got his bill here.'

'Got it,' came the mumbled reply from the bedroom. 'He left it on charge on his bedside table. I guess he didn't want us to get hold of it.'

'Is it switched on?'

'Yeah.'

'Then bag it and bring it in here quickly.'

Garfield appeared, looking slightly flustered.

'Have you tried to do anything with it?'

'No.'

'Good.' Warren took the plastic evidence bag containing the smartphone and placed it in the microwave. 'It's unlikely, but just in case, we don't want somebody remotely wiping data from it.'

'I never even thought.' Garfield looked chastened.

'What else did you find in there?'

'Well, he could have started his own museum of England and Chelsea football shirts and I sincerely hope he'd planned on washing his bedsheets before he brought anyone around to stay the night.'

'Nothing else?'

'Nothing I didn't expect. His choice of bedside reading is a biography of José Mourinho and a couple of dirty magazines. Nothing too exotic.'

'None of these fine tomes then?'

Warren inclined his head towards the bookshelf, with its collection of paperbacks, which aside from a handful of sports memoirs, were mostly far-right polemics. A couple even bore swastikas on the spine. Pride of place was a hardback edition of *Mein Kampf*.

Garfield was dismissive. 'Don't be fooled. Look at the spines, they've never been cracked. These idiots get all of their propaganda from websites and grubby little underground magazines. These are just for show. There's no way Tommy Meegan read himself to sleep at night with Albert Speer's memoirs. Especially in the original German.'

* * *

DSI Grayson had pulled a few strings and by the time Warren and Garfield had finished in Tommy Meegan's flat, four Detective Constables and an experienced DS from the Metropolitan Police were waiting at the local police station to help with door-to-door inquiries with his neighbours.

After a quick briefing from Warren, the five officers piled into a people carrier and headed out, with orders to report back to Middlesbury.

Warren looked at his watch. Two o'clock. Less than forty-eight hours had elapsed since the discovery of Tommy Meegan's body and the pace was starting to increase. On balance, Warren felt that they had started pretty well. He stifled a yawn, immediately triggering a similar response in Garfield.

'I'd forgotten how punishing the first couple of days could be,' admitted Garfield as he got his phone out. Warren smiled politely; it had barely started. He'd once thought of a murder investigation as a marathon, not a sprint and tried to pace himself accordingly. But experience had shown that to be somewhat facile. The first forty-eight to seventy-two hours were the 'golden hours'. To that end, Warren would work himself and his team hard during that magic window, maximising the returns from their efforts, before easing into a more sustainable routine. To return to the running analogy, they'd start the race with a sprint, trying to build a commanding lead over their opponents, before dropping the pace to a steady rhythm, with quick bursts of speed when they needed it.

'I'm going to deposit the laptop and mobile phone at Welwyn, do you want me to drop you off there, and save you a train journey?'

'Sounds like a plan,' agreed Garfield, stifling yet another yawn.

'Good, you can keep me awake with amusing stories about our far-right friends.'

'Take the scenic route, there's plenty.'

Chapter 19

By the time Warren arrived back at Middlesbury, the DS in charge of canvassing Tommy Meegan's neighbours had phoned in that nobody had reported any disturbances or suspicious characters hanging around. In fact, most had been surprised to find out the man's identity.

This wasn't unexpected according to Theo Garfield on speakerphone from Welwyn.

'For all his bluster, he isn't going to tell the world where he lives. These guys have to take their security seriously. For the most part, it's all part of the mythos, "look how important we are, we need protection", but we have spent taxpayers' money on consultants to advise them.'

'What about regular visitors?' asked Garfield.

'A woman resembling Annabelle Creasy had been seen occasionally, but not recently, and there was no evidence of her kid.'

'Fits with the state of his bedroom, I can't imagine there's been a woman in there lately,' observed Garfield.

'Other visitors match the description of his brother, Goldie Davenport and Bellies Brandon. They used to come around quite regularly, Brandon in particular, which fits with him staying there for a time, but they haven't been seen for a few weeks.'

'Hard to mistake Bellies,' noted Garfield.

'Anything from your files that hints that he may have been having an affair?'

'Nothing yet. I doubt it's important though, I think the murder weapon tells us most of what we need to know.'

'You're probably right, but keep me posted, Theo,' Warren ordered.

Despite Warren's words, he didn't like leaving loose ends and he wanted to know what Meegan had been doing on the evenings he was unaccounted for.

His stomach rumbled. He'd skipped lunch and his last dose of caffeine was wearing off; he decided to go grab a coffee, stretch his legs and then have something to eat.

A couple of years ago, he'd managed to sweet-talk the canteen staff into making him plain cheese sandwiches on brown bread without margarine or mayonnaise. But twelve months ago they'd sold the franchise and now the sandwiches were all delivered pre-made in a chiller van with a picture of a bread-basket on the side. Every day he had to dismantle the sandwich to remove the endless layers of tomato or lettuce it was stuffed with. Not only did the salad make the bread soggy, Warren really resented paying extra money for ingredients that ended up in the bin. The nutritional quality of Warren's lunch had become a bone of contention between him and Susan in recent months.

The kitchen area where the sandwiches used to be prepared had been given over to a chain coffee stall. Warren had yet to buy a drink there – his own small protest against the creeping privatisation of public services. Why was it, he asked himself as he threw a fifty-pence piece into the near-empty honesty jar, his colleagues were so reluctant to pay a few pence to keep the communal coffee area running, yet quite happy to pay several pounds for a single cup?

Warren was ruminating on this as he re-entered the office.

'We've got a positive match for the fingermarks on the Kirpan found at the scene.'

Gary Hastings held the printout like a trophy. Immediately all thoughts of the coffee in his hand, or the content of his sandwich, evaporated.

'Who have we got?'

'One Binay Singh Mahal. Twenty-seven years old. Historic convictions for vandalism and taking without consent. Last known address is the other side of the Chequers estate from Mary Meegan.'

Warren felt a thrill run through him; this was what he loved about his job.

'Get a team together in the main briefing room in one hour. I'll get the warrants processed.'

* * *

The forced entry team leader was Sergeant Roger Gibson who Warren had worked with previously. The suspect was presumed to be dangerous so the safety of the arresting officers was paramount. He might have forensically significant material that he could be trying to destroy even as they spoke, so they needed to plan and execute the operation as quickly as possible. Warren was happy to hand over the planning of such a complex operation to an expert.

'According to council tax records, he lives on the ground floor of Bevan Tower which will make entry easier. We've done a walk past and a red Ford Focus registered to him is parked outside and the TV is on, so we expect him to be in.'

He pulled over a sheet of paper with a crude floor plan printed on it.

'According to the letting agent, entry is via a communal hallway and opens into the lounge. The living area is to the left with an open-plan kitchen immediately to the right. Next door along that wall is a small bedroom. Keep going directly through the lounge to a passageway and the large bedroom is to the left and the bathroom to the right.

'We don't know if he's alone and he may try to destroy evidence, so we shan't be ringing the doorbell, ladies and gentlemen. We'll go in hard with the ram, full body armour, two to a room. Arrest anyone present and make sure the scene is secure, including any computer equipment.' He turned to the officer on his left, a young lad who barely looked out of his teens. 'Callum is our computer expert. Don't let his youthful appearance fool you, DCI Jones – he has a GCSE. He'll be in charge of waggling the mouse to stop the screensaver coming on and locking us out. I don't know what we'd do without him'

A number of good-natured chuckles rippled around the room as the young lad blushed.

'They run computing courses at the library for the old folks, I'll book you a place, Sarge.'

Gibson gave the young man's shoulder a fatherly squeeze. 'Cheeky sod.'

Turning serious again he continued with the briefing. Despite the speed with which the plan had been conceived, it was thorough, with only a couple of technical questions asked before Gibson pronounced them ready.

Although Warren had delegated the responsibility for the operation to Gibson, he was still the officer in charge and so it was to him that the sergeant turned for final approval. Warren ignored the familiar butterflies that seemed to have taken up residence in his gut again.

'OK, let's do it.'

* * *

Murderers tend to be rather paranoid and prone to overreaction, so the forced entry team converged on Bevan Tower in two

124

unmarked vans. A fully staffed ambulance was less than one minute away and back-up patrol cars were around the corner where they were unlikely to raise suspicion. A scenes of crime unit sat waiting for the all-clear to secure any evidence.

Warren and Hastings stood behind one of the vans. Both men wore stab vests and a full equipment belt with retractable baton, handcuffs and incapacitant spray.

The radio in Warren's hand crackled. Gibson.

'Confirm all units are in position and ready.'

A rapid sequence of confirmations filled the airwaves.

Warren licked his lips.

'Execute.'

* * *

A single blow with the steel ram had been enough to smash the cheap plywood door off its hinges.

'Police, drop all weapons,' screamed Gibson, his shout echoed by his officers as they piled through the open doorway, followed seconds later by Warren and Hastings, batons drawn, Warren brandishing a warrant.

'Binay Singh Mahal, you are under arrest on suspicion of murder.'

The man sitting in the armchair was wearing a T-shirt and shorts; the choc ice he'd been eating as his door flew into his living room sat melting in his lap as he stared in disbelief at the intruders. In the sudden silence, Warren heard the distinctive sound of the *Countdown* quiz show clock coming from the TV in the corner.

* * *

'Well, that was an anticlimax.'

'Would you have preferred he put up a fight and stabbed someone?'

Hastings flushed slightly. 'Point taken.'

Despite his rebuke, Warren sympathised with his younger colleague.

Within seconds the forced entry team had confirmed Binay Singh Mahal was alone and less than a minute after their entry he was in cuffs, his hands covered in plastic bags to stop any trace evidence being lost from his fingernails.

By now the shock had worn off and he was alternating between insisting there had been a mistake, demanding to speak to a lawyer and calling any police officer in earshot a variety of four-letter words. Neither Warren nor Gibson were impressed; when it came to foul-mouthed tirades Mahal was a strict amateur compared to some of the people they'd arrested over the years.

Their job done, the forced entry team had vacated the flat and been replaced by a team of white-suited scenes of crime officers. One of them was already placing the contents of a laundry basket into a paper evidence sack. Was that a smear of blood on the leg of a tracksuit?

'Sir, I'm going to have to ask you to remove your clothing and put on this protective suit. My colleague will assist you since your hands are restrained.'

This time even Warren was impressed with the suspect's choice of language.

Chapter 20

'My client would like it placed on record that he intends to sue Hertfordshire Constabulary for wrongful arrest and damage to property, specifically naming you, DCI Jones, as Senior Investigating Officer.'

Warren could see that it took all of the young solicitor's self-control not to roll his eyes. Daniel Stock had matured somewhat since the first time he and Warren had first crossed paths – when his client had vomited over his lap. However, he still looked too young to be shaving on a daily basis, let alone representing someone on a serious criminal charge.

Warren decided not to antagonise the man sitting opposite him any further by explaining that he had legally executed a properly authorised warrant. He assumed his legal counsel had already tried to do so without success.

'Everything in this room is on the record, Mr Mahal.' Warren pointed towards the PACE cassette recorder, which he'd already explained when formally starting the interview and reading him his rights.

'I prefer Singh.' It was the first words the man had uttered since they'd started the interview. It was also the first sentence he'd said since his arrest that hadn't been either shouted or loaded with profanity.

'OK, Mr Singh. First question, would you mind telling me what you were doing on the afternoon of Saturday the nineteenth of July?'

'No comment.'

Warren studied the man opposite him, who stared back at him unblinking.

On the scrawny side of skinny, he stood a shade under six feet tall. The skin on his arms was a dark brown, except for a paler band on each wrist. The man's beard was black and thick, with no hint of grey hairs. The hair on his head was neatly tucked under a dark blue patka. The black cloth turban he'd been wearing at the time of his arrest was in forensics, along with the rest of his clothing.

Most striking were the two black eyes and swollen cuts across the top of his nose. The injuries looked to be a few days old, about the same age as the bruises that covered his ribcage. One of the first things the custody sergeant had done was arrange for the police surgeon to take a look at them and photograph them. The last thing they wanted was any exaggeration of the level of force required to arrest him.

'I want my Kara, Kangha and Kachera back. You are violating my religious freedoms.'

'Your bracelet, comb and underwear are currently being tested by the forensic unit, along with the rest of your clothes and your watch. They will be treated with respect and if possible returned to you.'

Was that a faint flicker of disappointment in the man's eyes? His deliberate use of the Punjabi names for three of the 'five Ks' central to Sikhism had clearly been done to flat-foot Warren, but you didn't work in West Midlands Police for any length of time without picking up such important knowledge. Had Warren scored the first point in this opening salvo?

'Mr Singh, I am sure that you are aware that there was a significant amount of civil unrest Saturday afternoon. If you could help me eliminate you from the inquiries by telling us where you were that would be very helpful. Then perhaps we could return your items to you and let you go on your way.'

'No comment.'

He sat back in his chair and stared defiantly at Warren.

'OK, interview terminated.' Warren stood abruptly, flicked off the PACE recorder and walked straight out the door without so much as a backward glance. 'Don't go anywhere, will you?' he tossed over his shoulder as the door swung shut behind him.

* * *

'That spooked him,' commented Tony Sutton as Warren joined him in the control room, where he stood in front of a bank of blank TV monitors.

'The look on his face was pure surprise before the door closed behind you and the screens shut off.'

'No doubt he was expecting me to go at him for longer.'

Sutton was largely working the Islamic Centre arson, however Warren wanted his perspective and requested he watch the monitors.

'What have you got so far?'

'We've got his Kirpan, covered in what we presume is Meegan's blood and Singh's fingerprints on the handle. SOCO did a presumptive blood test on some smears on a tracksuit from his laundry basket and they tested positive at the scene. I'm going to ask Grayson to authorise a quick turn-around for DNA tests. It'll be worth the expense if it means we get a suspect in custody and can scale back the investigation.'

'Sounds sensible. Any CCTV yet? Jimmy Meegan claimed he saw an Asian man wearing a turban hanging around the rear of the shops near the alleyway.'

'Nothing. We haven't even found him at the protest.'

'Mobile phone?'

'It's being looked at as a priority. It's a smartphone so hopefully we'll be able to track its location. We'll need an extension to custody though.'

Sutton frowned. 'You'll get it, but they're going to ask you to place him directly at the scene eventually.'

'I'd settle for somewhere nearby or even in the crowd at the moment.'

Warren glanced at his watch.

'I'll let him sweat overnight, then I'll go and rattle his cage again. Maybe if we show him what we've got so far he'll confess.'

Warren agreed with Sutton's sceptical look – his gut was telling him that Binay Singh Mahal wouldn't break so easily.

Tuesday 22nd July

Chapter 21

Eight a.m. and Warren was finishing his second cup of coffee. He'd been late home again the previous night, having stayed to watch *Newsnight* with the team. ACC Naseem had done his best, but the interview had been a bruising experience for Hertfordshire Constabulary. Not surprisingly, the BAP had declined to take part and so the interview had ended up with the increasingly uncomfortable senior officer taking fire from both Councillor Kaur and a representative from the Muslim Council of Britain, with nowhere to deflect it.

'Superintendent Walsh will step down within twenty-four hours,' predicted Tony Sutton after the interview was concluded. 'They're going to agree with Councillor Kaur that her decision to redeploy the officers from outside the Islamic Centre left it vulnerable to attack and hang it all on her.'

'Well, it did,' Hardwick said. 'Surely that was the one place under the most threat from the BAP? I can't understand why she decided to pull the officers away from there.'

'The BAP weren't a threat to the Islamic Centre at the time,' said Sutton. 'They were over a mile away in the town centre. As far as Walsh knew, all forty-three of them were fighting protestors and her riot control officers, she couldn't have known that some sneaky bastard with a can of petrol was on the loose.'

'The whole day was a debacle,' opined Hastings. 'If you ask me, much of the responsibility lies with Inspector Garfield's team. Superintendent Walsh was given duff intelligence on the numbers attending and she planned accordingly. If their figures had been even close, she'd have had triple the number of officers there and they could have kept a presence at the Islamic Centre. I can't imagine those cowards would have torched the place with two officers sat outside.'

Hardwick wasn't convinced. 'Surely Walsh could have used her initiative? The numbers of counter-protestors predicted in her briefing must have sounded suspiciously small. Why not err on the side of caution and deploy more officers?'

Sutton beat Warren to the punchline. 'Money. An operation like that costs tens of thousands of pounds. If she'd ignored the intelligence and doubled the number of personnel deployed, and been proven wrong, she'd be in front of the Chief Constable justifying all the money she squandered. She was stuck in an impossible position.'

'Which just confirms what that masked protestor was saying about our priorities; we'll be spending a fortune next week protecting Tommy Meegan's mates as they turn his funeral into a bloody Nazi rally. You can see why people are so upset,' said Hardwick.

'Not to mention the need to protect all of our other minority communities from reprisals when the nature of the murder weapon becomes public knowledge,' said Hastings.

'Damned if we do, damned if we don't,' summarised Tony Sutton.

'What do you think, boss?' asked Hastings.

'I think it's about time we all went home and got a good night's sleep.'

In truth, Warren thought that all of them had raised good points, but he was the most senior officer in the unit after Grayson and he didn't feel it appropriate to share his views with junior ranks.

One thing was certain – the pressure to solve the two cases was only going to intensify.

Unfortunately, Binay Singh Mahal didn't intend to make it easy for him. A night in the cells hadn't changed his attitude and true to form he went on the attack immediately. Again, his lawyer didn't look as though he fully agreed with the decision.

'My client would like to file a complaint about a lack of sensitivity towards his religious needs.'

Warren repressed a sigh. He already knew where this was going, the custody sergeant had tipped him off.

'And what have we done to offend Mr Singh now?' Warren tried to keep his voice professional; it was all being recorded and could be obtained through a Freedom of Information request. The police had a bad enough reputation when it came to the treatment of minority ethnic suspects as it was.

'My client was offered halal food. He is a Sikh not a Muslim and his religion specifically forbids the consumption of ritually prepared food. He finds this lack of cultural awareness offensive and feels that an organisation such as Hertfordshire Constabulary should be investing more in training rank and file officers to understand the needs of the entire community that they serve, even those that make up a relatively small proportion of the population.'

Singh had barely moved a muscle since Warren had restarted the interview. Now the faintest of smiles played around his lips.

'Mr Singh was offered a choice of food from our standard menu, which contains food items suitable for a wide-range of needs, both religious and medical. Food can be prepared to comply with halal and kosher requirements if requested, but is not routinely served as such. And of course, vegetarian options are available if inmates want to be certain that they are avoiding *kutha* meat.'

Again the flicker in Singh's eyes. That was two points Warren had won in the battle of wills between the two men, but he had yet to elicit anything important.

'Mr Singh, I asked you to describe your whereabouts on Saturday afternoon. I am offering you that opportunity again.'

Singh took up his habitual pose of folded arms and said nothing.

'My client has already chosen not to comment on that matter, as is his right.' The solicitor looked pointedly at his watch. 'Mr Singh was arrested at 6 p.m. yesterday, over twelve hours ago. I'm sure that I don't need to remind you, DCI Jones, that you will need to release my client when twenty-four hours have elapsed or request an extension for a further twelve hours.'

'Don't worry about that extension, Mr Stock. I already have it.' Warren opened the manila folder he had brought into the room and passed over the sheet with DSI Grayson's neat signature at the bottom.

'On what grounds? You've arrested my client on what appears to be the flimsiest of excuses and have presented no evidence of any wrongdoing. Why exactly is my client under arrest?'

Warren opened the folder again and removed a colour photograph of Tommy Meegan.

'Do you recognise this man?'

Singh looked at the photograph. He licked his lips and glanced towards his lawyer, whose eyes had narrowed slightly. Warren watched with interest. Singh clearly wanted to deny any knowledge, but the dead man's features had been all over the news and the internet for hours before Singh's arrest. He'd have had to have been living in a cave in the middle of nowhere not to have seen it.

'Yes.'

'Could you name him for the record?'

'He's that Meegan bloke. The fascist who runs the British Allegiance Party.'

'And have you ever met Mr Meegan?'

'No. Never.'

'Again, would you describe to me your whereabouts on Saturday afternoon?'

Now the look on Singh's face was one of incredulity.

'Are you fucking serious?'

Stock cleared his throat.

'No comment.' Singh resumed his familiar pose, affecting a look of bored disinterest. But Warren could now see something else in his eyes. Worry. It was as if it was only just dawning on the man that his arrest the previous day had really happened. That he was potentially in a lot of trouble.

Warren pushed another photograph across the table. An establishing shot of the mouth of the alleyway where Meegan had been found. Blue and white crime scene tape hung limply across the entrance. The body had been removed, but splashes of red were still visible.

'Do you know where this is?'

Singh ignored the picture.

'No comment.'

'Have you ever visited this location?'

'No comment.'

'What about on Saturday afternoon?'

'No comment.'

Stock cleared his throat again. 'DCI Jones, Mr Singh has made it clear that he does not wish to disclose his whereabouts on Saturday afternoon and I would ask you to stop badgering him.'

Warren ignored the man. Stock was no fool, he knew exactly where this was heading – as did his client – and he was desperately trying to stall for time. No doubt there would be a request for a break any moment to regroup and formulate a strategy. It would be an exaggeration to say that Singh was on the ropes, but he was certainly heading that way and Warren wanted to land another couple of punches before they rang the bell.

'Mr Singh, you are a baptised Sikh, am I correct?'

'Yeah, of course.'

'And so I assume you follow the five Ks? Obviously you wear a Kara and Kachera and carry a Kangha. You wear a turban, so I presume your hair is Kesh?'

Before Singh could answer, Stock interrupted.

'I fail to see what Mr Singh's religious observances have to do with the matter at hand.'

Yesterday, the lawyer had apparently been largely ignorant of his client's beliefs, but he'd probably spent a few hours on the internet since then. He no doubt suspected where Warren was headed.

'Do you carry a Kirpan, Mr Singh?'

Again, Stock interrupted.

'As you are no doubt aware, DCI Jones, there are exceptions in common law for observant Sikhs to carry a ceremonial knife under their clothes as part of the requirements of their faith.'

'Do you carry a Kirpan, Mr Singh?'

'Sometimes.'

'You weren't wearing one when we arrested you yesterday. Could you tell me where the knife is?'

Singh's eyes darted towards Stock, who looked helpless.

'No comment.'

'Perhaps you could describe the knife to me?'

'No comment.'

Warren removed the final photograph from the folder.

'Do you recognise this knife, Mr Singh?'

'I want a break.'

* * *

'Nice sucker punch.'

Tony Sutton had been watching the interview on the monitors again. He passed over a mug of coffee.

'But is it enough?'

Sutton sighed. 'I doubt it, I don't think he's going to confess based on what you've shown him.'

'He's a weird one,' said Warren. 'I arrested him on suspicion of murder yesterday and yet today it was as if he was only just realising we were serious, and not just arresting him because we didn't like him.'

Sutton looked thoughtful. 'I agree, it's a strange reaction all right. If he's guilty you'd think he'd have been shitting himself from the moment you smashed his door in, not now.'

Warren looked at his watch. Even with an extension, the time was ticking away. Since the custody clock didn't stop during rest periods and Singh Mahal was entitled to a reasonable amount of sleep, realistically they would need to make a decision to charge or release that night. Warren had submitted everything to the Crown Prosecution Service earlier and was awaiting their decision. To proceed, there had to be a reasonable chance of a conviction and, at the moment, Warren was worried that it wasn't enough.

'What have the CPS said?'

'They're reserving judgement. If we can match the bloodstains on the tracksuit to Meegan then it's a definite. Otherwise they want some corroboration that he was at least near the scene.'

Warren took a swallow of the coffee. He'd start drafting a request for a further extension. Even using fast-track, the results of the DNA tests were some hours away and who knew when – or if – any CCTV or mobile phone evidence would appear. It could be days, weeks or months.

Warren looked at his watch again. Were Singh and his lawyer just stalling for time now? Sometimes the accused tried to run out the clock, like footballers trying to hold onto a one-goal lead during injury time, but Stock had to know that wouldn't work here. He might have managed to stall long enough to get a busy custody officer to give up and award police bail for a minor offence, but extensions for serious offences like murder were almost always granted. And the longer he remained in custody, the more likely it was that evidence would emerge that would guarantee he would be charged. Despite all his bluster, Singh and his lawyer were dancing to Warren's tune and they knew it.

* * *

'I was mugged.'

Singh pointed at his black eye.

'When?'

'Wednesday night. They took my wallet and my Kirpan and left me with this and bruised ribs.'

'Did you report it to the police?' A rhetorical question; nothing was recorded on the Police National Computer.

'What do you think? Asian bloke gets mugged on the Chequers estate late at night. What are you going to do, phone Sherlock Holmes? Why bother? You lot couldn't give a shit. I only had a tenner in the wallet anyway.'

'Can you describe your attackers?'

Singh shrugged.

'Two of them. White, wearing hoodies and tracksuits.'

'Anything else? What about how they spoke?'

Singh shrugged again. 'Normal. They weren't foreign or from anywhere with a weird accent.'

'What about their builds? Were they tall or short, fat or skinny?'

'I don't remember. It was dark. They pushed me from behind and I fell on my face. I managed to roll onto my back which was when I got kicked in the chest. One of them opened my jacket, took my wallet and removed my Kirpan.' He stared at Warren pointedly. 'It's fixed in its sheath – I couldn't stab anyone even if I wanted to.'

Warren looked at him hard. Sutton had been correct. No way was Singh going to confess. The excuse sounded flimsy, but the bruising on Singh's face and torso looked consistent with an attack a few days earlier.

'Did you tell anyone else that you had been attacked?'

'Not really. I told my girlfriend I'd tripped on the kerb.'

'What about the bruising on your ribs?'

Singh sneered slightly. 'We aren't married, she hasn't seen me without my shirt on.'

'What about co-workers?'

'Nobody asked me about it.'

'Whilst we're on the subject, where do you work?'

Singh paused.

'Durban's, the vehicle repairs garage up on the industrial estate.'

'Interview suspended. Get something to eat, Mr Singh. We're not done yet.'

* * *

Warren climbed slowly up the stairs. Reaching his office, he phoned the CPS lawyer about charging. He knew exactly what she'd say.

'Not enough. Now he's claiming he was mugged and the knife wasn't in his possession?'

'So he says. He never reported it.'

'You say he has bruises consistent with being mugged? That's pretty strong.'

'Again, he never reported it.'

'Well, unless you can catch him directly in a lie, we'll have to take his claims seriously. Can you find somebody who might have seen him with the Kirpan after he was supposedly mugged?'

'I don't think it's likely. He wears it under his clothes.'

'What about at night? Did he put it on the nightstand?'

'Maybe, but he lives alone.'

'Well I'm sorry, DCI Jones, but you're going to have to get another extension and see what else you can come up with.'

Warren thanked her and hung up. The excitement of the arrest yesterday seemed a long time ago.

Turning to his computer he opened a blank application form for an extension to the time in custody. A local magistrate would need to authorise any further detention for up to seventy-two hours.

Warren just hoped that it was long enough.

Chapter 22

DC Gary Hastings pulled onto the patch of gravel that served as the forecourt for Durban's vehicle repairs and tried to clear his head. Karen had been sick again. He'd been Googling her symptoms, even though he knew he shouldn't. He reckoned it was unlikely to be bowel cancer, but could it be irritable bowel syndrome? Or what if she was a coeliac? He had an aunt who had developed the gluten allergy when she was about Karen's age and it had been life-changing.

Stop being silly, he ordered himself, *focus on the job.* He slipped his sunglasses off, returned them to the case attached to the sun visor, and looked around. To his left was a BMW with a crumpled left wing, to his right a fluorescent yellow Fiat, emblazoned in signs advertising cut-price MOTs.

The front of the garage was open, with two vehicles on raised platforms and a third with its bonnet open. Rap music echoed off the concrete walls as workers in blue coveralls and white rubber gloves fussed over their charges.

Large signs forbade members of the public from entering the workshop, so Hastings followed the arrow to the reception area. The faint tinkling of a bell when he entered must have been amplified inside the workshop, since within seconds a door marked 'Staff Only' swung open and an older man dressed in trousers and a shirt greeted Hastings. His name badge identified him as Jim Durban, owner.

'What can I do for you, lad?' The man's voice still bore traces of a Scottish upbringing.

Hastings introduced himself and was promptly invited into the back office.

The small room was pretty much what Hastings would expect a vehicle repair office to look like; shelves of lever arch folders interspersed with technical manuals. The desk was cheap, dark brown MDF and the chairs were well worn but comfy. Except for the laptop and printer, it could have been from any time in the last thirty years. That and the fact that his nose told him nobody had lit a cigarette in here in recent memory. And the up-to-date calendar was about as un-titillating as possible – assuming that full-colour photographs of different alloy wheels weren't your thing.

'I'm enquiring about one of your employees, Binay Singh Mahal.'

Durban's expression became guarded. 'Is he in trouble?'

'It's just a routine inquiry. Mr Singh gave your business as his place of work.'

Durban waited in silence for a few seconds, but soon decided that Hastings was not going to assuage his curiosity.

'Sure, Binay works here. He's a mechanic, been here about five years. He should be in today, but I haven't seen him since last week. Says he has the flu. You haven't spoken to him lately, have you? I'm getting a little worried.'

'Like I said, I'm just confirming his details. Does he work full-time?'

'Pretty much. We're open Monday to Friday, eight until five. We also have a rota for Saturday mornings, everyone does one week in four; a bit more if we've got a lot on.'

'I see. How well do you know Mr Singh?'

Durban shrugged. 'He's a quiet bloke. Pleasant enough, I suppose, but doesn't say a lot.'

'What about the other workers. Do they get on with him?'

'He's not the most sociable. He tends to sit in the corner and just eat his sandwiches at lunchtime.' Durban looked a little uncomfortable. 'He's never said anything, but I get the feeling he doesn't really approve of some of the banter and jokes between the lads. He tends to read or play on his phone.'

'What sort of banter?' Hastings chose his words carefully. 'Could it perhaps be seen as a bit... racial?'

Durban looked genuinely shocked. 'Christ no! I wouldn't be having any of that crap in here. Besides we've got a couple of black lads, they wouldn't stand for it either.' He paused, then his eyes widened and he sat up straight. 'Wait, he hasn't complained has he?'

Hastings raised his hands. 'No, no, nothing like that. Please don't be concerned, I'm just trying to get a fuller picture of what Mr Singh is like.'

Durban leant back in his chair.

'I don't suppose you know what he does outside of work? If he has any hobbies? Do you know anything about his family?'

'Not really. I think he has a girlfriend, but he doesn't say much about her.' He scratched his chin thoughtfully. 'I think he visits his parents for Sunday lunch most weekends.'

'And nothing else? No mention of hobbies or interests?'

'Not really. He doesn't talk about politics and doesn't seem to watch the same stuff on TV as everyone else. I know he likes cricket, but that puts him in a minority of one in here – we're strictly football and rugby, I'm afraid. He's pretty strict about his religion, he's a Sikh, he wears his turban and has those bangles. He doesn't drink either, which I thought was a Muslim thing, but apparently some Sikhs don't. Oh, and he's a veggie.'

'You said you haven't seen him since last week. Can you remember when exactly that was?'

Durban thought for a moment. 'Wednesday. He seemed fine, no evidence of the flu. He sounded a bit nasally when he called in sick on Thursday, but that's it.' Durban's expression suggested he had increasing doubts about his employee's story.

Wednesday was the night Singh Mahal claimed to have been mugged, and a swollen nose would probably account for his voice. Why would he try to hide that from his employer?

Hastings closed his notebook. He'd taken plenty of notes, but he doubted any of them would be of use; hopefully his next stop would prove more fruitful. On the surface of it all, it sounded as though Binay Singh Mahal was just a normal guy trying to make a living. A bit antisocial perhaps, but if they ever made that a crime they'd be locking up a lot of people, not least Hastings' own father.

Chapter 23

Binay Singh Mahal's parents lived on the opposite side of the town to their son, in an area as far removed from the squalor of the Chequers estate as one could imagine. Dr Jag Singh Mahal was a GP, practising in Cambridge. His wife, Professor Dalip Kaur Mahal, was a consultant paediatrician at Addenbrooke's, with a thriving private practice on top of her NHS work.

The front living room occupied an area roughly equivalent to the total square footage of the flat Hastings shared with Karen Hardwick, with a carpet that probably cost more than the couple's entire furnishings combined.

'When was the last time you saw your son, Dr Singh?' asked Hastings.

The older Singh Mahal eyes narrowed slightly.

'Why do you ask?'

'I'm just making some routine inquiries,' said Hastings. Unfortunately, the doctor wasn't as easily placated by the detective's dismissal as his son's boss had been.

'He came around for Sunday lunch the weekend before last,' said his mother.

'And that was the last time you saw him?'

147

'Yes, he would have been around this weekend but he said he had the flu.'

Hastings was aware that Singh Mahal hadn't answered the question.

'What about you, Dr Singh?'

The man paused.

'I saw him Friday.'

Professor Kaur blinked in surprise at her husband's revelation. 'You didn't say. Why did you see him?'

Singh looked over at his wife, plainly unwilling to say too much in front of her. However, it was clear that she wasn't going to let it drop.

'He said he had the flu. I'm a GP, I dropped by to check on him.'

'Well, how was he?'

Singh licked his lips, his gaze flitting between his wife and Hastings.

'Jag…'

'He was fine.' He paused. 'He didn't have the flu.'

'Then why didn't he want to come around?' Kaur sounded hurt.

'He got into a bit of a fight. He didn't want us to worry.'

'A fight!'

'Well, more of a mugging.'

'When? When did this happen?'

Hastings leant back in his chair slightly, trying to make himself invisible. It looked as though the couple would answer all of his questions without any intervention from him.

'Wednesday night.'

'Well, did he report it?'

'No. They didn't take very much, he said it wasn't worth complaining about. Besides, you know how he is about the police.'

As if remembering they had a guest, the two parents turned back to Hastings.

'Is this why you are here?' asked Kaur. 'Has he decided to report it?'

'Not exactly. Dr Singh, could you tell me what the muggers stole?'

'Not a lot, from what I can tell. They emptied his wallet of a few pounds, but then they threw it and his mobile phone over a wall and he retrieved them later.'

'Did they injure him?'

Singh nodded reluctantly. 'A couple of black eyes, a cut to his nose and some bruising to his ribs – nothing serious,' he added hastily.

'Did he describe his attackers to you at all?'

'He said there were two of them, that was all.'

'Did he suggest any sort of motive?' asked Hastings.

Again Singh paused, but the glare from his wife prompted him to continue.

'He said that one of them called him an "effing Paki".'

Kaur put a hand to her mouth.

'Why didn't he report it to the police?' asked Hastings.

Singh paused and it was his wife that replied.

'Binay had some trouble with racists when he was younger. He never felt the police took him seriously. Then when he was a teenager he was arrested for being in a stolen car. He believed that the police were quick enough to deal with him when they thought he was a criminal but weren't interested when he was the victim. He still thinks that.'

'Can you remember if anything else was stolen?'

Singh started to shake his head, before stopping. 'Hold on. When I saw him, I insisted that he took his shirt off to show me the bruises. I remember he wasn't wearing the holster that he keeps his Kirpan in. He's baptised and takes that very seriously. I asked him where it was and he changed the subject.'

Chapter 24

DS Mags Richardson's career had travelled almost full circle. Her first specialist role in the police had been with traffic; she'd left the road safety unit for CID as video surveillance was really starting to take off. Now she was increasingly becoming Middlesbury's go-to person when a case involved the analysis of large volumes of CCTV and other video footage.

'As you know, forty-three BAP activists arrived in Middlesbury at approximately noon on a privately hired coach from Romford. Our colleagues in the Met gave them a warm send off a little after 10 a.m. and took some video of everyone who got on the bus. All but three have been positively matched to faces on Inspector Garfield's database.

'The coach driver comes from an Essex-based firm, and he wasn't best pleased to find out who he was driving. Unfortunately, he felt too intimidated to object to them walking around the coach and drinking beer. They spent about thirty minutes stuck in traffic and had a fifteen-minute comfort break after exiting the A10. As far as he can tell, the same half-dozen or so that went to the toilet returned and everyone that got off for a smoke got back on again.

'We've compared the Met video against the video that we took as they left the coach and the faces match. Nobody left or got on the coach after it left Romford.'

'OK, so what about during the march and rally?' asked Sutton, 'Could anyone have slipped away and made it down to the Islamic Centre during the twenty-six-minute window when the fire was set?'

Richardson shook her head.

'No. The BAP were escorted along the entire march, until they reached the rallying point outside the council house. They were then corralled there until everything went tits up and the protestors breached the cordon at 14.32. I can guarantee that nobody left that area before then.'

'What about the three unknowns?' Hardwick had arrived late, her face pasty under her make-up. Warren was going to insist that she made a GP appointment if she didn't perk up later. The last thing he wanted was for one of his best officers to work herself into a month's sick leave.

'We are looking to see if they appear on the PNC for any other offences. We're also trying to get other BAP members to identify them, but they aren't being helpful.'

'Could there have been any other BAP members that travelled to Middlesbury under their own steam?' asked Warren.

'Quite possible; not all of the BAP members are based in London and the South-East and only about two-thirds of the members we know about were on that coach. But if they did, they didn't join the march. At least they tend to show their faces, unlike the counter-protestors.'

Warren looked at the next question in his notepad.

'What about the counter-protestors? How many have we identified? Are there any interesting suspects?'

'We're doing what we can, but there were over five hundred of them. Based on the number of people wearing anti-BAP T-shirts we reckon there were up to two hundred organised anti-fascists. It's a little hard to tell since they've taken to wearing two face masks and swapping them around. The rest were a mix of students, concerned locals and casual lefties on a day trip.'

'We do have a database of the biggest agitators,' said Garfield, 'but it's pretty poorly populated. For the most part these guys behave themselves and are only added if they get arrested or commit a violent act.'

Warren puffed out his lips in frustration. He'd caught a few minutes of the news as he'd wolfed down a sandwich in his office. The increasing rhetoric on social media showed no sign of easing off, with increasingly inflammatory posts coming from all sides. The longer both cases dragged on, the more likely that online fights would spill over onto the streets, with Middlesbury the likely epicentre.

'What about the surrounding streets?' he asked.

'It was still a Saturday afternoon. The shops and businesses in the immediate centre were closed down on police advice, but there were plenty of folks wandering around enjoying the sunshine. Apart from the obvious, it's hard to work out who is a protestor and who is a member of the public. There were lots of people in the vicinity of the alleyway where Meegan was found in the time running up to the line being breached, but we haven't managed to find anyone acting suspiciously. We could really do with some CCTV from that area, but we've got nothing.'

'So watch this space?'

'Pretty much. I know we have a blank cheque, but unfortunately there are only so many trained analysts and even fewer super recognisers not busy with counter-terrorism. We barely get a look-in.'

Chapter 25

'The marks on the knife match Singh Mahal's prints; there's blood on the blade that matches the victim—' Warren raised a finger and Sutton corrected himself '—*probably* matches the victim – the autopsy states that the wound is consistent with a bladed weapon similar to the Kirpan and there's blood on his tracksuit. I say we wait for the DNA on the tracksuit to match and push the CPS to charge. We can worry about the CCTV or mobile phone footage later. We've got a whole horde of the great unwashed from the protest out on bail, I'm sure someone will be able to ID him.'

The two men were sitting in Warren's office and taking the opportunity to refresh their coffee cups and eat a pastry.

Sutton brushed some crumbs off his jacket.

'Hiding the evidence?'

Sutton scowled. 'It's fine for Marie, she gets a regular lunch break, with plenty of time to eat healthily. None of this grabbing food on the hoof and trying to get a sugar boost when you can.'

'Well it seems to be working for her,' said Warren. 'Susan told me she said she'd lost half a stone last time we met up.'

'Yeah, and I've found it.' Sutton looked over his cup at Warren. 'Don't look so smug, boss. You're past forty now, your days of eating like Gary Hastings are coming to an end.'

The jibe stung more than Warren cared to admit; maybe if he'd taken a bit more care of his diet over the past few years he and Susan wouldn't be facing the problems they were struggling with now.

Warren forced himself back to the topic at hand.

What Sutton had said was probably correct; nevertheless, Hastings' failure to catch out Singh Mahal in a lie about his mugging and the loss of his Kirpan worried Warren.

'If it turns out that he really was mugged, then we have to find out who did it, and if they did take his Kirpan,' said Warren. 'Get Hutch to organise some door-knocking on the Chequers estate and see if we can find some witnesses.'

'I wouldn't hold your breath, the police aren't exactly welcome there,' warned Sutton.

'Which poses a problem for us,' said Warren.

'You're thinking the mugging might have been staged? To give him an alibi?' said Sutton.

'Not impossible,' replied Warren, keen to let his friend work through the holes in the theory.

Sutton took another bite of his pastry.

'I'm struggling to make that work,' he mumbled, spilling yet more crumbs down his front. 'The mugging supposedly happened in the middle of last week – which his wounds are certainly consistent with, yet the murder happened Saturday. So it was definitely premeditated.'

Sutton's wife was probably right to nag him, thought Warren. He'd put on a fair bit of weight in the three years that they'd worked together and he definitely seemed to be more out of breath when he climbed the stairs from the ground floor. Maybe the two of them should try and exercise together? Perhaps a regular run? He'd suggest it when this case was over, he decided.

Again, Warren forced his attention back to what Sutton was saying; he was going to have to call it a day soon. His shortened attention span was a symptom of his tiredness; he'd start making mistakes soon.

'So why would he use his own Kirpan? It seems a bit sloppy for someone taking that much care to set up an alibi,' finished Sutton.

'A message to the BAP from the Sikh community? "We stand with our Muslim brothers"?' suggested Warren.

Sutton chewed thoughtfully. 'I can kind of see that, but why use his own Kirpan? Surely he could have just got hold of another one? One without his own fingerprints, for a start?'

'Perhaps he wants to take credit for the attack?' said Warren, although the suggestion sounded even weaker when he said it out loud.

The two men lapsed into silence. They needed more evidence. And more sleep. Warren had laid out his case to the magistrate and was awaiting a decision to extend the custody to seventy-two hours. It wasn't a done deal. In the meantime, Singh Mahal was back in his cell, apparently catching forty winks. Warren envied him.

The phone rang. It was Andy Harrison.

'I thought I'd better ring you myself.'

'That was quick, I thought it'd be another twelve hours before they matched the DNA.'

'There's no match.'

'What? Then whose blood is it on the knife?'

'The knife is still being tested, the blood probably is the victim's. I meant the tracksuit.'

Warren was confused. 'Wasn't the Kirpan sent off first?'

'It's not blood on the tracksuit.'

'But you did a presumptive blood test at the scene.'

'I'm really sorry, it was a false positive. The test looks for the presence of haemoglobin in blood, but it can also change colour in the presence of iron oxide – rust. You're supposed to add the reagent first and wait to check there's no colour change before you add the hydrogen peroxide. The technician didn't wait. I'm really sorry, sir.'

Warren felt sick. He'd been so certain that the blood test would link Singh to the murder. Now it seemed it wasn't even blood. Singh was a mechanic, he probably came home covered in rust.

'What about his other clothes?'

'We're going over the lot. It'll take time, but if there is blood on them we'll find it.'

Warren hung up, unsure what else to say. There was no use ranting about it, Harrison was clearly mortified at the error. In the years that Warren had known him, he'd never known Harrison – or his team – to make such a fundamental mistake. But then it wasn't his team, was it? The Forensic Science Service was gone and services were being outsourced to the cheapest bidder. Who knew what other errors they'd made?

The revelation pretty much scuppered their chances of the magistrate granting a further extension to custody, based on their current grounds. They now had until the following morning before the current extension ran out. If they didn't come up with something soon, Singh would walk. And for the first time since Warren had arrested the man, he was beginning to wonder if it was all a big coincidence.

Wednesday 23rd July

Chapter 26

Six a.m. and Warren wanted nothing more than to wipe the smirk off Singh's face. The remainder of the extension had elapsed, and, as expected, the magistrate had declined his request for a new extension the previous night. Warren had gone home leaving strict instructions that he was to be called immediately if anything else turned up, so that he could apply again for the extension, but he'd known it was unlikely.

Depressed and unable to face cooking at that hour, he'd stopped off for a kebab. Unfortunately, Susan had anticipated him being late and had prepared a tasty, healthy vegetable stew and left it in the fridge. Whether she was more annoyed at him for not answering her calls earlier that evening or his unhealthy choice of dinner was unclear. Regardless, she hadn't offered him a goodnight kiss. He'd slept in the spare room to avoid waking her when he got up the next morning. The two of them had been on edge for the past few weeks, and the stressful nature of Warren's current case wasn't helping matters. Yet again, he vowed to make it up to her; yet again, he couldn't see when that would happen.

Singh's solicitor had made a perfunctory objection to his release on bail, insisting he should be released without conditions, but Warren had stood firm. Until he knew exactly what had taken place on that Saturday, and until he had confirmation that Singh's Kirpan was not in his possession when it was used to kill Tommy Meegan, he had no intention of absolving his only suspect. Warren didn't believe in coincidences.

Was it too early for a second cup of coffee?

* * *

At the other end of the CID office, DI Tony Sutton was having a better start to his day. The door-to-door inquiries organised by DS Hutchinson in the streets surrounding the community centre had yielded a couple of leads, but most of the houses were empty for the summer during university vacation. Relations between the Islamic Centre and the local neighbours were generally pretty good. Most of the worshippers lived within walking distance and a nearby bus route meant that the parking was generally adequate. Nobody had reported seeing any graffiti beyond the usual brainless 'tags' that the local youths felt compelled to spray everywhere, with most of those weeks or months old. No one recalled any racist slogans and certainly no swastikas.

Sutton made a note; it looked as though Imam Mehmud was correct and the graffiti was only added a few days before the fire. SOCO had photographed the images and passed them on to Garfield's team in the hope that they may produce a match from their database.

'Most people that were around were either out enjoying the weather or didn't hear anything until the sirens started.' Hutchinson flicked through his notebook.

'One of the neighbours a few doors down reported seeing the police car sitting outside from early morning but she didn't know why it was there since she never reads the local paper. She confirms that it left a bit after 2 p.m.'

'What about strangers in the street?' asked Sutton.

'Another neighbour reckons that there are always a lot of

160

strangers around, since the Islamic Centre is the only one for miles around. On Saturday, there seemed to be a lot more people around in the morning. Then when the police arrived to keep an eye on the place, a load of the men walked off in the direction of town. She assumed that they were going to the protest. Most of the women stayed behind at the centre.'

That matched what Imam Mehmud had told Sutton about the events that day.

'One resident did spot something a little unusual. He took his dog into the garden about half twelve and spotted a car sitting around the corner on Buzzard Lane. It'd have been out of sight of the patrol car on Sparrow Hawk Road. He said you get all sorts visiting the centre, blacks and whites as well as Asians, but the car's white occupant didn't seem to fit.'

Sutton stroked his chin thoughtfully. Had the fire been the act of an opportunist who had simply come across the unguarded centre? Sutton didn't think so. The fire had been set in a thirty-minute window between the patrol car being called away and the first emergency call. He couldn't see how somebody could have arranged the attack from scratch at such short notice.

'Let's go and see him. I want to see what he remembers.'

* * *

Stanley Buchanan was a retired postman who'd lived on the corner of Sparrow Hawk Road and Buzzard Lane for most of his adult life.

'I remember when the centre opened back about ten years ago.' He looked a little uncomfortable. 'I have to admit we weren't sure about it at first. I didn't know much about Muslims, except what I saw on telly and read in the newspapers. You hear about stuff, you know. How they treat their women and all those hate preachers, but we never saw anything like that. The lead fellow, Imam Mehmud, runs a cricket team for Muslims and non-

Muslims and they're trying to get a girls' football team up and running. Nice bloke, always has a word if he sees us in the street.'

'So there were never any tensions?'

Buchanan shrugged. 'None that I saw.'

'What about vandalism?'

'There's been a bit of graffiti, but no more than anywhere else and nothing offensive. Just the local idiots, if it doesn't move they think they have the right to spray their signature on it. They did my shed last year, the little shits.'

The man's account was matching what they'd been told by Imam Mehmud and others. The centre had been a well-regarded neighbour with little or no trouble.

'What did people think about the proposed mosque and community centre?'

Buchanan shrugged. 'It's on the other side of town so it won't really affect me.' He looked thoughtful. 'If anything, I'll probably miss them. They kept the place tidy and they didn't have a bar kicking drunks out at all hours.'

'Tell me about the strange car that you saw in the street.'

Buchanan frowned. 'I didn't really think anything of it to be honest, until you guys appeared and started asking questions.'

He shifted in his seat.

'I took the dog out to do her business in the front garden about half past noon and saw them parked up.'

'Do you usually take the dog out?'

Buchanan smiled slightly. 'I wouldn't normally, but we're having a conservatory built out the back and she's only a puppy. She hasn't quite figured out where to go out front. Call it a professional courtesy to my former colleagues at the Royal Mail.'

Sutton smiled.

'So why did you notice the car?'

He shifted slightly. 'I don't want to sound racist, but there aren't that many white folk coming in and out of the centre. They're mostly Asians and that. Usually the white guys tend to have beards and wear those little caps, I guess they feel they have to try a little harder to look the part, but this bloke didn't.'

'How do you mean?'

Buchanan paused. 'I'll be honest, he looked like a thug. You know the type, shaved head, England shirt and arms completely covered in tattoos.'

Chapter 27

'We've a new suspect, sir.'

Hastings had called Warren and Sutton over to his workstation.

'The Social Media Intelligence Unit and the Hate Crime Unit have been watching groups like the BAP for years. They also keep an eye on the other side of the coin, to try and get a heads up if there is any trouble in the offing.'

'They didn't do such a brilliant job this time, did they?' noted Sutton.

'No, sir. They dropped the ball on this one. They knew what the BAP were planning – it was all over their Facebook page and Twitter – but the counter-protestors are a bit more sophisticated. They announced their intention to attend via Facebook and got about a hundred or so likes, so policing was planned accordingly. But behind the scenes they were using platforms like Snapchat, which are transient and delete the conversation after a few seconds. In the end, closer to five hundred turned up and caught us with our pants down.'

'So who is this new suspect?'

Hastings turned to his computer and pulled up a headshot.

'Philip Rhodri. He's a veteran protestor – you name it, he

protests against it: animal experimentation, hospital closures, the Iraq War. However, he has a particular beef with the far-right and the BAP and Tommy Meegan in particular.'

Hastings opened another screen.

'He has a couple of dozen different social media profiles, since he keeps on getting banned. This one cropped up on the BAP's Facebook page in the comments section of the announcement about the protest march. The conversation was saved before Facebook deleted it and blocked the profile. It makes for interesting reading: Meegan calls himself TrueBluePatriot and Rhodri goes by the imaginative FascistKiller.'

FascistKiller:	You coming out to play on Saturday?
TrueBluePatriot:	Yeah going to fuck up some muzzer lovers.
FascistKiller:	Big words when you have the pigs watching your back.
TrueBluePatriot:	No need for the pigs, I've got my crew.
FascistKiller:	What crew? Your queer brother and some fat fuck who waddles like a duck. If he wasn't such a chubster you could fit your whole crew in the back seat of a Mini.
TrueBluePatriot:	How many suicide bombers have you got lined up?
FascistKiller:	Don't need any. Come to Middlesbury and you'll get cut.

'How poetic,' said Warren. 'So what's so special about Rhodri? The BAP get death threats all the time.'

'I agree, but Rhodri is one of the most experienced organisers in the country when it comes to these sorts of counter-protests.

He regularly gives advice to other groups on everything from how to coordinate before, during and after, to knowing your rights if you're arrested, even how to deal with tear gas. He practically carries a business card. He took the lead in organising this one, since it's personal and local.'

Hastings switched to a CCTV image of a male protestor in a black, long-sleeved T-shirt with 'Fascists Out' across the chest. His lower face was covered with a black face mask decorated with the logo of a CCTV camera in a circle with a line through it. His eyes were hidden by black glasses, and his hair covered with a red cloth. Despite the hot weather, the man wore dark blue gloves.

'As you can see he tries to make it difficult for us to identify him, but we were able to track his movements once we'd isolated him.'

'How do you know it's Rhodri?'

'He drove in with some other known activists and left his car at the Park and Ride. CCTV footage shows him stepping out of his car and putting his face mask on before joining up with some more protestors and walking into town.'

'OK, so why else is he a suspect? He can't be the only one there to say nasty things about Tommy Meegan on the internet.'

'We know he travelled to Middlesbury – and we have images of him at the Park and Ride. But he doesn't get on the bus and walks towards the centre with other activists. And then we lose him.'

'What do you mean?'

'There is a half mile or so that isn't covered by cameras on the walk. He enters the blind spot and doesn't re-emerge. His party keeps on walking and reappears at roughly the time we'd expect if they didn't stop or make any detours. But eleven enter the blind spot and ten emerge.

'Sir, this man was the main organiser of the protest and has a personal history with the BAP and Tommy Meegan. So what could be so important that he wouldn't be on the front line with the rest of his troops?'

* * *

According to his file, Philip Rhodri was thirty-six years old, although his appearance suggested an age anywhere between mid-twenties and forty. For a man who liked to make it difficult for police to keep track of him, his build was perfect; he pretty much ticked 'average' for any physiological characteristic that you'd care to measure, and Warren could see no distinguishing features on display as he manipulated the brake levers on an ancient bicycle.

Ask someone to describe student digs in Cambridge and the rambling, yellow brick building close to Parker's Piece and within easy walking or cycling distance of most of the colleges would probably fit the bill nicely. Rhodri wasn't a student – he'd left school at sixteen with few qualifications – but he shared the property with his landlord, another known activist, and a handful of like-minded students from the university. Of course, Rhodri's name didn't appear on any official paperwork, which was why he'd managed to avoid paying council tax for the past five years.

'Mr Rhodri, my name is DCI Jones and this is my colleague, DC Hastings. Could we have a word, please?'

'Whatever you want to talk about, speak to my lawyer first.' The man's accent retained a slight Welsh drawl.

'I was rather hoping that we could simply clear up a few things without needing to go down that route.'

Rhodri fished in his back pocket and pulled out a battered nylon wallet with the remains of a fluorescent surfboard pictured on the front. Without saying a word, he passed over a business card for a local law firm. Pointedly turning his back on Warren and Hastings he picked up an Allen key and continued fixing the bicycle.

Ten minutes later Rhodri sat in the back of a Cambridgeshire

Constabulary police car under arrest on suspicion of sending malicious communications.

* * *

Despite the protestations of his solicitor, the warrant to search Philip Rhodri's flat was valid and Warren was determined to execute it. The first thing the evidence recovery team did was seize Rhodri's laptop and mobile phone. Unfortunately, the warrant didn't extend to the other occupants of the house and so if he had given any other equipment to his housemates for safe-keeping, they were going to struggle to retrieve it.

Fortunately, the warrant did include communal areas of the building and his car, which Warren ordered impounded. Nobody covered in bloodstained clothes had been reported walking around the area where Tommy Meegan was killed and Warren was determined not to miss something obvious.

Philip Rhodri's housemates had initially been obstructive, refusing to let the evidence recovery team into the property. However, the flashing of a warrant and the threat that they'd enter by smashing the door off its hinges if necessary, not to mention arrests for obstruction, soon ended that stalemate, although not before the sound of a flushing toilet was heard upstairs. Warren felt a twinge of sympathy. Somebody was going to have to go down the sewers to check that out, but he wasn't expecting much more than a few joints and maybe a couple of bags of something stronger.

Rhodri and his landlord shared the house with three students. The owner of the property lived in the large double room downstairs at the front of the house, with Rhodri in what had probably been a dining room when the house was first built. Upstairs, the three students – all female and in their early twenties – lived in small single rooms, sharing a miniscule bathroom. The cistern was refilling as they entered the tiny room. A root around the downstairs bathroom, which Warren noted was at least twice the size of the upstairs room, showed no evidence of female occupation.

Rhodri and his landlord, Bryan Thornton, were in their thirties; none of their flatmates were older than twenty-one and, Warren couldn't help notice, very pretty. It was creepy, but they were all adults so it was none of his business.

The house smelt of stale tobacco and weed and it didn't take long for SOCO to find a couple of discarded joints down the back of the fridge. The amount of drugs was negligible and they'd never work out who they belonged to – regardless, they could always be used as a lever. Rhodri and Thornton would know that the police wouldn't go to the expense of linking DNA from saliva on the filter to the user, but their housemates might not...

Philip Rhodri wasn't the most fastidious man and his room was filled with dirty laundry; the bed was covered in sheets that looked as though they hadn't been washed in months. The smell of sweat added to the stale smoke and the ripe stench of an unfinished takeaway curry.

A quick look in the overflowing laundry bin revealed it contained clothes similar to those seen on Saturday's CCTV footage and so the entire bag was simply photographed and placed into a large evidence sack. If any of Tommy Meegan's blood had found its way onto the clothes, they'd find it. But Warren was worried. Rhodri didn't strike him as a fool; if he had been wearing those clothes when he stabbed Meegan on Saturday, would he really be silly enough to leave them unwashed in the laundry basket?

Chapter 28

Philip Rhodri's posture in custody was a carbon copy of that shown by Binay Singh Mahal; arms folded and an expression of mild disinterest. Unsurprisingly, his solicitor, a smarmy young man who seemed to know Rhodri well, was significantly better prepared than Dan Stock.

'DCI Jones, I have yet to see convincing evidence that my client is in fact the person that sent those allegedly abusive messages over the internet to the late Mr Meegan. Furthermore, I object strongly to the search of Mr Rhodri's property and the seizure of his motor vehicle on such a flimsy premise.'

'All in good time.'

The truth was, Warren wasn't especially bothered about a bit of abusive to and fro on social media, the allegation was simply a useful way to get a search warrant.

'As I am sure you are aware, Mr Rhodri, the person that you were engaged with on social media was killed on Saturday, 19 July. Much of what was said in that conversation could be interpreted as threatening. Did you threaten Mr Meegan?'

'Don't answer that,' interjected his solicitor. 'As I have already stated, there is no evidence that Mr Rhodri is responsible for those messages.'

Predictable.

'Have you ever met Mr Meegan?'

'No comment.'

'OK, Mr Rhodri. Could you tell me your whereabouts on Saturday afternoon?'

'No comment.'

The man's face was a mask. Time to try something different.

'We have CCTV footage that places you in Middlesbury on Saturday afternoon. Could you tell me what you were doing?'

Was that a flicker of surprise? It was too fleeting for Warren to tell.

'No comment.'

'Were you meeting anybody?'

'No comment.'

'Do you recognise this man? For the record, I am showing Mr Rhodri photograph 12A.'

Rhodri's eyes barely moved.

'No comment.'

'Try taking a closer look, Mr Rhodri.'

'No comment.'

'Does the name Binay Singh Mahal mean anything to you?'

'No comment.'

Warren stared hard at the man for a few more seconds. Rhodri met his gaze, unblinking.

Warren stood up. 'Interview suspended.'

* * *

'He's hiding something.'

Gary Hastings had been watching the interview on the monitors.

'No argument there. The question is what and is it significant? Rhodri hates the police, he sees us as little more than state-sanctioned terrorists – his words on his Facebook page.

He wouldn't cross the street to piss on us if we were on fire.'

'So you think he might have nothing to do with the killing?'

'I honestly have no idea. He could be completely innocent, he could know who did it, he could have stood next to Binay Singh as he stabbed him or he could even have done the stabbing himself. I genuinely have no clue. Contact Social Media Intelligence and get them to look for any link between Binay Singh Mahal and Philip Rhodri.'

Hastings looked at his watch. 'We have about twenty hours to figure it out or come up with enough to get an extension to custody.'

Warren sighed. That seemed to be the way that this was case was destined to go.

Chapter 29

'Rhodri's computer is password protected, and so is his mobile phone. Unless he chooses to cooperate with us, it'll take us time to trace the threatening messages back to him.'

Warren thanked Pete Robertson, the head of Welwyn's Forensic IT unit. Rhodri had shown no evidence of any willingness to cooperate and the clock was ticking. Hopefully they'd have better luck with some of his associates.

Of the ten people that Rhodri had hooked up with on Saturday afternoon at the Park and Ride, six had been arrested at the scene, including two of those he had driven from Cambridge. The remaining four had been identified from Garfield's database.

The six arrested at the scene had been released the following day without charge. Ultimately, the CPS had decided that it wasn't worth the expense of taking them to court over a bit of spitting at police officers and abusive language. Warren wondered how the officers who had been spat at felt about that decision.

Pulling the ten activists back in for questioning hadn't been entirely straightforward, since they were not under arrest, but they had eventually been persuaded it was in their interest to help voluntarily or Warren and his team would dig until they found something to arrest them for.

So far Warren, Hastings and a detective constable on loan from Welwyn had been met with a wall of silence or 'no comments'. It was what he'd expected, but nevertheless Warren had warned Tony Sutton in the canteen that he was likely to strangle the next person who uttered the phrase. Hastings, who'd interviewed two witnesses himself, agreed.

They were down to the last three, one in each of the interview suites. Warren downed his coffee.

'Well, folks, as much as I'd love to spend another hour listening to these delightful individuals refusing to cooperate, I see that we have three witnesses left and if I count myself and DI Sutton, four officers. I shall bow out here and leave it in your capable hands. My inbox awaits.'

The interview team groaned but reached for the three files left on the table.

The door opened and one of the civilian support workers poked his head in.

'Gary, I have a call for you. It's about your sergeant's interview.'

With a sigh, Warren reached for Hastings' file.

'Wipe the grin off your face, Constable.'

* * *

Despite his earlier cynicism, Warren was generally an optimist and having read the file of Alois Kernaghan, he'd felt a stirring of excitement.

Kernaghan was one of the students that Rhodri had driven to Middlesbury from Cambridge. According to the notes he had in front of him, the first-year natural sciences student at Homerton College had been distraught at being picked up at her first demonstration. Whether it was the risk of being kicked out of university or the reaction of her parents back in County Mayo, the nineteen-year-old had cried from the moment she'd been bundled, handcuffed in the back of a police van, to when she'd finally been released without charge after a night in the cells.

Judging by the state of her mascara, the tears had been flowing again this morning, although she had dried her eyes and blown her nose by the time he sat down in front of her. It was a change from the hard-faced sneers of her fellow protestors.

After the preliminaries had been completed, Warren started with his questioning. Despite being appraised of her right to representation, Kernaghan had waived her right to a solicitor, no doubt wanting the whole thing over with as soon as possible.

'Tell me, Ms Kernaghan, where were you on Saturday afternoon?'

'No comment.'

Hardly unexpected, but Warren was only just starting. Her voice was clear and confident.

'Really? You were arrested Saturday afternoon during the protests against the BAP.' Warren allowed a flicker of annoyance to cross his features. 'I have that written down in black and white by my colleagues. Do you really want to waste everyone's time by refusing to acknowledge something already agreed upon?'

She said nothing, affecting a look of bored disinterest.

He flicked through her file.

'I see that Saturday was the first time you've been arrested in the UK. If I were to contact the Gardaí, would I find anything of interest?'

'No.'

It was the first time she'd said anything other than 'no comment'. Even on Saturday, in floods of tears, she'd said little more.

'Are you certain? I'm sure your college would be able to look on my behalf.'

'No, nothing.'

Her voice had a strong Irish lilt.

'OK. Let's take it as a given that you were at the counter-protest. How did you get there? Did you come from Cambridge?'

'No comment.'

Warren sighed dramatically. 'We'll all be out of here a lot sooner if you stop this "no commenting" nonsense. I just want to know how you travelled to Middlesbury on Saturday. Did you come by train?'

She shook her head.

'What about bus? We have footage of lots of protestors getting off the bus.'

She nodded, almost eagerly.

'For the record, Ms Kernaghan claims to have travelled to Middlesbury on the day in question by bus.'

'How did you get to the scene of the protest? Did you travel alone?'

'Yes.'

'Could you tell me roughly what time you arrived in the centre of Middlesbury?'

'No, I didn't look at my watch.'

Warren shrugged slightly. 'No matter, I can get that off the CCTV cameras.'

He leant back in his seat slightly.

'Look, Alois. I really don't care about some silly student who gets caught up in a protest and finds herself in over her head.' He sighed. 'Protesting is a rite of passage. When I was at uni we marched against Tory cuts to student grants.' He smiled ruefully. 'Had bugger all effect. We also protested against the council closing down our favourite nightclub – similar result.'

He looked over at her. 'All I want to do is to track people's whereabouts that afternoon. I'm sure you've seen the news and know what happened. As you can imagine there were hundreds of people in town that day. I just need to eliminate as many as I can. That's all I'm asking. Will you help me?'

The young woman sitting across from him chewed her lip.

Warren said nothing. He had to let her make up her own mind; to think it was her decision.

Eventually she nodded.

Warren opened a manila envelope containing a couple of dozen individual headshots. All of the protestors who she had met at the Park and Ride were included, along with Rhodri, a few of the other protestors who had been arrested, and a number of unrelated 'control' photographs.

'We're trying to work out who was at the protest and may have seen something suspicious. Do you recognise any of these individuals?'

The headshots were all custody photographs. If she was on the ball, she might question why they had these photographs if they didn't know who they were. She didn't.

The photographs were slightly larger than those used for passports, and similarly devoid of humour, and she started to divide them into two piles.

'I recognise these guys.' She pointed to the pile on the left. All of the protestors that she'd walked in with were included, plus a couple of others who had also been arrested.

'What about these?'

She signalled 'no' but didn't meet his eyes. The pile included a couple of known protestors, plus the 'control' group. And Philip Rhodri.

'Some of these guys were arrested at the scene of the protest – are you sure that you don't recognise them?'

'No, I never met them.'

'OK. Now just so we're clear, I am in charge of a murder investigation. If any of the information you have given me is incorrect, you may well be charged with perverting the course of justice.'

Kernaghan blanched slightly, but her voice remained steady. 'I understand.'

'Tell me again how you got to the protest.'

'Bus.'

'And were any of these individuals on that bus?'

She paused for a moment before pulling out the pictures of the individuals who she had met at the Park and Ride.

'Can you remember what number bus you caught?'

She paused. 'No, sorry.'

'That's OK. I'm sure the CCTV footage will tell us.'

She bit her lip again.

'And the bus stopped in the middle of town?'

Another pause.

'Yes.'

'Could you tell me even roughly what time it arrived?'

'No, sorry.'

'That's fine, we have CCTV footage of the bus station, we'll pick you out easy enough.'

Kernaghan clasped her hands in her lap, but not before Warren saw that they were trembling.

'Where did you pick the bus up from? Cambridge?'

Warren could see the fear in Kernaghan's eyes. How much deeper would she dig the hole that she found herself in?

She nodded, her voice barely audible.

'Whereabouts in Cambridge? I believe the main bus route to Middlesbury has several stops?'

It was time to stop digging. She knew it, but he could see that she was terrified, with no idea how to extricate herself. A more experienced person would have started 'no commenting' now and Warren didn't want her to start that again, so he decided to make it easier for her.

'Let's start again, shall we? Tell me the truth and I'll consider not arresting you for attempting to assist an offender.'

She slumped in relief.

'First of all, how did you get to Middlesbury?'

'We drove to the Park and Ride.'

'Who is we?'

She pointed to two of the protestors, a woman about the same age as her and a man a few years older.

'Anybody else?'

She picked through the other pile until she found Rhodri's photograph.

'He drove us.'

'And what's his name?'

'Philip. That's all I know.'

'OK. What else do you know about him?'

She shrugged. 'Not a lot. We met at a Students Against Fascism meeting a few months ago.'

'Is he a student?'

'Yeah, although I don't know what he studies or which college he belongs to.'

Warren said nothing. Philip Rhodri had five GCSEs to his name and when he wasn't claiming Jobseeker's Allowance, he pulled pints in local pubs.

'What happened when you got to the Park and Ride?'

'We met up with these other guys. I assumed that we were going to jump on the bus, but Philip said it was only a mile or so and he'd rather walk.'

'So Philip was the leader?'

'I guess.'

'And did you walk all the way into town together?'

'Yes.' The tremble was back.

'STOP LYING TO ME, ALOIS!'

The young student rocked back in her chair in surprise at Warren's sudden bellow.

'You were doing so well.' Warren's voice was soft again. 'I don't want to arrest you again, but I will if you don't start telling me the truth.'

The tears were back.

'What happened on the walk into town?'

She rubbed her nose on her sleeve.

'About halfway in, a car pulled over. Philip said he had a meeting to go to and that we should go ahead, he'd meet us in town later.'

'Then what?'

'He got in and they drove off.'

'Who was in the car?'

'I don't know, I didn't recognise him.'

'Just one person?'

'Yeah, an Asian guy.'

'What did he look like?'

She shrugged helplessly. 'I dunno. Youngish I guess. Long black hair and a beard. He was wearing sunglasses, I couldn't see him clearly.'

'What about the car?'

She shrugged again.

'Normal. White, I think, not very big.'

Warren could see that he was unlikely to get much more out of her.

'Why did he pull over there? Why not pick him up at the Park and Ride?'

She looked at the table.

'Alois?' Warren's tone was sharp.

'Philip said there were too many cameras at the Park and Ride.'

'And there were none on the road he was picked up on?'

'No.'

'How did he know that?'

Kernaghan said nothing.

'Alois…' This time Warren's voice was low, warning.

'There's a website. It tells you where surveillance cameras are.'

'Thank you, Alois. Interview suspended.'

Chapter 30

'So what else have you found?'

CSI Stewart Beattie and his colleagues had spent the past few hours completing a search of Philip Rhodri's house and were now heading back to Welwyn with their spoils. Since he practically had to drive past Middlesbury, it hadn't taken much more than the offer of a decent coffee to get Beattie to take a detour.

'We didn't find anything in Rhodri's room of great interest, but you were right about them flushing drugs.' Beattie held up a plastic evidence bag. 'It'll need testing, but that looks like a fair few grams of cannabis resin to me.'

'I'm surprised it didn't flush away completely.'

'Well, it probably would have done, but the drain was partially blocked and it snagged on the way down.'

Warren grimaced. 'Spare me the details.'

'So you don't want to see what blocked it?'

Warren eyed him suspiciously. 'If this is going to put me off my dinner, I'm not interested.'

'Depends how strong your stomach is, sir.'

He pulled out another baggie.

'What the hell is that?' Despite himself, Warren was intrigued. He ignored the unpleasant-looking stains.

'I'll know more when I get it back to the lab, but it looks like a lump of partially melted nylon.'

Warren frowned.

'Well, since she was the one responsible for flushing the drugs down the toilet, perhaps his housemate Laura Tufnail can some shed light on the mystery. I think she's spent enough time sweating in the custody suite.'

* * *

Bryan Thornton, Philip Rhodri's landlord worked for the housing department in Cambridge City Council, somewhat ironic given that he had been claiming Rhodri was a student, for council tax purposes, during the years that they'd lived together. Despite Hastings' implicit threat to reveal the fraud – which would almost certainly have cost him his job – he denied all knowledge of Rhodri's whereabouts on the day of the murder, claiming to have been visiting his sister. His record revealed a number of run-ins with the police and he was a known face on the protest scene; however, unlike Rhodri, he'd managed to avoid being charged, which explained how he'd kept his job. By the time Hastings called time on the interview they'd learnt nothing more and it was far from clear if he was genuinely ignorant or simply lying.

Two of the three students that shared the flat with Rhodri and Thornton had driven into Middlesbury with Rhodri and had already been interviewed. Despite their relative youth, the two women were experienced and had simply repeated 'no comment'.

The third student, Laura Tufnail, had been away the day of the protest. The moment Warren saw her in the interview room, screwing up a polystyrene cup, he knew they had their weak link.

After reminding Tufnail that she had the right to legal representation and confirming that she was not under arrest, Warren started by asking her what she knew of Philip Rhodri's whereabouts on Saturday.

'No comment.' The faintest traces of an American accent coloured her words.

'Tell me, Ms Tufnail, do you enjoy being a student at Cambridge University?'

She said nothing.

'I imagine your parents are pretty proud of you.'

No response.

'I didn't go to Cambridge, so help me out here. You're a member of a college first and foremost, which then means you are a member of the university. Is that right?'

'Close enough.'

They'd broken the impasse. Tufnail no doubt thought that answering such a question was harmless, but Warren's experience had shown that simply moving someone away from 'no commenting' often made it more difficult for them to return to their previously uncooperative state.

'Which one are you a member of?'

'Fitzwilliam.'

'Oh I know that one, it's up on Huntingdon Road next to Newhall, isn't it?'

'Yes.'

'And the house that you share with Mr Rhodri and Mr Thornton is college property, I assume?'

'No, Bryan owns it.'

'Oh, OK. I thought he was a student like you and Mr Rhodri.'

'Philip isn't a student.'

Warren made a point of looking hard at the papers in front of him.

'Sorry, my mistake. But it doesn't matter if the college owns the house you live in, does it?'

Her brow furrowed. 'I don't know what you mean.'

'I mean that just because you don't live in a college-owned

property, you still have to follow university rules and regulations, right? For example, you can't own a car within the city limits without written permission from the college.'

'I don't own a car.'

'I know, but Philip does. That confused me, but I guess if he isn't a student he can do what he likes.'

'Sure.'

Warren placed the evidence bag containing the joints from the kitchen on the table between them. He said nothing.

'I assume you know what these are.'

The draining of colour from her face made the smattering of freckles across her nose and cheeks suddenly noticeable. 'Cigarette ends?'

'Try again.'

She sighed. 'I guess they're spliffs.'

'Correct. They were found down the back of the fridge.'

'I don't know anything about them.'

'I sure hope that's the case, because I believe that colleges like Fitzwilliam take matters such as arrest for drug possession very seriously. Now how about you tell me who the drugs belong to?'

'I don't know.'

Warren looked at her long and hard. She was starting to perspire, but he couldn't tell if she was lying or just scared.

'You can save us a lot of time and money by telling us who they belong to, rather than making us perform expensive DNA fingerprinting.'

'I've said I don't know.'

'Hmmm,' said Warren, his tone implying that they'd be revisiting the subject.

'When we arrived at the property, we were delayed entry by your landlord, Mr Thornton. During that time, the toilet was flushed by somebody upstairs. We're retrieving evidence from the drains as we speak. You were upstairs. Would you care to tell me what you flushed down the toilet?'

'Nothing. I didn't flush anything down the toilet.'

'Then who flushed it? Mr Thornton was talking to me at the front door and Mr Rhodri was already in custody. Was it one of the other girls?'

'No comment.' Her voice was reedy and there was no conviction behind the dodge.

Warren leaned back in his chair.

'Look, Laura, I'm not with the drugs unit. I'm not interested in a bit of puff and whatever you flushed down the lavatory. That's not the focus of my investigation. A man was brutally murdered on Saturday afternoon. It is my job to find his killer.'

'He got what he deserved.'

'Well, I'm not qualified to make that decision and neither are you,' snapped Warren. 'And neither was his killer. No matter what Mr Meegan is alleged to have done, or whatever views he may have held, we have rules in this country and they apply to all of us.'

The rebuke had the desired affect and Tufnail lowered her eyes.

'Now what can you tell us about Saturday afternoon?'

'I was away, I didn't go.'

'Are you sure about that? We are trawling the CCTV as we speak. Being charged with a bit of drug possession is nothing compared to lying and perverting the course of justice. You'll never set foot inside college again if you end up charged with that.'

'I was visiting my friends that weekend.'

'Where?'

She sighed. 'At Jesus College.'

Warren blinked. 'Jesus College? As in Jesus College, Cambridge?' She nodded.

'But that's barely down the road. I'd hardly call that going away.'

'It's what I told Philip. I didn't want to go to the protest, but

I was too scared to tell him, so I said I was going to a wedding in Edinburgh.'

Her eyes were starting to shine. Warren handed her a tissue and gave her a moment.

'Why don't we start from the beginning?' he suggested gently.

She sniffed and when she started again her voice was croaky. 'It's all such a mess. I don't know what to do.'

'Why don't you tell me all about it and maybe we'll see if I can help.'

She smiled gratefully. 'You're right, Mum and Dad are proud that I got into Cambridge. They wanted me to go to university ever since I was a little girl. And when I gained a place studying Maths they were so proud.

'I spent my first year in college, but the cost is crippling. With tuition fees on top, I'll be over forty thousand in debt before I even graduate. And I really want to do a doctorate, which means I won't be earning proper money for years. My parents keep on saying they'll support me, but they can't afford it. I'm the youngest of four and Mum and Dad want to retire back to the States. I have a job at the museum and work some shifts in a restaurant, but I still needed a way of reducing my fees.'

'Rhodri?'

'Yeah. I met him at a Students Against Fascism demo in my first year. They seemed a pretty cool bunch and I joined up. When I came to the end of my first year, I saw the bill for the next year if I stayed in college. It was astronomical. But Philip told me he lived in a house down near Parker's Piece with a load of other students. It was a bit basic, he said, but it was less than half what college was charging.'

'So what happened?'

'Well it was OK at first. It was pretty convenient, I could cycle to college easily and I enjoyed being with other people who shared the same beliefs as me. But it soon started to get a bit scary. Philip and Bryan smoke a lot of weed. The house stinks of the stuff. I tried it a couple of times but I don't like it.' She looked down at the table. 'That was me flushing the loo. I knew where Philip kept his stash and I panicked. I didn't want to be associated with that stuff, so I tried to get rid of it.'

'And that's all you flushed?'

'Yeah.' She bit her lip; she'd draw blood soon if she wasn't careful. 'I think there might be other stuff in the house though.'

'Why do you think that?'

'There was a weird stink coming out of Philip's room Sunday night. Sort of like burning plastic and I could hear him coughing. I've no idea what it was, I've never smelt heroin or crack or anything before.'

Warren was unsure what melting nylon smelt like, but he imagined it was similar to burning plastic. Sorting through his evidence folder, he found a photograph of the mysterious lump Stewart Beattie had fished out of the sewer. Tufnail looked at it before shaking her head. Warren believed her; it had been a long shot anyway.

'OK, tell me about Saturday. Why didn't you go to the protest?'

'I was scared. I've been on marches and stuff in the past and it's a lot of fun. Everyone wears face paint and carries placards. We stand behind the barriers and shout a bit, but this was the first time we were going to actually confront some of these thugs and try to disrupt their march. At first it sounded exciting, I'd seen them on TV. The police stand in the middle and both sides shout at each other, but nobody gets hurt.'

Warren fought the urge to roll his eyes.

'What changed?'

'Philip was boasting about it one night. He doesn't usually drink, but when he does he likes to show off. He said that they had figured out how to stop the pigs – sorry – hearing about our plans in advance and that this time there were going to be so many of us, they'd never know what hit them.'

'And you didn't want to be part of that?'

'It wasn't just that. I want to leave the house. I've been looking for somewhere to move to for my final year. I might even move back into college and sod the cost.'

'The drugs?'

'In part, but the house isn't what I expected. Philip isn't what I expected.'

'Oh. I see.'

'I was such a fool. It all seemed a bit romantic you know, I guess I had a bit of a crush. But then there were the drugs and the lies – I'd been living there for two months, can you believe, before I realised that him and Bryan weren't mature students? Philip doesn't even have a proper job.'

'And Philip didn't return your affections?'

'No, quite the opposite; that was the problem. I realised very quickly that my crush was just that and that he wasn't my type at all. Which was fine, I didn't make a fool of myself or anything. But it soon became clear that he and Bryan choose their flatmates very carefully.' She paused to see if Warren understood.

It seemed that his suspicions had been correct.

'One of the other girls, Carly, worked that out to her advantage pretty soon – I'm convinced she doesn't pay any rent. Our other flatmate, Rosie, made it clear fairly quickly that she isn't interested in sharing a bed with Philip, Bryan or *any man*. I don't think they saw that coming.' She smiled bleakly, as if recognising the humour but not fully appreciating it. 'Which just leaves me. I fitted a lock to my bedroom door – Bryan claimed that if we had locks on our rooms they were classed as separate residences and we'd all need our own TV licence, but I don't care – but I still don't really feel safe.'

'OK. So let's go back to Saturday. You weren't there, but what else can you tell me about what happened that day and where Philip in particular went.'

She shrugged helplessly.

'I've no idea. When I said I wasn't coming, he got the hump

and didn't really speak to me. All I know is he was planning to meet at the Middlesbury Park and Ride and walk into the town centre. He spent a lot of time on his mobile using Snapchat to arrange the meetings. I didn't get back until Sunday night and he was already in his room. That's when I noticed the weird smell. I saw him the next morning when I was getting ready to go to work, but he didn't seem to want to talk. He didn't even try to see down my dressing gown, which was a pleasant change.'

'All right, what about in the weeks before the march? Did you notice anything strange? Were there any unusual visitors?'

'The whole place was strange and people were always coming and going. That's another reason I got a lock for my door. Some of them I recognised. I'm pretty sure I know the guy who he and Bryan get their weed from. Some of the other visitors I recognised from SAF meetings or other marches.'

Warren pulled out a headshot of Binay Singh Mahal.

'Do you recognise this person?'

She looked hard at the picture before shrugging. 'I really don't know. He might have been around the house or hanging around SAF socials, but I'm really not sure.'

'OK. Well thank you for your assistance. We'll be sure to call you if we need any more help.'

She blinked. 'Is that it? Can I go?'

'Yes. But do yourself a favour, Laura. Find yourself some new digs and some new friends.'

Chapter 31

'Sir, we have identified the car that picked up Philip Rhodri Saturday morning.'

'Well done, Mags, that was quick.'

'Well, don't get too excited, sir, it might not be any use to you. The road that he was walking along has no direct CCTV surveillance. However, it's a straight road, with only one additional junction. ANPR cameras on traffic lights either end of the blind spot and on the entry junction photographed thirty-six vehicles in the twenty-seven minutes that Rhodri and the rest of the protestors were in the blind spot.

'Based on what Kernaghan told us, it was a white car, which narrowed it down to three possible vehicles.'

'OK, that certainly sounds promising, what's the problem?'

'Well, two of the cars are registered to rather unlikely types; the first is a Motability vehicle with adapted controls for its elderly owner.'

'It could have been borrowed by someone else.'

'I agree and we'll conduct interviews to rule that out.'

'What about the other cars?'

'The next one has been tracked continuing through Middlesbury, in the opposite direction to the town centre, onto the M11 motorway and eventually over to Bristol. Registration documents show it to be owned by a young couple. We picked up some still images in a motorway service station on the M4 and you can clearly see two small children in car seats.'

'Sounds doubtful. What about the final car?'

Richardson sounded reluctant. 'I'd bet a week's pay on this being the one, for what it's worth. The licence plate doesn't exist.'

'Fake?'

'Looks like it, the index was never issued. I've put a search out to see if it has been picked up on any other ANPR cameras, but nothing yet.'

'Bugger.' Warren thanked her.

This was the time that Warren hated most in any investigation. More than four days had passed since Meegan's murder and the arson at the Islamic Centre and after a quick start, it had now turned into a waiting game. Waiting for forensic analysis of seized items; waiting for the analysts in Welwyn to finish trawling through hundreds of hours of video footage and thousands of social media posts; waiting for his colleagues to uncover that small link that would open up the case. It would happen, the two crimes would be solved, of that Warren was certain. But how long would it take? It could be months or even years.

It was time that he didn't have. Grayson had confirmed that the crematorium had been booked for 1 August and members of the far-right, at home and abroad, were planning on taking full advantage. In life Tommy Meegan had been little more than a mouthy irritant. In death he was being seen as a martyr to the cause. At the moment all the chatter was roughly evenly split between those that blamed Muslims for his death and those that were pointing the finger at anti-fascists. Nobody was looking forward to the reaction when the nature of the murder weapon was made public.

Warren looked at his watch. It was 6 p.m. To hell with it, he had a mobile phone, he could even access his email if necessary.

It was halfway through the first week of the school holidays and he had barely seen his schoolteacher wife, since he'd been going to bed after her and rising before her. They weren't planning on going away until the end of August, but he'd hoped they might enjoy at least a few summer evenings in the garden that they had been working so hard on over the past year.

Grabbing his jacket, Warren headed out to his car. Fifteen minutes later he emerged from Tesco with a shopping bag bulging with a curry meal, a bottle of Susan's favourite wine and a bunch of brightly coloured flowers. He'd learnt from bitter experience that going to a restaurant or the theatre at this stage of a case was tempting fate, but hopefully tonight's surprise would be uninterrupted.

Placing the bag on the passenger seat, he inserted the key into the ignition. A simultaneous double beep and vibration heralded the arrival of a text message. Warren swore mightily. Could he not get a moment of peace with his wife? Was that too much to ask?

He turned the key and put the car into gear vowing to ignore it. His promise lasted as far as the supermarket's recycling station before, cursing his weakness, he pulled over by the bottle bank and took out his phone.

The use-by date on the curry was three days away and the wine would taste better after twenty-four hours chilling in the fridge. The flowers would be a nice surprise for Susan on the kitchen table when she got up for breakfast the next morning. Warren just hoped that he was back in time to kiss his wife before she went to sleep.

He opened the text message.

Gone to the cinema with the girls. Don't work too hard and get an early night, big day tomorrow. Susan xx

Thursday 24th July

Chapter 32

Warren was in even earlier than normal the following morning; the expiration of the first twenty-four hours of Philip Rhodri's detention was looming and he had a lot to do that day. A good night's sleep would have been nice, but he'd lain awake for hours until Susan had come home, full of cocktails and giggles. Warren hadn't mentioned his thwarted plans – it was hardly her fault – and the next twenty-four hours promised to be stressful enough for the both of them without more recriminations.

Two Singapore Slings and a Cosmopolitan had worked their magic and within ten minutes Susan had been sound asleep, leaving Warren alone with his thoughts. Either they charged Rhodri, released him, or applied for an extension. DSI Grayson was able to authorise another twelve hours, but he had to have valid grounds. At the moment Rhodri was locked in a 'no comment' cycle.

Warren's insomnia hadn't been helped by another vitriolic interview given to BBC *Look East* by Councillor Kaur, which had condemned the police for both the mishandling of the riot and their subsequent investigation into the Islamic Centre arson. To listen to her speak it was easy to forget that the investigation was only four days old. In addition, she managed to imply that the failures of the police the previous Saturday had emboldened the far-right so much that it was their fault that Jewish headstones in the local cemetery had been defaced by swastikas and other anti-Semitic graffiti the night before.

Fortunately, the technician who answered the phone to Warren was an early riser also.

'I'm afraid that Mr Rhodri is rather more computer savvy than most.' The Forensic IT analyst was apologetic.

'We managed to bypass his log-on and access his laptop's hard drive, but it's encrypted. Nothing too fancy, but unless he actually gives us his password, which acts as the encryption key, we can't get in.'

'There's no way you can decrypt it?' Warren tried not to sound too desperate.

'Not unless you have a friend at GCHQ. The software is cheap and widely available, but it's effective.'

'What about his phone?'

'We've managed to unlock it, but that's all. He uses a secure email client and has a secure instant messaging app installed.'

'What exactly does that mean?'

'It means messages are deleted from the sender's and receiver's phones and the communication company's servers immediately after being read.'

'OK. But I thought they say that when it comes to computers, nothing is ever truly deleted. Can you retrieve it?'

Was it Warren's imagination or did the young-sounding technician speak a little slower, as if explaining something to an elderly grandparent?

'No. The app uses end-to-end encryption. That means it's encrypted on the sender's handset and only decrypted by the receiver. And before you ask, even if the company who designed and run the app keep a copy of the file, they don't possess the necessary encryption keys to read it.'

'OK, well can we at least figure out who he was talking to?'

'Nope. Again, that's encrypted. You'll need his password to gain access.'

Warren thanked her and hung up, dejected. The chances of getting Rhodri to voluntarily give up his passwords seemed remote. He could apply for a warrant to compel him, but even if it was granted, his lawyer would no doubt contest it. Regardless, he was unlikely to get the information he wanted before it was too late.

Chapter 33

'What do we do with Philip Rhodri?'

Gary Hastings, Theo Garfield and Warren were sitting in John Grayson's office.

'You seem pretty confident that Rhodri is involved in Meegan's murder.' Grayson was leaning back in his chair, fiddling with a golf ball. Whether this was the man's equivalent of doodling or a subconscious telegraphing of his desire to be elsewhere, Warren was never entirely sure.

'We're waiting on forensics to see if they can find any traces of blood on his clothes or in his car. However, even if he wasn't present at the killing itself, he's involved somehow.'

Grayson waited, saying nothing.

'We know that he and Meegan exchanged heated and threatening exchanges online. We also know that he was instrumental in organising the protest march. Usually he is in it up to his neck—' Warren glanced towards Garfield, who confirmed it with a nod '—but this time he seems to have sat it out, disappearing before the protest kicked off, picked up by a stranger in a car with fake licence plates.'

Even to Warren's ears, it sounded weak.

Grayson sighed and placed the golf ball back on its wooden plinth.

'For what it's worth, Warren, I trust your gut on this, but you know that's not enough. You have until two o'clock to find me grounds to extend your questioning by another twelve hours or you'll have to release him on bail.'

The three officers trudged out of Grayson's office. Warren was philosophical. 'He's right. We have nothing on him at the moment beyond hearsay, some internet abuse and no alibi. Unless we can place him near that alleyway or forensics find a speck of blood, it's all circumstantial. We don't even have any real evidence that he was picked up by the car with fake plates.'

'Are you going to put that to him?' asked Garfield.

Warren pulled at his bottom lip as he leant against the wall.

'No. Not for the time being. That lawyer of his is sharp enough to call our bluff on the lack of real evidence and I can't see him breaking his silence. Besides, the last thing we want is for him to tip off his accomplice and get them to ditch the car.'

* * *

Eleven a.m. The morning briefing had revealed no new evidence linking Rhodri to Tommy Meegan's murder. No witnesses claimed to have seen him, and his face had yet to appear on any of the hours of video footage examined so far. The only remaining hope was forensics; traces of blood – it didn't need to be identified as Tommy Meegan's at this stage – would be sufficient for Warren to get another twelve hours to question the man.

The phone on Warren's desk warbled and he felt his pulse increase. He recognised the extension number.

Ten minutes later, Warren picked up the phone and called down to the desk sergeant in the custody suite.

'Prepare to cut Rhodri loose. I'll be down in five to prepare his bail.'

Chapter 34

The alarm on Warren's phone was set to vibrate and the sudden rattle against the wooden surface of his desk made everyone jump in surprise.

'Sorry, I have another meeting,' he said. It wasn't technically a lie, although it had nothing to do with work. He felt a sudden urge to pick up the phone and text his apologies; to claim that he was too busy. He was in the middle of a murder investigation and overseeing an arson attack that could become a murder any moment. That would qualify as busy in anyone's book.

He shook himself mentally. Man up, he ordered himself.

'OK. Any idea when you'll return?'

Warren and Sutton worked very closely together and Warren usually shared all his plans and movements with him. But not this. This was private.

'No idea. I've put it in the diary. I'll let you know when I'm back.'

With that, he plucked his jacket off his chair back and headed out.

The traffic was quiet this time of day and he made much better time than he'd expected, arriving a few minutes early. Sitting back in his seat he pinched his eyes shut with his thumb and forefinger.

There were so many questions that he needed to answer; so many loose ends that needed to be tied up. Normally he'd relish a few quiet minutes on his own to just think things through. Sometimes you just needed to let your subconscious off the leash, to see where it led you. But in an investigation as fast-paced as this, such contemplation time was a luxury he could rarely afford. Small wonder that his brain, starved of such a valuable activity, kept him awake at night.

But today was different. He just couldn't concentrate. Today, thinking about the case had been a distraction; an activity that kept him focused, stopping him from dwelling too much on anything else.

That had been easy in the pressure cooker of the CID office. The ringing phones, the pings of arriving emails, the taps on his office door. All of them had conspired to keep him on track. Even yet another nagging call from finance had been a welcome diversion. He'd never thought of his job as a displacement activity before, and he wasn't sure he liked it.

The crunch of gravel and grumble of Susan's diesel engine disturbed his reverie. He opened his eyes at the creak of her handbrake and took a steadying breath, before opening his own door, a high-pitched beeping reminding him to remove his keys from the ignition.

Slamming the door behind him, he circled the rear of his wife's car to greet her with a kiss as she stepped out. Although it was a Thursday, it was the school holidays so Susan wore a light summer dress with the sort of heels that would have crippled her if she'd tried to wear them all day in the classroom. She'd still been asleep when he'd left and she looked a lot more rested than he felt.

'Sorry I couldn't give you a lift,' Warren apologised again.

Susan squeezed his hand. 'Don't be silly. You're far too busy to trek halfway across town to pick me up, then drive all the way over here.'

Warren didn't mention that he'd briefly thought about using his workload as an excuse to cancel altogether. For her part, Susan didn't suggest that she should have perhaps driven to pick Warren up. They both knew that would have risked more questions for Warren. Questions that Warren at least, wasn't ready to answer yet.

'Ready?'

Warren forced a smile.

'Absolutely.'

Susan stared at him, searching his face to work out his true feelings. Not for the first time, Warren thought that she'd missed her calling. He pitied the poor teenagers who tried to lie about their homework to her. They didn't stand a chance.

'It'll be OK.' She squeezed his hand again. 'Whatever they say in there, we'll be fine. We'll deal with it.'

Warren leant forward, his lips brushing her forehead.

'I don't deserve you,' he whispered.

'I know you don't.'

Despite himself, Warren smiled.

With one last squeeze for good luck, Warren turned. Time to man up, he repeated to himself. Leading the way, they crossed the car park and entered the clinic.

Chapter 35

'We've identified the brand of petrol that was used in the fire at the Islamic Centre; ESSO, regular grade.'

'How certain are we?'

'Very, the volatile part of the petrol has burnt off obviously, but there were enough of the additives and detergents remaining to identify it with some certainty.'

Tony Sutton thanked the forensic chemist and hung up. There were ESSO forecourts across the UK, but assuming the petrol hadn't been siphoned out of a car's petrol tank, how often did customers fill a canister these days? He looked across the office at the back of Mags Richardson's head. The team at Welwyn were already poring over thousands of hours of CCTV for the Meegan murder. How much more time would it take to analyse the footage from all the ESSO garages that had sold petrol in a container over the past few weeks? He had a suspicion Mags would let him know in no uncertain terms.

* * *

The waiting room was like any other that Warren had sat in; pale blue walls, with matching comfy chairs and cheap plywood tables piled with ancient magazines. In the corner, somebody had attempted to brighten the room with a vase of vivid flowers that looked a lot like the bunch he'd picked up on a whim from the supermarket the previous week. Behind the door opposite sat the consultant whose pronouncement would determine the course of their lives for the next few years, if not forever.

Susan squeezed his hand again. Despite her bravado outside, Warren knew she was as worried as him, but that was what marriage was all about. You took the rough with the smooth and worked as a team.

The move to Middlesbury three years previously had been far from easy, the pace in that first year had been relentless for both of them. No sooner had Warren got his feet under his new desk than he'd found himself embroiled in his first murder investigation, whilst at the same time dealing with the mess left by his predecessor. His situation was mirrored by Susan who had unexpectedly found herself in charge of a failing department in a struggling school. Within months of the conclusion of his first case, Warren had to take charge of the hunt for a serial murderer and rapist, whilst at the same time dealing with the sudden loss of his beloved grandmother. When he thought back on what they'd dealt with over the past few years he knew that neither of them could have survived without the other.

Nevertheless, he felt shame. It was largely his fault that Susan had had to deal with the biggest challenge of her life. It was his past that had come back to haunt them two years ago; his past was the reason Susan still flinched when a stranger came to the door or when a maddeningly elusive electrical fault set the burglar alarm off without warning. It was his past that meant that her parents – who had once been so overbearing – hadn't invited themselves down to stay since it happened.

He vowed to man up more – his phrase of the day – and start supporting his wife like a husband should. He squeezed her knee.

The door opened and Warren flinched.

The consultant exited and Warren tensed his legs, ready for their names to be called. Ignoring them, the doctor picked up another overflowing folder from the pile on the reception desk. The dark green cover had been filled in with biro and Warren had no hope of reading it from across the room.

The doctor exchanged a few quiet words with the middle-aged woman at the desk, who laughed, before he returned to his office. The door closed behind him with a quiet click.

Warren let out a breath. Beside him, he felt Susan relax.

'We're still a little early.'

The receptionist's phone warbled. The ringtone was different to the previous calls. Did that mean it was internal, rather than external? There was no way Warren could overhear what the caller was saying. The receptionist glanced across the room.

'Yes, they're here.'

Warren was on his feet before she'd hung up.

Chapter 36

'We've narrowed it down to sixteen possible.' Karen Hardwick hadn't realised there were so many ESSO petrol stations in the local area. Neither had Tony Sutton, or he wouldn't have asked Mags Richardson to pull in all the CCTV – a request that had been politely, but firmly, refused.

'These stations have all sold petrol in a can in the past two months. Some have footage of the cars and driver on the forecourt. Others, their licence number from the ANPR cameras. Some have CCTV of the shop at approximately the time that the petrol was bought.'

'What about payment?' asked Sutton.

'Most used cards – we're pulling them now to see if any interesting names pop up, but a few paid cash.'

'Start with them. If I was going to buy petrol to use in an arson attack, I doubt I'd be daft enough to pay for it with my credit card.'

* * *

Hardwick had a printout of petrol stations to visit. By the time she had reached number six she was sick of the sight of petrol forecourts. The fumes were giving her a headache and making her feel nauseous again and she'd bought some painkillers and antacids at the last stop.

The ESSO station on the Cambridge road had four pumps and a tiny kiosk selling junk food and tobacco. The teenager behind the till steadfastly avoided eye contact with Hardwick until his manager arrived. He'd hastily slid a pack of rolling tobacco behind a stack of newspapers when she'd flashed her warrant card. She doubted he'd be going outside for his break until he was certain she was no longer downwind of him.

'Hello, DC Hardwick, I'm Maureen, we spoke on the phone.' Hardwick shook her hand.

'We don't get that many requests for petrol in containers here and I remember this one because Ethan—' she nodded towards the nervous youth '—hadn't served it before and called me over for assistance.'

'What can you tell me about the sale?'

'It was for cash, so we don't have a credit card receipt. He bought an approved green canister and then went back out and filled it with five litres of unleaded.'

The story wasn't much different to one she'd heard several times already today.

'Do you have any video in here?'

'Unfortunately no, it was over a month ago and the shop cameras are erased and recorded over.' Hardwick made a note. She'd heard of a case recently where supposedly erased video footage had been retrieved by forensics.

'What about on the forecourt?'

'No CCTV since he didn't drive to the pumps to fill up, but the ANPR cameras snap anyone driving in. It won't have an image of the driver, but you'll get the licence plate. You'll need to contact head office for that.'

'That's great, thank you for your assistance.' Hardwick added it to her list. She'd be spending quite a bit of time on the phone to ESSO's head office.

'You said that you remembered the transaction. I don't suppose you could tell me anything about the person who bought the fuel?'

'Sorry, love,' said Maureen. 'It was weeks ago and I see a lot of different customers.'

'I remember him.'

Hardwick turned towards the teenage assistant and tried to look encouraging. The boy flushed pink, making his acne stand out even more.

'He had really sick tattoos. All the way up his arms.'

Hardwick's breath caught slightly.

'What else do you remember?'

The lad stammered slightly. 'Mostly the tattoos, but I remember he had a shaved head. Oh, and he was wearing an England shirt.'

Chapter 37

'Nice work, Karen.'

Tony Sutton was starting to feel as if the case was finally going somewhere. The recollections of the petrol station attendant and the retired postie, Stanley Buchanan, were pointing the finger at a shaven-headed man with tattoos and an England shirt. It was almost like a uniform for the far-right.

'We'll see if forensics can retrieve anything from the garage's CCTV. In the meantime, let's see what the ANPR camera has.'

'If this is the right person, it suggests that this was planned for some time. The petrol was bought five weeks ago,' said Hardwick. 'It could also mean the arsonist is local. Why else would they buy the petrol in Middlesbury so far in advance?'

'True, although he could have been visiting on a reconnaissance mission, so let's not limit ourselves to suspects with a local connection'

Hardwick conceded the point.

'Let's see if young Ethan can remember any more. We'll show him our scrapbook of the far-right's finest and see if any of these handsome gents jog his memory.'

'OK, but can I nip downstairs and freshen up first? I stink of petrol.'

Ethan Westwood was both nervous and excited as he sat in the interview suite. Despite appearances, he was eighteen years old.

'The tattoos were pretty cool. They stretched from his wrists to underneath his T-shirt.'

'Can you recall the pattern?'

'I only got a quick look, but there were some pretty awesome eagles and loads of gothic-looking script.'

'I don't suppose you can remember what the script said?'

Westwood shook his head. 'Sorry. I remember it looked like numbers or dates mostly.'

'Were there any other patterns you can recall?'

Westwood frowned in concentration.

'There were some of those pretty cool-looking symbols you see on old war films. You know with the red background and the black cross with the right angles.'

Sutton looked hard at the youth to see if he was pulling their leg. He stared back guilelessly.

Hardwick took a pencil and sketched what he had described.

'Yeah, that's the one. What are they called?'

Hardwick and Sutton exchanged a glance.

'You didn't pay much attention in history at school, did you, Ethan?'

Hardwick and Sutton showed the petrol attendant a book of headshots of known far-right activists, but after half an hour he claimed not to recognise any of them. However, given that he apparently hadn't known the significance of a swastika, neither detective was prepared to rule out any of the men completely.

* * *

'This skinhead is certainly looking promising,' mused Sutton as he and Karen Hardwick drank coffee in his cubicle. Hardwick agreed, trying not to make too much of a mess with the Danish pastry he'd insisted on buying them in celebration.

'We really need to identify him. It's a shame that Mr Buchanan couldn't tell us more about the car he was sitting in, he didn't even seem too sure that the car was white.'

'That's the downside of witness statements. At least he was honest enough to admit it, rather than sending us on some well-intentioned wild goose chase,' said Sutton.

'Hopefully forensics will be able to pull at least a couple of images off the CCTV's hard drive, and then Inspector Garfield can run them through his far-right database,' said Hardwick hopefully.

Sutton shrugged. 'Let's not rely on that, it might not work with the system that they have in the garage. Besides, we don't know how much it'll cost. The bean counters might not cough up, given that it's not a murder inquiry.'

Hardwick washed the remains of her pastry down with her coffee.

'There is one thing that bothers me about Stanley Buchanan's account.' She flicked through the notes Sutton had made when he interviewed the retired postman. 'It says that he saw the tattoos because the man's left arm was hanging out of the car window.'

'Which means the suspect was seated in the passenger seat,' finished Sutton.

'Exactly, so assuming Mr Buchanan was correct it raises the question, "who was the driver?"'

'And where was he or she during this time?'

'Well, let's hope the ANPR camera comes up with a name for the registered keeper, then we can ask them directly who they both are.'

Sutton smiled tightly and raised his cardboard cup in salute. 'Here's to hoping.'

Chapter 38

'Thank you for coming, Mr and Mrs Jones. May I call you Warren and Susan?'

'Of course,' said Susan. The man in front of them held their future in their hands; being on first-name terms seemed only right. He looked younger than either Warren or Susan, with a startlingly pale complexion that matched his slight Scandinavian accent.

'My name is Peer Ingersson and I am a senior consultant.'

Warren made a reappraisal of the man's age. He was reminded of the old saying that you knew you were getting old when policemen started getting younger. Warren had been facing that reality for years. In fact, he'd had a sudden jolt when he'd realised that he was actually old enough to be the father of some of his probationary constables. Maybe he could change the saying to 'you know you are getting old when you find that you're older than your consultant'.

'I believe that you saw my colleague, Michaela Reyes, last time and that she ordered some tests to see if the course of treatment she'd prescribed improved matters?'

'Yes, I gave a sample last week,' said Warren, his mouth dry.

'Well I'm sorry, Warren. The lifestyle changes that she prescribed have had no significant effect.'

Warren had suspected as much. Nevertheless, hearing it confirmed was a hammer blow.

'What next?'

Susan had taken over, her voice measured and calm. Warren felt an irrational flush of shame, he'd let her down. He'd let them both down.

'Well, as you know, tests have shown that you are still fertile, Susan, but time is ticking. Statistically a woman of thirty has a roughly seventy-five per cent chance of becoming pregnant within twelve months of trying; by thirty-five the likelihood of a successful pregnancy will have dropped to two-thirds. You turn thirty-six in a few weeks and the odds are starting to stack against you.'

'So IVF is the only option.'

Dr Ingersson leant back and looked over his glasses at them. He pursed his lips.

'It's not the only option. For example, we could concentrate Warren's sperm and try artificial insemination, but I have to warn you that when a man has a low sperm count, it can also be an indication of lower quality sperm. Increasing the density of the sperm may not significantly increase the likelihood of successful fertilisation.'

Susan nodded; she was a biology teacher and Warren knew that she understood these things better than he did.

'If we can remove some of your eggs and freeze them, Susan, then we have more options. If only to buy us some more time.'

Warren could see that Susan was torn.

'Let us think about it,' he said.

'Of course.' Dr Ingersson smiled tolerantly. 'I have read your notes and I understand your concerns. If it is any help to you, I have leaflets that discuss the Catholic Church's views on IVF.'

Warren and Susan thanked the consultant for his time and agreed to a follow-up appointment in a few weeks.

They walked back to their cars without speaking.

Warren turned to Susan; he didn't know what to say, but he couldn't stand the silence any longer.

'I'm sorry,' he started.

'Don't,' Susan snapped, before softening. 'I've told you to stop apologising. It's a medical condition. You know that. You wouldn't be apologising if you had cancer or heart disease.'

'I know, but they wouldn't affect you like this does.'

'Warren, listen to yourself, of course I'd be affected! I'm your wife.'

She waved her hand in a vague gesture towards the clinic.

'This is nothing. So what if we can't have a baby? It's not the end of the world.' Her defiant words were betrayed by the catch in her voice.

Warren enclosed her in a massive hug. 'Now who needs to listen to themselves?'

His own voice caught in his throat. 'You've wanted this for years. If only I hadn't been so selfish. You heard what Dr Reyes said last visit. Men have a biological clock, just like women. I turned forty in January, but I've been so wrapped up in my career, I might have scuppered our chances of having a family.'

Susan pushed herself back slightly and glared at Warren. 'Don't you dare take all of this on your own shoulders. We both delayed this for the sake of our careers. Hell, I'm a biologist, I knew that every year that passed after I turned thirty I was rolling the dice. It was just chance that your fertility was affected more than mine. I could have insisted that you took a fertility test before we delayed any further.'

Warren hugged her again; unsure what to say, he just held her. After a few moments he heard her sniff, signalling the end of her tears.

'Let's go home and get some lunch,' he suggested. He'd blocked out several hours in his work diary and he was determined to use them. They had a lot to talk about and sometime over the next few days they would need to make some difficult decisions.

His phone was set to silent, so he just ignored the pulsing in his jacket pocket, willing it to stop.

Susan stiffened. 'Is that your phone? I thought you'd booked time off.'

'I did.'

'Well, aren't you going to answer it?'

'No, my diary clearly says "unavailable" until late afternoon.'

'So it must be important then. At least check and see who it is.'

Warren conceded to her logic reluctantly, already compiling a mental list of who he'd answer to and who could damn well leave a message on his voicemail.

Sutton.

He might not know what Warren had booked time off for, but he wouldn't be calling unless he thought it was important.

Warren answered the call.

'Sorry to interrupt, boss.'

'It's OK, Tony, I'm sure it's important.'

'It is.'

Chapter 39

Warren was waylaid on his way back to the office by Janice, the support worker who acted as his unofficial PA.

'Chief, you have a visitor in reception.'

'Oh, I wasn't expecting anyone. Who is it?'

'Councillor Kaur, sir.'

'Great. Come to apologise, has she?'

'I didn't get that impression, no.'

'Well, we're under strict instructions to refer all contact with the media and the public to the press office. Give them a heads up and tell them to treat her nicely; maybe she'll support us for once.'

'She asked for you by name, sir.'

'Shit.'

Warren had a nasty feeling that he was going to be the focus of the publicity-hungry councillor's next TV appearance.

* * *

Councillor Kaur was a short, sturdy woman of about fifty. Dressed in a sharply tailored grey suit, with a dark blue neck scarf, her hair was neatly pinned in an elaborate bun, with surprisingly few hints of grey around the temples.

Warren forced a smile as he crossed the reception area and held out his hand.

In person, Lavindeep Kaur was not only shorter than she appeared on TV, but seemed, at first glance, a lot less sure of herself. Her grip was less firm than Warren expected and slightly moist. The reception area's air conditioning only had two settings: ineffectual and arctic blast. Today it was set to the latter, with the support worker pulling desk duty wearing a woolly jumper. Kaur had been there for a few minutes by all accounts, why was she still perspiring?

'Pleased to meet you, Councillor Kaur, I'm sorry you had to wait.' Warren offered no explanation. Kaur was on his territory and Warren had no intention of playing politics with a self-important local official. Regardless of what assurances Warren gave the woman, he was in no doubt that the councillor's tame reporters would spin the story to her benefit, whilst also getting a dig in at Hertfordshire Constabulary.

'Not at all, DCI Jones, thank you for taking the time.' The politician's tone was smooth, practised; more like the woman off the television.

'Please come with me, I'm afraid the air con is pretty fierce out here.'

Before coming downstairs, Warren had run a comb through his hair and organised some biscuits and fresh milk for the smart meeting room. Situated at the far end of the building from CID and Warren's office, the room was decorated with light, calming pastels and padded, comfy chairs. Away from the bustle of the rest of the station it was better suited to the more delicate and private aspects of policing – such as the breaking of sad news and dealing with tricky elected officials. Its complex hot drinks machine also served the best coffee in the building – John Grayson's private stash notwithstanding.

Lavindeep Kaur was a tea drinker, black, one sugar, and so the machine obligingly spat out a cup full of boiling water. For his part Warren selected the strongest roast available. After what seemed like an age of huffing, puffing and grinding it belched out a thick black liquid. Carrying it back to where Kaur was seated, Warren reminded himself again to figure out where the hell the foil sachet disappeared to after use; the machine didn't seem large enough to store more than a couple of them, yet he'd seen it serve meetings of over a dozen people.

'Please help yourself to a biscuit.' Warren would have preferred a custard cream or a garibaldi over the usual packets of shortbread and ginger stem biscuits, but it was called the 'smart meeting room' for a reason. Kaur shook her head in polite refusal.

'I assume that you are here for an update on the investigation into the Islamic Centre fire?' Warren doubted she gave two hoots about the progress of the investigation into the murder of Tommy Meegan.

'Actually, I'm here about the arrest of Binay Singh Mahal.'

Shit, Warren thought. Suddenly, he was no longer fobbing off a local politician. It looked as though Binay Singh Mahal had been as good as his word and was going to complain about his treatment.

Ordinarily the matter would be dealt with quickly and efficiently. The warrant had been legally executed, with minimal force and Singh had been treated appropriately in custody. However, the involvement of Councillor Kaur – and no doubt the local press – would necessitate a more transparent approach than usual. Warren would probably be interviewed and waste hours filling in paperwork, whilst the media would doubtless enjoy the opportunity to recycle old news stories.

'The arrest of Mr Singh was part of an ongoing investigation and I'm afraid I can't comment on the matter.' It was worth a try, Warren decided.

'I understand that Binay's arrest was because you suspected him of involvement in the murder of Tommy Meegan?'

'Again, it would be inappropriate for me to comment on an ongoing investigation.'

Kaur continued as if Warren had said nothing. 'And that you suspect his involvement because of the presence of his Kirpan at the scene?'

'Again…'

Kaur cut him off with a wave of her hand. 'Yes, I understand, Chief Inspector, however I have information that you may find interesting.'

'Go on.'

Warren took a swig of his coffee, using the opportunity to look over the woman seated across from him. Kaur licked her lips.

'I believe that Binay was less than cooperative in the interview.'

Warren said nothing.

'That he refused to tell you where he was at the time of Mr Meegan's… demise.'

Again, Warren said nothing.

'What if I told you he was with me?'

'That's an extraordinary claim, Councillor.'

'Not really. We often spend time together.'

'So you and Mr Singh Mahal are acquaintances. May I ask the nature of that relationship?'

'Certainly. The Sikh community in Middlesbury, as I am sure you are aware, is very small, barely a hundred. I pretty much know everyone. I've known Binay since he was a child. For the last few years he has been helping with langar. We are often rostered together.'

'Feeding those in need.'

'Exactly, every Sikh's duty. Middlesbury doesn't have as large a homeless problem as some places, but we still have a few dozen regulars who come to us for a hot meal. As you know, race or creed is unimportant.'

'So what were you and Mr Singh doing on Saturday?'

'We were on food preparation duties. We have a rota system with two shifts. The first shift prepares the food. It's not that difficult, two people can easily chop the vegetables and get the food cooking in a couple of hours, we're pretty well practised. The second shift then takes over, there are three or four and they serve the food from early evening and wash up.'

'I see. And were you and Mr Singh often partnered together?'

'About once a month. Most of the shifts are done by the older, retired members of the community or those with more flexible schedules.'

'What about Mr Singh?'

'Binay works Monday to Friday, so he does a couple of weekend shifts a month. Our rotas would coincide periodically.'

'What time were you and Mr Singh working together?'

'Food preparation starts at 3 p.m. and takes about two hours.'

The last photograph of Tommy Meegan was taken after two-thirty. Even if he was killed only minutes after that, there was no way Singh could have made it from the alleyway to the Sikh Community Centre by 3 p.m. Not to mention the fact that he would have been covered in blood.

'OK, Councillor, so why didn't Mr Singh tell us this when he was interviewed?'

Kaur sighed and removed her rimless spectacles, rubbing them with the end of her scarf.

'Binay hasn't had the happiest relationship with the police over the years.'

'Go on.'

'You don't need me to tell you that he was a troubled young man, with arrests and brushes with the law. In recent years, he's put all of that behind him. He has a good job and has spent a lot of time helping the community. I've even persuaded him to look into college; he's a very bright young man.

'Nevertheless, he still doesn't trust authority. He believes the police are against our community. Not without some justification'

It was the first dig she'd made since arriving and Warren decided to ignore it. But Kaur obviously had more to say on the subject.

'Tell me, Chief Inspector, how many non-white police officers do you have in Middlesbury? How many in CID? Would you say the make-up of your department reflects the community you serve?'

It was a fair question. The demographics of the Hertfordshire population were significantly less diverse than that of the West Midlands where Warren had grown up and started his career. The lack of Sikhs was especially noticeable. When Warren was a small child in Coventry he remembered assuming that turbans were part of the uniform for bus drivers. By comparison, the sight of a bearded man with a turban was rare in Middlesbury. Yet even measured against that low bar, Middlesbury police would still struggle to claim it fully reflected their local community.

Warren said nothing, knowing that there was no satisfactory way to answer the question without landing himself in hot water. Kaur smiled slightly; she knew that she'd scored a point.

'So for that reason, he refused to give an alibi that could have removed him from the investigation immediately?'

Kaur gestured the futility of any answer she could give.

'It's fair to say he has a bit of a blind spot when it comes to the police. That's why he wouldn't report being mugged earlier in the week.'

'Which mugging was that?'

Kaur smiled thinly.

'The one last Wednesday night that left him with two black eyes, a cut nose and bruised ribs. And that resulted in his Kirpan being taken.'

'I see. And when did Mr Singh tell you about this alleged mugging?'

'I asked him about his black eyes on Saturday.'

'Did you not try to persuade him to report it to the police?'

'Of course. But he refuses to have anything to do with you.'

'On that note, I find it a little surprising that Mr Singh wasn't present at the protests.'

'As I said before, Binay is making an effort to get his life back on track. Just as well, really. I see that more counter-protestors were arrested than the far-right activists who were inciting hatred. And despite being unable to spare two officers to protect the centre last Saturday you are somehow able to find a half-dozen constables to keep an eye on visitors paying their respects and delivering flowers. Doesn't cast a very good light on Hertfordshire Constabulary's community policing initiatives, does it?'

Chapter 40

Karen Hardwick's favourite day of the working week was Thursday, because unless they had to work overtime, she and Gary always finished shift together. She'd taken to referring to it as 'date night', although Gary still contended that was something that old, married couples with tribes of under-fives did. Despite that, he was as enthusiastic about planning their weekly fun as her. Tonight's schedule of DVD and wine had just been shelved, however.

'Shit.' Hastings sat down at the table and put his head in his hands. 'That's just what we need.' Wordlessly he passed over the letter from their landlord.

Hardwick did some quick mental arithmetic. 'After tax, that's more than double September's pay rise. How can she justify that sort of increase?'

Hastings shrugged helplessly. 'It's true what she says, we haven't had a rent increase in the two years we've lived here.'

'Can we afford it? We've already changed our phone contracts and ditched the cable TV. And my car isn't going to sail through next month's MOT.'

'We'll just have to cut back on how much we're saving towards a deposit and see what overtime the boss decides to throw at the Meegan killing and the arson.'

Hastings slumped back in his chair.

'You know, I thought we were going to finally start growing that pot.' He squeezed Hardwick's hand. 'I know you shouldn't count your chickens and all that, but I did some sums and I worked out that if I pass sergeants' selection and bank the pay rise, we might be able to save enough for a deposit in five or six years rather than ten. Now I'll need the promotion just to stand still.' He smiled ruefully. 'No pressure.'

* * *

On the other side of town Susan Jones ended her phone call, her self-control abruptly collapsing as she burst into tears. Warren slid across the settee and took her in his arms. He didn't know what to say. The relationship between a mother and a daughter was complicated at the best of times, but when your mother was Bernice…

After a few seconds, the tears subsided.

'I'm sorry, I'm being silly.'

'No you aren't. Bernice is the one being silly. It's the twenty-first century for crying out loud.'

'I've already told her that and you know what she said.'

Bernice had made her views quite clear and they matched those of the Catholic Church; IVF and other assisted reproduction techniques were a sin. End of discussion. And it didn't matter what century they were in, God's word was eternal.

'Find me the passage in the Bible where it says "thou shalt not mix sperm and eggs in a petri-dish".'

Despite herself, Susan smiled slightly.

'And Lo it was said, "the use of a turkey baster shall only be at Christmas".'

'Eww, that's gross.'

Warren squeezed her shoulder.

'I wish I'd never said anything,' Susan repeated for at least the tenth time.

'Don't be daft. She's like a bloodhound, your mother. There's no way you could have hid it from her. I'm trying to persuade Grayson to employ her as an interviewer.'

Susan smiled weakly at his continued attempts to cheer her up.

'I could have chosen my moment a bit better though. In a restaurant, after most of a bottle of red wine, probably wasn't the best time.'

'I thought you were remarkably restrained. The ticking clock jibe was below the belt and bringing up your sister Felicity's latest pregnancy was disgraceful. I think that's the first time I've ever seen your old man contradict your mother in public.'

Susan frowned. 'I can imagine the drive home was a bit frosty.'

'Have you spoken to Dennis since?'

'He texted me and said he'd talk to Mum when she's calmed down.' She gestured towards the phone. 'Judging by what she just said, it doesn't look as though he's had much success yet.'

She sniffed loudly. 'So that's it. I'm not going to call again until she apologises.'

Warren gave her another squeeze. God knew Bernice was hardly the easiest person to get on with and probably still felt Susan could have married better, but over the years Warren had also seen the warm, caring side of her. He'd never forget the kindness she'd shown his Granddad Jack, especially since the death of Nana Betty. He hoped Susan and Bernice would work this out before it was too late. If there was one thing Warren had learnt, when your parents were gone, it was the things you wished you had said rather than the things you wish you hadn't that haunted your dreams.

Chapter 41

One a.m. and Warren stared at the ceiling. Over the hours he'd been lying awake, his eyes had adjusted slowly to the darkness; what had started off as impenetrable, uniform blackness had steadily gained texture. The coal black was now interspersed with the occasional dash of the deepest charcoal.

Insomnia at this point in a case wasn't unusual for Warren, and this time around the stakes were as high as they'd ever been. The town he loved could well be ripped apart by the twin blows of the Islamic Centre fire and the murder of Tommy Meegan. Even if they were somehow able to prevent Meegan's funeral from turning into a massive rally for the far-right, rumours were already circulating that this week's Friday prayer session – wherever it may be held – was likely to attract Muslims from all across the region. Warren doubted that even the charismatic young imam that Sutton had spoken to would be able to fully keep the lid on the boiling emotions.

In either event, it would be his colleagues in the middle of things. Trying to keep things calm, whilst allowing all of those present to vent their feelings and exercise their democratic right to free speech. All in front of the critical gaze of the nation's – if not the world's – media.

None of this had anything to do with Middlesbury CID or Warren – and everything to do with him. Never in his career had Warren wanted more to hand over a case, but even if that was possible, he knew that he couldn't.

Everybody from the Home Secretary downwards wanted the murder of Tommy Meegan solved. To the politicians, and the senior officers in his own force, the man's death was an embarrassment and a brewing headache. Already they were planning damage limitation should the killer turn out to be one of the town's minority ethnic residents.

But to Warren, he was first and foremost a victim. The man had been deeply unpleasant, and few outside his immediate circle would miss him, but that wasn't the point. He had been murdered – brutally and in cold blood. Even a man like Tommy Meegan had people who loved him, and Warren had seen the pain in their eyes. It was his duty to bring the man's killer to justice.

Similarly, they also needed to find the arsonist. In some ways, it would be easy if the fire could be pinned on the far-right, but it was still going to raise a lot of awkward questions. The force would need to work with the local communities to rebuild the confidence lost when somebody decided to remove protection from a vulnerable target to stop a group of racist thugs getting lynched. Warren understood the pressures faced by the Gold Commander that day and knew that she had faced an impossible decision – but he could see how it must look to outside observers.

And what about Binay Singh Mahal? The man was still on bail and despite the intervention of Councillor Kaur, Warren's instincts were telling him that he was still a person of interest. As Sutton had predicted, no witnesses to the man's supposed mugging had come forward, and Warren didn't believe in coincidences.

Hopefully forensic IT would have better luck with Binay Singh Mahal and Tommy Meegan's laptops and mobile phones than they'd managed with Philip Rhodri's. If they didn't then Warren knew that the pressure would be on him to cancel Singh Mahal's bail restrictions; he was in no doubt that if he didn't, Councillor Kaur would fully capitalise on the situation.

In times like this, Warren would usually take solace in the sleeping form of his wife beside him. Listening to her soft breathing, he could usually convince himself that no matter what challenges the day ahead might bring, for the next few hours at least, the woman sharing the bed beside him made everything right with the world.

But tonight even that was denied him. Susan had been tearful as she'd come to bed, the fraught phone call with her mother still hanging over her. When had having a baby become such a big thing? At first it had been fun: their little secret. They'd known it probably wouldn't be immediate and the two had resolved to enjoy the journey as much as the destination. After all, if the horror stories some of their friends had told them were true, once the baby arrived spontaneous lovemaking sessions whenever the mood took them were probably out of the question for eighteen years until their offspring left for university.

'I just hope they don't decide to take a gap year,' Warren had mused as they lay in bed one night. 'I'm not sure I can wait nineteen years.'

'Maybe they'll go travelling.'

'We should start saving money to buy them plane tickets for their eighteenth birthday.'

They'd both laughed at that. After all they'd only been trying for a few weeks. Or was it months? Time had slipped by and slowly the process became more urgent. Susan started keeping a diary, taking her temperature and using ovulation testing kits from the chemist, applying science to the problem.

When had lovemaking become a chore? Warren asked himself. When had it changed from a joyful, fun experience into a duty that needed to be performed whether they were fully in the mood or not?

It had taken eighteen months before the couple finally admitted they might need help. Although the guidelines suggested that they should wait a further eighteen months, their GP had been sympathetic and referred them on the NHS to a local fertility clinic for investigation.

Warren and Susan had been relieved when the results showed that she still had a healthy store of eggs and no reason why she should be infertile. However, the news for Warren had been less encouraging. As before, Susan understood the science better than Warren but, in a nutshell, he had crap sperm.

'I feel like half a man,' he'd confided in Susan one night, ignoring her protestations. 'Every day I see evidence that becoming a father is easy. You only have to meet some of the feckless idiots that populate our custody suites to realise that it shouldn't be a challenge. Some of these guys couldn't even tell you the birthdays of half their kids.'

Tests ruled out anything obvious and the advice had been to eat a healthier diet, reduce stress levels and cut back on alcohol. Reducing his stress levels at work was all but impossible and Warren flatly refused to take up yoga, but he'd tried his best to change his work-life balance and the couple had resolved to spend their free time more carefully. A brief dalliance with decaffeinated coffee had caused an increase in stress, or so he'd claimed, and the experiment had soon been abandoned. Warren wasn't a big drinker, didn't smoke and didn't indulge in long, hot baths, so that left only diet.

Five pieces of fruit a day and trying to eat more vegetables were achievable; however, despite Susan's entreaties, salad was out of the question and oily fish made him gag. Nevertheless, he'd been deeply disappointed when his latest test results had shown no improvement in sperm quality.

Disappointed and ashamed.

Friday 25th July

Chapter 42

Warren had asked Tony Sutton to lead the morning briefing.

'This is our prime suspect in the Islamic Centre fire. Assuming it is the same person, he bought petrol from an ESSO filling station a little over a month ago, the same brand used to start the fire. He was then seen in a car near to the centre in the hours preceding the fire.

'Unfortunately, the eyesight of one witness isn't the best and the petrol station attendant isn't the brightest bulb in the chandelier, but this is what we have so far.

'Both describe full-length tattoos on at least one, probably both arms. Details are limited, but it would seem that they are neo-Nazi in nature, with swastikas and gothic script, possibly including key dates significant to the movement. Aside from that he was white with a shaved head and the obligatory England shirt. Unfortunately, we have no more physical descriptors other than a rather vague impression that he was of average height and unremarkable build. It is possible, but not confirmed, that he may have had an unknown companion as he waited outside the centre.'

'Does the description match anyone on the bus and were they all accounted for at the time of the fire?' questioned a detective sergeant from Welwyn.

'No and yes. We can vouch for them all. Whoever this person is, he didn't come up from Romford with any of the BAP protestors. The Hate Crime Intelligence Unit are going through their files to see if the description matches any other known players, either affiliated to the BAP or another far-right organisation.

'Our witness at the filling station didn't get much of a look at the car. Unfortunately, there's no CCTV of either the car or the suspect, but ESSO are currently trawling their ANPR records for us and should be able to supply us with an index shortly. We'll cross-reference it with the wider ANPR network and see if we can reconstruct its journey. We might even get lucky and find some images of the driver.'

'Thank you, Karen and Tony, good work. Check the job board folks, we've got a busy day.' Warren dismissed the team. Day six was just starting.

* * *

'What do you mean the plates don't exist?'

'They've never been registered. Sorry.'

Sutton resisted the urge to slam the handset down. It wasn't the technician's fault. He leant back in his seat and rubbed his eyes. The closing of that potential lead had taken the shine off an otherwise productive twenty-four hours.

Karen Hardwick looked over. 'The car at the petrol station had fake licence plates?'

'Apparently.' He paused. 'What do you think the odds are that two cars, both of them with fake licence plates, are unlinked?'

'I'll find out.' She was already turning back to her computer.

* * *

'I've been on to the DVLA about the fake licence plates.' Hardwick had a printed email in her hand.

234

'As you know, it's quite difficult to get them made up, at least on the high street, you need the vehicle's registration documents. That's why thieves normally try and nick plates off other cars. In this case, they either wanted a quick fix, or didn't fancy the risk.'

She laid the printout down on the table in front of Warren.

'The two index numbers, from the car that we believe picked up Philip Rhodri and the car that bought the petrol, only differ by two digits. Unfortunately, we don't have high resolution photographs that can spot the tampering directly, but we can make a pretty good guess at what they did.'

She pointed at the two numbers.

'You can see how on this plate there are two letter Rs. However, on this one the remaining five characters are the same, but instead of two Rs we have two letter Bs.'

'It's been changed with black tape,' said Warren.

'Exactly. It probably wouldn't pass close inspection by eye, but it's good enough to fool ANPR cameras.'

'Do we know what the original index is likely to have been?' asked Sutton.

'There are a few permutations, but the most likely candidate is two modified letter Ps, which leads us to this car, a white 1998 Vauxhall Corsa, owned by a sixty-seven-year-old Mr Mansfield in Bedford.'

'Good work, Karen,' praised Warren, 'although I have my doubts that the registered keeper is our man. Do you have an address?'

'Unless he's moved since the last tax disc was issued back in December.'

'Check it out.'

* * *

'Sir, Tommy Meegan's mobile phone provider have given us the call log for his smartphone.' Hastings was clutching a wad of A4 sheets. 'I'm still waiting to hear back from the network that his ancient Nokia was registered to.'

Warren looked up from his computer. 'Any clue if he was playing away from home?'

'It looks like it.'

Hastings had marked almost a third of the entries with a fluorescent pink highlighter pen. A single number had been either called or sent text messages almost twice a day for the three months covered by the log.

'The entries follow a pattern. A text first thing in the morning and either a text or a lengthy call each evening.' Hastings looked a touch embarrassed. 'It looks a lot like the pattern Karen and I followed when we were first dating.'

'Ah, modern love. Back in my day, Susan and I had to rely on carrier pigeons. I assume the number isn't that of his beloved Ms Creasy?'

'Nope.' He passed over another piece of paper, this time with the owners of the numbers listed. Again, he'd highlighted a number in pink.

Warren whistled.

'Well, that is interesting.'

Chapter 43

'Mr Mansfield died back in May. His widow sold the car through a private listing in a newspaper in mid-June.' Hardwick sounded frustrated.

'Why is it still registered to him?' Warren made to perch on the edge of her desk, then reappraised the structural integrity of the cheap MDF and thought better of it.

'She admits to being a bit overwhelmed by everything and not being a driver herself, didn't really know what to do. She said that the man who bought it offered to fill in the paperwork for the transfer of ownership.'

'So she met the man she sold it to. I suppose it would be a bit too much to hope for a name or bank details?'

'Sorry, sir. She thinks his name was Richard. He paid her three hundred pounds cash and drove straight off. But she does have a description.'

'Go on.'

The frustration in her voice eased somewhat. 'White, shaven-headed, wearing an England football shirt…' she paused '… with full-length arm tattoos.'

'Sounds familiar. Now we just need to figure out who this person is,' said Warren.

'Knock, knock.' Theo Garfield rapped his knuckles against the wooden divider between Hardwick's cubicle and the next. The grin that he wore threatened to split his face in two. Tony Sutton looked similarly pleased.

'We may be able to help you. We've got a hit on the database.' He waved a piece of paper in the air.

'Shaven-headed with full-length arm tattoos is a surprisingly rare combination amongst our far-right friends. A properly done tattoo sleeve could easily cost a thousand pounds or more per arm, although given the designs they favour, I'd imagine they probably aren't popping into the local high street parlour. Either way it's a pretty hefty investment for most of these guys.'

He passed the printout to Warren.

'Mr Robert Lynton, fifty-two years old, Haverhill, Suffolk. He spent some time at Her Majesty's pleasure for assault in the early Nineties. Not a lot since then, but he occasionally crops up at protest marches.'

He passed across a colour photograph.

'This was taken at a rally in 2012. It's blurry, but you can see he has ink covering his right arm.'

'The one raised in a Nazi salute?'

'Yeah, he's a pleasant boy.'

'Well, Haverhill is less than an hour's drive away and on the opposite side of Middlesbury to the direction they will have been driving up from so it makes sense that he wasn't on the coach,' said Sutton.

'It also makes sense that he'd be the one that knows Middlesbury well enough to be put in charge of torching the Islamic Centre. Any other evidence? Has he said anything on social media?'

'No. It doesn't look like he's a big one for using the internet. Or at least we haven't managed to link any of the accounts we monitor to him,' said Garfield.

'Do we have an address?' asked Warren.

'Yes, and council tax records show it to be current.'

'Then why don't you and Tony pay him a visit? Be sure to pass on my regards.'

* * *

The sort of man who would spray petrol through a letter box after blocking the exit with a metal bin was a coward and probably wouldn't put up much resistance. Nevertheless, Sutton and Garfield were taking no chances, neither of them wanting to find themselves on the wrong end of a knife. Both men wore stab vests and a van full of similarly attired constables on loan from Suffolk Constabulary sat around the corner ready to respond to any trouble within sixty seconds.

Robert Lynton lived in a well-maintained, semi-detached, four-bedroom house on the outskirts of the town. A white Mercedes soft top sat on the gravelled drive.

'I'm sure Alois Kernaghan would have mentioned if the car that picked up Rhodri was a sports car,' said Garfield. 'But then I suppose it would be too much to hope for a Vauxhall Corsa with dodgy licence plates to be sitting in plain view.'

Sutton looked around appreciatively at the neatly landscaped front garden. 'This guy hardly conforms to the stereotype.'

'Some don't. They wear long sleeves in summer to cover their tattoos and keep their views to themselves in polite company. Plenty of men shave our heads these days, myself included. They travel away if they want to go on marches. They don't shit in their own nest.'

The doorbell, a melodious affair, also confounded Sutton's expectations, as did the tastefully decorated hallway visible past the woman that opened the door to them.

'Whaddya want?' The woman's harsh, gravelly tones contradicted her immaculately coiffured hair and meticulously applied make-up. At first glance her smooth, wrinkle-free complexion suggested a woman closer to thirty than fifty, however the way that her sneer seemed to stop halfway up her face hinted that her youthful appearance wasn't entirely natural. A glance at her throat, visible above her plunging neckline, confirmed that her true age was probably closer to sixty than fifty.

'Mrs Lynton?'

'Who wants to know?'

'I'm Detective Inspector Tony Sutton, and this is my colleague.' As usual, Garfield was keeping a low profile.

'Is Mr Lynton in?'

She smiled, her lips curling the part of her face that hadn't been paralysed by Botox.

'Of course he is.'

'May we speak to him?'

'Doubtful.'

'We do have a warrant to enter these premises and speak to Mr Lynton, but we'd rather avoid any unnecessary unpleasantness.'

She shrugged. 'Knock yourself out.'

Stepping to one side, she called out. 'Rob, you've got visitors. Two lovely gentlemen from the police would like to speak to you.'

She gave her half-smile again. 'Go in. I won't bother boiling the kettle.'

* * *

'Well, that was a waste of bloody time.'

Sutton tried hard to keep the frustration out of his voice as he pulled away from the Lyntons' house with a squeak of tyres.

Garfield looked embarrassed. 'Sorry, our database isn't always as up-to-date as we'd like.'

Sutton breathed out in a sharp hiss.

'Not your fault. You weren't to know the poor sod was in that state.'

240

'Yeah, looks as though he can't lift a spoon these days, let alone raise a Nazi salute.'

According to his wife, Robert Lynton had suffered a massive stroke two years previously. They'd check out his story, but both men knew the lead was a dead end; you'd need to be an Oscar-winning actor to fake the man's symptoms that convincingly.

The two men lapsed into silence.

'Karma, wouldn't you say?' said Garfield after a while. 'The man was a nasty piece of work. I guess what goes around comes around.'

Sutton said nothing. He wasn't sure anybody deserved that.

Chapter 44

Sutton and Garfield were deflated when they returned to the station and Warren shared their concern. As did the Chief Constable, by all accounts.

'We could have done with a bit of good news,' muttered DSI Grayson. He'd turned his computer screen through one-hundred-and-eighty degrees so the gathered officers could see the BBC News he was streaming.

Behind the same journalist from earlier that week, a crowd of fifty or so protestors had gathered, some with placards bearing the now ubiquitous #Justice4Muslims hashtag, whilst a dozen or so police in fluorescent green vests stood a watchful guard.

'Imam Danyal Mehmud leads prayers at the Middlesbury Islamic Centre, which was subjected to an arson attack at the same time as the riots in the town centre. What can you tell me about the mood of the local Muslim community, particularly in the light of these recent attacks, both at the site of the fire and online?'

The young imam was clearly nervous and Sutton looked on with sympathy. He'd grown to like the young man and had been on the phone with him that morning as he'd prepared for holiest day of the Muslim week.

'Obviously we are still very shocked and saddened by Saturday's events and we continue to pray for our sister and her great-grandson who remain in hospital. We are worried that there are plans for yet more far-right extremists to come to our town to mark the funeral of Tommy Meegan and after the despicable defacing of this community memorial, we urge the police and the authorities to do all they can to prevent future attacks on all of our communities.'

To underscore his point, the image switched to one of the pile of flowers and soft toys that well-wishers had been leaving against the centre's front gate since the weekend. Red paint had been splashed all over the makeshift memorial and crude swastikas sprayed on the wall behind. 'Terrorists Out' and 'No Muslims in Middlesbury' were the only two slogans that the BBC hadn't blurred out for decency reasons.

'The Social Media Intelligence Unit have reported the sudden registering of over one hundred Twitter and Facebook accounts in past twelve hours, all using the murder of Tommy Meegan to call for everything from the banning of the burqa to forced deportation and worse.' Garfield was grim, reading an email on his phone. 'The service providers are doing their best to shut them down as soon as they are reported, but these guys are damned sophisticated. IP addresses for those setting up the accounts are scattered across the continent and even the US, involving at least a dozen different groups. This level of online coordination is almost unprecedented. If they can carry it over into the real world, Tommy Meegan's funeral could be an even bigger flashpoint than we feared.'

Back on screen, the reporter turned her microphone towards the woman on her left. 'Councillor Lavindeep Kaur is a prominent member of the local Sikh community and represents many of the ethnic minority residents in Middlesbury, including Muslims. What are your thoughts on what took place last Saturday and on more recent events?'

Councillor Kaur had dressed for the cameras, her hair now covered in an elaborate red and gold headscarf and her trouser suit replaced with a flowing salwar kameez.

'Well, first I should clarify that I represent all of the citizens of Middlesbury, not just members of our minority communities, and you can see from the crowds behind us that the events here have united people from across all faiths.' The BBC correspondent acknowledged the rebuke with a nod of the head. 'However, I join our Muslim brothers and sisters in praying for those still in hospital and I echo Imam Mehmud's call for action from the authorities ahead of the funeral of Mr Meegan. We must ensure that our peaceful town is not overrun again by the nasty, racist individuals who perpetrated this cowardly act.'

To her credit, the reporter didn't let the assertion go unchallenged.

'As yet, the police have not been able to establish who was responsible for the arson attack on the Islamic Centre and the British Allegiance Party have denied all involvement.'

Kaur assumed a grave expression, but Warren fancied he could almost feel the woman's glee at the opportunity to address her favourite subject.

'Well, so far the police have singularly failed to inspire confidence in many of the communities I represent. They have yet to announce any leads in their investigation, and after meeting with the Senior Investigating Officer, I get the impression that they seem to be far more interested in the killing of Mr Meegan. After all, it was their carelessness that led to Saturday's fiasco in the first place and the criminal damage that took place last night.'

Warren bit his tongue, as the reporter again challenged her sweeping comment. The veteran politician brushed her protests aside.

'Look behind you. There are dozens of police officers policing a peaceful protest by our Muslim brothers and sisters, yet on the day that a coachload of Islamophobic thugs came to our town, hell-bent on trouble, Hertfordshire Constabulary saw fit to post only two officers in a car outside what was an obvious target for their hatred and violence. They then redeployed them in a failed attempt to shore-up their under-resourced response to the riot threatening to wreak havoc on our town centre. After Saturday's attack, they again turned out in force to police those individuals paying their respects. Then, suddenly, last night withdrew all officers from here, allowing this disgraceful vandalism to take place. Their lack of planning and foresight calls into question the competence of those senior officers involved and their commitment to keeping the entire community safe.'

Grayson inhaled sharply. 'The hypocritical…' He paused for a moment. 'It was Councillor Kaur's constant pressure on ACC Naseem that resulted in the withdrawal of a police presence yesterday evening. Now she's trying to blame the cockup on us?'

Unfortunately, the interviewer hadn't picked up on the discrepancies in Kaur's statement.

'Are you saying that the police's response, or rather lack of it, was responsible for the fire that took place here last weekend and the attack last night?'

Kaur paused for a moment and Warren could almost see the political calculations taking place behind her eyes. When she resumed speaking her tone was more conciliatory.

'What I am saying, is that there needs to be a full, independent inquiry into what has happened over the past week and whether the dangers faced by minority communities are being taken seriously by the authorities, including the police. Furthermore, I call on the Home Secretary to consider using her powers to stop the funeral of Tommy Meegan becoming a flashpoint for yet more violence.'

'What powers?' exploded Grayson. 'She can't ban a funeral, for Christ's sake!'

The reporter turned back to Imam Mehmud. 'Mr Mehmud, what are your final thoughts?'

The young man looked uncomfortable.

'I would echo the councillor's calls for an inquiry, but in the meantime would urge our brothers and sisters to remember that Islam is a religion of peace and that we should refrain from taking the law into our own hands.'

The journalist thanked both interviewees before handing back to the studio.

Sutton was the first to speak. 'Imam Mehmud is out of his depth, he said as much to me. He's worried that things are going to turn ugly. They're going to hold their Friday prayers in a church hall and he said that a lot of angry young men that he doesn't recognise are arriving. He's concerned that some are going to use it as an excuse for violence.'

'Which plays into the hands of the BAP and their ilk,' concluded Garfield.

Warren agreed. 'The slightest sniff of any trouble and the right-wing press will have a field day. All people will see on the front pages of the newspapers are angry Muslims protesting. And you just know the photos they use will be of the hardcore troublemakers carrying placards saying "Death to the West". People like Danyal Mehmud won't get a look-in.'

'And whoever is policing the event is going to be under impossible scrutiny,' said Sutton. 'If they set a foot wrong, they'll be out on their ear. I wouldn't be surprised if there are a few wannabe martyrs looking to find themselves on the wrong side of a baton and the right side of a camera.'

'Well, politics isn't our concern,' Grayson reminded them. 'All we can do is get to the bottom of this and the killing of Tommy Meegan as quickly as possible and hope that the politicians and community leaders can mend fences and keep a lid on things.' He grimaced. 'What I will say is, I wouldn't want to be in the shoes of whoever ultimately carries the blame for Saturday's cockup.'

Chapter 45

Warren had again decided to leave his office and get his hands dirty. Grayson hadn't said anything about Warren's lengthy absence from the office, which he took as tacit approval for his actions.

However, he was getting thoroughly sick of the A10. For that reason he had pulled rank and tuned the car radio to Heart, much to the disgust of Gary Hastings, who'd spent the whole journey staring at his smartphone with headphones in. It reminded Warren of seemingly endless car journeys to the South of France as a child, staring out of the window, trying to ignore the crackling of Radio 4 longwave as his father kept abreast of the cricket scores. Happy days. At least they had air conditioning now.

The dilapidated council house on the opposite side of Romford to where the late Tommy Meegan had lived showed little evidence that it had once been occupied by a trained painter and decorator. A snarling Rottweiler had greeted Warren and Hastings at the front door; the aptly named Cerberus. The beast certainly looked as though it would be more than capable of guarding the gates of Hades, even with only one head. Warren wasn't a big dog lover at the best of times and he was relieved when the dog's owner,

Paige Brandon, had dragged the huge animal into the kitchen and locked the door, all the while reassuring Warren and Hastings that 'he wouldn't hurt a fly'.

That done, the woman turned to them and appraised them.

'Guess you're here about Tommy?'

Warren estimated she was in her late thirties. A pretty, slim – verging on skinny – brunette, she was surely evidence that opposites attract; she couldn't be any more different from her estranged husband, Harry 'Bellies' Brandon. Only the glimpse of a tattooed England flag on the top of her shoulder hinted at her allegiances.

'Yes, we're just looking at his background, trying to work out who might have had a reason to harm him and trying to retrace his movements on the days leading up to his death,' said Hastings.

She shrugged, heading back into the lounge. Warren and Hastings followed.

A packet of cigarettes was on the mantelpiece and she took one out, her back to the two officers.

'I didn't know him that well. I'm not sure how much help I can be.' Her hand shook slightly, and it took three clicks of the lighter for her to ignite the cigarette, the flame pitifully small. When she finally turned around, it was to sit down in a thread-bare armchair and pull over an already overloaded ashtray.

Warren took that as an invite and he and Hastings sat down on the mismatched couch opposite. He noticed with some dismay that the house clearly didn't operate a 'no furniture' rule for its canine occupant. He'd have to get the lint roller out when he got back to the station.

'Any information you can give us would be helpful, Ms Brandon,' encouraged Hastings.

'Whatever.' She stared at the scratched coffee table.

'I assume that you knew Mr Meegan?'

'Yeah, I suppose. He worked with Harry, my husband.'

'Doing what?'

'Harry runs a painting and decorating business. He hired Tommy and a couple of others to help him out.'

'How well did you know him?'

The coffee table still seemed to hold a fascination for her.

'We met a couple of times, obviously.'

Warren made an 'mm-hmm' noise and scribbled a few lines in his notebook.

'How well would you say your husband knew Mr Meegan?' Hastings continued.

The cigarette was barely half gone, its acrid smoke filling the air between them. Nevertheless, she stubbed it out and removed another from the packet. Again, it took several attempts for her to light it.

'Well, they worked together for the last few years and they'd go to rallies and that.'

'So they were friends?'

'Yeah, I guess so.'

'How involved are you with the BAP, Ms Brandon?'

She must have been expecting the question, nevertheless she fidgeted awkwardly.

'Not much, that was mostly Harry's thing.'

'But you support their goals and ideals?'

Now the awkwardness turned to defiance. 'It's a free country.'

'Of course.' Hastings' tone was placating. Warren remained silent.

'Not everyone feels that way though, do they?'

She said nothing.

'Were you aware of any threats against your husband and his friends, in particular Mr Meegan?'

''Course. There were always people online, stirring up shit.'

'Did Tommy ever talk to you or give you any names?'

'Not really, he usually told me not to worry about it.'

The look in her eyes told them that she knew she'd misspoken as soon as she closed her mouth.

'So you did know Mr Meegan?'

She sucked hard on the cigarette.

'Like I said, he was a friend of my husband's. We met occasionally.'

'When did you and your husband split up, Ms Brandon?' It was the first thing Warren had said since introducing themselves.

She started slightly, before recovering. 'Who says we've split up?'

He pointed towards the mantelpiece. 'I noticed there are no pictures of the two of you. Not even a wedding photo.'

She said nothing, but the rate at which she was sucking on her second cigarette meant she'd be finished with that pretty soon also.

'Harry doesn't like having his photograph taken.'

'Were your husband and Mr Meegan close?' asked Hastings.

'I suppose. They worked together every day, so I guess so.'

'What time did your husband leave for the rally on Saturday?' Warren again.

She looked away. Warren wondered if she knew how much time she let pass when she dissembled.

'I don't know.'

Warren raised an eyebrow in surprise.

'You don't know? Can you give us a ballpark figure?'

She bit her lip.

'About eight-ish, I guess.'

Warren made a show of looking at his notebook.

'Are you sure?'

Another long pause.

'Maybe...' A sudden look of relief crossed her face. 'I'm a heavy sleeper. He was gone when I woke up. He could have left sooner.'

'You woke up about eight then?'

'Yeah, it was the weekend. I had a bit of a lie-in.'

They'd given her enough rope to hang herself, Warren decided. He closed his notebook with a snap.

'According to the coach driver, the coach left for Middlesbury at ten o'clock sharp. Your husband is a pretty distinctive man and the coach driver clearly remembers him arriving just before they left. I've looked at the map and it is less than thirty minutes from your house to the pub car park. I can't believe your husband left the house before 9 a.m.'

'He probably met up with some of the lads before they got on the coach, you know to have breakfast in a caff or something.' A note of desperation had crept into her voice.

'Nope. The coach driver says he arrived alone.'

Hastings now took over, his voice more gentle.

'Why are you lying, Paige? We know that the two of you have been separated for some time. Why are you protecting him?'

She fumbled for another cigarette; this time her hand was shaking so badly, she dropped the lighter down the side of her seat. She scrabbled to retrieve it from between the cushion and the arm of the chair but it refused to light, the dry snick of the flint filling the silence between them. After a few moments, Hastings stood up and handed her another lighter he'd spotted on the mantelpiece.

She inhaled so deeply she coughed, before immediately taking another hit.

'You don't know what time he left because he wasn't here, was he?'

A slight shake of her head.

'DCI Jones was correct when he said you were no longer together, wasn't he?'

Her eyes were moist; it could have been from the smoke or the coughing, but Warren doubted it.

'How long?'

She sniffed. 'About six months.'

'And have you spoken to him since?'

She shook her head. 'Not really, not for a while.'

'Has he spoken to you about Saturday? Asked you to say anything to us about him?'

This time the shake was emphatic. 'No.'

'So why did you lie about him being here on Saturday morning? Why did you lie about not knowing Tommy Meegan? We know that he lived with you and your husband when he first moved down here,' said Hastings.

She said nothing again.

'Did you start your affair with Mr Meegan before or after you split up with your husband?'

The blood disappeared so quickly from her face Warren wondered if she was going to pass out.

'Oh, God…' was all she managed.

Warren reopened his notebook. 'According to mobile phone records, the two of you had been calling and texting each other twice a day for months. Did your husband know?'

Her latest cigarette had burnt almost to the end, a long tube of ash half the length of a man's thumb was starting to bend under its own weight. She flicked it into the ashtray, the motion automatic.

'No.' It was a whisper.

'Are you sure?'

She ignored the question. 'You mustn't tell him.' Suddenly the tears were flowing.

'He mustn't know,' she repeated.

Warren opened his mouth to reply, but she cut him off.

'Promise me you won't tell him? He can't find out.' There was panic in her voice.

'Why, Paige?'

'He'd kill me.'

Chapter 46

Hastings and Warren had retired to a café a few miles away to have lunch and compare notes. They'd driven there with the windows open in an attempt to dispel the smell of cigarette smoke that lingered on their clothes after the visit.

'She's clearly terrified of Brandon. I guess that's why she tried to cover for him at first.'

Warren agreed. 'It sounds as though he has a nasty temper on him. Add to that the fact that he must weigh more than three times what she does and it's no wonder she didn't want us to tell him about her affair with Tommy Meegan.'

'Do you think he knew? It would be a hell of a motive. From what he said in interview, he and Meegan were really good friends. He even said that he'd kipped on his couch when he and his wife split up.' A thought suddenly occurred to him. 'Bloody hell, you don't think Tommy was sleeping with her whilst Brandon was living with him do you? Can you imagine how furious he'd be if he found out?' Hastings looked excited. 'It'd be hard to keep that sort of thing a secret from your house guest.'

Warren raised a cautionary hand. 'We don't know if he knew, or if the affair overlapped with Brandon staying with him, but you're right about it being a powerful motive.'

Hastings acknowledged the gentle rebuke, tackling his half-baguette for a couple of moments, before starting again.

'The thing is, he may be big and strong, but he's so unfit; do you think he'd be able to kill Tommy Meegan?'

'I don't see why not. Assuming he didn't tip him off that he knew about the affair he'd probably have the element of surprise. But I think there are bigger questions that need to be answered.'

Hastings thought for a moment. 'Where did he get the Kirpan from? Surely Binay Singh Mahal would have said if Bellies Brandon was the person that mugged him?'

'Exactly. And why was Tommy Meegan in that alleyway anyway? We're pretty confident he was lured down there. Did Brandon set it up?'

Hastings snapped his fingers. 'Could he have been working with Singh Mahal? Singh Mahal lures Tommy to the alleyway and supplies the Kirpan…' His voice tailed off. 'No, wait. That doesn't make any sense. Why would Singh Mahal incriminate himself in that way?'

'I don't know, the whole affair is getting increasingly complicated. Let's see if we can exclude Brandon first by checking his alibi. Depending on what time he was lurking in that pub garden, we may be able to rule out his involvement entirely. I sent Hutchinson to check that out, I'm expecting a call any moment.'

Hastings looked troubled. 'You realise that if Hutch doesn't give us enough to clear him we're going to have to interview Brandon again?'

Warren knew exactly what the young officer was concerned about and he couldn't help feeling the same way.

'We'll deal with it sensitively of course, but I don't see how we can avoid bringing up Paige Brandon's affair with Tommy Meegan. We need to see his reaction.'

'It's not his reaction in the interview suite I'm worried about. If he is innocent, we'll be releasing him back out there having just told him that his dead best mate was shagging his wife. Estranged or not, that's going to piss anybody off.'

The two men lapsed back into their own thoughts. Eventually Hastings broke the silence.

'Speaking of complicated, the BAP are an incestuous lot. You've got Tommy Meegan shagging Bellies Brandon's missus, whilst at the same time Goldie Davenport is busy with Tommy Meegan's girlfriend.'

Warren agreed. 'It's not surprising, I suppose. I imagine they're all fishing in a pretty small pond. Their views don't make them the most attractive catch for most folks, I shouldn't think.'

'Good point. They can't even use online dating; what would they put in their profile? Hobbies and Interests: extreme racism, xenophobia and bad tattoos?'

'They could use the lonely hearts column in the local newspaper I suppose, "Right wing fascist, GSOH seeks similar. Must like dogs and hate foreigners."'

* * *

David Hutchinson called Warren just as the two men finished lunch.

'None of the bar staff at the Middlesbury Tavern can recall seeing Bellies Brandon at the time of the murder. When the trouble kicked off they got their customers inside and locked the doors.'

'Seems sensible. Would any of the locals remember if Bellies was hanging around outside?'

'Unlikely. The landlord reckons that most of the regulars were absent, probably because they didn't fancy coming into town that day. It was also pretty rowdy as there was a bunch of lads on a stag do watching the Formula One qualifiers on the big screen.'

'Traceable?'

'Doubtful, the landlord reckons they all sounded Welsh. God

knows why they were in Middlesbury; they must have got lost on the way to Cambridge.'

'What about CCTV?'

'She was adamant that nobody matching Bellies' description came inside. We've taken the footage in the bar in case image analysis can do something with it, maybe they can catch his reflection in a window or something, but I think we're grasping at straws.'

'He claimed he asked for directions from drinkers in the beer garden. Were there any cameras outside?'

'There were, but they were over the back entrance, pointing downwards. They only cover an area three or so metres from the door. I've seen the video and nobody walks into shot between them closing the doors and reopening them when it calmed down. She reckons that a few of the stag party immediately went outside to smoke. I had a look at the footage and one of them does wander out of the range of the camera as if going over to speak to someone. I suppose he could have been going over to talk to Brandon.'

'Brandon said he was asking for directions. If the guy he called over wasn't local, how could he have helped him?'

'The lad had a smartphone. I suppose he could have used Google Maps on his phone to give directions. He was out of shot for a couple of minutes, long enough to look something up for him.' The sergeant was apologetic. 'Sorry, boss. That's all I've got.'

Warren thanked him and hung up.

The patchy information didn't confirm or contradict Brandon's alibi. It looked as though the man's name was staying on the whiteboard for the time being.

Chapter 47

Bellies Brandon was back in Romford. Given his antipathy towards the police, getting him to voluntarily travel back up to Middlesbury was pretty much a non-starter. So Warren got DSI Grayson to call the Met and ask for some favours, seeing as he and Hastings were already down there.

Although Warren had hinted that he was prepared to arrest Brandon if he didn't attend his local station, it had been a reluctant threat. No matter how discreetly he tried to detain him, there was always the risk that the word would get out. The custody clock would start its ticking and people might start panicking. Incriminating pieces of evidence might find themselves at the bottom of the River Rom. Far better to keep everyone guessing as long as possible.

At least his colleagues at Romford Police Station shared his love of good coffee.

'A bit hands-on for a DCI, aren't you? Is Hertfordshire short of detective constables?'

Warren returned the woman's friendly grin and swallowed his coffee.

'No, ma'am, we just don't follow the Met's policy of promoting anyone who's past it to chief inspector or above and locking them in an office where they can't do any more harm.'

Chief Superintendent Sawjani, who had been so generous with the use of her interview suites and the loan of warm bodies, let out a short bark of laughter.

'I don't know whether I should be jealous that you're getting so much fresh air or commiserating that you've been handed this nest of vipers to deal with. I suspect that time will tell.'

Warren drained his coffee and said nothing.

Sawjani lowered her mug slightly and eyed him through the steam. 'Tread carefully on this one,' she said quietly. 'Dot the i's and cross the t's.'

Warren silently acknowledged her use of his favourite phrase.

'The Met's had its fingers burned too many times when it comes to race, I'm sure Hertfordshire has been watching and learning. I don't usually recommend officers spend too much time second-guessing themselves, but in this case you need to assume that any decisions you make will potentially be questioned in an inquiry.'

'Yeah, I'm starting to get that feeling.'

Sawjani forced a smile. 'Well as far as I'm concerned, you're doing us a favour, Warren. If you can lock up some of these BAP idiots for a few months, I will personally buy you and all of your team a drink. If nothing else, I'll be able to redeploy some of the Neighbourhood Policing Team elsewhere for a bit. Anything you need, just call me.'

Thanking Sawjani for the hospitality, he shook her hand again before leaving her office. Spying Hastings at the far end of the open-plan office, chatting to a group of fully kitted uniformed officers, he made his way over.

'Come on, Constable, our date's waiting downstairs.'

'Sure thing, boss.'

'And stop playing with that Taser before you electrocute someone.'

* * *

258

'You are aware that you are not under arrest and that you are free to leave any time?'

Harry 'Bellies' Brandon was doing his best to appear nonchalant as Warren placed the legal niceties on record.

'We're just trying to pin down some missing details from Saturday the nineteenth of July. According to your statement, you were one of the last to arrive at The Feathers pub?'

'I guess.'

'Roughly what time was that?'

Brandon shrugged, the ubiquitous England flag above his left breast jiggling.

'Dunno, I don't wear a watch.'

Warren scanned the man's pudgy wrists; sure enough, the slightly tanned skin bore no traces of him sporting a watchstrap either currently or in the recent past.

'Remind me again why you were so late.'

'I didn't know how to get to The Feathers, so I waited in a beer garden to ask for directions.'

'And you can't tell me how long you were there for?'

'No.'

Warren could see the man was getting irritated. He made a show of looking over his notes.

'We're trying to work out who might have threatened Tommy in the weeks and months before last weekend's events. Now you said that you lived with him recently. Can you tell me if you saw anything suspicious? Did he mention anything worrying him?'

'Like what?'

'Unexpected phone calls that upset him, online threats? Did his demeanour change at all?'

Brandon's brow furrowed.

'I was only with him for a few weeks, but I didn't see anything.' He paused. 'There was some shit posted online on the Facebook page and he blocked a couple of trolls on Twitter, but nothing unusual.'

He paused. 'No wait. He did get the hump one night about

something. We were watching telly and he got an email on his phone. He got really angry. I asked him what the problem was and he got really pissy and told me to mind my own business. Then he went in his room for about an hour before storming off somewhere. He didn't come home that night.'

'And you've no idea what it was about, or who had upset him?'

'No. But it usually took a lot to get him that annoyed. I figured it was probably his missus.'

'Why?'

'Well, he didn't come home. He had to stay somewhere, didn't he? They probably made up and he stayed the night.'

'And did you and Tommy ever argue?'

'Nah, he was a good bloke. He was a bit of a slob, but he was letting me stay for free and listening to me whinge, so I couldn't really complain.'

'So aside from you, did he have many other guests?'

'Not really. Goldie came over once or twice to watch the footie, but we usually went to the pub. He wasn't really the entertaining type.'

'What about his girlfriend? Did she stay over?'

'Annie?' He gave a short bark. 'Are you kidding? You've seen the state of his room, she might not be the classiest of birds but even she has standards.'

'So he used to stay around there then?'

'Sure.'

'How often would you say he stayed? Was it a regular thing?'

'I don't bloody know, I'm not his mum.'

'Fair enough, we're just trying to establish his usual patterns.'

'I guess he used to go around a couple of nights a week. It depended if she had her kid over or not.'

'And there was nobody else?'

'What do you mean?' His eyes narrowed.

'Was it possible Tommy was seeing somebody else. As well as Ms Creasy.'

'Why do you ask?'

Warren tried to read the man in front of him. Was he truly ignorant of his friend's betrayal? Had he suspected that something was going on and decided to mind his own business? Perhaps it had been an open secret? Or perhaps Bellies Brandon had known full well that his friend and confidant had been seeing his estranged wife behind his back and had hatched a plot to kill him in revenge? Warren needed to know.

'We have evidence to suggest that he may have been having an affair with somebody else as well as Ms Creasy.'

Brandon let out a puff of air. 'Dirty bugger.'

Brandon's tone was neutral.

'Did you have any suspicions?'

Brandon paused for a moment.

'I suppose it doesn't really matter. Yeah, I figured something might be going on.'

'Why?'

'Sometimes the phone would ring in the evening. He'd always answer it with "Hello, Annie", but then he'd be like a bloody teenager and disappear into his bedroom for an hour. Other nights he'd announce he was off to ring her and go to his room. I'm not being funny, but him and Annie had been together for years. What the hell did they still have to talk about?'

'And do you have any idea who it might have been?'

Brandon shrugged. 'None of my business who he's shagging.'

Warren looked at him carefully.

'What if it was somebody you knew?'

The room was so quiet that Warren fancied he could hear the whir of the twin cassettes in the PACE recorder. Two red dots had appeared on Brandon's cheeks.

'Who?'

* * *

261

Warren took a long, steadying sip of his coffee and winced as his battered left shoulder protested. He'd only finished his latest round of physiotherapy on the abused socket a year ago and he hoped he'd not done anything too serious.

'If he's released after all of this, you're going to need to either persuade Paige Brandon to move away from the area or get your Domestic Violence Unit involved,' said Warren to a concerned-looking Chief Superintendent Sawjani.

It was unclear if the volcanic explosion from Brandon had been consciously directed towards Warren or whether he was just in the way. Regardless, by the time three custody officers had burst in and managed to subdue the raging man mountain, the PACE recorder would never be used again and they were going to need new chairs.

'I should have let you bring that Taser in with you,' Warren joked weakly.

'Do you think he did it?' Hastings looked a little pale. He'd managed to avoid Brandon's colossal temper tantrum and had dragged a stunned Warren to the corner of the room as the man rampaged around the suite, screaming incoherently.

'Well, he's certainly capable of murdering someone,' said Warren, 'but is he capable of biding his time long enough to set up something as elaborate as Tommy Meegan's murder? He doesn't look like a man in control of his impulses to me. And where the hell did he get that Kirpan from?'

Chapter 48

As Brandon was cooling his heels in a police cell, facing charges of assault, a search of the depressingly small, one-room studio flat he'd occupied since he'd given up Tommy Meegan's sofa bed was executed. It hadn't taken the scenes of crime team on loan from the Met long to perform. Most of the man's belongings were still at the house he'd shared with his wife. It was a fair bet that trace evidence from Tommy Meegan would be all over the flat; what they wanted was a smoking gun.

The head of the search team called Warren at home that evening, where he was recovering from a shoulder massage. Was it his imagination, or had Susan's ministrations been a little more forceful than usual? She'd certainly not been happy when he'd returned home battered and dishevelled.

'A shirt we found in the laundry hamper matches the description of the one he was wearing the day of the killing.' An accompanying photo sent to his email showed a large white football shirt held aloft by another white-suited technician. 'There were small traces of what could be blood on the sleeve. We've bagged it and sent it by courier to Welwyn for your own team to process, along with the rest of the hamper.'

Warren thanked her, but the recent debacle over the rust on

Binay Singh Mahal's trousers meant he wouldn't be happy until somebody had confirmed it was actually blood, ideally with the owner's DNA profile attached.

'There wasn't much blood,' noted Hastings when Warren called him. 'From the autopsy and CSI reports the killer should be covered in the stuff, assuming he didn't cover himself in protective gear first.'

'Protective gear that we have yet to find,' said Warren. 'Mind you, the spots could be secondary transfer, in which case if it matches Tommy Meegan, his lawyers will have fun explaining it away.'

* * *

At Susan's insistence, Warren had stopped reading his email, enjoyed a hot bath and taken some ibuprofen. However, he'd been unable to resist turning on the late-night news to see what was happening in Middlesbury before retiring for the night. To his relief, it was now only third on the news agenda behind the ongoing conflicts in Syria and Ukraine. The arrival of some more influential and experienced imams at the Friday prayer sessions had quelled some of the tempers and strategic policing had pre-emptively removed a few known troublemakers from the mix. So far, it had been a noisy but peaceable evening.

The rattling of Warren's phone against the arm of the sofa disturbed the mood.

Sutton.

Warren swiped to receive the call.

'Sorry to disturb you, Chief, but I knew you'd want to know.'

Warren's stomach tightened.

'Imam Mehmud just called. His grandmother Mrs Fahmida, the old lady injured in the fire, just died. The arson has just been upgraded to homicide.'

Saturday 26th July

Chapter 49

Saturday marked the end of the first week since the murder of Tommy Meegan and the arson at the community centre. It also marked the two-week anniversary of Warren's last full day off. At Warren's insistence, Susan had agreed to meet her father to discuss how they were going to persuade her mother to be more supportive of the couple's decision.

If ever there was a time that Warren should be by his wife's side, it was now. Unfortunately, it was out of the question. The death of Syeda Fahmida had hit social media within hours of Sutton's phone call, and by the time Warren had given up on sleep and left for the office, there were already reports that protest marches were planned for the following day.

The ongoing vigil outside the Islamic Centre had swelled significantly in number overnight and there had been several tense confrontations between the police and attendees. So far, nobody had been arrested and no officer had felt threatened enough to take out their baton, but Warren worried that it was only a matter of time before somebody provoked a conflict, either through frustration, or deliberately. Imam Mehmud had arrived briefly to lay flowers and thank those present for their support but had left quickly when it became apparent that his grandmother's death was becoming politicised. Warren felt sorry for the young preacher, who had been thrown into the centre of such a storm.

Pulling into the car park, Warren noticed that some early riser had spray painted 'fascist pigs' on the main gates to the police station; a reminder that not everyone was supportive of the police's actions.

'We've finally got the call log from the phone found on Tommy Meegan's body.' Gary Hastings slid the paper across Warren's desk. 'Sorry it took so long, but it was a pay-as-you-go from some little start-up company run out of a bloody garden shed.'

'Anything interesting?'

'Hard to say. It's only been used a few times over the two years that he owned it. Or that we presume he owned it,' Hastings corrected himself. 'The phone is left switched on, but never moves from the same location for months on end – I looked it up on Google Earth and it corresponds to his flat. When it does move, it's the same days that the phone is used. There tends to be a flurry of short duration calls or texts over the course of a few hours then nothing.'

'Which suggests that it's an unregistered phone he used when he was doing things he probably shouldn't, with little in the way of incriminating evidence if we got hold of it. Check with Garfield and see if the dates and locations coincide with known BAP activities. Now explain the spring in your step and the fluorescent yellow highlighter on some of the entries.'

Hastings grinned. 'This is where it gets interesting. Most of the calls are from other unregistered mobile numbers. I'm guessing that if we confiscated all the rest of his friends' phones we'd probably account for them. But one stands out.' He turned the sheet around.

It took Warren a second to see what he meant, two highlighted calls – approximately a week apart. 'That's a Middlesbury area code.'

'Yep. Better than that, it's a payphone.'

'Where?'

'The shops opposite the Chequers estate.'

* * *

The row of shops opposite the Chequers estate were the very definition of a 'food desert'. Consisting of a fried chicken takeaway, a tanning salon, and three betting shops, the only business selling anything approaching nutritious food was a Costcutter – and even that sold more brands of pork scratchings than varieties of fresh fruit and vegetables. Exactly how people without a car or the means to travel the mile or so to Tesco were supposed to have anything approaching a balanced diet was unclear.

The proprietor of the Costcutter simply turned his lip up and sneered when Warren and Hastings requested access to the only surveillance cameras in the vicinity of the badly vandalised phone boxes outside.

Hastings cocked a head towards a group of teenagers smoking and drinking on the wall outside. Either they hadn't realised that the two men were police officers or – more likely – they didn't care.

'They don't look eighteen.'

The shopkeeper shrugged. 'Nothing to do with me.'

'Really? So where did they get the fags and the booze?'

'Beats me.'

'Because as far as I can tell, you're the only person around here selling tobacco and alcohol.'

'So? You can't prove anything. Ask them.'

'If I want to prove anything, I can just take a look at your CCTV. I'd say there's reasonable grounds to seize the videotape, wouldn't you, Chief Inspector?'

'Definitely.'

The shopkeeper blanched. The cameras were positioned to

show who came in and out of the store, and what they were carrying. There was probably enough evidence on the tapes to earn him a massive fine at the least and maybe even close his business.

Hastings let the thought sink in a little.

'We aren't here about your lax ID checking. We just want a look at your CCTV footage.'

From that moment, the shopkeeper couldn't have been more obliging.

'Nice work, Constable,' whispered Warren as the little man led them out the back. Hastings just hoped he could impress the interview panel at his promotion board as easily as he'd impressed DCI Jones.

* * *

The video from the shop was grainy and the angle was wrong, the camera designed to deter shoplifters or vandals hanging around outside. The very edge of the telephone box was just in shot, but maddeningly, it was impossible to see who was inside making a call.

'Let's hope that whoever used the box walked up the high street, rather than down,' said Hastings as he fiddled with the security system's remote control. The thick layer of dust and grime covering the small black and white monitor suggested it had been set up to keep the shop's insurance provider happy and then forgotten about. Unfortunately, the shop only stored the previous six weeks before automatically writing over the disc with new footage. Nevertheless, videos of the last call from the phone box should still be available on the system.

The time stamp in the corner of the screen was jumping upwards towards 18.26 almost too quickly to read. Every so often a person would flicker into shot and back out. An old lady with a wheeled shopping cart walked across the screen at the speed of an Olympic sprinter. A cyclist blasted through in the blink of an eye.

Five minutes from the time the call was made Hastings slowed the speed to eight times, then normal speed. Thirty-seven seconds before the call was started a figure ambled into shot. Head down, a hoodie hiding any features, the unknown individual crossed the camera's field of view, before lifting an arm to grab the door handle.

Warren's breath caught in this throat as the target glanced towards the camera, their face clearly visible for just a fraction of a second. It was enough.

'Why the hell are they calling Tommy Meegan?'

Chapter 50

'I have a list of Binay Singh Mahal's internet browsing history and activity on his social media profiles,' said Garfield, his voice echoing over the speakerphone.

'Give me the highlights,' instructed Warren. A caffeine headache had settled over his right eye socket.

'It seems that Mr Singh led something of a double, indeed triple, life.'

'How so?'

'His laptop has three user accounts, one for his day-to-day activity and two others for his rather less savoury online personas. They have separate social media profiles, email and web-browsing. It seems that he's very careful to ensure that the three don't overlap.'

'Intriguing.'

'IT are unable to access any private messages, since they need a password, but now we know his online identities it's easy to track what he posted on different forums and discussion groups.

'To put it mildly, he has rather extreme political views, which he is happy to share on his public profile. He is a strong supporter of Sikh separatism, following some of the more militant Punjabi forums and Sikh rights in particular. But it's his other profiles that are more illuminating.

'On the one hand, he is engaged in some quite vicious flame wars with far-right groups, including the BAP. He's been an outspoken critic since they first appeared. He also follows and joins in discussions with a number of anti-fascist and anti-racism groups. He was very vocal about the BAP's visit to Middlesbury, joining in calls for counter-protests almost as soon as they announced the date of the march.'

Warren wasn't particularly surprised.

'Any link to Mr Rhodri?'

'It looks as though they posted in the same forums and followed the same Twitter feeds. Unfortunately, if there were any more direct communications they took place either privately through Facebook Messenger or via other secure applications.'

'Which can't be tracked.'

'Precisely, although we've put a request in for access to their Messenger accounts and Twitter direct messages. Alas, neither have used anything as quaint and old-fashioned as text messaging.'

'Anything of note in his call logs or GPS?'

'I'll send you his call history, but nothing jumps out. Interestingly, on the day of the riot, his smartphone never left his flat.'

'Well, that's suspicious in itself. He is supposed to have been serving langar that day, so we know he went out. What twenty-something leaves the house without his mobile phone these days?'

'Somebody who watches *CSI* and needs an alibi?' suggested Garfield.

'What about his other user accounts?'

'Well, that's where it starts to get even more interesting.'

Chapter 51

Karen Hardwick swallowed another antacid, although they didn't seem to be making much difference. Hastings got up from where he was seated in front of the TV and rubbed her shoulders.

'Tummy playing up again?'

Hardwick nodded, then wished she hadn't as a wave of nausea passed over her.

'I just don't understand it,' mused Hastings for the umpteenth time. 'I got sick first – it was definitely that omelette I had in Montmartre, I hadn't eaten anything else all day. But within twenty-four hours it was finished.' He looked apologetic. 'I'm sorry, sweetheart, I must have passed it on to you.'

Hardwick said nothing, it was hardly his fault, but the way she felt right now she didn't trust herself to speak.

Failing to pick up on her unspoken cues to drop the subject, Hastings was now warming to the topic. 'I was looking online and recurrent poisoning is rare but not unheard of. It usually clears up in a few months. It's a bit unusual the way it seemed to go away for a few weeks then come back though.'

Hardwick groaned. Hastings was now in full flow. 'They say that you need to avoid recontamination, so every time you have an episode you need to make sure that everything you come in contact with is disinfected or disposed of properly.'

Please change the subject, Hardwick pleaded silently. She lurched to her feet, heading for the bathroom again.

At least the diarrhoea had stopped, but the regular vomiting was making her life a misery. The French doctor had said her symptoms suggested a viral infection, rather than bacterial, making treatment more difficult. Quite how Gary had escaped the same fate was a medical mystery that she was unable to contemplate right now. She'd have to see what her GP had to say, if she could ever get an appointment. She'd try again first thing Monday. If that failed, she'd take herself to the walk-in centre. This couldn't continue.

Exiting the bathroom, she returned to the living-cum-dining area of their small apartment. Gary was back in front of his laptop, surrounded by textbooks.

'How are you feeling?'

'Fine,' she lied.

The last thing Gary needed right now was to be worrying about her health. He had interviews for sergeants' selection in the next few days. Rumour had it that after the recent cutbacks the ratio of shortlisted officers to vacancies for this round of selection was more than three to one.

'I'm going to take a bath and have an early night.'

'OK.' He was already engrossed in his textbook again.

Hopefully the soothing water would ease her constant feeling of sickness. Then she might just be asleep by the time Gary joined her. The last thing she wanted to do was share the duvet when she felt so ill, but the only alternative was the couch. She knew that if she asked, Gary would grab a pillow and blanket without complaint, but he needed a decent night's sleep as much as she did.

Maybe when Gary got his promotion they could afford a bigger flat. Buying in a town less than an hour on the fast train from

London was all but impossible for two junior police officers, even if Gary got a pay rise. They could just about afford the mortgage repayments on a two-bedroom flat, but they'd never raise the deposit necessary to secure such favourable terms.

Gary had spent hundreds of pounds on online courses and textbooks to prepare him for the written OSPRE legal exams that he had passed last year. Now he was trying to anticipate the sorts of questions he might be asked in interview. If – when – he was successful, he'd be temporarily promoted to sergeant for twelve months, before gaining a substantive, permanent promotion.

Hardwick had flicked through the textbooks herself and had been surprised at how straightforward it seemed. Gary had several years more service than her, since she'd done a Master's degree before joining the police, but that was no obstacle. She decided that as soon as Gary had gained his promotion, she'd also apply. Perhaps with two sergeants' salaries coming in they could finally start saving for that deposit.

Sunday 27th July

Chapter 52

'Financial crime have found something interesting in Philip Rhodri's credit card history.'

Mags Richardson stood in Warren's doorway clutching her ever-present bottle of water in one hand and a piece of paper in the other.

'Come in, let's have a look.'

Warren shoved a pile of paperwork to one side. He still wasn't sure where Philip Rhodri fitted into the whole affair, and anything that might shed a light on the man's involvement was welcome.

'The warrant to search his premises didn't extend to his online banking unfortunately, but he hasn't switched to paperless statements for his credit card and so they were fair game when the search team found them on the mantelpiece.'

'What's he been buying?'

'We can't be a hundred per cent certain since it only lists the companies' trading names, but this payment here stands out.' Richardson had highlighted an entry about halfway down the page. The company's name happened to be its web address.

'PrinceofInk.com, is that what I think it is?'

'Yes, it's a tattoo parlour.'

Warren thought back to when they'd arrested the protestor.

'I didn't see any tattoos on him. Did the custody officer record any when he was searched?'

'None at all.'

Warren scratched his chin.

'That seems quite cheap for a tattoo. Could he have paid for somebody else? Or is that a booking fee?'

Richardson smiled. 'Not unless he was planning to travel to the Willamette Valley, Oregon USA.'

'What? That doesn't make sense. Why would he book a tattoo session in the US?'

'I doubt he did. I visited their website and it seems they also have a thriving mail order business.'

'How can you order tattoos by post?' Now Warren was even more confused.

Richardson came around Warren's desk and accessed the website on his computer.

The homepage proclaimed that it was the state's number one provider of personalised body art and custom body modifications. A link invited visitors to read the testimonies of satisfied customers. A second link invited visitors to book an appointment for a consultation.

'These guys are pretty popular. There's a three-month waiting list.'

'So you won't be getting a Stevenage FC tattoo any time soon?' teased Warren.

'How do you know I don't already have one?' replied Richardson.

'So if he didn't book a tattoo, then what did he buy?'

Richardson reached over and clicked a link entitled 'custom merchandise'.

It took just a few seconds for Warren to spot it.

'Very clever,' he breathed.

'Factor in the exchange rate and the cost of international postage and packaging and the price matches the amount charged to Rhodri's credit card.'

Warren slumped back in his chair. It seemed that he had almost certainly been completely wrong about Rhodri. But where one door closed, another opened. He resisted the urge to punch the air.

'Great work, Mags.' He rose to his feet and leaned out his door into the office.

'Tony, I need you in here.'

Chapter 53

Philip Rhodri was more nervous and fidgety the second time he was called in for questioning. The smug sneer that he'd worn as Warren had released him on bail a few days ago was now just a faint shadow of itself. Even his solicitor's slick veneer seemed tarnished, he was surely experienced enough to realise that they wouldn't have recalled him so quickly unless they had a significant new line of inquiry. Nevertheless, the lawyer went on the attack the moment Sutton finished setting up the PACE recorder.

'I assume that you have called Mr Rhodri here to remove the unjustified bail conditions that you have imposed upon him?'

Warren ignored the man's bluster; he had no desire to take part in the lawyer's grandstanding for the benefit of his client.

'Mr Rhodri, on Saturday the nineteenth, you travelled to Middlesbury to take part in the protest march against the BAP. Could you tell us what time you arrived?'

Rhodri said nothing, just glanced over at his solicitor.

'Mr Rhodri made it clear that he did not wish to discuss his whereabouts on the date in question at his previous interview. I hope that you are not intending to waste his time by simply going over the same ground yet again.'

'No matter. We have video footage of you arriving at the Park and Ride at two minutes past ten. We also have witnesses that saw you there and confirmed your arrival. Could you tell us where you went after meeting there?'

'No comment.'

Unperturbed, Warren continued. 'Again, no matter. Eyewitnesses have said that you decided to walk into Middlesbury and video footage shows that you didn't wait for the shuttle bus into town. Why? You'd paid for a ticket.'

'No comment.'

Rhodri had folded his arms.

'Which route did you follow when you walked into town, Mr Rhodri?' asked Warren.

'No comment.'

Warren shuffled the papers in front of him.

'Again, we have eyewitness reports that say you set out walking up Lansdowne Lane. I wouldn't say that was the most direct route to town. Why didn't you walk along Claverton Road? That's the route that the shuttle bus takes.'

Again Rhodri said nothing, glancing at his solicitor who, on cue, leant forward. 'I would remind DCI Jones that my client has declined to discuss his whereabouts on the day in question.'

'Be that as it may, we have eyewitness reports and CCTV footage that place him on that route.'

Rhodri and his lawyer exchanged glances again.

'It was a hot day. I didn't fancy a sticky bus ride.'

The buses that served the Park and Ride route all had air conditioning, but Warren let that slide.

'Why did you choose such a strange route into town?' It was the first thing Sutton had said since the interview started.

Rhodri shrugged. 'I don't live here, do I?'

'Did you walk directly into town from there?' Sutton asked.

Rhodri paused for a moment, a brief look of indecision flashing across his face.

'Yeah, pretty much.'

'Lansdowne Lane, then onto Oakfield Street?'

'If you say so. I don't know the names of the roads around here.'

Sutton nodded, as if he'd confirmed something then sat back.

Warren shuffled the papers in front of him.

'Tell me, Philip, who was driving the car that picked you up on Lansdowne Lane?'

Rhodri started slightly.

'I don't… No comment.'

Warren sighed. 'Come on, Philip, don't start playing that game again. We know that you were picked up by somebody in a white Vauxhall Corsa, we have eyewitnesses. Where did you go?'

'No comment.'

'Did you have something better to do? You'd spent ages organising that march, what could be more important than attending it? Getting stuck in with your mates against those fascists, surely that was the point of Saturday?'

'No comment.'

'Who was driving the car?'

'No comment.'

Rhodri's solicitor's eyes had been narrowing more and more throughout the questioning.

'I would like to request a break to talk to my lawyer,' said Rhodri.

'Interview suspended.'

* * *

'What do you think?'

As usual, Sutton and Warren had taken the opportunity to fulfil their caffeine needs.

'It'll go one of two ways,' replied Sutton. 'Either he'll dig his heels in and we'll need to drag it out of him, or he'll confess.'

The custody sergeant poked his head around the door. 'They've finished their break.'

Warren looked at Sutton. 'Shall we let him sweat for a bit?'

'I think so. Fancy a pastry from the canteen?'

'Just this once.'

* * *

By the time Warren returned to the interview suite, Rhodri had shredded his polystyrene cup into tiny fragments. The bulging folder Warren carried under his arm had been bulked out with two blank paper pads, but he placed it on the desk as if it contained the key to Rhodri's future. Both Rhodri and his lawyer struggled to keep their eyes off the cardboard envelope as Warren took his time setting up the PACE recorder.

'Is there anything you would like to tell me, Philip?'

'My client has nothing to add to what he has already told you.'

'Are you sure about that, Philip?'

Rhodri said nothing.

'Let's go back to two o'clock that afternoon. Could you tell us your whereabouts at that time?'

'No comment.'

'Are you certain? It would certainly help clear things up if you could account for where you were. Perhaps the person who picked you up in the car could be an alibi?'

Rhodri's lawyer stirred immediately. 'I wasn't aware that my client needed an alibi. In fact, at this moment in time, my client has not been accused of anything concrete. I would like to request that my client be advised of what you are investigating, so that he may properly address the issue.'

'Of course, I'm sorry. We're currently investigating a death linked to Saturday's events.'

Rhodri's eye twitched and his breath caught in his throat.

'If you can verify your whereabouts on Saturday afternoon, this could help eliminate you from the inquiry.'

Warren could see that the solicitor was suspicious. He hoped that he didn't suggest his client request another break to think over his response, or worse than that, ask to see evidence.

'No comment.' The man's voice was a lot less confident now.

'The car that picked you up – that eyewitnesses saw you being picked up in – had fake licence plates. Why?'

Beads of sweat had appeared on Rhodri's forehead.

'I had nothing to do with any death.'

Warren ignored him.

'Tell me, Philip, do you know anybody with tattoos?'

The sudden change in questioning caught both the suspect and his solicitor off guard.

His solicitor responded first. 'Of course my client knows people with tattoos. Half the population have them.'

'Sorry, let me be more specific. Do you know anyone with full-length arm tattoos?'

Rhodri relaxed slightly. 'A bloke who lives near me has a full sleeve on one of his arms.'

'Could you describe it?'

'One of those thick, black tribal decorations, I think.'

'Nothing with Germanic script? Pictures of eagles, swastikas, that sort of thing?'

Rhodri sneered slightly. 'Hardly my scene. Why don't you look on your little database? See if anyone interesting pops up.'

'Why did you cut your hair, Philip?'

Again, Rhodri's solicitor stepped in. 'I hardly see what that has to do with anything.'

Warren and Rhodri ignored him.

'I fancied a change. Hot weather and all that.'

'I'm surprised, it must have taken years to grow that amount of hair. When did you get it cut?'

He shrugged. 'A couple of months ago.'

'And it had nothing to do with trying to disguise yourself more easily when taking part in protests?'

'DCI Jones, I don't like this line of questioning.'

'Presumably you are a lot less recognisable on CCTV. I'll bet it was quite hard to cover your head with all that hair.'

'No, of course not.' The bravado was back; after all, cutting one's hair was hardly a crime was it?

'Tell me, do you have tattoo sleeves, Mr Rhodri?'

The solicitor nearly choked. 'DCI Jones, my client is wearing a short-sleeved T-shirt. If you can't see that his arms are bare of any decoration, I think you should consider an eye test.'

'Answer the question please, Philip.'

The man's face had paled slightly.

'This questioning is ridiculous. I'm going to demand an end to this farce,' snapped the lawyer.

On cue, Sutton opened one of the manila folders and removed a colour photograph.

'Do you recognise this, Philip?'

'What the hell is that?' asked his lawyer.

The solicitor was starting to get on Warren's nerves. 'Let your client answer, please.'

The man scowled but sat back.

'No.'

'Are you certain? It was retrieved from the drain in your house.'

'I live with flatmates.'

'Have you ever heard of PrinceofInk.com?'

'No.' His voice caught in his throat and he reached for his solicitor's polystyrene cup without asking.

'Really, because your credit card statement shows that you purchased something from them. What did you buy?'

Sutton produced a photocopy of the statement, the purchase highlighted.

'No comment.'

Sutton produced a screenshot of the company's website.

'We looked at how much you paid, factored in the exchange rate on the date of purchase and the cost of international postage and packaging and it seems that you could only really have bought one thing from their website. So I ask you again. Do you recognise this item, found in your drain?'

Rhodri said nothing, instead staring at the table top. His fingers had started the cup shredding again.

'According to a preliminary lab analysis, it appears to be melted nylon, similar to ladies' tights, with a mixture of different inks soaked into the material. The results are consistent with bespoke fake tattoo sleeves. The website markets them as suitable for fancy dress parties or testing out a design before committing to the real thing. What pattern did you ask them to print on them? Swastikas? Germanic script?'

Rhodri continued to stare at the table.

'Never mind, we'll get the details of your order from the company.'

'So far I don't see anything other than circumstantial evidence here.' The solicitor was back on the attack again. 'There are a dozen perfectly innocent reasons why my client might have such a thing in his possession.'

'What about this?'

The next photograph looked like a flesh-coloured melted rubber bathing cap.

Rhodri remained mute.

The next photograph was an England football shirt.

'We found this in your wardrobe, Mr Rhodri.'

'Yeah, so? Owning an England shirt is hardly a crime.'

'I tend to agree, but then you're a proud Welshman.'

Chapter 54

Philip Rhodri looked beaten. He sat back in his chair, gnawing his thumbnail.

'You've got the wrong man.'

'A man with arm-length tattoos, a shaved head and an England shirt was seen by several witnesses. You have no alibi, were picked up by somebody in a car with fake licence plates and have consistently refused to confirm your whereabouts on Saturday afternoon. In your house we find evidence of fake tattoo sleeves, what appears to be a rubber cap designed to mimic a shaved head – both of which have been partially destroyed and flushed down the loo – and an England football shirt, even though you are supposedly a Welsh rugby fan.'

'Still all circumstantial,' interjected the solicitor. Warren glared at him and he quietened.

'Tell us who picked you up and where you went or I'll have to start drawing some unpleasant conclusions.'

Rhodri continued staring at the table. Warren waited patiently, the only sound in the room a faint whir from the PACE recorder.

'I was picked up by a mate and driven to the other end of town.'

'Why?'

He shook his head.

'Philip, I already know that you were picked up. I have witnesses and number plate records. Where did you go?'

'We went to his house.'

'Why?'

'We were going to play Xbox.'

'Do you seriously expect us to believe that? That you decided to ditch a huge counter-protest that you'd been organising for weeks to play video games? Come on! No, I think you got changed there. You put on your bald cap – so much easier now you've had a haircut, then changed into your England shirt. Or did you put your fake tattoos on first? What next? Sunglasses? I'll bet your mother wouldn't even have recognised you.'

Rhodri looked close to tears. Warren continued to press.

'Where next?'

Nothing.

'Come on, Philip, you got changed at this mate's house and then what? He got out the dressing-up box as well?'

Again nothing.

'Who was this friend of yours?'

The only sound was the whir of the tape recorder.

'We have more than enough to charge you.'

The solicitor shifted in his chair but said nothing.

'I was down the other end of town, I wasn't anywhere near the town centre.'

'Where? Give us some times and locations and we'll see if we can place you on CCTV. Tell us your friend's name and we'll see if his story matches yours. You can clear all this up right now.'

Rhodri licked his lips.

'Buzzard Lane. Between about noon and two o'clock.'

'And what were you doing there?'

'Nothing. I just sat in the car and listened to the radio.'

'For two hours?'

Rhodri said nothing

'So you didn't get out?'

'That's right. I just sat in the car and listened to the radio for a bit and then drove home.'

'Were you alone?'

He paused, visibly conflicted. If he admitted that someone was with him in the car, then that person could verify that he was nowhere near the alleyway that Meegan was killed in, at the time of the murder. On the other hand, Rhodri couldn't be certain what his companion would tell Warren about their whereabouts or what they were doing.

However, by refusing to admit to the other person being present, he was effectively hanging himself out to dry. He looked over to his solicitor for advice; none was forthcoming. His solicitor was ethically obliged to urge his client to tell the truth.

'No comment.'

Warren glanced at his watch. One o'clock.

'Why don't you have a think about it, Philip?'

* * *

Philip Rhodri was formally re-arrested, starting the custody clock again, but Warren wasn't bothered. He had more than enough to charge him there and then, but there was more to the story and Warren was in no rush. A twelve-hour extension to the initial twenty-four hours was guaranteed; he'd probably get the full seventy-two hours if he really wanted it. Unfortunately, as soon as Rhodri was charged he'd be up in front of the court. Bail was unlikely, but the details would be splashed all over the newspapers. Warren's instincts told him that minimising publicity for the time being would be prudent.

Chapter 55

'Good news; defeating the swipe-lock on Tommy Meegan's smart-phone was a doddle, he left dirty fingerprints all over the touchscreen,' started Pete Robertson. It was a Sunday afternoon, but Warren knew from past experience that once the IT specialist got involved in something really interesting he wouldn't let it go. Warren wondered what Mrs Robertson thought about her husband's dedication. In fact, was there a Mrs Robertson? Warren tried to picture the man's long fingers – did he wear a wedding ring?

'We've accessed his Facebook, Twitter and email accounts and his internet browsing history. I can even tell you what cinema tickets he's booked.'

Warren sat up straight immediately, all ruminations about Robertson's private life evaporating. 'Bloody hell, Pete.'

'I'll let you trawl through them at your leisure, DCI Jones, but just to whet your appetite, it seems that contacting Mr Meegan for some one-to-one is as simple as sending him a private message on Facebook and leaving a phone number or an email address for him to contact.'

'You are kidding, right?'

'Nope. I'll bet they didn't advocate that sort of behaviour in those personal security seminars Inspector Garfield's team spent so much taxpayers' money sending him on.'

* * *

Commandeering a conference room at headquarters on a Sunday wasn't difficult, so Warren opted for one with a large table, whiteboards with plenty of different coloured pens, and a hot drinks machine. The coffee for the machine was supplied by Theo Garfield whose office was only a stone's throw away and Tony Sutton conjured up some biscuits. Pete Robertson had offered to bring some mugs, but Warren had politely declined the offer – he'd seen the state of the man's office – and borrowed some from Garfield.

Warren had known Pete Robertson for three years, yet the IT specialist's height still surprised him every time they met. Warren had suggested that Robertson take off and enjoy the rest of his Sunday, but he was having none of it.

'You'll only end up having to phone me anyway, it'll be quicker if I'm here. I'll record it as flexi-time. Besides which, my boyfriend is away on a rugby tour, I'll only get bored.'

Tommy Meegan's phone turned out to be the proverbial goldmine and within the space of a couple of hours, the team had pieced together a rough timeline of what had taken place over the past few weeks.

The large table had gone from being covered in dozens of printed transcripts from Meegan's different internet accounts to a series of neat piles and a multicoloured timeline now adorned the whiteboard.

By 6 p.m. Warren had taken a photograph of their handiwork and was writing a report for DSI Grayson. As usual, his superior's phone went straight to voicemail. Repressing an unprofessional sigh, Warren left a message and requested a meeting the next morning.

He looked at his watch. Maybe he and Susan could finally get an evening together. They really needed to talk.

Monday 28th July

Chapter 56

It was still only eight-thirty in the morning, but Warren had been at his desk for almost three hours and a similar number of cups of coffee.

Susan's talk with her father the day before had resulted in limited success. They'd enlisted the support of her sister, but according to Dennis, her mother was unwilling to even discuss the situation. The drive to and from the Midlands had taken the better part of five hours and Susan had been emotionally and physically exhausted when she returned.

Warren hoped that Bernice would soon see her overreaction for what it was, but he worried that she seemed to be digging her heels in deeper. The situation weighed heavily on his mind, along with everything else and after yet another sleepless night, he'd decided at 5 a.m. to do both him and Susan a favour and go into work; she'd barely acknowledged him, rolling over and burying her head in her pillow.

Also contributing to his insomnia was Binay Singh Mahal. Until the revelations about his online activities had come to light, Warren had been unsure what it was about him that set his teeth on edge. Was it his arrogance in the interview room, or the way that he had refused to confirm his whereabouts during Tommy

Meegan's murder, despite having a solid alibi? He could have saved them a lot of footwork by getting his friend Councillor Lavindeep Kaur to vouch for him from the start.

Warren had voiced his frustrations to Susan as they lay in bed that night.

'I've been going through his file. There are entries dating back to April 2002 when he broke another kid's nose in the playground. The parents filed a police report for assault, but eventually dropped it and let the school deal with the incident.

'Then, less than six months later, he's cautioned for shoplifting, and a few weeks after that for vandalising a community centre down on Lilac Lane. The last entry was theft of a motor vehicle and criminal damage. Luckily for Singh, he was the youngest passenger in the car by several years and managed to avoid a custodial sentence. Then nothing until his Kirpan turned up at Tommy Meegan's murder.'

'It sounds as though that playground fight was the start of something. Perhaps his teachers know more about what was going on?'

'Maybe. Normally I'd call the school, but this was twelve years ago. I doubt they even remember him.'

'Don't be so sure. I can remember some of the first kids I ever taught; it sounds as though he made an impression.'

'Maybe you're right, but I can't wait until everyone comes back in September to chase this down.'

'You mightn't need to. I've been into school twice these holidays already to prepare for next year and the main office is still fully staffed. Our senior leadership team stagger their breaks away so that there is always somebody available in an emergency. You might be surprised who you can get hold of.'

The central switchboard at Dame Etheridge Academy rang several times before it was picked up. A week into the school holidays and all of the end-of-term trips had probably returned and the parents demanding the school be turned upside down to locate their offspring's wayward PE kits appeased.

Warren explained who he was and what he was looking for. The bemused woman took his number, promising to get somebody with enough seniority to call him back.

Warren drained his coffee and walked over to his Superintendent's office.

DSI Grayson was just hanging up his own phone.

'The early morning call didn't go down well, but I hinted that we were just aiming to tie up a few loose ends.' He grimaced slightly. 'There'll be a solicitor in tow.'

Warren shrugged, 'It'll save us time later, I suppose.'

'What about Mr Singh Mahal? No courtesy call for him, I presume?'

'Nope. He's in the back of a car as we speak. That should minimise any chance for them to get their stories straight. However, he's already demanding his own brief, so he'll have to wait for a little while.'

'What about Mr Rhodri?'

'He's keeping his mouth shut so far, but we have more than enough to charge. I'm running down the custody clock as I want to delay him appearing in court and everything going public.'

'Good, let's hope the rest of the day goes as smoothly.'

* * *

Barely an hour after Warren's call to Dame Etheridge Academy, his phone rang. This time the voice at the end of the line was Mrs Sims, the headteacher.

'It's an unusual request, DCI Jones, but yes we do have records of our students going back to that time period. However, I would have to be convinced, along with the chair of governors, that the request was appropriate. You are aware that it is the summer holidays? Tracking down staff or governors at this time of year can be very hit and miss.'

'I appreciate your assistance, Mrs Sims.'

'Let me see what I can do, I don't think our chair is planning to go away until the end of August. I'll see if I can get hold of him.'

* * *

'You need to tread very carefully, here.'

The warning was unnecessary, but DSI Grayson felt compelled to issue it anyway. A look of pain had crossed the man's face when Warren had outlined his proposed course of action that morning, before he'd even had a chance to remove his jacket. If Warren was wrong and complaints were made, they would rocket to the top of the tree and Grayson would be standing shoulder-to-shoulder with his DCI explaining why he'd authorised such a reckless course of action.

The potential for career-limiting fallout was the reason Warren had decided not to involve Hastings. The last thing he wanted was the young officer embroiled in controversy whilst he was in the middle of his sergeant application.

Hastings had protested of course – after all he'd done much of the legwork that led to this moment – but Tony Sutton had told him not to be silly; he'd get the credit he was due and hope-fully none of the blame if everything went pear-shaped.

Warren took a deep breath and pushed open the door to the interview suite.

'Thank you for coming, Councillor Kaur.'

Chapter 57

Councillor Lavindeep Kaur seemed smaller than before in the bare room. Despite the air conditioning, she'd hung her jacket on the back of her chair. Beside her sat her solicitor; a slim woman almost six feet tall.

'Is this really necessary?' asked the lawyer as Warren set up the PACE recorder. 'My understanding is that Councillor Kaur is merely here to help your inquiries.'

Warren smiled politely. 'I always think it's a good idea to keep these things on the record, don't you?'

Kaur glanced over at her lawyer, who gave an almost imperceptible shrug.

After completing the preliminaries, Warren started the conversation.

'When you visited me on Thursday, twenty-fourth of July, you did so to help us eliminate Binay Singh Mahal from our inquiries, which we appreciate.'

Kaur inclined her head slightly.

'For the record, would you mind telling me what you said then?'

The request was perfectly reasonable but Kaur squirmed slightly. It was her lawyer who spoke up; Warren noted that Kaur, aside from confirming her name for the tape, had yet to speak.

'Is this really necessary? I'm sure you took appropriate notes at the time.'

'If you wouldn't mind, Councillor.'

Kaur removed her glasses.

'I explained that on the day of the riot, Mr Singh Mahal was with me preparing langar, the daily feeding of the poor.'

'And what time was that?'

'Our shift was food preparation before those serving the food took over.'

Warren made a mark in his notebook.

'And you were rostered together?'

'Yes.'

'Just the two of you?'

'Yes, it doesn't take much preparation. Mostly just peeling and chopping vegetables then getting the pans of water heated.'

'I'm not a big cook, what are we talking here? Two hours?'

'About that.'

'And you started about 3 p.m.?'

'About then…' Kaur paused. 'I picked up the keys from Mrs Maninderjeet Kaur.'

'Yes we know, we spoke to her.'

Kaur looked even more uncomfortable.

Warren made a note on his pad.

'So you and Mr Singh Mahal worked together for about two hours. And then the next shift took over, to do the actual serving?'

'Yes.'

'And what time was that?'

Kaur let out a little huff of air.

'As I said before, about 5 p.m.'

Warren made another note. Kaur shifted in her seat, before ostentatiously looking at her watch.

'I'm very sorry, DCI Jones, I have an important council meeting in a few minutes. If I don't leave soon, I'll miss the start. If you have any further questions, please don't hesitate to call me.'

Kaur's solicitor followed her cue, closing her briefcase and standing.

'Sit back down please, Councillor, we haven't finished yet and I would rather you didn't go anywhere.'

'My client is here voluntarily, DCI Jones, you don't have the authority to stop her leaving. If you wish her to stay any longer, you will need to arrest her and interview her under caution.'

'If that's what you want,' said Warren quietly.

Both women stopped in their tracks.

Chapter 58

Binay Singh Mahal was even more sullen than the first time he had been arrested. The same lawyer, Dan Stock, who had accompanied him on his previous visit sat beside him. He didn't look happy.

'Before we start, my client would like to protest in the most vigorous fashion that the imposition of bail conditions, based on purely circumstantial evidence, are a breach of his human rights and yet more evidence of the institutionalised racism demonstrated by the police as a whole and Hertfordshire Constabulary and you, DCI Jones, specifically.' It was a long sentence, delivered in one go, with an impressively straight face. Warren ignored him.

Warren turned to Singh Mahal. 'Mr Singh, why didn't you tell us that you were serving langar on Saturday afternoon with Councillor Kaur? It would have saved us all a lot of wasted time and effort.'

Singh Mahal sneered. 'None of your business, was it? Why should I do your job for you?'

'Regardless, based on what Councillor Kaur has stated, it would seem very unlikely that you were in a position to kill Mr Meegan on Saturday, given the estimated time of death.'

'So I'm free to go then?'

'Not just yet, I have a few more questions I would like answered.'

'You have just said that my client was not involved in the death of Mr Meegan. I must insist that you release him from his bail conditions or re-arrest him.'

'I said no such thing.'

Tony Sutton cleared his throat.

'Mr Singh, have you ever met Tommy Meegan?'

'I said no last time and I meant it.'

'So you and Mr Meegan have never had a conversation?'

A fraction of a pause.

'No, of course not. The guy's head of the BAP. Why the fuck would I be talking to him?' The man's indignation sounded real, but his eyes told a different story.

'So you and Mr Meegan have not been in contact?'

'No.'

'Can you tell me your whereabouts at approximately six-thirty on Monday, sixteenth of June?'

Singh Mahal shrugged. 'Not a clue.'

'What about Sunday, eighth of June?'

His eye twitched. 'No idea.'

'OK, we'll come back to that.'

Warren took over again.

'You know, there's a problem here. You say that you never had contact with Mr Meegan, but we've had a look at your social media and it would seem that isn't true.'

He slid a transcript across the table.

'This appeared on the BAP's official Facebook page. Do you recognise any of the user accounts here?'

Singh Mahal barely glanced at it. 'No comment.'

'OK, let me help you out. This account here—' Warren pointed to the person who had originally started the thread, calling for supporters to sign a petition against the proposed mosque and community centre '—belongs to Tommy Meegan, the late leader of the BAP.'

He ran his finger down the list of replies beneath the original article. 'We've linked a dozen of the other accounts to other BAP supporters, as well as several well-known anti-fascist protestors. I must say that some of these replies are likely to be in breach of Facebook's own community policy, if not the law.'

Singh Mahal affected nonchalance.

'This reply in particular is pretty strong. It could be construed as a death threat.'

Singh Mahal said nothing.

'Do you recognise the user account, Mr Singh?'

'No comment.'

'What about these posts, from the same user account on a different thread?'

'No comment.'

'What about this different user account? Very similar views are expressed.'

'No comment.'

Sutton sighed theatrically. 'OK, quit the stalling, Binay. We found the login details for both of these accounts stored in your phone's browser and on your laptop. We know that you wrote all of these posts. You threatened to kill Tommy Meegan if he set foot inside Middlesbury.'

Singh Mahal stared at the wall, before looking over at his solicitor.

'Yeah, I joined in a couple of flame wars.'

'And that was the only contact you had with Tommy Meegan? You didn't meet up with him?'

'No.'

'I hardly think that overblown rhetoric typed in the heat of the moment on Facebook is sufficient cause to continue wasting taxpayer's money.' Singh Mahal's lawyer started to rise. 'We've already established that my client was nowhere near the alleyway where Mr Meegan was found at the time of his death. I must formally request that he is released from his bail conditions and allowed to continue his lawful business.'

'Have we established such a thing?' asked Warren mildly. 'Tell me again, Binay, where you were on the afternoon of Saturday, nineteenth of July?'

Singh Mahal glared across the table. 'I was at the community centre preparing food for langar.'

'Was anybody else there?'

'Yes, Councillor Kaur.'

'This has already been established, DCI Jones,' snapped Stock.

'Has it?'

Sutton took over again.

'Think very carefully, Binay. According to the printed rota pinned to the wall in the community centre, you weren't originally due to work that Saturday. However, you switched with somebody else to cover that shift alongside Councillor Kaur. You can see the change in blue biro.' Sutton passed across a printout of a photograph taken on Hastings' cameraphone the previous day.

'So? People switch around all the time. As long as there are two people on duty and nobody takes the piss, everyone is cool with it.'

'But you didn't turn up for that shift, did you?'

Singh Mahal paled slightly. 'Sure I did. Ask Councillor Kaur.'

'We did and she corroborates your story.'

'So what's the problem?'

'She's lying.'

'That's rather a serious accusation, DI Sutton.' Stock turned to Warren who ignored him

'According to those coming on shift to serve the food,' continued Sutton, 'you were nowhere to be seen when they arrived just before 5 p.m.'

Singh Mahal raised a hand dismissively. 'I nipped off a few minutes early, didn't I? We was done.'

'Reports in the media say Mr Meegan's body was found at approximately six-thirty,' said Stock. 'Assuming he had died some time before then, I don't believe it would be possible for my client to cross the town centre from the community centre to the alleyway where Mr Meegan was killed, given the police presence and the closed roads,' interjected Stock again.

'Statements from those taking over claim you weren't done though. Councillor Kaur was still busy chopping vegetables and the others had to help her finish. In fact, they had to delay serving the food by half an hour.'

Singh Mahal licked his lips. 'I wanted to get home in time to watch the footie. She said it was OK and she had it all covered. I'd have stayed if I knew it was going to cause so much trouble.'

'Which match?'

'Sorry?'

'What match did you want to see?'

Singh Mahal coughed. 'I can't remember.'

Warren dismissed it with a wave of his hand. 'No matter, we'll look at the records on your Sky box.'

Singh Mahal rubbed his hands together; a faint sheen of perspiration lingered for a moment on the shiny table top where his hands had rested.

'So you left a few minutes early because Councillor Kaur said that she had it all in hand?'

'Yes.'

'So why is it that when the next shift arrived, Councillor Kaur was swearing about you not turning up at all and complaining that you never answer your phone?'

Binay Singh Mahal had been caught in a lie, but he was determined to wriggle out of it. After a short pause he put his hands up.

'I've been seeing someone.'

'Someone other than your girlfriend?'

'Yeah. I skipped preparing langar so we could spend some time together.'

'I see. Could you tell me the name of this person that you were seeing?'

'No comment.'

'Really? This person could provide you with an alibi for the time that Mr Meegan was killed.'

It was clear to everyone in the room that Singh Mahal was lying, that his story was in its death throes. How long would he continue to deny his involvement? Even his lawyer looked fascinated.

'No comment. I don't want to get her into trouble.'

'All we need is for her to confirm your whereabouts. It's unlikely that we'd need to speak to anyone else.' The recording would show that Warren was giving him every chance.

For the first time since he'd been brought in, Singh Mahal's eyes betrayed something other than arrogance.

'OK, I'll let you have a think about that. Why don't we come back to it later?' Warren cleared his throat and shuffled the papers in front of him.

'Let's go back to your relationship with Mr Meegan. You say that you only had contact with him online? Some back and forth on Facebook, a few tweets?'

'Yeah.'

'My client has already confirmed that the contact was nothing more than a bit of overblown rhetoric, said in the heat of the moment.'

Strictly speaking that wasn't true. Singh Mahal's *solicitor* had said that was the case.

'Was that the extent of your interaction, Mr Singh?'

Stock picked up on Warren's subtle emphasis on 'Mr Singh' and took the hint, letting his client answer for himself.

Singh Mahal paused for a fraction of a second.

'Yeah.'

'In that case, could you explain why we have CCTV of you calling Mr Meegan from a payphone opposite the Chequers estate?'

* * *

Binay Singh Mahal had slipped back into his 'no comment' routine again and so Warren formally arrested him on suspicion of perverting the course of justice and arranged for him to be sent to the cells to have a bit of a think.

John Grayson and Theo Garfield had been watching the interview on the monitors.

'Softly, softly, catchy monkey?' asked Garfield.

Warren nodded. He was mentally exhausted from juggling both interviews.

'I don't want either him or his solicitor to get wind of everything we've got. I don't trust that lawyer of his not to contact Lavindeep Kaur's brief and swap notes. He's getting a little too involved for my taste.'

Grayson looked at his watch.

'You won't have any trouble getting an extension to custody for either Rhodri or Binay Singh Mahal, but you'll need something more if you want to keep Councillor Kaur here even for the initial twenty-four hours.'

Warren agreed; truth be told, he doubted that Kaur was guilty of anything more than lying about her friend's whereabouts, and that was almost certainly after the fact. He'd seen little evidence of a conspiracy and after charging he would have to release her on bail; there was nothing to justify remanding her in custody until her court appearance.

'Gut feeling, Warren: did Binay Singh Mahal have anything to do with the death of Tommy Meegan?'

'Difficult to say. We know that Meegan and Singh Mahal had a lot of contact on Facebook and then later over the phone. We can't know what they discussed over the phone, but late last night Pete Robertson contacted me again.'

'That man's worth every penny of the overtime he earns.'

'There was nothing of interest in Meegan's email folder on his phone, but Pete was looking at his browsing history and found that he used another, different web-based email account which wasn't synchronised with his phone's email app.'

'So emails to that account aren't stored on his phone.' Grayson smiled tightly. 'Seems as though I did learn something useful in that cybersecurity workshop they made me attend.'

'Precisely. Fortunately, Pete Robertson isn't one to ignore a challenge.'

'Don't tell me, he managed to crack the password. Was it the name of his cat?'

'Nope, no cat and no cracking. The silly sod had clicked yes when his browser asked if he wanted it to remember his password. It redirected Pete immediately to his inbox.'

Grayson gave a short bark of laughter.

'The account was set up within hours of his first phone call with Binay Singh Mahal and only exchanged emails with a single contact. You can guess who.'

'So what were they talking about?'

'Singh Mahal claimed that he had another fifty so-called patriots willing to join in the march. That would have more than doubled the total. All they had to do was meet up beforehand.'

Grayson whistled. 'Don't tell me, fifty patriots all queuing in an alleyway between the chippy and the nail bar?'

'No, the coach park. The alleyway came later.'

'Are you deliberately speaking in riddles?'

'The last batch of emails, sent two days before the march, seem to be the lure that enticed Meegan down that alleyway. To cut a long story short, he convinced Meegan that he had been in contact with other "concerned patriots" about the possible impact of the new mosque on local businesses. Complete bollocks of course, but just the sort of thing that people like the BAP would lap up. Anyway, he claimed that these people were willing to help fund the party's "patriotic fight".'

'But it had to be done discreetly and they couldn't be seen to help publicly,' interrupted Grayson. 'Let me guess – brown envelopes in a back alley?'

Grayson closed his eyes and rubbed the bridge of his nose at Warren's confirmation.

'We knew these folks were idiots, but even so, this has to be worthy of a Darwin Award.'

'Theo Garfield says that these guys are such true believers that they can't imagine that the rest of the world doesn't see things the way they do. It wouldn't occur to them that the other person may have different views and might not be on the level.'

'Confirmation bias, I believe they call it. Anyway, what about the coach park? There weren't fifty shaven-headed white supremacists waiting for the BAP when they turned up Saturday. Where did they go? Did they cancel?'

'No idea. Besides which, they weren't shaven-headed white supremacists.'

Grayson looked surprised.

'Back up a second, what do you mean they weren't white supremacists?' Another thought occurred to him. 'And how on earth did Singh Mahal and Meegan even hook up? The two of them were tearing chunks off each other all over Facebook. I can't imagine Meegan accepting a friend request from somebody who had threatened to kill him.'

'That's where another of Mr Singh Mahal's online identities comes into play.'

'Could this get any more complicated?'

Warren opened to his mouth to reply when Janice poked her head around the door. 'Sorry to interrupt, a Mrs Sims from Dame Etheridge Academy is on the phone.'

'Sorry, boss, I've been waiting for this call all morning. I'm following a hunch that could help us clear up everything.'

Grayson sighed. 'Fine. But I want a full briefing when you get back. I don't like being in the dark when we have an elected politician cooling her heels in one of our cells.'

Chapter 59

After arriving at Dame Etheridge Academy, Warren signed the visitors' book, donned a badge and followed Jenny Sims, the headteacher, to her office. Through the windows, he could see at least three of the tower blocks that made up the Chequers estate. Assuming that Newington Lane Comprehensive, as it had been then, was the only school in the vicinity, it was quite possible that a decade or so previously Tommy and Jimmy Meegan had also been pupils at the school.

The chair of the school's governing body was a gangly man in his early sixties, Warren estimated, fighting a losing battle against baldness.

'Peter Etheridge – no relation, it's a common name in these parts,' he said quickly. 'You realise that under data protection rules, there may be limits to what we can tell you, even though Mr Singh has not been a pupil for many years?'

'Of course, Mr Etheridge, I understand. Anything you can give me would be appreciated.'

'May I ask what this is about, Chief Inspector?' asked Jenny Sims.

'Just routine inquiries,' Warren replied smoothly.

'Hmm,' was all she had to say. However, she wasn't daft; routine inquiries didn't usually involve visiting a school in the summer holidays to ask about a pupil who had attended over a decade earlier.

'What can you tell me about him?'

'Not huge amounts I'm afraid. Although we were already using computers back then of course, we were still transitioning from paper to digital. Pretty much everything is stored electronically these days, but at that time most records were still hard copy.'

'Are those records archived?'

'No, we securely destroy them five years after the student leaves or when they turn twenty-one, whichever comes later. Key data is kept obviously, in case of requests for references, helping replace lost exam certificates, or child protection issues, but the reams of paper about a student's behaviour, their internal test scores etc. are destroyed. We just don't have the space.'

'Mr Singh attended around the turn of the century. What records do you have on him?'

Sims pulled across her laptop and input a password.

'He joined us in September 1998 as a year seven, from one of our local feeder schools. He left us in July 2003 after completing year eleven.'

'So he didn't stay on to sixth form? Where did he go after finishing here?'

'I'm afraid that information isn't recorded on our system.' She paused. 'Binay didn't really fit. He sat his GCSEs, but as I recall he didn't live up to his potential.'

Warren was surprised. 'You remember him?'

'I never taught him, but some pupils you never forget. I was newly qualified when he started. Let's just say he made a name for himself and built quite a reputation over the years.'

'Not in a good way, I take it?'

'No. I don't recall most of the details, but his name was

almost permanently on the detention list and I remember him getting into trouble for fighting a lot. He also stood out in appearance.'

'Because he was Sikh?'

'Yes, he started school wearing one of those small cloths that young Sikh lads wear before their hair is long enough to need a full turban, I think they call them patkas. By the end of year eleven he had a full beard and turban.'

'Was he the only Sikh pupil?'

'As far as I remember. Things are different now of course. He had a sister, but I think he'd left by the time she came in. I taught her – sweet girl.'

'Do you know if he was especially observant back then?'

'I'm sorry, there have been rather a lot of students since.'

'I can imagine. My wife is a teacher, I don't know how she remembers so many ex-pupils. Is there anyone else who might remember him?'

Sims pursed her lips. 'We lost a lot of staff a few years ago.' She smiled ruefully. 'Let's just say it wasn't our decision to convert to an academy. A lot of teachers decided they couldn't face being under special measures and jumped ship.'

'But you stayed?'

There was a sudden flash of steel behind her smile. 'I like a challenge.'

Etheridge cleared his throat. 'And you've certainly met that challenge. Deputy Head, then Head. Last year's OFSTED inspection was a good with outstanding features.'

Warren acknowledged her accomplishment then continued. 'And did anyone else remain?'

'A few, but unfortunately we don't keep timetable data on past pupils so I couldn't tell you who taught him.'

Warren tried to hide his disappointment.

'No, wait, hang on, it says his form group from year seven to eleven was HS – that's Henry Schneider. He still teaches maths and computing three days a week. He's retiring next summer.'

* * *

Warren's luck was holding, it seemed. Despite a warning from Sims that he usually spent the summer vacation in the South of France with his wife's family, Henry Schneider agreed to meet Warren that day.

'Our daughter has just had a baby – our first grandchild – so we decided to spend the first half of the holiday playing Grand-Mère and Granddad before going to France.'

Schneider didn't look old enough to be a grandfather, with the healthy glow that came from an active lifestyle, good genes and the pride of a new grandparent. To Warren's untrained eye, the mountain bike propped against the hallway looked like an expensive piece of kit, and the man's baggy shorts showed off an impressive musculature for a man of any age, especially one approaching retirement.

'Jenny Sims tells me you want to talk about one of my old pupils.' He led Warren into the kitchen and handed him a glass of icy water from a cooler in the fridge. Warren gratefully swallowed half of it in one gulp. The weather had cooled slightly over the past few days but it was still uncomfortably warm.

'Binay Singh Mahal.'

Schneider sighed. 'Such a waste. I remember him very clearly. He was in my first form group when I joined the school. I can still picture them on their first day in year seven; blazers too big for them, pencil cases full of brand-new equipment, scared stiff that they were going to get a detention for not doing their homework and still putting their hand up to ask if they needed to underline the title and date.'

He smiled fondly. 'Of course it doesn't last. By the end of year ten, some of them had spent so much time in the isolation unit

316

they deserved a blue plaque from English Heritage and tried to avoid me where possible. Of course, at the year eleven leavers' ball they all wanted a photograph with me and there were tears.' He smiled unselfconsciously. 'Me too, I'll admit.'

Warren smiled back. Susan felt the same way; complaining about the behaviour of some of her pupils all year then trying not to cry on the last day of term when they moved on.

'What do you remember about him?'

'He had a lot of potential, but it all came to nothing. There were moments that I really thought he wouldn't make it to the end of year eleven. Fighting, defiance towards teachers, refusing to do homework. I had his parents in at least once a month towards the end. When he turned sixteen we sent him home on early study leave – it was either that or wait until he did something really stupid and got himself permanently excluded. I didn't think he'd turn up for his exams, to be honest, but he did and despite everything, didn't do nearly as badly as I'd feared. Enough to get him onto a college course or into a job, at least.'

'And did he?'

Schneider shrugged. 'No idea.' He smiled sadly. 'You know what teenagers are like. They live in the moment. Despite all the promises, very few keep in touch after they've gone. I did ask his sister what he was doing, but she didn't seem to know.'

'So do you know what went wrong? Why did he change? Was it just a teenage thing, do you think?'

Schneider shook his head. 'No, I can tell you exactly why he changed and even the date when it happened.'

'The date?'

'Yes, a single day. September the eleventh 2001.'

Chapter 60

Tony Sutton was struggling to keep the frustration out of his voice.

'Why am I only just being told this now?'

'I'm sorry, we're in chaos at the moment. Fire investigation is outsourced to a different supplier to trace evidence collection. Since they were two different cases, nobody thought to join the dots until I did a case review.'

Sutton let out a calming breath. It wasn't Harrison's fault, and he should be grateful that the experienced CSI had made the connection. At least this time. Would they be able to rely on this happening in the future?

'Thanks, Andy, sorry I snapped.'

'Completely understandable, sir.'

Sutton hung up. Despite everything he was starting to feel excited.

The phone rang again and Sutton braced himself for more bad news. This time it was the custody sergeant and the news was good.

'Rhodri's found his tongue,' Sutton told Hastings. 'I guess that smarmy lawyer of his has finally persuaded him that this won't disappear after twenty-four hours like last time and he'd better start being helpful. He's going to be in for a nasty little surprise.'

* * *

Warren eyed the councillor coolly. The woman's bluster about being kept in the station for several hours like a common criminal whilst Warren disappeared off was just that. The earlier threat of arrest still hung in the air and the last thing Kaur wanted was for the affair to go any further than this room. There was a knock at the door. Tony Sutton.

'Sorry to interrupt, I knew you'd want to know this immediately.'

Warren stood up.

'Interview paused. Don't go anywhere, Councillor, we haven't finished yet.'

Ignoring the protests of Kaur and her lawyer, Warren followed Sutton out of the room.

'Forensics just got back to me.' He handed over the report that had been emailed.

Warren read it silently, a slow smile spreading across his face.

'Good work, Tony.'

'I spoke to the Super on my way down. We've got enough. He's on the phone to the CPS as we speak. But we may want to hold back, Philip Rhodri's lawyer has indicated that he's ready to talk.'

Warren took a deep breath. 'Good. Listen to what he has to say, then arrest him. I'll join you as soon as I've finished here. Now stand back and get ready to duck, the shit's about to hit the fan.'

He reopened the door to the custody suite.

'This is intolerable, DCI Jones. You have no right to insist that my client remain. I shall be lodging a formal complaint with your superior officers.'

Warren ignored the furious lawyer, turning instead to the heavily perspiring local councillor.

'Lavindeep Kaur. I am arresting you on suspicion of conspiracy to pervert the course of justice…'

* * *

In a different interview suite, at the opposite end of the building, the name of Philip Rhodri's accomplice in the white car, when it came, was barely audible, and Tony Sutton insisted that he repeat it for the benefit of the tape.

'I didn't do it.' Rhodri's voice was close to breaking.

'Didn't do what, Philip?'

'I didn't kill Tommy Meegan.'

Sutton smiled slightly. There was no warmth in his expression.

'Who said anything about Tommy Meegan?'

Rhodri blinked in surprise.

'Philip Rhodri, I am arresting you on suspicion of arson and for the murder of Syeda Fahmida…'

* * *

Two arrests in the space of one hour meant that Warren and Sutton had a huge amount of work to do in a very short period of time.

Sutton had worried that once Philip Rhodri realised that he was no longer trying to defend himself against his implication in the murder of Tommy Meegan, and was now on the hook for the deadly arson at the community centre, he might clam up and start 'no commenting' again.

The opposite was true. Through floods of tears he'd laid out everything that happened. By the time he finally finished, it was well after 10 p.m.

'If what he says is true then it means that we got it all wrong about the murder of Tommy Meegan.' Warren's groan turned into a yawn; the two men had reviewed each other's interview transcripts to make certain that they both had the complete story.

Tony Sutton tried to stifle his own yawn.

'I'll get some blank paper and turn the coffee urn on.'

'And I'll get an extension to custody sorted, I think we're going to need some more time to sort this mess out.'

'Grayson will be pissed; he thought the whole thing was wrapped up.'

Chapter 61

'Are they trying to bleed us dry?' Gary Hastings was rarely a shouter, but the letter from the water company on top of the landlord's bombshell had left him in despair. It was already after 10 p.m. and he'd hoped to do another couple of hours of preparation for his interview on Wednesday before bed, but he knew he'd have to be in the office early the next morning. He thrust the bill onto the table, where Hardwick was seated. It must have been delivered after she returned from the walk-in centre otherwise she'd have picked it up from the mailbox herself.

'Gary…' she started.

'Seriously? Three per cent? For doing what?'

She tried again, but Hastings was in full flow now. 'I was looking at our council tax bill the other day and they claim that that rise is due to an increase in the council's contribution to policing. Really? What are they spending it on? Not us, that's for sure, we're getting a one per cent pay increase this year. Maybe we should become Members of Parliament, they're asking for eleven per cent.'

'Gary, we need to talk.' Her voice was almost drowned out by the roar of the tap as Hastings filled the kettle.

'I spoke to DCI Jones today about overtime and he said I

should be concentrating on my selection interview.' He sighed, loosening his tie. 'I suppose he's right.'

'Gary…' Hardwick tried again.

'I know you've been feeling ill, but do you reckon you'll be able to pick up any extra hours?'

'Gary. *I'm pregnant.*'

The sudden silence was broken only by the sound of running water.

'Shit.'

'"Shit"? I tell you I'm pregnant and you say, "Shit"?'

'No. I mean, that's wonderful,' Hastings stammered. 'Bollocks.' The kettle had now overflowed and was spraying water all over the counter. He hastily shut off the tap, before grabbing a tea towel to mop up the mess.

'I can't believe you.'

Hastings dropped the tea towel.

'I'm sorry. I was stressed about money and I said the first thing that came into my head.'

'That was the first thing that came into your head? How much money a baby – our baby – was going to cost?'

'No, of course not.'

'Don't lie to me, Gary. You're no good at it.'

Hardwick stood abruptly.

'Karen, I'm sorry.'

She marched towards the bedroom, pausing only to throw over her shoulder. 'It's due in March by the way, assuming you give a toss.'

The door slammed.

Hastings sat down heavily.

Pregnant? He couldn't believe it. More importantly, he couldn't believe what had just come out of his mouth. He placed his head on the table and groaned.

Tuesday 29th July

Chapter 62

The main briefing room was standing room only. Warren and Sutton had stayed up until the early hours and were now confident that they could explain much of what had happened on the fateful day. A dry run with Grayson had received his approval, and they had been given the go ahead to charge by the Crown Prosecution Service.

Philip Rhodri had already confessed to his role in the day's events and Councillor Kaur was taking legal advice; the question was whether Binay Singh Mahal would put his hands up. A confession wasn't necessary, but Warren knew he wouldn't feel fully satisfied unless he got one. Furthermore, there were still significant unanswered questions. Today would bring some closure, but the case was far from complete.

Unfortunately, Hastings had pre-booked personal leave to prepare for his upcoming sergeant's interview and would likely miss out on the fruits of all his hard work. However, Warren was pleased to see that Karen Hardwick was back, although she looked very pale under her make-up.

After running through the state of the case so far, Warren assigned everyone their roles and wished them luck, before dismissing them.

As everyone filed out of the room, John Grayson made his way to the front, accompanied by Theo Garfield, who looked grim.

'Good work, Warren. But before you get stuck in, we need to have a chat.'

* * *

Warren had been half expecting the conversation, nevertheless he was surprised at the number of senior officers packed into Grayson's office.

'Good work, Warren,' started ACC Naseem, rising to shake his hand.

'Well, I had a lot of support from my team and Inspector Garfield.'

'Of course. I've spoken to the Crown Prosecution Service and they seem confident that the charges will stick. Are you similarly confident?'

Warren hid his surprise. 'Of course, sir. Do you have doubts?'

He sighed. 'No, John has shown me everything and it looks as though you've got your man. Or rather, men.'

Warren said nothing. He could guess what had kept the senior officer awake last night.

'You know this is going to be explosive?'

It was a rhetorical question.

'If we handle this wrong the BAP and the far-right will leap on it.'

Warren felt the last vestiges of satisfaction start to ebb away. However, he was unsure what was expected of him; he said as much.

'Do your job, Warren. Solve these damn cases. And keep it quiet. The last thing we need is the BAP and other groups playing the victim card.

'We need to control how this information enters the public

domain. I'll be briefing spokespeople from all of the different communities and groups involved this afternoon with a view to developing some sort of strategy to minimise the inevitable shit-storm heading our way. We do not need anybody from inside the investigation helping their favourite journalist scoop his or her rivals. Do I make myself clear?'

'Crystal.'

'Spend whatever you need, jump whatever queues need to be jumped, this is our number one priority. On August the first Tommy Meegan is going to be buried in his local church and every nasty little racist on the continent is planning on turning up for the wake.'

Chapter 63

Binay Singh Mahal's opening salvo was as bombastic as usual. Warren batted away his solicitor's observation that Singh Mahal had been in custody for almost twenty-four hours with reference to the extension he'd had authorised that morning.

'Mr Singh, we can put an end to this very quickly if you could tell us your whereabouts on the afternoon of Saturday, July the nineteenth.'

'No comment.'

'According to your previous statement and that of Councillor Kaur, you were preparing langar at the Sikh Community Centre – a statement that she has now admitted was false. You also stated that you left early to watch the football but were unable to recall the match.'

Warren handed over a printout.

'Hardly surprising, since the football season is over and there were no matches being shown on Sky or Freeview at that time.'

Singh Mahal licked his lips.

'I got confused, I thought there was a Champions League game being played.'

'OK, we'll come back to that.' Warren let the threat hang in the air.

'Now, when you were arrested on Monday twenty-first we took a number of items of clothing for forensic testing.'

'Which proved negative for bloodstains,' interrupted his solicitor.

'That is correct. It would appear that the stains are in fact iron oxide, or rust.'

Singh Mahal shrugged.

'Could you explain why your clothing was covered in rust, Mr Singh?'

The suspect paused for a moment, his eyes darting around as he tried to think of a reason why Warren was so interested, a question that his solicitor put to Warren.

'If you could just answer the question, Mr Singh.'

'I work at a garage don't I? I'm working with rusty cars all day.'

'So you've worn these trousers to work?'

Warren pushed over a high-resolution picture of the tracksuit bottoms.

'Guess so. Could have been in the laundry for ages.'

'Did you wear them on Saturday?'

Singh Mahal's eyes narrowed slightly. 'Dunno. Maybe.'

'OK, we'll come back to that later.'

The solicitor frowned. He could see that Warren was letting his client build a house of cards and he didn't like it.

'Yesterday, we discussed your social media activity. I'd like to revisit that.'

Singh Mahal was clearly unhappy, but a glance towards his solicitor held no answers for him.

'We have traced this rather inflammatory Facebook profile to you. In it you threaten Mr Meegan on several different threads, along with another user. Could you name this user, we'd very much like to speak to him or her?'

'No comment.'

'Are you sure about that, Mr Singh? You use pretty threatening language, that some might see as concerning, but it's nothing compared to this person.' Warren leaned forward slightly. 'If I'm honest, I think this person is far more interesting. We've identified several profiles linked to him and he sounds like a pretty scary guy. Are you sure you can't help us identify him?'

'No comment.'

'Are you protecting him?'

'No comment.'

'OK we'll come back to that.' Warren took a moment to retrieve some papers from the folder in front of him. When he looked back up he could see faint beads of sweat on the man's forehead.

'Last time we spoke, you claimed not to have had any contact with Tommy Meegan. However, we then established that you had in fact had several phone calls with Mr Meegan, as well as private messages through Facebook.'

Singh Mahal said nothing.

Warren passed over the printouts.

'Do you recognise these emails?'

'No comment.'

'For the benefit of the tape, I'm showing Mr Singh exhibit 26A, a series of emails between an anonymous email account and an email account on Mr Meegan's smartphone, suggesting that the author could arrange for up to fifty members of an organisation called Sikhs Against Jihadis to accompany Mr Meegan and the British Allegiance Party on their march through Middlesbury. Do you recognise these emails, Mr Singh?'

'No comment.'

'As you said yourself, these emails are anonymous. They could be from anybody.'

Warren ignored the solicitor's interjection.

'Mr Singh?'

'No comment.'

'Why would Mr Singh email Tommy Meegan, a known racist and leader of a far-right organisation that is likely to attack him on sight?' asked his solicitor.

'Why indeed?'

Warren let the statement hang in the air for a moment.

'Besides which, how would Mr Singh obtain Mr Meegan's private email address? I would imagine that he doesn't exactly advertise it?'

'A good question. How did you get his email address?'

Binay Singh Mahal glared at Warren and Sutton.

'OK, Binay, time to stop messing us about.' Sutton leant forward. 'We know that you called Tommy Meegan on his mobile phone at least twice from a payphone on the Chequers estate. An email account was set up by Mr Meegan immediately afterwards, for the sole purpose of contacting you. We have the evidence, so stop wasting time and let's move on.'

Singh Mahal glared at Sutton, saying nothing.

The two officers sat back and waited. Even his lawyer knew better than to say something at this point.

'Yeah, OK. I emailed him to offer support for his march against the Muslims. It was a prank. I wanted to see if he was dumb enough to believe that there were fifty Sikhs willing to march alongside him and the BAP.'

Singh Mahal's lawyer had been rapidly reading the emails and transcripts.

'Aside from some inflammatory language, I see no evidence here that my client was in any way involved with the murder of Mr Meegan, and we have already established that there are no forensics tying him to the murder scene.'

'Except for his Kirpan.'

'Which was stolen when Mr Singh was mugged.'

'And his lack of an alibi.'

The lawyer snorted. 'Oh, please. You know full well that if you were to stop one hundred people on the street and demand proof of their whereabouts at any given time, most wouldn't be able to oblige.'

'I've been looking at this evidence. A fresh pair of eyes, if you will and I've got an interesting theory.'

Singh Mahal turned his gaze on Sutton

'You see, I reckon you probably didn't stab Mr Meegan, although I'd be interested to know how your Kirpan turned up at the murder scene.'

'Yet again, my client has—'

Sutton cut him off. 'Whatever. Anyway, I don't think you were in the alleyway when he was killed. However, I do think you were involved. I reckon you called Mr Meegan and invited him to meet up in Middlesbury on the day of the protest march. You lured him to that alleyway, where he was then killed by your accomplice, whilst you arranged your alibi.'

'No, I had nothing to do with Tommy Meegan's murder.'

Sutton continued as though he hadn't spoken.

'Why did you go for a fake alibi, by the way? I mean, if you weren't involved in the killing, surely it would have been safer to actually go and do your shift? Perhaps then we wouldn't be having this conversation.'

Singh Mahal shook his head vigorously. 'No, you've got it all wrong.'

'What were you actually doing in that time? We all know you weren't meeting up with some mysterious lady friend. Perhaps you just couldn't face actually working, and decided to skip langar in the end.' He looked over at Warren. 'I get that. I'd probably find it hard to concentrate on peeling potatoes if I knew my mate was sticking someone with my Kirpan on the other side of the town.'

'No, it wasn't like that.'

'I guess that's why you didn't speak to Councillor Kaur beforehand. Which seems a bit rude if you ask me. I'd be pretty annoyed if somebody called me without warning and asked me to give them an alibi for the same time that somebody was being murdered, no questions asked. Or were there questions asked? Did Councillor Kaur ask for a bit more information before committing herself to perjury?'

334

Singh Mahal was breathing heavily.

'No comment.'

Sutton tapped his teeth thoughtfully with a biro.

'What do you have on Councillor Kaur? What do you know about her that could possibly make her risk everything to cover your arse? You aren't related. I can't believe it's just because you're a fellow Sikh – the woman's a politician, I don't imagine she'd be that loyal. What did you use to blackmail her?'

'I must protest at this line of questioning. I think it highly inappropriate,' appealed the solicitor.

Warren ignored him, taking over from Sutton. 'We've discussed your social media profile at some length. Tell me, do you have any other accounts? Are you a member of any groups for example that aren't directly connected to opposing far-right extremism?'

Singh Mahal had paled even further.

'No comment.'

'What can you tell me about this group, Sikhs Against Jihadis?'

'No comment.'

'They would seem to have rather extreme views. Tell me, Mr Singh, are you a member of this group?'

'No comment.'

'Are you aware of the inflammatory – some might even say Islamophobic – views expressed within this group?'

'No comment.'

'Let me read you a few of the recent posts: "The Government should ban the teaching of Islam in schools. Share if you agree." "All Muslims entering this country should be registered and tracked to make it easier to stop terrorists. Like to show your support."'

'Those posts were started by many different users, you can't possibly claim that my client is responsible for all those profiles.'

Warren continued without pausing. 'This one is pretty topical, "Say no to the Middlesbury SuperMosque. No more terrorist training schools in our cities." It got quite a few likes and at least one share—' he looked up '—by the British Allegiance Party. Who would have thought that they'd be sharing posts from Sikhs Against Jihadis, eh?'

'Again, DCI Jones, I have yet to see any evidence that my client is linked to this site, and even if he is, what that has to do with the murder of Mr Meegan.'

Warren pushed another pile of printouts across the table.

'A search of Mr Singh's laptop and smartphone reveal that not only is he a regular contributor to this group and its associated website, he is also a founding member and group moderator, going by the name StopTheJihadis911. Nothing makes it onto this group or gets shared without his say-so. We also have evidence that he communicated directly with Mr Meegan in the run-up to his death using this account.'

Warren slid another set of printouts across the table. 'These are transcripts from Mr Meegan's Facebook Messenger account, where it can be seen that Mr Singh and Mr Meegan hold a surprising number of common positions on politics. The final two messages include Mr Meegan's mobile phone number and the address for a newly set up email account. The same email account from which this message was sent, arranging to meet up with Mr Meegan privately in the very alley where he was killed.'

Singh Mahal's eyes bulged and his mouth opened and closed repeatedly, like a fish out of water.

'I would like to request a toilet break,' he gasped eventually.

'Interview suspended.'

* * *

'My client is prepared to admit that he may have been involved in some indiscreet and possibly inflammatory language, which may have some overlap with the views expressed by the British Allegiance Party and the late Mr Meegan. However, we do not feel that his personal political views are relevant to this investigation and he again denies all knowledge of the killing of Mr Meegan.'

Binay Singh Mahal stared at the table, his jaw clenched.

'So how do you explain the message arranging to meet Mr Meegan? It rather looks to me as if you were luring him there to his death.'

'I didn't kill Tommy Meegan.'

'OK. Who did kill him? Who did you arrange for him to meet?'

'I don't know. I've never seen that message in my life. Somebody must have hacked my email.'

'Oh, come on, Binay, you don't expect us to believe that do you?' Sutton's voice was dripping with disdain.

'Either it was hacked, or you lot are trying to stitch me up.' Some of the fire had returned to Singh Mahal's eyes.

Grasping firmly at the same straw as his client, Stock demanded access to the original files, so that he could investigate their provenance. Warren agreed – the rules of disclosure were very clear in this case. Seeing that Singh Mahal was unlikely to budge on that point, Warren decided to move on.

'OK. Just to be clear, you have strong views against the Muslim community. How long have you held them?'

'No comment.'

'As I already said, we do not believe them to be pertinent to this investigation,' repeated his solicitor.

'Tell me, Mr Singh, how did your classmates' attitudes change towards you after the events of September the eleventh 2001?'

'DCI Jones! Your ignorance is staggering. My client is a Sikh, not a Muslim.'

Warren ignored him.

'Brown skin and a turban is still brown skin, right?' Singh Mahal's voice was strangulated, his words bitten short.

To his credit, Singh Mahal's solicitor picked up the thread of Warren's argument quickly.

'I'm not sure that this is the place to reopen old wounds, DCI

Jones. There were many unfortunate consequences arising from the events on that terrible day, ignorance and bullying of other members of the Asian community being just one of them.'

Singh Mahal scowled at the man next to him.

'So to be clear, you feel that you were a victim of the backlash experienced by other members of the Asian community, not just Muslims,' asked Sutton.

'Will you stop using that phrase,' shouted Singh Mahal. 'What does it even mean, "Asian community"?'

Warren, Sutton and Dan Stock all recoiled in surprise at the man's vehemence.

'There's no such thing. What you white guys actually mean is "the brown community". Go on, admit it. You're no different to those bastards in the BAP or the EDL or the BNP or whatever they're calling themselves this week. You see brown skin and you think "Asian". You see someone on the TV with a cloth wrapped around his head and you think a turban's a turban. Bin Laden was a fucking Saudi, he was from the Middle East, he wasn't even from Asia. He wore a turban because he was hiding in the desert. I wear a turban because I'm a Sikh and I let my hair grow as a symbol of the perfection of God's creation.'

Singh Mahal leant forward in his chair.

'There is no "Asian community". It's like grouping Scots and Greeks together and calling them the "white community". It's just laziness. To the police and the government and the BBC we all have brown skin, so we're all the same. Those kids at school were ignorant, I get that, but they wanted to be ignorant. It didn't matter how many assemblies the school held or how many visitors they had in to speak to us, the moment they got home their parents turned on the TV or bought a copy of the *Daily Mail* and it went in one ear and out the other. I was called "Binay Laden" every day until I left school.

'The British public see brown skin and they think Muslim. They see brown skin and a beard and they think terrorist. For years after the London bombings, every time I got on the bus with a bag, people saw me differently. Sometimes it was obvious – people would stand rather than sit next to me – other times it was like a bad spy movie with everyone peeking over their newspapers or pretending to look at their phones.'

The man's voice broke slightly.

'You know, ever since September the eleventh we've been bending over backwards to accommodate Muslims. You can't turn on the TV or look at the BBC without some earnest reporter desperately telling us that Islam is all about peace. The government spends millions every year trying to "integrate" Muslims or other "minorities".

'But what about the rest of us? What about those of us who are already integrated? I'm a Sikh. My family is from India, not Saudi Arabia or Pakistan or Somalia. But you know what, that doesn't matter, 'cos I'm British. I was born here, I've lived here all of my life. I'm as British as that bastard Tommy Meegan. I'm as British as you.

'Where are our millions? Where are our super mosques? Our community centre is a converted church hall with a leaky roof; the building's listed so we've been refused planning permission to make it more suitable. If we want to hold a wedding, the nearest gurdwara is Letchworth. We've applied for funding from the National Lottery three times, but each time we've been knocked back. That bloody great mosque has been promised half a million quid, and planning permission is pretty much a shoo-in. Well, maybe it's about time the rest of the so-called "Asian community" made sure their voices were heard.'

Warren took a deep breath. He could see that Sutton was stung.

'You are quite correct, Mr Singh. My colleagues and I shall attempt to use more appropriate language in future.'

Singh Mahal folded his arms and stared sullenly at the table.

'Let's go back to your online accomplice. Philip Rhodri, I believe he is called.'

'No comment.'

'I haven't asked a question yet. Now why would you be protecting him?'

'It hasn't been established that this Mr Rhodri is an accomplice, or even an acquaintance of my client.' Stock had been visibly chastened by Singh Mahal's outburst also.

'Yes it has. In fact, Mr Rhodri is sitting in a cell just a few metres from here. He's been very chatty. Now what do you think he has been telling us?'

'That is not a reasonable question to ask my client. He cannot possibly know what this Mr Rhodri has been saying.'

'Then tell me about those rust stains on your trousers, Binay. How did you get them?'

'I'm a mechanic.'

'Is it normal for you to end up with rust all over your clothes after a day at work?'

'Sometimes.'

'Tell me, Binay, what made you vandalise the Lilac Lane Community Hub in 2002?'

'That was a long time ago. My client was just a teenager, DCI Jones, and I fail to see what that has to do with Mr Meegan's murder.'

Warren turned slightly towards the solicitor.

'You're right, it has nothing to do with Mr Meegan's murder. I've already said that I don't believe that Mr Singh, or for that matter Mr Rhodri, killed Mr Meegan. Their involvement is a question that remains to be answered. However, Mr Meegan's killing was not the only attack that day.

'Back in 2002 the Lilac Lane Community Hub was Middlesbury's central meeting point for the Muslim community. A community that has since moved to the Middlesbury Islamic Centre. Which was set on fire at approximately the same time as Mr Meegan was being murdered. What were you doing at that time, Mr Singh?'

'DCI Jones, my client has admitted that he has somewhat ambiguous views towards Islam, and in the past – as a youth – was involved in some petty vandalism. However, I don't think it automatically follows that he was involved in that arson. The town was overrun by racist thugs espousing Islamophobic rhetoric only a couple of miles away from this tragic incident. Surely they are more likely culprits.'

'Please let Mr Singh answer the question,' responded Warren, trying his best not to let his growing irritation with the solicitor show.

'No comment,' said Singh.

Warren passed over photographs of the rear of the community centre.

'This wheelie bin was pushed in front of the rear exit, making escape impossible.' He tapped the picture. 'You can see how rusty it is.'

'It has already been established that my client has perfectly legitimate reasons for the rust marks on his clothing.'

Warren bit his tongue; the solicitor was really starting to get on his nerves.

'Are you sure that the rust on your clothes came from your workplace and not this bin, Mr Singh?'

'Yeah.'

Warren passed another colour photograph across the desk.

'When we visited your workplace, your workmates were adamant that you and your colleagues all wear overalls. And disposable gloves. In fact, according to one of your co-workers, you are quite fussy about making sure you don't get dirty.'

'No comment.'

'This evidence is circumstantial.'

'Mr Stock, this is not a court of law and you are not a barrister. Please do not answer on behalf of your client again, or I shall be forced to terminate the interview.'

Stock flushed bright red, but wisely said nothing.

Tony Sutton cleared his throat.

'The rust stains on Mr Singh's trousers weren't the only interesting thing about this piece of clothing. This is an image of the trousers under a high-powered microscope.' He passed over yet another colour photograph. 'You can clearly see that in amongst the fibres are tiny, microscopic spheres. I'm told by forensics that they are melted nylon from the polyester that makes up the material. One interpretation is that you were a bit clumsy when you slopped the petrol through the letter box of the community centre and when you lit it there was a very brief flash as the fuel burnt off, leaving behind these melted spheres. You were bloody lucky you didn't set yourself on fire.'

Singh Mahal's eyes widened slightly.

'No, I had an accident at work.'

'Try again,' snapped Warren. 'You wear overalls at work.'

'We sent the clothes off for petrol branding,' continued Sutton. 'The lab tests identified trace residues on the clothing as matching the petrol used as an accelerant in the community centre fire. The same brand of ESSO petrol that your accomplice, Philip Rhodri admitted to buying on the seventeenth of June.'

'Would you care to comment?' asked Warren.

Singh Mahal's body language radiated defeat. The defiance and arrogance was gone. It took over an hour for him to describe the events that had taken place over the past few weeks and months, his story matching that of Philip Rhodri's perfectly and confirming much of what the team had suspected. By the time he finally finished he was exhausted.

Warren was unsympathetic.

'Binay Singh Mahal, I am charging you with the murder of Syeda Fahmida…'

Chapter 64

The atmosphere in the CID unit was a mixture of relief, satisfaction and weariness. Somebody had found some cheap fizzy wine and was trying to divide it fairly amongst the dozens of officers present.

'Tony, would you like to say a few words, since you led on this?' asked DSI Grayson, uncharacteristically forgoing an opportunity to bask in the limelight.

Sutton cleared his throat and clambered onto a table, before raising his polystyrene cup.

'Well done, everybody, for putting in the hours and bringing this to such a speedy close. I'd also like to thank our visiting colleagues from Welwyn for their support and assistance.' A ripple of applause ran around the room as Sutton took the opportunity to thank a few individuals by name.

Warren smiled his congratulations, but inside he knew the job was only half finished. The events of the week before had resulted in the deaths of two people. Nobody in their right mind would claim they were both innocent victims, but Tommy Megan had still been unlawfully killed; in a civilised society he was as deserving of justice as anyone, and it was Warren's duty to deliver it to him. Raising his cup one more time he turned towards his office; he'd let the team celebrate a little longer and then try and get everyone back into work-mode.

Unfortunately, the team had different ideas and despite his protestations, Warren found himself being pushed towards Sutton's impromptu stage. The cheap office furniture creaked alarmingly under the weight of the two men but held.

'I'd just like to echo everything that Tony said,' he started. 'It's hard to be too upbeat after the sad news that Mrs Fahmida didn't make it, but we can at least be satisfied that we did everything in our power to bring her killers to justice.' A few muted 'hear hears' showed the room's agreement.

'On a more positive note, her great-grandson Abbas was moved to a regular ward this morning and the prognosis is a full recovery.'

After taking another swig of the too sweet liquid, Warren asked for quiet again.

'The full story will emerge in due course, but I'm sure many of you are aware that the motive for the fire was in large part religious and could well be classified as a hate crime.' He had everyone's attention now.

'The details have *not* yet been released to the press. I'm sure that you will all understand the potentially explosive fallout from this incident and agree with the Chief Constable's insistence that we continue to refer all press enquiries to the press office. We're sitting on a potential powder keg here. Keep away from reporters and keep your mouth shut online. Make sure that you aren't the spark.'

A chorus of muted 'yes, sirs' signalled compliance.

'This is still an active investigation. So drain your thimbles and get back to work, we've got another killer to catch.'

A smattering of polite applause followed him as he hopped awkwardly down and finally headed towards his office. Sutton fell in behind him.

'Beautiful, boss. You have the soul of a poet and don't let anyone tell you otherwise.'

'Sod off.'

* * *

'What a bloody mess.' Assistant Chief Constable Mohammed Naseem was on speakerphone in John Grayson's office. After congratulating Warren and his team on their success, the senior officer's voice turned sombre.

'At least Binay Singh Mahal's legal team won't be able to plead it was a spur of the moment. He and Philip Rhodri were planning this for weeks. Did he say what the trigger was?'

'An article was posted anonymously on the Sikhs Against Jihadis website when news of the proposed "super mosque", as they insisted on calling it, was announced. He was pretty incensed about it and he decided to share it with the BAP,' replied Warren. 'It looks as though he created a Facebook profile just for the occasion. He'd read somewhere about the Meegan brothers being from Middlesbury originally and it seems he had a flash of inspiration.'

'So where does this Philip Rhodri come in?'

'That's the interesting bit,' said Warren. 'Singh Mahal and Rhodri had never met in real life before, but the two of them worked as part of an online collective who trolled far-right social media sites with fake profiles. Rhodri was also involved in real world direct action, with groups such as Students Against Fascism and was well known in the anti-racism movement. Theo Garfield and his Hate Crime Intelligence Unit have been following him for a few years and he's been arrested enough times to carry business cards for his lawyer as a matter of routine. Rhodri claims that he had no idea that Singh Mahal was also a member of Sikhs Against Jihadis, and for what it's worth I believe him.'

'Sounds like he was duped by Singh Mahal?'

'Yes and no. I don't think he had any idea that the BAP's decision to come and march on Middlesbury was so heavily encouraged by Singh Mahal, and he certainly didn't know that Singh Mahal had decided to gamble and connect directly with Tommy Meegan. However, when Singh Mahal proposed that they use the march as an opportunity to frame the BAP for some sort of attack, Rhodri went along with it immediately.'

'Say what you like,' interjected Grayson, 'but that was a pretty ballsy decision by Singh Mahal. He must have known that the likelihood was that the moment Meegan realised that Singh Mahal was an Asian himself he could have turned around and gone for him.'

'Perhaps, perhaps not,' interjected Garfield. 'We'd already been picking up indications that Tommy Meegan was a lot cleverer and nuanced than most of these idiots; Singh Mahal may well have got the same impression. Either way, the gamble seemed to work.'

'OK, so Binay Singh Mahal puts the idea into Tommy Meegan's head to do a protest march on Middlesbury, surely that's job done? Why did he need to contact him again? Was it to lure Tommy Meegan down that alleyway to kill him?'

This time Sutton answered. 'Singh Mahal claims not. He denies sending the email that arranged the alleyway meeting and seemed pretty confident that anything we can get from Facebook won't implicate him in Meegan's murder. Forensic IT are treating it as top priority.'

'What about their phone calls then?'

Warren took up the story again. 'Unfortunately, we can only ever have his word for it, but he reckons he rang Meegan to discuss the logistics of the march. He claimed to have promised Meegan the support of a few dozen of the local Sikh community on the day of the march, which we know was a complete fabrication. In reality, he was making sure that Meegan didn't change his mind and back out. The BAP have cancelled a couple of marches in the past because of low turnout.'

'And Meegan fell for it?'

'These guys have a real blind spot. They are so convinced that they are in the right, that they have no problem believing that everyone else will see the light eventually,' said Garfield.

'What I don't understand is why he nearly scuppered the whole thing by picking Rhodri up in front of a load of witnesses in that car with fake plates?' asked Naseem.

'Rhodri claims that wasn't part of the original plan. He says that his role was to lay a trail pointing towards the BAP. He ordered those neo-Nazi tattoo sleeves online and cut his hair so he could easily wear a bald cap, then made sure he was seen buying petrol, and purchasing the car. He even sprayed racist graffiti on the community centre wall and took out the security cameras, although it seems that nobody actually witnessed him doing that.

'The plan then was to attend the rally as himself and build his alibi. Then, later that night, Binay Singh Mahal was going to sneak back to the Islamic Centre and start the fire. He reckoned that as long as he took his turban off, nobody would think anything strange about seeing an Asian man hanging around the local Islamic Centre.'

Warren grimaced slightly, remembering Singh Mahal's earlier tirade. He suspected the man was probably right.

'So what changed?'

'I think Binay Singh Mahal got cold feet. He figured that the police would want more evidence that the BAP had set the fire, so he called Rhodri and insisted that he pull out his dressing-up box and do his far-right turn again near the Islamic Centre at the same time that the BAP were in town, making sure plenty of people saw him.'

'And Rhodri went along with him? Why? He must have seen it was a bad idea?'

'Rhodri claims that Singh Mahal threatened him. He knew where he lived and said that if Rhodri tried to back out, he'd let

Tommy Meegan and the BAP know the address of one of their least favourite people.' Warren paused for a moment. 'If you ask me, I think Rhodri is a bit of a coward. He'd get involved in protests, but only when there's a line of burly coppers standing between him and his targets. He's never actually been done for assault, just resisting arrest. He's what my mother used to describe as "all mouth and trousers"'.

'Sounds about right,' agreed Garfield.

'So what happened?'

'They turned up and found that there was a police car around the corner. Rhodri wanted to just abandon the plan, but Singh Mahal insisted they wait, if nothing else it would increase the likelihood of Rhodri being spotted near the scene. Singh Mahal cranked the seat back and hid himself from view.'

'Makes sense,' interjected Grayson. 'They'd have made a pretty odd couple.'

Warren continued. 'Rhodri was using Snapchat to keep in touch with friends in town and was aware of what was happening and they decided to wait and see if the police guard got pulled away to assist. It seems that decision was the correct one.'

'From their perspective, maybe,' muttered Naseem darkly, his tone reminding Warren that solving the case so quickly wasn't going to get the force off the hook for some of the poor decisions it had made that day and since.

'So how culpable is Rhodri in what happened next?'

'He knew that Singh Mahal was going to set a fire, and of course he bought the petrol, but he swears the original plan was to do it late at night when it was empty. Obviously he agreed to the change of plans to during the day when the centre was occupied, but he claims to have been horrified when he found out that Singh Mahal had poured the petrol through the letter box. It's why he tried to get rid of his disguise down the toilet and left the car with the spray cans he'd used to graffiti the community centre in the boot and the keys in the ignition where he knew it'd be nicked. I thought he was going to have a stroke when I told him that Singh Mahal had blocked the rear entrance.'

'We'll let the courts and the CPS decide if they want to nail him for murder or manslaughter. Now, one last little matter.'

Warren knew exactly what he was hinting at.

'In light of everything that Singh Mahal and Rhodri have told us, Councillor Kaur has decided to make a clean breast of it. Or so she tells us. She claims not to have known anything about the plans in advance and knew nothing until Binay Singh Mahal phoned her after his release and demanded that she give him an alibi.'

'Be that as it may, she must have had a suspicion why he needed an alibi, if not for the arson then the murder of Tommy Meegan. Why did she give him one?'

'She claims that it was because she had known Singh Mahal since he was a young child and that she was convinced that he was of good character. She said that Singh Mahal had claimed to be scared that the police were framing him by finding his Kirpan at the scene and that she had been naive enough to support Singh Mahal whilst she got to the bottom of it. I think she may even believe herself.'

The noise from the other end of the conference line was halfway between a snort of disbelief and a guffaw.

'In reality, Singh Mahal claims that his parents have been supporting her re-election bid, both financially and through their influence in the local community. Draw your own conclusions.'

'That sounds more like it. I'll bet she's furious with Singh Mahal right now. If he hadn't had cold feet at the last minute, she'd never have been involved,' said Grayson. 'Well, even if she squirms her way out of a prison sentence, at least we can be sure that her political career is over. We'll be a lot better off without her popping up on TV every five minutes telling us what we're doing wrong and how we're all closet racists.'

'I'm sure they could find her a place in House of Lords, they'll let anyone in there,' said Garfield.

'I'll pretend I didn't hear that.' Naseem's voice boomed out of the speakerphone, before hanging up.

Warren looked at his watch reluctantly. The day's result had been hard won and he knew his team wanted to savour it a bit longer, but there was still work to be done.

'I want a briefing in one hour. Binay Singh Mahal still claims that he knows nothing about Tommy Meegan's murder and if his story holds up, there was no way either Philip Rhodri or he could have killed him.

'Somewhere out there is a cold-blooded killer, twisted enough to try and frame Binay Singh Mahal. We need them off the street.'

* * *

Despite their success in solving the community centre blaze, Warren couldn't risk the team falling into a slump. The murder of Tommy Meegan was still unsolved and he wanted everyone to raise their game again. Warren snagged Hardwick to help him roll a wheeled whiteboard into the main briefing room. The force had invested heavily in case management software and Warren was a keen advocate of its use, in particular HOLMES2 – nevertheless, sometimes marker pens, Post-it notes and Blu Tack could help make sense of the bigger picture more easily. He pretended not to hear the stage whispers about clay tablets and Mount Sinai from the more technologically savvy members of his team.

Warren and Sutton had spent the past half-hour drawing parallel timelines for the day of the murder. The top line, in blue, included key time-points related to the murder of Tommy Meegan. A red line at the bottom of the board did the same for the fire. Between the two, they'd used a range of different colours to mark the whereabouts of key suspects during the day.

'Right, folks. Whilst it is remotely possible that both of

Saturday's events were unrelated, a message luring Tommy Meegan to that alleyway was sent from Binay Singh Mahal's email account. I want everything entered into HOLMES ASAP, but I also want it on the whiteboards.' He held up a large packet of multicoloured Post-it notes. 'I didn't steal these from my wife's school bag for nothing.

'There are a lot of suspects and there's still a huge amount of CCTV to trawl through, so we need to keep on top of everything. In other news, the results for the blood tests on Bellies Brandon's shirt show no match to Tommy Meegan.'

'So Brandon's off the hook?' asked Hutchinson.

'Not necessarily, he still has no alibi, has a colossal temper and plenty of motivation, so he stays on the board for now.'

Warren pointed a thumb over his shoulder. 'If you haven't already done so take a look at the timeline and the suspect list and see if you can spot some new avenues of investigation.

'The involvement of Binay Singh Mahal brings in an unwanted complication; tensions between the Muslim community and our far smaller Sikh community are inevitable. The last thing we need is the far-right wading in with their hobnailed boots and making a bad situation worse.

'The clock's ticking, folks. Tommy Meegan's funeral is still scheduled for August the first, a key date in the far-right calendar, and we need answers before then.'

Chapter 65

Mid-afternoon and all eyes were on BBC News as ACC Naseem held a press conference.

The information relayed to the assembled reporters had been terse, and short on detail, merely confirming the arrest of two suspects and their subsequent charging. Unfortunately, the rumour mill was already flowing freely and there was a flurry of questions about the arrest of Councillor Kaur and stories about a plot by radical Sikhs to stop the building of the new mosque and terrorise the local Muslim community.

Naseem's refusal to either confirm or deny the reports merely fed into the speculation. By mid-afternoon the leader of Middlesbury council had been forced to confirm Lavindeep Kaur's suspension pending an inquiry and Imam Mehmud was being door-stepped by journalists from across the country.

Within hours *Channel 4 News* announced they would be running an extended piece on tensions between different factions of the Asian community, particularly between Muslims and Sikhs. Warren couldn't help think that even in death, Tommy Meegan would be looking on with glee at the seeds of discord sown that day – even if they had yet to bring his own killer to justice. Certainly his former compatriots in the BAP weren't slow to seize the initiative.

The announcement that the suspects charged over the fire at the Islamic Centre had nothing to do with them provoked a predictable response from the far-right organisation. A hastily posted press release cited everything from the systematic dismissal of the views of patriots to an establishment-led conspiracy involving the government, the police state and the Muslim-dominated liberal elite, facilitated by the mainstream media, in particular the BBC, known to have been infiltrated by homo-sexuals and communists since the Forties.

For his part, Assistant Chief Constable Mohammed Naseem was directly accused of trying to brush the killing of Tommy Meegan under the carpet as part of yet another Muslim-led conspiracy.

'I'm surprised they haven't included the worldwide Zionist conspiracy and the Illuminati,' commented Grayson.

'I imagine that even the BAP would struggle to place Islamist extremists and Zionists in the same boat,' suggested Warren.

'Give them time.'

Their last tactic though, appropriating the Twitter tag #Justice4Tommy in a deliberate reference to the already trending #Justice4Muslims, seemed to have backfired somewhat as Theo Garfield gleefully reported.

'Say what you want about Twitter; some days it's downright vile, but other days it can be magnificent.' The hashtag had been tweeted about a hundred times in the hour after the press release, mostly by accounts known to be run by far-right extremists. In the next six hours, it was tweeted over ten thousand more times, mostly followed by pictures of the scene of Tommy Meegan's murder, with a second hashtag #JusticeDone. Warren didn't think such gloating by a senior officer such as Garfield was entirely appropriate. He wondered if the man would feel different if he'd had to sit opposite Mary Meegan?

* * *

A phone call from Pete Robertson, from Forensic IT, supplied a welcome distraction.

'Pete, I hope you have some good news for me,' said Warren, doing his best to sound upbeat.

'Depends on what you mean by good news. We've been looking at those emails sent to Tommy Meegan by Binay Singh Mahal in more detail and we've spotted a discrepancy.'

'Go on.'

'We traced the routing information for each message and found that the first few emails, discussing the organisation of the march and promising the participation of Sikhs Against Jihadis, were sent from a different account to the later emails promising financial backing for the BAP and ultimately luring Tommy Meegan to the alleyway where he was stabbed.'

'What? But they all had StopThe Jihadis911 in the From: line.'

'That doesn't mean anything. It's child's play to change that. It's a feature used both legitimately by big organisations managing their email, and in those phishing emails from criminals that claim to be from your bank.'

Warren thanked him and hung up.

Yet again the sands were shifting. It was looking as though Binay Singh Mahal had been telling the truth when he denied all involvement in Tommy Meegan's murder. So who had sent the emails?

* * *

'How did it happen? We were both so careful.'

It was eleven o'clock and Gary Hastings and Karen Hardwick were curled up in bed. Much to Hastings' relief the big bunch of flowers and king-size box of Karen's favourite chocolates had bolstered his heartfelt apology enough for Karen to forgive his thoughtless outburst the day before. The plan had been to get an early night in preparation for his interview the next day, but the excitement of the last twenty-four hours had made sleep all but impossible.

Hardwick sighed. 'We weren't careful enough. You remember when I got ill in Paris?'

'How could I forget?'

'Well, I felt better in the last couple of days, so we decided to make the most of it.'

Hastings smiled at the memory. They'd finally had the romantic break they'd planned. They'd splashed out on a meal as they cruised down the Seine, climbed the Eiffel Tower in the dusk and finished off with cocktails. Then they'd returned to their little hotel room and spent the rest of the night making love.

'But you're always so careful about taking your pill.'

'And I'd also just spent three days throwing up.'

'Shit, it can happen that fast?'

'Apparently so.'

Hastings thought about that for a few moments. 'Wow.'

Hardwick giggled. 'I know. We're going to be parents.'

'When can we tell everyone?'

She sighed.

'Not yet. It's bad luck, just in case, you know…'

'But you can't keep it completely quiet. What if you need to go running after somebody or you get into a confrontation?'

'Gary, we're CID, not uniform. I'm not going to be chasing shoplifters or taking down drunks on a Saturday night.'

'Yeah, but still, you need to let DCI Jones and DI Sutton know just in case.'

She sighed. 'I know. But let's enjoy it for the time being. It's our secret, let's keep it that way for a bit longer.'

Hastings rested his hand on her still flat tummy. It was hard to believe that growing inside her was their future. He sighed and kissed her neck, before closing his eyes.

Tomorrow was going to be a big day and he needed his sleep.

Wednesday 30th July

Chapter 66

Hastings' interview wasn't until eleven, down at the forces' headquarters in Welwyn Garden City. Nevertheless, Warren was not pleased to see him at 8 a.m., wearing his uniform and standing at the back of the morning briefing.

'What the hell are you doing here?' asked Tony Sutton, beating Warren to the punch.

'I've been preparing solidly for this thing for weeks. If I'm not ready now, I'll never be. I'd rather be here than sitting at home or in Welwyn twiddling my thumbs.'

Warren could sympathise, after all he'd been using work to distract him from his own worries lately.

'Well, make sure you're not late.'

As Warren outlined the day's plans and filled the team in on Pete Robertson's revelation the previous evening that Binay Singh Mahal might not have been responsible for the emails luring Tommy Meegan to his death, he noticed Hastings talking quietly to one of the DCs on loan from Welwyn. The constable was a huge Scottish lad with a beard – what was his name? DC Ruskin? The two men had their notebooks out and were busy comparing them with the timeline.

At the end of the briefing, Hastings crossed the room,

'Boss, how confident are you about these timings?' He pointed to the times that the BAP members arrived at The Feathers pub.

'They came from interviews. Why?'

'We spoke to the landlord, Micky Drake, and he more or less agrees with the time that most of them arrived and confirmed that Bellies Brandon arrived last, but you've grouped Goldie Davenport's arrival in with most of the rest of them.'

Warren opened his own notepad. 'According to my notes, Marcus Davenport claimed that he stayed with Jimmy Meegan since he didn't know the area and they were amongst the first to arrive at the pub. What did Drake say?'

'He reckons Goldie Davenport arrived just before Bellies Brandon.'

Warren fought to keep his voice calm.

'If you are right, then what was Goldie Davenport doing in that time and why did he – and Jimmy Meegan – lie about it?'

Chapter 67

'No comment.'

This was the fourth time that Marcus 'Goldie' Davenport had refused to answer a direct question since the interview had started. Gone was the confident swagger and arrogance, and in were the folded arms and solicitor.

Things had moved fast since Hastings' observation and barely three hours later, Davenport had found himself sitting opposite Warren and Tony Sutton in interview suite one. He'd still been in bed, when colleagues from the Met had banged on his door; it seemed that work was going through a sudden dry spell. As he'd been led out of the flat, Mags Richardson and Theo Garfield had headed in, along with an evidence recovery team. A phone call to Forensic IT had resulted in an email with Davenport's mobile phone records.

Warren had expected such an answer to his question about Davenport's whereabouts immediately after the BAP protestors had scattered. He passed over a transcript of their previous interview.

'We're simply confirming what is already on record, Mr Davenport.'

Davenport's solicitor, a middle-aged woman who had locked

horns with Warren on numerous occasions, looked at the transcript as if she hadn't already read it before they started.

'This interview was given without legal representation.'

Warren pointed to the first paragraph. 'Mr Davenport was being interviewed as a witness and was not under arrest. As you can see, he declined the offer of a solicitor.'

The skirmish was little more than a verbal shot across the bows. But Warren took heed of the warning. He could expect resistance from all quarters today. Good, he was evidently onto something.

Davenport looked over at his solicitor who remained stony-faced.

'After the police let those scum attack us, we ran towards the war memorial.'

'I wasn't present for the original interview, could you remind me who "we" is?'

If Davenport realised that Tony Sutton's interjection was merely a play to get him to slip up and contradict his previous statement he didn't seem bothered.

'Me, Jimmy, Tommy and Bellies.'

'And what happened next?'

'We split up. Me and Jimmy headed towards BHS and Tommy headed towards Marks & Spencer. Bellies stopped at the war memorial to catch his breath.'

'Did you see anybody else around?'

'No one.'

'OK, tell me what happened after you reached BHS.'

'Me and Jimmy went through the alleyway between BHS and Next, then crossed the road and went between the key-cutter's and the newsagent. Then we walked to The Feathers.'

'My client has confirmed exactly what he stated before, I fail to see what going over old ground will accomplish.'

Sutton ignored her.

'What route did you take to The Feathers?'

Davenport squirmed slightly in his chair. 'Dunno. I followed Jimmy, he knows the area.'

'But would you say you went there by the most direct route?'

'My client has already stated that he doesn't know the area, so how could he possibly know that?'

'Sorry, my mistake, I worded the question a bit clumsily.'

The solicitor's eyes narrowed.

'If I were to walk from Stafford Road to The Feathers, by the most sensible route, I reckon it would take about ten minutes. Does that sound about right?'

Davenport licked his lips. 'Yeah, I guess so. Maybe a bit longer.'

'OK, a slow walk. Call it fifteen minutes.'

He shrugged.

'That's rather speculative, DI Sutton.' The solicitor turned to Warren. 'I'd prefer that we deal with hard facts.'

'OK.' Warren made a show of looking at the interview transcript. 'Was the pub already full when you arrived, Mr Davenport?'

The pause was so long that Warren was convinced that he was going to damn himself by 'no commenting'. In the end, he shrugged helplessly. 'I can't remember.'

Warren turned the transcript through one-hundred-and-eighty degrees and pointed with his ballpoint.

'You said in the original interview "We were pretty much the first." Do you agree with that statement?'

Davenport looked over at his solicitor helplessly.

'Do you agree with the statement that you originally gave?'

He cleared his throat. 'No comment.'

Warren let him stew for a moment.

'I have spoken to others from the pub. They say that you arrived at least thirty minutes after most of your friends. In fact, you were almost the last to arrive. Is that true, Mr Davenport?'

'No comment.'

'What were you doing in those thirty minutes or so?'

'No comment.'

Warren could see that he had locked Davenport into a 'no commenting' cycle.

Sutton picked up on Warren's cue.

'Mr Davenport, you said that you are unfamiliar with Middlesbury?'

Davenport bobbed his head.

'Have you ever visited Middlesbury before?'

Again he paused.

'Not that I recall.'

'I take it that means you definitely haven't visited recently?'

'No.'

'So you weren't in Middlesbury on the evening of Wednesday, sixteenth of July this year?'

Davenport shook his head, but his voice was unsteady. 'No.'

'Are you absolutely certain, Mr Davenport?'

He nodded.

'According to a witness report, a man matching your description was involved in the mugging of an Asian man that night on the Chequers estate. Were you involved in that assault, Mr Davenport?' Warren knew that he was taking a gamble. What little description Binay Singh Mahal had provided had been vague to say the least, and no other witnesses had come forward yet. If they couldn't get Davenport to admit to the assault, then when his solicitor asked for the witness reports in disclosure, they could undermine Warren's credibility.

'No.' Davenport was barely audible.

Sutton pulled a sheet out of the manila folder sitting in front of him.

'Do you own a Samsung Galaxy smartphone?'

'Yes.'

'And is this the telephone number of your phone?'

Davenport thought about it, before deciding that a denial or refusal to comment would be a waste of time.

'Yeah.'

'According to cell tower records, this handset was in Middlesbury – specifically the area adjacent to the estate where the assault took place at the time of the attack. Are you sure that you have never been to Middlesbury, Mr Davenport?'

'No comment.'

Warren decided to take over again.

'The victim's wallet was taken, along with his Kirpan. Do you know what a Kirpan is, Mr Davenport?'

'No comment.'

'I'll ask you again, were you involved in that assault, Mr Davenport?'

'No.'

'I am showing Mr Davenport a photograph of a Sikh ceremonial knife known as a Kirpan. Are you familiar with this type of knife, Mr Davenport?'

'No comment.'

'This knife was used to kill Tommy Meegan at sometime between 2.36 p.m. and approximately 6.30 p.m. on Saturday, nineteenth of July. Can you account for your whereabouts at that time, specifically between approximately 2.36 and your arrival in The Feathers pub roughly one hour later?'

'No comment.'

'I should warn you, Mr Davenport, that, as we speak, officers are executing a search warrant on your apartment in connection with the murder of Tommy Meegan. Is there anything that you wish to tell me at this time?'

The man looked terrified.

Picking up on his unspoken cue, his solicitor leant forward.

'I'd like to request a comfort break.'

'Interview suspended.'

Chapter 68

Warren and Sutton made straight for the coffee urn. Neither man was in the mood to wait for the barista in the coffee concession to faff about with a needlessly complicated machine then charge them nearly three pounds for the privilege.

'What do you reckon? Think he'll confess?' Sutton was heaping several spoonfuls of sugar into his mug. 'I need the energy,' he protested at Warren's raised eyebrow.

'You'll need a dentist. And in answer to your question, I really don't know. On the face of it, we don't have enough to charge. His solicitor has to know that, why do you think she paused the interview?'

'Well, we have more than twenty hours remaining on the clock and we'll definitely get an extension if we ask for it. Let's see what forensics find. Meegan bled out, there must be at least some trace.'

Warren chewed his nail. 'But is it enough to charge? You know what the CPS are like. They practically want it gift wrapped.'

Before Sutton could reply, the custody sergeant poked his head around the door.

'His solicitor is now requesting a meal break. He hasn't eaten since he's been here, I can't really deny it.'

Warren glanced at Sutton. The solicitor was clearly stalling for time. But why?

Sutton thanked the sergeant then turned back to Warren. 'Well, I don't know about you, boss, but I could do with lunch myself. They have some tasty-looking tuna melts in the canteen.'

Warren wrinkled his nose. 'Eat it down there, I'm not having it stinking out my office like last time.'

Sutton grinned and headed for the door.

'Haven't you forgotten something?'

Sutton looked blank.

Warren inclined his head towards the coffee urn.

Sutton shrugged his shoulders. 'Give us a clue.'

Warren waggled his coffee cup.

Sutton shook his head. 'You'll have to spell it out, boss, I'm obviously a bit thick today.'

Warren sighed. Three years he'd been fighting this particular battle; today obviously wasn't the day he'd win it.

Sutton didn't even try to conceal his grin as Warren's pound coin rattled into the empty honesty jar.

* * *

Goldie Davenport was a surprisingly fastidious man. Mags Richardson had searched plenty of houses over her career and it was obvious whether a person was naturally tidy or had simply blitzed their flat to give a good impression. The CSIs had done their thing, bagging any suspicious items of clothing, including the contents of the laundry basket and the trap from the back of the washing machine. Now it was up to her and Garfield to retrieve anything else of interest.

'And my husband accuses me of having expensive tastes,' opined Richardson as she gazed at the inside of Marcus Davenport's wardrobe.

'I know, these jeans aren't from Primarni,' agreed the young DC on loan from the Met.

'I was thinking more of these football shirts.' Richardson fingered the team tops. 'They're the real deal, you can tell by the stitching on the label that they aren't counterfeit – no spelling mistakes for a start. I bought my daughter the England one for Christmas, it cost me fifty quid and she'll be wanting the latest Stevenage FC for the start of the season. He's got Chelsea home and away, plus England replica shirts for the past eight years.' She pulled open a drawer. 'Plus tracksuits and hoodies. He's nothing if not dedicated.'

The young DC wrinkled her nose. 'That's one word for his kind.'

Richardson looked around the room; it was a curious blend of grown man and teenage boy, with glossy posters of the current England and Chelsea line-ups jostling for space with rather more amateur flyers for death metal bands unlikely to bother the music charts any time soon. If he ever brought anyone back, they knew exactly what they were getting.

'Where the hell do you even buy a pillow case with a swastika on it?'

'You'd be amazed what you can get on the internet if you look hard enough,' said Garfield from the doorway.

'Anything interesting, sir?' asked Richardson.

'Not much, I found an ancient Nokia brick that I imagine we'll be able to link to the march on Saturday. I found his phone bill and it matches his smartphone. All the utility bills are in his name, on the surface he seems to be living here alone.'

'On the surface?'

'He doesn't strike me as the sort of man who needs two toothbrushes; nor does he smell strongly of Sure for Women deodorant.'

'So who is staying over regularly enough to leave her own toiletries?'

'I think we can guess.'

* * *

The hoped-for confession wasn't forthcoming.

'So far it would seem that you have pulled my client in here

368

based on a discrepancy in his time-keeping. As I am sure you can appreciate, Saturday was a very emotional day for Mr Davenport and he, and his friends, were rather the worse for drink. They may have become a little confused.'

Warren waited.

'My client recognises that you have a job to do and that you are simply trying to solve the brutal killing of his good friend. He will of course assist your inquiry in any way he can, including allowing you to search his apartment.'

A pointless gesture; they had a search warrant.

'Thank you. Now, Mr Davenport, why don't you tell us about your relationship with Annabelle Creasy?'

Davenport blanched. 'What do you mean?'

'I mean just that. I presume you know her?'

'Uh yeah, sure. She was Tommy's girlfriend.'

'I see. And how often did you sleep with her?'

'DCI Jones!'

Warren ignored the solicitor's yelp.

'Did you take the opportunity to spend the night every time Tommy visited his mistress? Or did she stay with you sometimes?'

'No comment.'

'Well, there's no point denying it. Unless you are in the habit of stocking your bathroom with women's toiletries.'

'Those toiletries could be anybody's'

'I imagine you didn't leave your own things around Ms Creasy's flat when you stayed over, for example on Friday night before Saturday's excursion. I imagine Tommy thought he was being really clever as well, didn't he? Telling Ms Creasy that women didn't usually come to BAP meetings, or claiming that he was going to stay at his brother's or his mum's place so he could spend time with his own mistress.

'Did you know about it?' Warren answered his own question. 'Of course you did, I'll bet you laughed like hell when he asked if he could use you as an alibi, I reckon you were around her flat like a rat up a drainpipe, knowing he was busy elsewhere.'

'No comment.'

Warren leaned forward slightly. 'But that wasn't enough, was it? What happened? Did you decide to get rid of him so you could live happily ever after? Was she in on it?'

'No comment.' It was more of a croak.

Warren looked at him contemptuously. 'You were scared of him, weren't you? It didn't matter that he was being unfaithful himself, you knew he'd never tolerate you screwing his girl. And what about Jimmy? He's a bloody psycho, he'd have been more than happy to join in teaching you a lesson.'

'No, that's not what happened.'

'Really, then tell me. Because from where I'm sitting it looks like the oldest story in the book. A classic love triangle, if you can forgive me being romantic.'

Chapter 69

Davenport and his solicitor had been doing more than enjoying overpriced coffee and a tuna melt during yet another comfort break. Unfortunately, the handwriting on the sheets of paper in front of the suspect was far too spidery for Warren to have a hope of reading it upside down.

'My client wishes to make a statement and cooperate fully with the investigation,' his solicitor started.

Warren fought to conceal his surprise, resisting the urge to glance towards Sutton.

Davenport cleared his throat. 'I did not kill Tommy Meegan, nor was I involved in his killing.'

Warren said nothing.

'I believe that Tommy was killed by his brother Jimmy.' He licked his lips. 'When we left the square Jimmy and me ran past BHS and through the alleyway next to the key-cutter's and onto the street behind. Then we split up. I got lost trying to find The Feathers pub and Jimmy was already there when I arrived. When I asked him what he'd been doing, he told me to keep my mouth shut. When the police arrived later in the day, I realised that he must have killed Tommy.'

Davenport sat back in his chair. The fear remained in his eyes, but Warren could see that a great weight had been lifted from his shoulders.

* * *

After a ten-minute consultation in the corridor outside, the two detectives returned, ready to hear Goldie Davenport's full statement. In the meantime, Warren's opposite number in Romford was arranging for the arrest of Jimmy Meegan and a full forensic search of his flat and anywhere else he could conceivably hide evidence.

'Start at the beginning,' suggested Warren.

'It was like I said before, we left Romford at about ten and got to Middlesbury about twelve. Jimmy was all wired, ready for action and Tommy was trying to calm him down. He's got a problem you know.' He touched his nose.

'Cocaine?'

'Yeah, Tommy's been on at him for ages to lay off it, says he's doing too much. Jimmy reckons he's got it under control, but he blatantly hasn't. We stopped at a service station for a piss and a fag and when Jimmy came back he was well jittery and annoying the fuck out of everyone, I thought Tommy was going to hit him.'

'What happened when you got to Middlesbury?'

'We had to stay on the coach for an hour whilst you sorted out the protestors and the muzzers and searched us, then we got off and lined up to walk to the rally point.'

'Were you all together at this point?'

'Yeah, Tommy and Jimmy were at the front with the banner and the loudhailer. Me and Bellies were with the rest of the troops with flags and signs.' He leered at the memory. 'Some raghead tried to drown Tommy out, but ours was louder.'

'Then what happened?'

'Well, it were all going well, we was having our say but the number of protestors was getting too big and there were hardly any coppers. Eventually some wankers started throwing stuff at us. Tommy got hit in the head.' He scowled. 'Perhaps you should have been searching the protestors instead of us.'

'Carry on, Marcus, what happened next?'

'Well, eventually you gave in to the protestors and we had to leg it.'

'OK. So far you haven't given me anything I didn't already know and nothing that tells me you weren't responsible for Tommy Meegan's murder.'

Davenport shrugged. 'What do you want to know?'

'How did Jimmy know his brother was going to be alone in that alleyway?'

Davenport looked uncomfortable. 'I'm not one hundred per cent sure, but I heard Tommy talking to Bellies on the coach after he'd tried to collect everyone's money for the coach. Some of the lads reckoned they hadn't got any on them – although they all seemed to be able to find enough to buy beer later – and Bellies said something about how we needed to raise some cash if we wanted to do this sort of thing more often. From the way Tommy was talking it sounded like somebody was going to help fund the party. I got the impression that he was planning on meeting this person after the march. I reckon it was Jimmy playing him.'

Sutton laughed. 'Oh come on. You expect us to believe that Tommy Meegan was daft enough to meet a stranger in an alleyway in the hope of getting some money?'

Davenport shrugged. 'I dunno, but Tommy always liked a bit of drama. Brown paper bags stuffed with cash are just his thing.'

So far Davenport's story matched the evidence. However, until they found out who had sent the emails, it remained speculation.

Warren took over again.

'So you went through the alleyway, then what?'

'We stopped for a breather, then Jimmy told me to carry on to the pub, because he had something to do.'

'What did you say?'

'Well, I asked him what was so bloody important he was going to leave me in the middle of fucking nowhere and he told me it was none of my business.'

'And that was it?'

Davenport looked down at the table. 'Yeah, he pointed me towards The Feathers and left me to it.'

Warren looked at the man hard. Despite his bluster, it was clear that Goldie Davenport was scared of Jimmy Meegan. But why?

'Which way did he go?'

'Up the street.'

Towards the alleyway that Tommy Meegan had been killed in.

* * *

Not only was Davenport a fool, it seemed he was also directionally challenged and too proud to admit it. Most of BAP's supporters had, by a combination of basic map skills, intimidation of local residents and blind luck, eventually stumbled across The Feathers and were supping pints and trading war stories within half an hour of the march breaking up. Goldie Davenport it seemed had wandered the streets getting progressively more and more lost until finally hailing a taxi who'd happily taken a fiver off him for a three-minute journey around the corner. Only Bellies Brandon, who'd shuffled there under his own steam, had arrived later.

'Where did Jimmy get the knife?'

Again, Davenport looked worried. 'You need to know that I didn't have any idea what Jimmy was up to. I was just helping a mate out. I had no idea that he was going to, you know…'

'Go on.'

'Jimmy said he needed help to sort out some Paki who'd been hassling his mum.'

'Did he give a name?'

Davenport frowned in concentration. 'I don't think so.'

'So when he said "sort out", what did you think that meant?'

Davenport shifted in his chair. 'You know, have a word.'

'And it took two of you to do that?'

Davenport squirmed.

'So what happened?'

'We drove up after work and arrived about eight. It was still light, so Jimmy told me to go to the chippy whilst he went and saw his mum.'

"What day was this?"

Davenport frowned in concentration. 'A couple of weeks ago . . .' He paused. 'It must have been a Wednesday, 'cos I was pissed we missed the karaoke down the Swan.'

The night Binay Singh Mahal claimed he was mugged.

'How long was he gone for?'

'About half an hour or so. I'd finished my food by the time he came back.'

'Whose car did you take?'

'We took the work van. I drove there.' He paused. 'I don't trust him not to snort something before he gets behind the wheel. He drives like an arsehole at the best of times.'

'When he returned what happened?'

'He said that his mum had given him the name of the bastard and that he knew where he lived. We got our hoodies out of the car, put some gloves on and walked to the estate.'

'Go on.'

Davenport peeked over at his solicitor who was visibly uncomfortable with him incriminating himself in such a way.

'There's a telephone box at the edge of the estate, near the shops. It's vandalised and covered in piss, but it still works. We hung around and eventually the bloke Jimmy was waiting for turned up.'

Davenport took a sip of his water and avoided his solicitor's gaze.

'We waited until he walked past, then Jimmy jumped out and punched him in the head.'

'Then what? Tell me exactly what happened.' Warren's tone was stern. He wanted to see if Davenport was prepared to incriminate himself in a serious racial assault. If he did, Warren might believe what so far seemed to be a rather fantastical tale.

'He fell on his face.'

Davenport was silent and Warren found himself holding his breath. If Davenport's story contradicted that told by Binay Singh Mahal, the lawyers would paint Davenport as an unreliable witness.

'And?'

'He rolled onto his back, so I kicked him in the ribs until Jimmy pulled me off and told me he'd had enough.'

'What did you do then?'

'I walked away. I was buzzing and I needed to calm down.'

'And Jimmy?'

'He knelt down and said something to him. I don't know what. Then he opened his jacket, took his phone and wallet and threw them over a wall.'

'Did you actually see the knife?'

'No, I just figured it out later.'

'So what happened next?'

'I wanted to leave right away, in case he called the police, but Jimmy reckoned he wasn't going to say anything. In the end we drove to the pub.'

'Which pub?'

'Dunno. The Rose or something.'

'Not The Feathers?'

'No, everyone recognises him in there and he wanted to keep our visit quiet.'

'What time would you say this was?'

'About half-nine, I guess.'

The cell-tower log placed his phone close to a small pub called the Rose and Crown from twenty past nine until shortly after ten-thirty.

Sutton interjected. 'If Jimmy was so worried about being seen in Middlesbury, why didn't you drive somewhere else?'

'Jimmy said he wanted to go and see his mum and tell her everything was sorted.'

'So he left you in the pub?'

'Yeah.'

Warren glanced at Sutton who took his cue. 'So basically you drove to Middlesbury on a Wednesday night to help your mate beat somebody up for his mum. You spent half an hour on your own in the chippy, then after you'd helped him assault a total stranger, Jimmy patted you on the head and told you to go and sit in the pub. Did he also give you some money for a packet of crisps and tell you not to talk to strangers?'

Davenport's mouth twisted and he glared at Sutton, before finally looking away.

'Why didn't you go and meet his mum?' Warren's tone was deliberately more conciliatory.

'He said she was getting on a bit and wouldn't want any fuss.'

That didn't sound like the Mary Meegan Warren had met and he could see from Davenport's expression that he realised that now also.

One thing was certain. Jimmy Meegan's whereabouts in Middlesbury were unaccounted for twice that evening. Assuming that he hadn't been visiting his mother as he'd claimed, that had given him plenty of opportunity to smash the CCTV camera overlooking the alleyway his brother had been killed in. Had he also stashed the murder weapon in the alleyway ready to use on Saturday? He'd been on enough marches to know that he would be searched.

'What you've said is all very interesting but you haven't answered the most important question; why would Jimmy Meegan kill his own brother?'

Davenport licked his lips, a sign that he was probably going to try and avoid telling the full story.

'He didn't like the direction Tommy was taking the party.'

'How do you mean?'

'Tommy was moving away from our beliefs. Jimmy saw him as a traitor.'

'In what way?'

'Tommy reckoned the future was in getting rid of Muslims. We all do of course, but he reckoned it was worth sacrificing your principles for.'

'How do you mean?'

'The BAP was founded on the belief that Britain is a white, Christian country and that immigrants should be encouraged to go home. We believe that Britain was only Great Britain when it was populated by the super race and that the mass uncontrolled immigration since the Second World War has brought this country to its knees. In the past seventy years we've diluted our bloodlines and given away our right to govern ourselves. And now we're paying the price; a collapsed economy, paedophiles and queers on every street corner and religious nutters threatening to kill us if we don't follow their rules. There should be no exceptions.'

'But Tommy thought differently?'

'He kept on talking about the "bigger picture". He reckoned that there were other organisations that felt the same way that we did about Muslims and that we might want to get them to help us in our cause.

'Jimmy found out that Tommy was talking on the internet with some group called "Sikhs Against Jihadis". They wanted an end to Islamic law being forced down their necks. He was furious. He thought that it was a betrayal of everything we stood for.'

'And did anyone else hold the same views as Tommy?'

'A couple. I reckon Bellies might be persuaded.'

So Jimmy Meegan was angry with his brother for changing the direction of the party. 'Now Tommy is gone, who will lead the BAP?'

Davenport shrugged. 'Take a guess.'

Chapter 70

Warren and Sutton had another five-minute consultation in the corridor.

'Would Jimmy really kill his own brother over his political views?' asked Warren.

'I'm sure it wouldn't be the first time. Cain and Abel set something of a precedent,' responded Sutton.

'I know, but these groups are splitting and reforming all the time – there must be something more to it.'

'Goldie could just be trying to pin all of it on Jimmy to save his own skin,' pointed out Sutton. 'We have nothing linking Jimmy to Middlesbury the night of the mugging. Goldie could easily be the killer, maybe even working alongside somebody like Bellies Brandon.'

'Brandon certainly has motive, given what we know about Tommy Meegan and his wife.' Warren twisted his lip thoughtfully, before making his mind up.

'Let's lean on him. Get him to give us more.'

'Usual roles?'

'Oh, yes.'

* * *

'I'm sorry, Marcus. Nothing you've told us makes me believe that you had no involvement in Tommy Meegan's death.'

Tony Sutton was less polite.

'Do you seriously expect us to believe that Jimmy Meegan murdered his own brother because of his political beliefs? This is Middlesbury, not the Garden of Eden.'

Whether Davenport's look of confusion was from Sutton's esoteric biblical reference or he was genuinely surprised that his story hadn't been accepted at face value was unclear.

'You are going to have to give us something a bit more concrete if you want to convince us that Jimmy Meegan was responsible for his own brother's death.'

Davenport squirmed in his seat, before looking at his solicitor. She shrugged slightly.

'There were some photos,' he finally managed.

'What sort of photos?'

'Jimmy is a shirt-lifter. I don't know if Tommy knew and just ignored it or he really had no idea.'

'Jimmy Meegan is gay?'

Warren fought to keep the surprise out of his voice.

'Yeah. Couldn't believe it when I finally figured it out. Especially since he'd been done for queer bashing a couple of years ago. But then loads of stuff started to make sense. We'd go out on the pull and he'd be chatting up the birds and all that, but he rarely took them home. I heard rumours that he was having a bit of difficulty keeping it up. I figured it was probably the coke and the booze you know. Then there were stories about when he was inside. I ignored it at first. People always talk shit about you when you've been to prison.'

'So what made you change your mind?' asked Warren.

* * *

'I found an app on his phone. He was a right bastard for posting stuff on Facebook if you left your phone unlocked and I wanted to get him back. He had a really easy swipe gesture to unlock the phone, so one day when he left his phone to go for a piss I unlocked it. He had that gay dating app on his home screen, with a load of notifications.'

'And that was a problem?' asked Sutton.

Davenport looked at him incredulously. 'You've visited our website, right?'

He answered his own question. 'Homosexuality is perverted and against the natural order of things.' He leant forward, a flash of the old fire returning. 'Mark my words. The worst thing this country ever did was make being gay legal. Now we have poofs teaching our kids and getting married for fuck's sake. No wonder there are so many paedos about.'

'So you told Tommy his brother is gay. I thought you and Jimmy were friends,' Sutton continued.

Davenport said nothing. Was that shame?

'How did he react?'

Davenport chewed his lip and maintained his silence.

'I don't believe you,' announced Sutton, leaning back and clasping his hands across his chest.

'What do you mean? I'm telling the truth.' The man's voice was an indignant squeak.

'Oh, I have no problem believing Jimmy is gay. All that homo-erotic, gay Nazi stuff that you guys are into, I figure the whole lot of you are hiding something.'

'Fuck off!' snapped Davenport, before a glare from his solicitor silenced him.

'No, what I find difficult to believe is that you had the balls to tell his brother. That you marched up to him and said, "Tommy, your brother's batting for the other team." He'd have punched your lights out.'

'DI Sutton, I find your choice of language offensive,' interjected Davenport's solicitor half-heartedly.

Sutton ignored her. 'Seriously. A nutter like Tommy Meegan would never believe you.'

'I had proof. I unlocked his phone and took a picture of the app on the screen.'

'Really, that's all you had? Tommy Meegan was no brain surgeon, but even he'd have demanded a bit more than that.'

Davenport fell silent and stared at the table.

Warren let the silence settle, before taking over from Sutton. 'What else did you have, Marcus?'

'I had other photos. Of him, you know…'

'How did you get them?'

'I looked on his phone again and saw he'd arranged to go to a gay bar in Basildon and meet some guy. So I followed him.'

'After you followed him into the bar, what happened next?'

Davenport's mouth twisted slightly.

'I didn't go in, I waited around outside.'

Davenport licked his lips again. If the man played poker, that would be his tell, Warren decided.

'Then what?'

'They went to the guy's car and got in. I thought they were going to drive off. But the car didn't move. Then I figured out what they were doing.'

'So what did you do?'

'I sneaked up to the car. I was worried he might see me, but he had his eyes closed.'

'What about the other man?'

'Can't you just use your fucking imagination?' snapped Davenport.

Warren gestured towards the tape recorder. 'For the record.'

Davenport scowled. 'He was getting a bloody blowjob in a car park behind a gay bar. I took photos. Satisfied?'

Chapter 71

'Do you have the photographs, Mr Davenport?' asked Warren after the skinhead regained his composure.

'No, I deleted them, I didn't want that shit on my phone.'

'Convenient. Was this before or after you showed them to Tommy?' asked Sutton.

Davenport said nothing.

Sutton continued. 'You see I still can't imagine you marching up to Tommy and showing him your snaps. I reckon he'd have put you in hospital. What did you do with them? Post them on Facebook and tag them both? Print them out and pin them to the noticeboard in the pub? How did Tommy Meegan find out about these pictures that you have so conveniently deleted?'

Davenport mumbled something as he stared at the table.

'Speak up for the tape,' instructed Sutton, sternly.

'Email.'

'You emailed them to him?'

'Not directly.' Davenport was staring at the table top like a scientist looking down a microscope.

Warren took over, ignoring his response for the moment.

'What puzzles me is what motivated you to do all this? Why go to all this trouble to prove Jimmy, your mate, was gay?'

Davenport said nothing.

'You've cracked the lock on his phone, opened up this gay dating app and used it to follow him to a gay bar. You've then waited around outside before sneaking up on him and his date and photographing them through the car window like a grubby little paparazzi. You're like some sort of twenty-first-century Miss Marple. Why on earth would you do that?'

Davenport remained silent.

'Frankly, Marcus, unless you can come up with a good reason for why you did this and show me some evidence, I don't believe you and as it stands I'll be recommending the CPS charge you with Tommy Meegan's murder,' said Warren.

It was a huge bluff and gamble and Warren could see Davenport's solicitor formulating her objections even as he opened his mouth.

'It wasn't my idea.'

At last. Warren's gut told him that he was finally getting to the heart of the matter.

'Whose idea was it?'

'I don't know.' Davenport sounded close to tears.

'You'll have to do better than that.'

'A few weeks ago, I got a private message on Facebook. I didn't recognise the user, the name was mostly gibberish.'

'Go on.'

'The person said "I know what you did March the twenty-second".'

'And what did you do on March the twenty-second?' asked Warren.

Davenport's solicitor clearly wanted to intervene. She obviously suspected that he was about to incriminate himself but had no idea what he was about to say.

Davenport licked his lips.

'If I tell you, I want a guarantee that I'll not be charged.' He looked towards his solicitor for approval who scowled back unimpressed.

'No chance. Carry on.'

Warren stared at him until his shoulders slumped and he returned his gaze to the table.

'There was a bit of a ruckus outside the Golden Eagle at closing time. A group of Asian lads started giving us some verbal, so we stuck up for ourselves. Anyhow, they called a few of their mates over. Bunch of fucking student layabouts. We chucked a couple of bottles in their direction and most of them pissed themselves and ran off.'

'Then what?' Warren prompted.

'One of the Asians was a bit more up for it and cornered me round the back where the bins were. So I had to defend myself.'

'How did you defend yourself?'

Davenport cringed slightly shrinking in on himself.

'I hit him with a broken bottle.'

Warren remembered the case now. A group of Asian students had been threatened by a group of, presumably, far-right thugs as they walked through one of the less salubrious parts of Romford. One of the Asian lads was hand-in-hand with his white girlfriend and this was believed to have been a trigger.

In the resulting melee, one of the students had been cornered around the back of the pub and glassed with a broken bottle. Surgeons had saved his sight but he would never be able to smile properly again. His attacker had taken the bottle with him as he fled and the CCTV images were too blurry for any suspects to be identified.

'So somebody claims that they knew you were responsible for the attack?' said Warren.

'Yeah.'

'And do you have any idea who the person is or how they know about the attack?'

'Not a clue. The Facebook profile was deleted shortly afterwards.'

'So what happened?'

385

'They said that they would go to the police with what they knew if I didn't do what they asked.'

'And what did they ask?'

Davenport sighed. 'They said that there were rumours about Jimmy and that they wanted evidence.'

'Why?' asked Sutton.

'I don't know, they didn't say.'

'Really? Did you think they wanted to sign him up for next year's Pride march?' Sutton responded.

'Look, I didn't really care, OK? All I knew was I was facing a long stretch inside and if I didn't do as I was told I was fucked.'

'So what did you do?' asked Warren.

'I started following Jimmy, but he was too careful and I was getting desperate. I really did stumble across the app on his phone, although I was trying to access his email at the time. I took a photograph of the screen, but there was no evidence it was his phone or that he used it for anything but a bit of queer bashing.'

'Again, what did you do?'

'The next time he left his phone I accessed the app then followed him to the gay club.'

'And what about the photos? Did you really delete them?'

Davenport nodded miserably, clearly realising that he might have disposed of the only piece of evidence that could prove his story.

'I assume that you sent them to this contact first?'

'Yeah, I sent it to some random Hotmail address.'

'Do you have the address?'

'I deleted it from my phone's sent folder. If Jimmy found it...'

* * *

Unfortunately for Warren and Sutton, Davenport was unable to give them any more help, other than furnishing them with a list of the other BAP members present during the attack. There were no new names to add to their list; Tommy and Jimmy Meegan and Bellies Brandon were already under investigation.

'It could still all be a load of cock and bull,' opined Sutton.

'Possibly, but why would he incriminate himself in such a way?' replied Warren. 'Until his admission in there, nobody had a clue who was responsible for that attack. He'd pretty much gotten away with it. Now he's under arrest and facing charges. He's also confessed to mugging Binay Singh Mahal, who again could make something of it.'

'Misdirection?' responded Sutton. 'What if Tommy was threatening to expose him and Goldie killed him to shut him up? Then he concocts some story about Tommy and Jimmy falling out over Jimmy's sexual orientation.'

'A bit elaborate don't you think? Secret photos, mysterious Facebook contacts, and anonymous email accounts? He should be in Hollywood writing spy thrillers. He doesn't strike me as that creative.'

Sutton let out a hiss. 'The whole thing seems implausible.'

'Well, let's see what Forensic IT have to say about it. Draft another warrant for Facebook, they should be able to retrieve those deleted messages,' ordered Warren.

Thursday 31st July

Thursday 1st July

Chapter 72

Unable to stomach the A10 yet again, Warren decided to practise his delegation skills and despatched Tony Sutton and Gary Hastings to oversee the Met scenes of crime team's search of Jimmy Meegan's flat. A forced entry team had found the flat empty the previous day. None of the man's neighbours could recall seeing him recently.

The drive down to Romford had been unusually quiet; ordinarily Sutton enjoyed spending a couple of hours in the car with Hastings. The two men had wide-ranging musical tastes and enjoyed discussing them; a complete conversational non-starter with their DCI. However, Hastings had seemed unusually preoccupied, and so after a few faltering starts, Sutton left him to stare out of the window.

Hastings' head was buzzing. At the start of the week he'd been worried about his upcoming interview, the ever-receding dream of owning their own home and Karen's mysterious illness, not to mention the pressures that came with any high-intensity investigation.

The pregnancy had turned all of that upside down and after the comedown from what he prayed had been a successful interview, he had started to prioritise what mattered most. To that end, the previous night he'd finally done something that he'd been delaying for far too long. He felt the edges of his mouth curling upwards.

'We're here,' announced Sutton as he applied the handbrake.

The younger Meegan brother was a cokehead; an observation confirmed by the preliminary drug tests performed on the traces of white powder found on the razor blade and the cracked mirror on the coffee table. Furthermore, it seemed that neither brother had inherited the tidy gene from their mother.

Piles of dirty dishes teetered precariously on every surface; empty food packets and crushed beer cans spilled from the over-filled recycle bin, whilst the smell from the overflowing general waste bin made Sutton wonder if losing your sense of smell was a consequence of snorting cocaine on a regular basis.

The bedroom wasn't much better. The room was close and stuffy, although given the local area Sutton couldn't blame him for not leaving the ground-floor window open; nevertheless a couple of air-fresheners wouldn't have gone amiss.

The wastepaper basket was as overloaded as the kitchen bin. However, aside from a couple of empty crisp packets there wasn't any food rotting amongst the used tissues and pocket litter. He pulled a face; it looked as though Jimmy Meegan suffered from regular nosebleeds. Sutton carefully emptied the bin into an evidence sack and sealed it; they'd need to ensure that the blood was Jimmy's. Holding the bag up to eye-level, he carefully manip-ulated its contents through the clear plastic.

It appeared that Jimmy had been on a bit of a shopping spree since the bin was last emptied. Two Sports Direct garment barcodes, complete with plastic tags, were half screwed up. He carefully straightened them out one at a time. No surprise there; the first was for a replica England shirt, reduced from sixty pounds to fifty. He twisted the second one around; another replica shirt, the same eye-watering price. The away kit? He frowned as he compared the two tags. They looked identical, even down to the barcode.

Further manipulation of the plastic bag revealed a screwed-up receipt. He smoothed it as flat as possible. Two identical shirts purchased three weeks ago, total cost ninety-nine pounds ninety-eight pence. Paid for with cash.

'Hey, boss, take a look at this.'

The voice came from the other side of the room where Hastings was holding a magazine aloft.

'There's a stack of them under the bed, well thumbed by the looks of them. A couple of them are still in plain packaging.' He squinted at the postmark. 'Amsterdam. I guess he likes his material old-school rather than through his internet service provider. I can see why.'

Sutton looked over at the magazine and blinked. 'Well, at least we know that part of Goldie Davenport's story was true.'

393

Chapter 73

'The unlock code is included on the Post-it note. The owner claims to have taken compromising photographs of Jimmy Meegan and then emailed them using his phone to an unknown Hotmail account. Naturally, he claims to have deleted the original images and the sent email. I need the images and the email address he sent them to if possible,' said Warren.

'Retrieving the photos shouldn't be too difficult, assuming he doesn't use software to encrypt and securely delete the data on the device,' replied Pete Robertson, already unzipping the evidence bag.

'He doesn't strike me as that sophisticated.'

'Retrieving the deleted email could be more tricky. If he accessed his email via the website, then everything takes place inside the browser or on Microsoft's servers and there are no footprints left on the phone, and tracing the owner of a web-based email account is very hit and miss.'

'He's been fairly cooperative, so he may be willing to give us his password.'

'Fingers crossed,' agreed Robertson, as he filled in a job sheet.

'What turn around do you want on this?'

'ASAP.'

'I'll do it myself as soon as we are finished here.'

'Thanks, Pete, I appreciate it. If what Goldie Davenport says is true, then those photos must have been emailed to Tommy Meegan at some point,' said Warren. 'Either from him, or by this mysterious third party. Presumably Davenport isn't so stupid as to use his own email address, so if we can find that incoming email, would you be able to trace the sender?'

Robertson rocked a hand back and forth. 'Depends on what route the email took. Sometimes it's easy, other times it's virtually impossible.'

'Well, do what you can.'

'With all the work you've been sending our way, it could take a while for us to get around to it, unless you want something else that's top priority to be put on the back burner for a while?'

Warren thought about it. The problem was that everything seemed equally important. 'I don't believe that you went through all of the other emails on Tommy Meegan's phone,' suggested Robertson. 'I only had a cursory scan, so I don't know if the photos you are looking for were sent to his usual email account or to another web-based account.'

Warren asked Robertson what he needed to do.

'I've transferred everything onto a tablet to make it easier to go through.'

Warren took the proffered mini-computer. He groaned; over eleven thousand emails were listed.

Robertson grinned. 'Welcome to our world, sir. As a default we also include the junk mail, sent items, unsent drafts and recycle folders in case we miss something.'

'Christ, where do I even start? I don't know the email address of the person who sent it or the subject heading.'

Robertson took pity on the detective.

'Well, we can narrow the search down to only those with an attachment, or link to a file-sharing site. Do you have a date range?'

Davenport had been vague as to when he received the mysterious contact; nevertheless, the list of emails immediately shrank, to just under five hundred.

'Well, I think we can assume that British Gas weren't sending Tommy Meegan compromising pictures of his brother,' stated Warren.

'Not so fast, sir. We already know that our killer can spoof an email address to something more likely to be opened by the target. If I were you, I'd have a look at everything on that list.' Robertson smiled sympathetically. 'There's a percolator in the corner and milk in the fridge. I'll get started on Mr Davenport's phone.'

Warren thanked him, but politely declined the offer of refreshment. A bout of poisoning from *E. coli* or whatever other bacteria Robertson was cultivating in that corner of the room would be inconvenient to say the least. Pulling up a chair, he lay the tablet on the table and started to read.

* * *

It took Warren twenty minutes to scan the emails. As he'd suspected, the communications from well known other companies were exactly what they appeared to be, with the attachment nothing more than the company's logo. The remainder of the attachments were largely crude images with racist slogans added, usually forwarded as part of a chain and preceded by lots of 'LOLs' or 'ROFLMAOs'. Warren made a note to pass the emails onto Garfield, he might find the list of addresses useful. Pretty soon though it became apparent that if the email had ever been sent to Tommy, it no longer existed on his phone.

The initial excitement of Goldie Davenport's revelations had worn off, leaving Warren dejected. He phoned Tony Sutton, to see if he had any thoughts or ideas before he left Robertson to his work.

'I figure that either the whole thing is bullshit and the photos don't exist – Pete should be able to retrieve them from Goldie's phone and answer that question at least – or they were sent to another email address that we don't know about. Pete's team are going to look at Tommy's laptop and see if there is evidence of any other email accounts.'

'Or the email was deleted,' finished Sutton.

'Maybe Tommy didn't even confront his brother. He knew what a headcase Jimmy was. Brother or not, would you have gone toe-to-toe with him?'

'You could be right. He might even have deleted them to protect him, although that's hardly going to be effective. By definition, the person sending them had copies.' Sutton sounded as frustrated as Warren felt. 'Maybe he didn't even receive them. Have you checked his junk mail?'

'Yep, nothing.'

'Well mine auto-deletes after seven days. Maybe the email was marked as junk then deleted.'

'In which case he might never have seen them.'

Warren chewed his lip, before calling across the room.

'Pete, if we go under the assumption that the email was sent to this email account and then deleted, would you be able to retrieve it?'

'It'll take time to reconstruct all the deleted data on the phone, assuming that memory sector hasn't been written over already.'

'If you were able to retrieve the email could you tell if he read it or if it was marked as spam?'

Robertson was silent, pinching his bottom lip thoughtfully. 'Maybe. I'll have to ask around.'

'OK, do it, fast as you can. I'll authorise the cost.'

Robertson looked troubled. 'I can do it, but even if you write me a blank cheque and I pass it on to one of our commercial partners, it's a big job. We're not talking overnight, or probably even in the next week.'

Warren hissed in frustration. His instincts were telling him that they had all of the pieces to the puzzle in their grasp, but if they didn't get this solved before Tommy Meegan's funeral who knew what would happen?

Chapter 74

Whilst he was in Welwyn, it made sense to catch up with others involved in the investigation, and so Warren headed next to Crime Scene Manager Andy Harrison's office. It was a gamble, the man could be literally anywhere in Hertfordshire, but as he knocked on his door, the Yorkshireman nearly fell off his chair, his grey ponytail swinging wildly.

'Bloody hell, I was just about to call you. Do you read minds?'

'I learnt it on a course.'

'Guess what we found?'

Warren had no chance to respond before Harrison answered his own question.

'A carrier bag stuffed full of clothes soaked in blood.'

* * *

'Sophie, one of my trainee technicians, spotted it.' Harrison gestured towards a large video screen showing an image of the crime scene.

'She was doing some blood spatter analysis, trying to pinpoint exactly where the victim and his attacker were standing.' He zoomed in. 'Anyway, there were some spots of blood on the wall of the fish and chip shop that didn't seem to fit the pattern. When she looked closer and panned over the image she spotted some more, smaller spots here—' he pointed to a place higher up the wall '—and here.'

Warren leaned in and squinted. 'Unless I'm looking at this wrong, that spot appears to be about three metres above the ground. That can't be right, surely?'

'Two point nine six metres to be exact. With another two spots even higher.' He minimised the image. 'Those were the only spots visible on the pictures we had, so we went back down there.'

He opened another image.

'There was a line of putative blood spots leading vertically up the wall as far as we could see.'

'The killer bagged his clothes and threw them onto the roof of the chippy?'

'Exactly. The roof was flat and less than seven metres above the ground, easy if you use the handles of the carrier bag to give you a little extra swing.'

'Fantastic, can I have a look?'

'They're being processed at the moment to identify the owner, but I can show you photos.'

Another click of the mouse and several pictures of blood-soaked garments appeared on the screen. The ubiquitous England shirt and jog pants were accompanied by a blood-soaked raincoat, waterproof trousers, latex gloves and what looked like protective overshoes. A bathing cap and face mask completed the ensemble.

'I'll give them credit, they did their best to minimise the blood that they took away from the scene. The protective outer gear pretty much kept their clothes clean, there isn't much on the shirt and jog pants, but switching them for fresh clothes was a good tactic. Somebody watches *CSI*.'

Warren sighed. 'I suppose it's too much to hope the owner's mum sewed name tags inside them?'

'No such luck, I'm afraid. We've tracked down the manufacturers, but they come up as generic and popular. The shirt is a large, but that doesn't narrow it down too much. For every person who wears the correct size, there's somebody who prefers the shirt loose and baggy or who is still in denial about middle-aged spread. I wouldn't even be certain it was worn by a man. We may be able to at least link the jogging pants to the thread found attached to the Kirpan.'

'DNA?'

'We're trying to get some samples from the wearer that haven't been mixed with the victim's blood but it isn't easy. I'll let you know when we get them.' He paused. 'It could be a while.'

'Keep at it, Andy, and pass on my thanks to that eagle-eyed trainee of yours.'

'Will do.'

Leaving the room, Warren called Sutton.

'No firm ID, but we can at least say with some confidence that the clothes don't belong to Bellies Brandon.'

Chapter 75

Warren walked to the lift, excitement and caffeine competing with fatigue to give him a slightly light-headed feeling.

'DCI Jones!'

Robertson's unusually long limbs weren't designed for running – an image of a baby giraffe from an Attenborough documentary sprung to mind.

'Thank goodness I caught you. I am such a bloody idiot. Tommy Meegan's laptop; was it switched off?'

'Yes, you received it in exactly the same state we found it.'

Robertson held up a piece of paper as they started back down the corridor. The man might not be the most graceful runner, but then he didn't need to be. His long strides meant Warren struggled to keep up without breaking into a trot.

'This is the scene log. It says the laptop was found, unplugged, under a pile of magazines and old clothes in the bedroom. Did it look as though it had been used lately?'

'Well, his room was an absolute pigsty, he could have dumped the magazines on it anytime. But I'd guess he hadn't used it for a while.' Warren felt the excitement returning, the weariness banished again as they re-entered Robertson's office. 'If he's anything like Susan and I, he probably did most of his surfing on his phone.'

'I agree, in which case, there's a good chance that his computer hasn't been turned on since before the email was deleted.'

'OK.'

'Well, if he used Microsoft Outlook or something similar, then the last time he used the computer it will have synchronised his inbox. If he deleted the email on his phone it might still be on his computer if he hasn't switched it on in the meantime.'

The idea was exciting, but already Warren could foresee a string of problems, not least how to access the computer without a password.

'Piece of cake.' Robertson snatched a screwdriver up in one of his huge hands and within seconds was unscrewing the bottom of the computer. 'Again, as long as he doesn't use encryption – and most folks don't – I can simply slot the hard drive into a USB caddy and plug it into another computer. It'll read it like a USB pen drive.'

'OK, but what if he did synchronise his email after deleting it from the phone? Wouldn't it no longer be on his computer?'

'Well, if it was deleted from the computer, I could still retrieve it. Unfortunately, if he received it and deleted it whilst the computer was off it won't have synchronised and there won't be any record on the laptop.'

Chapter 76

Warren was exhausted by the time he returned to CID and he vowed to do no more than a quick circuit of the office before heading home. Checking his phone, he groaned; a text from Susan.

Looking forward to tonight, sexy man xx.

He vaguely remembered glancing at the colour-coded calendar in the kitchen that morning, but the red sticker on today's date hadn't registered.

Perhaps it would do him good? A few hours with his wife might perk him up a bit; he just hoped she wouldn't object to him having a quick nap first…

His plan was scuppered by Mags Richardson the moment he entered the office.

'Sir, the team have been looking at some of the body camera footage from the riot and we've spotted a discrepancy.'

Richardson was not easily excited.

'I'm sorry it took so long, but the material was filmed late that evening by the uniformed officers who went to The Feathers pub to break the news about Tommy to his brother and his friends.'

'What did you find? Actually, no. Just show me the images, let me see if I can spot it myself.'

Richardson placed her tablet computer on the table in front of them both,

'These are the best screenshots I have. These ones are from The Feathers.' She pointed to a slightly blurry picture of Jimmy Meegan, Marcus Davenport and Bellies Brandon sitting at a dark wooden table, its surface covered in pint glasses. Meegan and Davenport faced the camera, their mouths open. It didn't look as though they were inviting the police officer to join them in a drink.

The next picture in the sequence showed the two men getting to their feet, both pointing at the approaching officer.

Richardson swiped the screen and called up a video clip, this time from the riot itself, shortly after the police line had broken down. The far-right activists were back-to-back, swinging punches at two approaching protestors, armed with what looked like bottles, who had broken through the police line.

A moment later, the two protestors had been successfully tackled by a team of riot police, batons drawn. At this point, the BAP activists ran off the side of the screen.

Richardson paused the video and opened the next sequence of screenshots. Warren took the offered tablet and flicked forward and back between the images of the pub and close-ups of the activists as they turned tail and ran.

It took him a few moments to see it.

Susan was going to have to wait.

'We've got him.'

Chapter 77

Warren hadn't known what to expect when he'd arrived on Mary Meegan's doorstep to tell her that he was confident that her eldest son Tommy had been killed by his brother Jimmy. Denial? Grief?

In the end there had been acceptance and anger. Not a raging, shouting anger, rather a quiet fury. For the first time since meeting her, Warren wondered if the simmering hatred expressed by her sons had at least some of its origins in her side of the gene pool.

'Jimmy was always the bad 'un.' Meegan's voice was low, raspy. Her hands shook slightly as she lit a cigarette, despite being inside. It was the first time that she had acknowledged her son's depravity without caveats.

'Tommy was a thug. I know that, he got it from his father.' Her eyes flicked towards the picture above the fireplace. 'His old man was his hero. From the moment he could walk, he'd follow Ray around like a shadow.

'When he was six tried to shave his head with his dad's electric razor.' She smiled briefly. 'He couldn't see the back and so by the time he'd finished he looked like he had mange and was missing an eyebrow. Ray thought it was hilarious.' The smile vanished. 'Obviously we had to finish the job, but Ray went further and used felt tips to draw tattoos on him then took him around his mates to show him off.'

Her eyes flashed with anger. 'A six-year-old with a swastika drawn on his neck. Can you believe it? I told him it wasn't right. That it wasn't funny. But he ignored me. As usual.'

She took a long drag on her cigarette, the Family Liaison Officer deftly passing her an ashtray before the ash spilled onto the carpet.

'Thank you, Kevin.'

Her eyes turned inward for a second, as if trying to retrieve her memories.

'Tommy was just a copy of his old man. If Ray had been a better man – a nicer man – Tommy could have been a lovely boy.'

'What about Jimmy?' asked Warren, eventually.

Meegan let out a long sigh. 'He was different. He… enjoyed it.'

Her eyes were misty and Warren could tell that this was the first time she had voiced thoughts that had lain upon her mind for years.

'The hatred was always there in Jimmy. From the day he was born, he seemed angry at the world. All babies cry, but when Jimmy was hungry he seemed so furious. Even Ray was surprised sometimes. If Tommy was upset, Ray would take him for a walk in the pushchair and he'd soon be sound asleep. Not Jimmy. If anything, he'd be screaming louder when he got back than when he left.'

Stubbing out the cigarette, she fished the handkerchief from her sleeve and blew her nose.

'Jimmy was unkind to other children.' Her tone dripped with understatement.

'Both boys liked a fight – and Ray encouraged them to stick up for themselves. But Jimmy fought dirty. I remember being called in by the school when he was in reception. He'd only just

406

turned five. There'd been some sort of disagreement. Nothing major, but it had ended up in a scrap. Despite his size, it took two teachers to drag Jimmy off the boy. Thankfully, nobody was seriously hurt.' She paused. 'A few days later Jimmy got himself a lunchtime detention for damaging the other boy's work. The teacher left him alone in the classroom for a few minutes; when she came back, Jimmy had taken her extra-sharp scissors from her drawer and had cut the other little boy's brand-new coat into little pieces.'

She shook her head, her gravelly voice barely audible.

'What sort of a five-year-old can hold a grudge that long and be so devious?'

It was a hypothetical question.

'People will say that it's our fault our boys turned out the way they did. Maybe they're right.' Her eyes snapped back, her stare penetrating him. 'I know why you're here. You're here because you're going to release Jimmy's name to the press. You're hoping to stop Tommy's funeral tomorrow becoming a magnet for every hate group in Europe. And you're here because you want my help. You think that Jimmy is going to turn up on my doorstep.' She sniffed. 'You want me to betray my last remaining child.'

'Mary…' Warren wasn't sure what to say. She was right. He was there because the press release was already hitting the inboxes of reporters across the country and he didn't want her to hear news of the developments second-hand.

And she was right; maybe Jimmy Meegan would turn up on his mother's doorstep, looking for her help. Had the drugs made him that unstable? Perhaps he'd just phone his mother. Warren admitted as much.

'Tomorrow I am burying my first child.' She paused for a moment. 'My second child is as good as dead to me. If you want me to help you bury him, just give me a fucking spade.'

Friday 1st August

Chapter 78

'Well done, Warren.' Even over the speakerphone the relief in ACC Naseem's voice was palpable.

'It was a team effort between Middlesbury and colleagues in Welwyn, especially Inspector Garfield,' replied Warren modestly.

'Of course. Is he with you?'

'I'm afraid not, he's got his hands full with the Hate Crime Intelligence Unit keeping an eye on the attendees for Tommy Meegan's funeral.'

'Well, I imagine that the revelation that he was killed by his own brother has taken the shine off that somewhat.' Was that a trace of a smile in the man's voice?

'I hope so.'

The decision to release a photograph the previous night of Jimmy Meegan and reveal that he was wanted in connection with his brother's murder had been as much a political decision as a policing one. The story had been reported by the late-night news and even one or two of the more nimble morning newspapers; equally importantly it had been picked up by social media and by the time Warren met his team in his office that morning, it was already being shared widely. The impact on the day's funeral had yet to be seen.

'So Jimmy Meegan lured his brother to that alleyway where he'd already stashed some spare clothes along with the stolen Kirpan. I presume that he was also responsible for the broken CCTV camera?'

'We assume so.'

'He then stabbed him, bagged his blood-soaked clothes and switched the England shirt he'd been wearing during the riot for an identical one, before chucking the bag of clothes onto the roof of the chippy and walking cool as you please to The Feathers for a pint. That's cold.'

Warren wondered if the details of these latest cases would end up in the book that the Assistant Chief Constable was rumoured to be writing, ready for publication when he retired.

'We're still waiting for forensics to prove that he was wearing those clothes, but there is plenty of circumstantial evidence linking him to them if the DNA is too mixed to separate. Not least the fact that video footage from the day of the riot shows him picking up blood on his England shirt from punching a protestor, and those spots magically disappearing hours later in the pub when he was informed of his brother's death. Hence the receipt for two identical England shirts in his waste bin. He could claim that he got changed in The Feathers, but he plainly has no bags with him during the day and apart from a couple of very brief trips to the toilet he wouldn't have had an opportunity to swap shirts.'

'Except during that period when he was finding his way to The Feathers.'

'The jury will laugh him out of court if he tries to claim that. They'll want to know exactly why he decided to get changed, where he got his spare set of clothes from and what he did with his old ones – given that an identical shirt was found concealed near the murder scene.'

'So the motive for the killing was a response to blackmail?'

'Possibly. We won't know for sure unless Jimmy confesses, but

I think that he and Tommy had a falling out over the political direction of the party. Jimmy's neighbours reported several late-night arguments between the two men about the time that Binay Singh Mahal started talking to him. Unfortunately, they couldn't make out what was being said. I think Jimmy threatened to expose his links to Sikhs Against Jihadis, which would probably have resulted in him being ousted as leader of the party.'

'How would Jimmy know about that?'

'Well, according to Marcus Davenport, Jimmy was well known for unlocking people's phones when they left them unattended and messing about with them. He could have stumbled across the messages. Alternately, Tommy could have told him; after all, he was expecting fifty Sikhs to turn up and protest alongside them. I can't imagine he was going to simply spring that on Jimmy at the march.'

'So what about these compromising photographs?'

'I'm still waiting for confirmation from Forensic IT that they aren't just a figment of Marcus Davenport's imagination, but I suspect that Tommy confronted Jimmy about them, and used it as leverage to make him keep his mouth shut about Tommy's flirtations with Sikhs Against Jihadis.'

'Which caused Jimmy to flip.'

'Maybe flip is the wrong word, given the complexity of the plan that he hatched. It certainly wasn't some heat-of-the-moment thing. We believe he hacked his brother's phone and impersonated Binay Singh Mahal to lure Tommy down that alleyway. He also fooled Singh Mahal into going out to make a call from that phone box, so he could be mugged.'

'Why did he rope in Marcus Davenport? That seems like a bit of a weak link. You know what they say about two people being able to keep a secret as long as one of them is dead.'

'Good question. I suppose he may have been planning to bump off Davenport at some point in the future, but the main reason I think was cowardice, because for all his arrogance I doubt he has the balls to pick a fight with an unknown person on his own. And he probably knew Davenport was too frightened of him to say no.'

'Well, it all sounds pretty plausible. Keep on plugging away, and let's hope Jimmy Meegan turns up soon. We'll speak face-to-face, later, after the funeral.'

Warren thanked him and hung up, before walking out to join the rest of the team. Despite everything, there were still things bothering him.

* * *

'So we accept that Marcus Davenport took compromising photos of Jimmy Meegan, which were then somehow emailed to his brother Tommy, and that this may or may not have been a factor in Tommy's killing?'

'That seems to be about the size of it, boss,' agreed Tony Sutton.

'So the question is, who else was involved in the transmission of the photos? IT are trying to trace the route that the photos took after they left Goldie Davenport's phone but we may need to go old school on this.'

Warren wanted his team to thrash their way through all the possibilities before Davenport's potential lies coloured their judgement.

'First possibility is that there's no such person and Goldie Davenport did it all himself,' Hastings suggested.

'He would certainly have a motive,' suggested Sutton. 'He knows what a psycho Jimmy is; he could have planned the whole thing to get rid of Tommy so he could have a clear run at his missus.'

'That involves a lot of assumptions on his part,' countered Hardwick. 'Could he really be confident that Tommy would confront his brother with them and then be killed by him?'

'Maybe he wasn't planning on the killing; maybe he just wanted to destabilise the party and take over himself? That Goldie

Davenport is a lot more intelligent than we're giving him credit for, mark my words. Plus it sounds like he had the ear of both brothers. Who knows what he was whispering in them?' Hastings was unwilling to let his idea be dismissed without a fight.

'It seems a hell of a gamble,' said Warren. 'By claiming he was blackmailed, Goldie has just implicated himself in a serious racially aggravated assault. He'll probably be charged with GBH and anything else the CPS can pin on him.'

'Bellies Brandon,' suggested Hardwick. 'He was probably present when the assault took place, so he'd know all about it.'

'What's his motive?'

'See above. I reckon there's a lot more going on there than meets the eye. Again he could be angling to capitalise on any disruption and take over.'

'I can't say he ever struck me as particularly ambitious.'

'Like I said, there's more going on there. Plus, it could be the same motive as we ascribed to Goldie; give him the photos of Jimmy, get him to confront him and get rid of the man shagging his wife.'

'See above, for objections,' said Hastings, receiving a dig in the ribs for his trouble. 'Besides which, he doesn't strike me as a man who believes that revenge is a dish best served cold.'

'His little temper tantrum when the chief broke the news about his wife's affair could have been staged,' suggested Sutton. Warren winced, his shoulder twinging on cue; it certainly hadn't felt like an act.

'OK, we'll put it to him and see what he says. Who else?'

'I guess anybody else who was there the night of the assault,' said Hardwick.

'Could any of the anti-fascist crowd have found out what happened that night? I can imagine the likes of Philip Rhodri would have been ecstatic if those photos had come into their possession,' suggested Sutton.

Warren frowned. 'I agree, but I'll need some help joining the dots. How would Rhodri or somebody similar know to even blackmail Goldie into taking the photos? I can't imagine he bumped into Jimmy whilst clubbing one night, suspected he might be gay and decided it was worth a punt.'

'I'm sure if we dig hard enough on the internet there are rumours floating around about Jimmy's preferences.'

'Even then, how did he, or they, know about the assault?' asked Hastings. 'I think we can agree that Goldie isn't making that part up, he's not that daft. Rhodri, Binay Singh Mahal or anybody else in their social circles are hardly likely to have been on a night out with Goldie when the attack happened and what are the odds that Philip Rhodri, or his brethren, were a member of the football team that just happened to stumble across a lagered-up Goldie and his gang? It's too much of a coincidence.'

'I tend to agree,' stated Warren. 'However, we should make it a priority to find out who was there that night. I think the paperwork accompanying the victim's statement listed his team mates and their girlfriends. Let's see if there are any interesting names. We'll re-interview Bellies Brandon and Goldie Davenport and see if they can make any suggestions. We should also try Philip Rhodri, seeing as he's so cooperative at the moment. And Binay Singh Mahal, for what it's worth.'

It had been some days since the last confirmed sighting of Jimmy Meegan and Warren was impatient to have him in custody so that he could be charged and the whole sordid affair finished. In the meantime though, the funeral of Tommy Meegan was only hours away and Warren was as nervous as everyone else about what lay in store.

Chapter 79

The scale of the security surrounding the funeral of Tommy Meegan rivalled that seen on match days; somewhat ironic given the man's convictions for football hooliganism. However, in the end it was unnecessary.

'It really took the wind out of the far-right's sails when they found out Tommy Meegan was killed by his own bloody brother. Apart from his old dear, the crematorium was empty. As for his status as a cause célèbre, my colleagues in the Social Media Intelligence Unit report lots of activity overnight,' said Garfield. He sounded jubilant, as he filled in Warren, Sutton, Grayson and ACC Naseem.

'The BAP looks as though it's dead in the water, with as many factions as they have members, whilst the rest of the three-letter acronym groups are scrabbling to disassociate themselves from the shitstorm. Intelligence had suggested that as many as thirty members of continental race hate groups were headed our way, but our colleagues at Dover report that none of them arrived in the end.'

'How is the search for Jimmy Meegan going?' asked Naseem.

'Early days, sir,' replied Warren, 'but we're confident. He's burnt a lot of bridges within the far-right community; these guys might fight like a sack full of rats, but Tommy Meegan was one of their own and it's doubtful Jimmy'll get a warm reception if he turns up asking for help. We're questioning all of his acquaintances again and we've even spoken to his mum, although from what I've seen, she's so angry she'll be calling us, not the other way around. He hasn't made any large cash withdrawals recently, so unless he finds a source of funding, he'll soon be skint.'

'Good work, keep at it. The sooner this bastard is locked up, the better. In the meantime, I shall be trying to repair some of the damage done to the local community.'

Unsurprisingly, the most senior Muslim police officer in the county had taken charge of rebuilding relationships. He'd already made a discreet visit to Imam Mehmud and passed on his condolences and best wishes to his family. Warren wished him luck.

There had already been some positive developments, even before the afternoon's much publicised meeting between the Muslim Council of Britain and Sikh Council UK. Local Sikh business owners, horrified at the actions of Binay Singh Mahal, had pledged several thousand pounds to help repair the damage to the Islamic Centre. A working party of young Sikh men had scrubbed the graffiti from the memorial that morning. Meanwhile, a local church had cleared out its under-used hall and invited Imam Mehmud to use it for as long as necessary. Numerous local councillors – including a prominent Jewish businesswoman – had pledged their unqualified support for the new mosque and community centre.

To think for one moment that the simmering tensions between the local communities could be solved overnight would be naive, but Warren couldn't help feeling optimistic for the future of his adopted town. And the irony that the hateful actions of a few might – in the long term – lead to less distrust between the people they tried to drive a wedge between made Warren feel better than he had in days.

Making their excuses, Warren and Sutton left Grayson's office.

'Sirs, can we have a word?'

Gary Hastings and Karen Hardwick looked nervous.

'We've got some news.'

* * *

With a loud ping, the champagne cork bounced off the light strip and everybody assembled in CID cheered. You could say what you like about DSI Grayson, mused Warren, but he was always generous. He'd sent his PA off to find three bottles of fizzy plonk and a huge engagement card in the half-hour since Hastings and Hardwick had shyly made their announcement and he was now busy filling polystyrene cups.

Warren looked around the room and smiled. The atmosphere had been heavy over the last few days, and the stresses and strains of his and Susan's repeated disappointments had robbed him of much of his own good humour. The brief respite would do the team good.

He glanced over to the far corner, where Hardwick was excitedly showing off her new ring to some of the support workers. To his left, Hastings was being teased by a couple of DCs from Welwyn.

'Pregnant is she, Gary? Did her old man march you at gunpoint to the jeweller's?'

Fortunately, Tony Sutton stepped in to spare the young officer his blushes.

'Well if she is, Johnno, at least we'll know he isn't shooting blanks like you.'

As the others laughed, Warren felt an irrational tide of shame wash over him again. *Stop it*, he admonished himself. Nevertheless, the mood was gone and after shaking Hastings' hand once more and giving Hardwick a peck on the cheek, he downed his wine and slipped back to his office.

To Warren's relief, his phone rang just as he stepped over the threshold, giving him the perfect opportunity to kick the office door closed behind him.

'We found the photos.'

Pete Robertson's voice was weary.

'A single email received by Tommy Meegan on the twenty-eighth of June, with a half-dozen photos of varying quality, showing what is unmistakably Jimmy Meegan enjoying fellatio from an unknown male.'

'Brilliant work, Pete. Have you managed to tell anything from the email?'

'Quite a few things. First, it was an anonymous Hotmail account, and the received email with the images wasn't forwarded. My guess is the photographer emailed them to one address and then the photos were copied into a new email by the recipient to obscure the original sender. There was no message other than the photos, and the subject line was "Family Photos".'

'At least the sender had a sense of humour.'

'Quite. I've stripped the headers from the new email and we're tracing it to see if we can work out where it was sent from. It won't take long. If you're lucky that might give you a clue as to the sender's identity.'

'That's great news, Pete.'

'There's more. It looks as though we can confirm the photographer was Mr Davenport.'

'How did you figure that out?'

Robertson sounded slightly smug. 'I looked at the photos' Exif headers.'

'You've gone techno on me again.'

'When a digital camera takes a photo it records lots of additional information in a part of the file called the Exif header.'

'Including the identity of the photographer?'

'Alas, rarely is it that simple. However, it does record the make of camera and this matches Mr Davenport's phone.'

420

'That's good, but that model is one of the most popular phones on the market.'

'True. But the header also records the photograph's precise time and location, if the phone's GPS and location tracking is enabled. These pictures were taken in a car park around the corner from one of Basildon's most popular gay bars at half past eleven on Saturday, 21 June. According to the location log on the phone and cell tower record, Mr Davenport's phone was within a few metres of that position at that time.'

* * *

Warren rubbed his eyes with his knuckles. It had been a long day, but Pete Robertson had been as good as his word, sending over the location that the email containing the photos had been forwarded from as soon as he had it. Hopefully, that would help answer at least one of the remaining unanswered questions – namely who had been responsible for sending the photographs of Jimmy Meegan to his brother? He'd send Gary Hastings down to secure evidence from the internet café used by the mysterious sender tomorrow. In the meantime, the most important question of who had killed Tommy Meegan had been answered, as far as Warren was concerned.

The problem was that nobody had seen Jimmy Meegan recently. His absence from his brother's funeral had all but confirmed what they already knew and social media chatter indicated that it had also laid to rest any doubts about his guilt within the far-right community. Did any of those people remain loyal to Meegan? Would any still harbour him, hiding him from the police, either because they agreed with what he'd done or just because?

It had been a hard few weeks and now that the case had become a manhunt, handled by specialist teams, Warren had taken the opportunity to send all but a skeleton team home for a decent night's rest. He'd been tempted to go himself – he was as tired as anyone and he knew Susan was waiting – but if he didn't take the opportunity to shift at least some of the paperwork that had been multiplying like bacteria on a Petri dish, he'd regret it.

Over in the corner, Karen Hardwick and Gary Hastings were pretending to be busy, although Hardwick's giggles suggested that whatever they were looking at on her phone wasn't entirely work related. He considered sending the two of them home also, but he didn't want to be caught under-staffed should the phones suddenly start going. And God knew, they'd be needing the overtime pay soon enough.

As if on cue, the phone warbled. An internal call.

'DCI Jones.'

The caller was the main switchboard.

'Sir, I have a Mary Meegan on the phone, she says it's urgent.'

Mary Meegan's voice was gravelly, the product of too many cigarettes, too little sleep and who knew how many tears, although from what he had seen of the woman, Warren suspected that they had been shed out of sight of the Family Liaison Officer.

'I think I know where Jimmy is.'

'Where?'

'I need to speak to you. I need to explain.'

'OK, Mary, are you at home right now?'

'Yes. Please come quickly.'

Warren grabbed his jacket. As he recalled, Hastings had developed something of a rapport with the old lady.

'Gary, you're with me. Karen, I want you ready to coordinate with everyone else in case we have to move quickly.'

Chapter 80

Hastings was on a high as they drove towards Mary Meegan's flat.

'I know it's old-fashioned, but I was really worried when Karen told me she was pregnant. Obviously, there's the money and all that but my biggest fear is what my mum and dad are going to say.'

Warren grunted politely and focused on his driving.

'The thing is they are quite old-fashioned. They love Karen to bits, but they weren't overly thrilled when we moved in together. Mum dropped several hints that Karen should have a ring on her finger by now.'

Warren nodded encouragingly; truth be told Hastings' predicament was a little too close to home for him. Nevertheless, as far as he knew, only he and Tony Sutton were aware of the pregnancy – it didn't sound as if they'd told their parents yet. The least he could do was let the lad sound off a little.

Hastings' next sentence confirmed it.

'Well, we're having a bit of a family get-together for Karen's mum's sixtieth next weekend. Both our parents will be going. At least if she turns up with an engagement ring, it'll soften the blow slightly.'

Warren looked over at the young DC, his eyes narrowed slightly.

'Gary, it's none of my business, but are you sure a shotgun wedding is the best reason to get married? It's a big commitment and you could probably put the money towards looking after the baby.'

Hastings sounded offended. 'Is that what people are going to think? I've been planning on proposing to Karen for months. That's why we went to Paris. I even had the ring wrapped in a sock with a note telling anyone doing a bag search to be discreet. Unfortunately, she was so ill, I decided to wait until our next holiday. I wanted the most vivid memory of the trip to be me on my knees proposing, not Karen on her knees in front of the toilet.'

Warren smiled slightly. 'Fair enough.'

'Anyhow, that was the plan. Then Karen said she was pregnant and I figured that's probably put the kibosh on going on holiday for a while, so I decided "sod it", no time like the present. Besides my parents have said they would be willing to pay for any wedding, so we don't need to worry about that.'

'You old romantic. I hope you asked her more nicely than that.'

Hastings laughed. 'Well, yeah. I knew what I wanted to say and Karen let me finish before she said yes, so that worked pretty well.'

'Good, I'm pleased for you both.'

'Thanks, sir.'

He leant back in his seat slightly and became more thoughtful.

'You know, it's amazing how finding out you're going to be a dad changes things. A few days ago, the biggest stress in my life was selection followed closely by how much our rent has gone up and whether we could ever afford a deposit for a house. But now everything is different.'

He looked a bit ashamed. 'I have to confess, I made a bit of a mess of it when she announced it. For a few moments, I thought "Shit, how are we going to afford a baby."'

'Please tell me you didn't say that?'

'Umm, not in so many words, no.'

Warren closed his eyes briefly. 'Bloody hell, Gary. And you still managed to get her to say yes when you proposed?'

Hastings chuckled. 'Yeah. How lucky am I?'

'She's a remarkable woman, Gary. I'd have been sleeping on the couch for a week.'

Hastings laughed in agreement. 'It was heading that way.'

He sighed, and looked out of the window. 'It's crazy I know, but we were in bed the other night using the iPad to look up baby names.' He laughed. 'We won't even know if it's a boy or a girl for months yet.'

'We're here,' interrupted Warren as they swung into the Chequers estate.

As always, most of the parking spaces were occupied either with residents' cars or rubbish. Warren parked in the only space available, flanked either side by a rusting washing machine and a badly ripped armchair.

Warren wondered if he could keep an eye on the car whilst they spoke to Mary Meegan, given that they were parked exactly below her balcony.

Hastings' phone rang. He glanced at the screen and blushed. 'Karen. I'll tell her to call back.'

'No, take it, it might be important.' Warren smiled tightly. 'She probably has cravings for pickled gherkins or something.'

Opening the door, he climbed out. If he was honest, he was glad for a moment's respite. Hastings was like a child waiting for Christmas, and whilst Warren was genuinely happy for the lad, his excitement just seemed to underscore his own personal frustrations. The very thought that news of a pregnancy could be met with anything other than absolute joy – not to mention relief – was unimaginable to Warren right now.

The sound of the massive earthenware plant pot smashing through the windscreen at the end of its ten-storey flight was like a bomb going off. Warren turned back towards the car in horror.

A barely coherent scream from above him broke his trance state and he looked up.

'Fucking pigs!'

Jimmy Meegan stood on his mother's balcony. Stripped to the waist, he wore only a pair of white, nylon shorts.

Warren threw himself backwards, as the second plant pot arced its way through the air towards him. He covered his face as a shower of stinging shards exploded around him. Looking back up, he saw Jimmy Meegan retreating back into the flat.

Scrambling back to his feet, Warren pulled the driver's door open. The inside of the car was awash with blood, mingled with soil, the remains of the windscreen surrounding the heavy container. Warren grabbed the car's radio. 'Code Zero. Urgent medical assistance required. Chequers estate. Officer down.'

Warren reached out and took Hastings' hand. On the seat beside him, Hastings' mobile phone remained on.

'Gary? What's happening, Gary? Are you all right, Gary?'

Hardwick's voice was getting louder, a note of hysteria creeping in.

Warren picked it up. He had no idea what to say.

Chapter 81

Warren knew he shouldn't stay in the car. Jimmy Meegan had disappeared back into his mother's flat. There had been two bonsai trees, but who knew what else he could hurl off the balcony? But he couldn't bring himself to move. The wail of sirens started in the distance. First one, then two, within seconds it seemed as if every patrol car in Hertfordshire was racing towards them. Code Zero. Officer down. Drop everything and get there as soon as possible.

But it didn't matter how fast they arrived. They were too late. They'd been too late the second the plant pot had all but removed Gary Hastings' head from his shoulders. Now all Warren could do was hold his hand and sit guard over his friend, keeping him safe from any further indignities.

* * *

Warren didn't need the paramedic to tell him he was in shock. He felt numb, his head was mushy. Nothing seemed to make sense. At some point they'd forced him to let go of Hastings' hand and moved him to the back step of the ambulance. Somebody else had put a blanket around his shoulders.

427

'Sir, your blood pressure is dangerously low. You really need to come with us to hospital.'

It was at least the third time somebody had said this to him. It could have been the same person, he had no idea.

'Not until it's over,' he repeated.

Exactly what that meant, he didn't really know. All he knew was that he couldn't leave yet.

How much time had passed since he'd heard that deafening crash and turned to see the remains of Gary Hastings, Warren couldn't say. Minutes? Hours? At some point, it had gone dark.

Warren looked across the estate. A hastily erected cordon kept the rubberneckers a reasonable distance away, the LEDs from their cameraphones twinkling like some sort of high-tech constellation.

Warren felt a flash of anger and he surged to his feet. Why hadn't they erected a tent? It was a crime scene with a victim, there should be screens preserving Hastings' modesty, giving him privacy. He wanted to wade into the crowds of onlookers, smashing their phones, deleting the images that he knew would be spreading across social media like a cancer.

The wave of dizziness had him sitting back down before the paramedic could react.

Warren waved her away.

A sudden whoop split the air and the barricade shifted out of the way to let a riot van through. A mixture of cheers and boos erupted from the crowd, as if the whole spectacle had been staged for their amusement, like some sort of macabre pantomime.

No sooner had the van pulled to a stop its doors opened, disgorging its occupants. Black-clad and grim-faced they lined up, all of them wearing utility belts with Tasers. Two also had assault rifles; they weren't taking any chances. Warren recognised Sergeant Roger Gibson, the forced entry specialist. The design of each tower block was essentially the same and his familiarity with their layout from the Binay Singh Mahal arrest would greatly speed up planning.

'Get those vultures back.' Warren recognised the angry clipped tones of DSI John Grayson. 'The last thing we want is somebody getting shot.' His tone suggested otherwise.

Warren had no idea when he'd arrived.

'Jesus, Warren.'

'None of it's his.'

Grayson and the paramedic were talking over him as if he wasn't there.

'Mary's still in there and the FLO.' The memory returned in a flash. Her voice had been low, fearful. Her son must have been in the room with her, making her speak. Making her lure the two officers in.

'Say again?' Grayson turned to Warren.

'Mary Meegan. She phoned us. Told us she had information about Jimmy's whereabouts. On her landline…'

'Bitch.'

Warren shook his head, ignoring the waves of nausea.

'No. I think he's holding her prisoner.'

'Shit.'

Grayson called over to Gibson. 'There may be two other people in the flat, an FLO and an older lady. She may be in on it, or she may be a hostage.'

'Understood.' Gibson turned back to his men, issuing new instructions.

* * *

Gibson and his team entered via the rear entrance of the tower block, out of sight of the Meegans' balcony. Teams of officers had already covered the nine floors beneath the Meegans', evacuating those residents that could manage the stairs and making certain that the less mobile stayed out of harm's way.

The whereabouts of Tommy Meegan's homicidal younger brother were unknown. Spotters with binoculars reported that he'd drawn the curtains and turned off the lights. They had no idea if he was even in the flat. Nobody had yet clapped eyes on Mary Meegan.

429

By now, Warren was starting to feel more connected to reality. 'What's happening?'

Tony Sutton's voice was tight at the end of the line. Warren filled him in as much as he could, aware that his sentences were disjointed and that he kept on repeating himself.

'Where's Karen?' he finished.

'She's with the surgeon, he's given her something. She collapsed and we thought it best under the circumstances to call the doctor.'

The circumstances. He meant the pregnancy. The child who would be fatherless before he or she was even born.

'Keep her safe, Tony.' It was all Warren could think to say; keep her safe the way I couldn't keep Gary safe.

Next to him, DSI Grayson's radio burst into life. It was one of the spotters with the binoculars.

'Fire. There's fire in the apartment.'

'Confirmed. That's fire at the window.' A second spotter jumped on the airwaves, her voice tense.

Warren looked up, an orange glow was now radiating out of the previously darkened window.

'Shit, evacuate all remaining residents,' Grayson ordered.

Warren strained his eyes. Even at this distance he could see the flames licking at the curtains. Suddenly they burst open and a figure stumbled out. Silhouetted against the fiery background, Warren could clearly see that it was a man, stripped to the waist.

The crowd cheered, like spectators at a sporting event. Jimmy Meegan stepped forward to the metal railing surrounding the balcony and started to climb.

The shouts of the crowd were all but drowning out Meegan's defiant screams. The cheap nylon of his football shorts caught alight, engulfing him in flames. The crowd screamed – whether in shock or delight, Warren couldn't tell.

Raising his arms, as if to take a last salute, Meegan took one final step into oblivion.

Saturday 2nd August

Chapter 82

Nine a.m. and the atmosphere in CID was oppressive. There had been a steady stream of colleagues, many off-duty, coming in to see if there was anything they could do.

Anything at all.

DSI Grayson had given up trying to persuade Warren to go home after he'd finally been given the all-clear by the hospital.

Despite himself, Warren found himself staring out of his office window towards the desk Gary Hastings had sat at since before Warren had moved to Middlesbury. A lone bottle of champagne sat forlornly on the table, next to a large congratulations card. Before anyone else took that seat he would have to tidy them away. What the hell would he do with them? He could hardly give them to Karen Hardwick, could he?

A quiet tap at the door disturbed Warren's reverie.

'I've just been to see PC Lederer.'

Warren must have looked blank.

'Kevin Lederer, Mary Meegan's Family Liaison Officer,' Sutton supplied. 'The details of what happened are a bit sketchy, but it seems the poor bastard was using the bathroom when Jimmy Meegan forced his way into the flat. He walked straight out of the toilet and straight into Jimmy's fist. For what it's worth, he doesn't think that Jimmy planned on killing his mum, he just wanted somewhere to lay low. But it all went tits up and escalated rapidly.'

Warren said nothing; it really wasn't worth anything. Sutton continued, regardless.

'Lederer's memories are a bit patchy, he hit his head on the way down, but he reckons Jimmy had no idea that his mother knew he'd killed his brother. God knows where he'd been for the past forty-eight hours.

'Anyway, Mary tore into him, screaming and calling him a murderer.' Sutton's mouth twisted. 'I'm sure the neighbours heard everything, but they aren't the sort to report these things to the police.'

The importance of his words hung in the air; perhaps if the neighbours had reported the violence from the flat next door, somebody would have called the Family Liaison Officer to check everything was OK. Perhaps Gary Hastings would be sitting at the desk next to his fiancée, not lying on a mortuary slab...

'When Jimmy realised that his mum wasn't going to help him, and didn't have any money lying about the place, he lost it and started smashing things up. She told him it was all over and if he was a real man, he'd give himself up and take it on the chin.' Sutton winced slightly. 'I guess she must have hit a nerve. Not her fault, she didn't know.'

Warren rubbed his eyes wearily. Everything they'd uncovered about Jimmy Meegan's private life suggested a man deeply conflicted about his true self; a closeted gay man trapped in an organisation that condemned him as a pervert and half a man, making his sexuality the butt of jokes, innuendo and insults. Hiding in plain sight, he'd worn his convictions for assault against homosexuals like a shield, using them to deflect rumours and allegations. Yet despite his best efforts, he'd been unable to entirely stifle his urges. Warren could only imagine the fury he must have felt when his brother confronted him with the photographs.

It was a wonder he hadn't killed Tommy there and then; that he'd waited so long before hatching his plan. But then Warren thought back to Mary Meegan's story about how he'd held a grudge against the little boy he'd fought in the playground all those years ago. Perhaps it wasn't such a surprise.

Warren shuddered; a conflicted, violent man, filled with hate and fuelled with drugs, but with the patience and deviousness to bide his time and plot his revenge. Jimmy Meegan was so much more than the violent knuckle-dragger he'd been dismissed as.

'So he decided to go out in a blaze of glory?'

'Seems so. Apparently, he did a line of coke right there on the coffee table. His mum objected and got a punch for her trouble.' Sutton looked pained.

'Go on.'

'He was mumbling something about "taking that bastard Jones" with him. That was when he told his mum to call you and get you to come over. She refused, even after he slapped her around a few times.' He paused. 'She was a brave woman.

'In the end, Jimmy realised that he couldn't beat her into doing what he wanted, so he fetched a knife from the kitchen and threatened to stab PC Lederer. That was when she folded and called you.'

Warren closed his eyes. He'd replayed the recording of her phone call a dozen times. Her voice had been grumbly. Had that been a note of fear? What was that sound, just audible in the background with the volume turned up to maximum? He remembered the thrill of excitement as she'd asked him to come around. Was that why he'd raced around there without back up? Should he have asked to speak to the Family Liaison Officer first?

Warren was too tired to hide his thoughts from his friend.

'I've heard the recording, Warren. Nothing out of the ordinary, nothing to suggest he was with her. Why would you have called ahead?'

Warren said nothing, not trusting himself to speak.

'After she'd phoned you, Jimmy tied his mum to the chair and stabbed PC Lederer. Obviously the wound wasn't fatal, but there was plenty of blood and the lad had enough sense about him to play dead. Jimmy went out on the balcony and Lederer said he heard a loud scraping noise, I guess he must have been lining up those big plant pots. Then he left the flat for a few minutes. Presumably that's when he moved that discarded furniture around to make sure you parked directly beneath the flat window.'

Sutton paused, struggling briefly to keep his composure.

'He was a wanted man, with blood staining his shirt, dragging old furniture around the parking area in broad daylight, and not one person picked up the phone.'

He took a deep breath.

'Lederer reckoned Jimmy mustn't have tied Mary up properly, but she wasn't quick enough to escape. He came through the door seconds too early.' Sutton sighed. 'It's all guesswork from here in; whether or not he was planning to kill himself in the end is anyone's guess. Either way, he stabbed his mother and the rest we know.'

* * *

Warren's phone rang. 'It's your wife, sir.'

Suddenly the thought of going home to his wife's comforting embrace was the one thing he wanted most in the world. But he couldn't. There was too much to do. Wasn't there? He looked through the window again. Tony Sutton sat grim-faced back at his desk, looking as if he couldn't decide whether to hit something or to cry; beside him, David Hutchinson was thumping away at his computer keyboard, keeping himself busy, needing to feel as if he was doing something.

'Tell her I'll be home as soon as I can.'

'Umm, she's already on her way up.'

* * *

Susan finally succeeded where others hadn't and after a half-hearted argument had driven Warren home to bed, where despite everything he had passed out within minutes of arriving.

It hadn't lasted long though, and despite Susan's protestations he'd been back at his desk by early afternoon, if not rested, then at least able to function again.

The phone rang and Warren snatched it up, eager for a distraction.

'I had a feeling you'd be at your desk. I don't suppose it's worth telling you to go home?' Professor Jordan was hardly in a position to talk; Warren knew for a fact that he'd been in the morgue since the night before.

'What have you got, Ryan?'

He heard the shuffling of papers down the phone. 'I have preliminary findings for all three of the deceased.'

The American's cool clinical tones were a balm, helping Warren to detach himself from the news he was receiving.

'I'll give you the highlights then email you the remainder of the report. First, Mary Meegan: I believe it likely that she was dead from a stab wound to the heart before she had the chance to inhale significant amounts of smoke. The pattern of the cut matches the blade of a bloodied kitchen knife retrieved from Mr Meegan's body.

'As for Mr Meegan, immediate cause of death was massive trauma to the cranium consistent with a fall of several storeys, head first. There were also fresh, second-degree burns to his lower body, both pre- and post-mortem, caused by the melting of nylon football shorts.'

Warren hoped with every fibre of his being that Jimmy

437

Meegan's last few moments had been filled with excruciating pain.

'A presumptive test on residue inside Mr Meegan's nostrils was positive for cocaine. Damage to the septum of his nose and an abnormally fatty liver indicate long-term drug and alcohol abuse.'

'What about Gary?'

Jordan's professional façade slipped slightly.

'Cause of death was significant trauma, consistent with a high velocity impact by a large, heavy object.' He cleared his throat. 'In my opinion, he died instantly. There was nothing you could have done, Warren.'

Warren thanked him and hung up.

'Nothing I could have done,' he repeated quietly.

If only he could believe that.

Chapter 83

Warren had to get out of the office. No matter how he positioned his chair, he could still see Hastings' empty desk through the window. Going home again was out of the question. What would he do? Watch TV? Read a book? Make small talk with his wife? He had to feel that he was accomplishing something, no matter how small.

Pete Robertson's report from the previous evening sat in his inbox; he'd been going to ask Gary to follow up on it. Ignoring the fresh surge of emotion, he forced himself to open it.

The person that had coerced Goldie Davenport into taking the explosive pictures and then sent them in an email to Tommy Meegan had been the catalyst for the whole affair. Warren felt certain that Tommy had confronted Jimmy over the images and the result had been catastrophic. Jimmy Meegan had ended up killing his own brother. Had that been the aim of the sender? Regardless of the blackmailer's intentions – or their culpability in the eyes of the law – the result had been the death of Tommy Meegan and the complete unravelling of Jimmy Meegan's already dangerously unstable mind. And ultimately the death of Gary Hastings.

Warren was in no doubt; the blood that had covered Warren's

hands as he sat next to the body of his friend and colleague also stained the blackmailer's.

Looking through the window, he could see Tony Sutton. The older man was leaning back in his chair, staring into space, his back to Hastings' desk. He looked as broken as Warren felt. Sutton had been at Middlesbury for years before Warren's arrival. Despite his sometimes rough exterior, he'd spoken on more than one occasion of the pleasure he got from mentoring junior colleagues. His calm, dispassionate demeanour as he'd finally persuaded Warren to leave the scene of Hastings' murder had broken as soon as they had returned to CID. When he'd returned from the bathroom, his eyes were reddened and his voice gruff.

Warren clambered to his feet, a renewed sense of purpose manifesting itself as a sudden surge of energy. Taking one last swig of the cold coffee next to the computer, he grabbed his suit jacket.

'Tony, get your car keys. Let's wrap this up.'

* * *

The trip down the A1 took barely thirty minutes. Neither man said a word, the silence eloquent in its own way.

According to Pete Robertson, the email had been sent from a computer situated in an internet café. Even in these days of a smartphone in every pocket, free public WiFi and cheap home broadband, more than half of the twenty PCs were occupied.

An expensive-looking coffee machine and a chiller cabinet kept the clientele watered, fed and caffeinated. Warren sniffed appreciatively at the air, but his hands were already shaking slightly and he didn't think any more coffee would be a good idea.

The middle-aged man behind the counter was so engrossed in his smartphone that Sutton had to clear his throat twice to get his attention. He didn't even attempt to hide his irritation at the interruption.

Warren flashed his warrant card. 'I'd like to speak to the owner, please.'

The man's expression didn't change. 'Yes.'

'We're trying to identify a customer that we believe used your premises a few weeks ago.'

'Got a warrant?'

'No, is that a problem?'

'I value my customers' privacy.'

The man's arrogance grated on Warren's nerves and he forced himself to breathe deeply before he responded. Beside him, he could feel Sutton shifting.

'I can get a warrant if necessary, but that will take time and I would appreciate it if you can help us now,' said Warren.

'No can do. It's against policy.'

Sutton leaned over the desk and Warren braced himself; he'd felt Sutton's anger radiating off him all the way down.

To his surprise, Sutton's tone was calm, his voice low as if imparting confidential information that he didn't want anyone to overhear.

'We understand that, sir. However, time is of the essence. We believe the person used your premises to send images which are of interest to a major, ongoing investigation. I'm sure that the last thing you want is for your business to be associated with such… unpleasantness.'

The man stared at him for a moment, before his eyes widened slightly.

'My God,' he whispered. 'I would never… I mean, we don't monitor our customers' usage. We have filters obviously to block those sorts of sites and of course we'd report anyone who you know…' The man was starting to flap and Warren silently applauded Sutton's skill; he'd merely let the man's imagination do all the work.

Suddenly the man couldn't be more helpful.

Warren passed over a heavily redacted copy of the report from Pete Robertson. 'Is this your IP address?'

The man fished a pair of small reading glasses from his pocket and squinted at the sequence of digits. He nodded.

'Would you be able to tell me which computer the person was using?'

'No, that IP address serves the whole café.'

'Would you be able to tell me the names of the customers that were using the café at the time the email was sent?'

The man thought for a moment. 'Maybe. These days a lot of people pay by card. I might have a record of that.'

He turned to his computer and clicked the mouse a few times.

'Here we are. Twelve of the computers were in use at the time. Seven were paid for by credit card and the rest cash. Before you ask, no we don't keep a list of names for the people who pay money.'

'But you have the credit card numbers?'

'Partials, but I'm sure the bank can confirm them.'

Warren made a note to get Hastings to chase that lead, before remembering why they were there. He pushed away the fresh surge of grief. It was unlikely that their blackmailer had used a credit card.

'Do you have CCTV?' asked Sutton.

'Of course.' The owner gestured towards a rather ostentatious ceiling camera in the far corner slowly panning across the room. It was mounted so that it could see the faces of everyone sitting at a computer, but not what was displayed on their screens. He licked his lips and leant forward, lowering his voice to a whisper. 'That's just for show, the real one is above the front door.'

'We'll need to see the footage from this date.'

* * *

The images on the screen were full colour, but poor quality. None of the faces of the customers already present in the café eight minutes before the email was sent were familiar and Warren worried that the individual who physically sent the email might not be their actual target. If the blackmailer had gone to all the trouble of using an internet café, stripping the images from one anonymous email and copying them to a new, anonymous message, they might have been careful enough to pay a stranger to do their dirty work for them.

The person just entering the café wore a shapeless hoody with a baseball cap pulled low. Aware of the ceiling camera, they took care to conceal their face as they paid cash to the bored owner. Head bowed, the new target walked briskly to a PC in the furthest corner, turning the chair slightly, to avoid facing the ceiling camera – and in so doing looked straight at the hidden doorway camera.

'Bastard,' breathed Sutton.

Chapter 84

'Why did you do it?'

The other man said nothing, staring into the distance. He was no fool. He knew it was over. The moment Warren and Sutton had appeared at his door it must have been obvious.

'Do what?'

'Don't play me for a fool.'

The conversation should have been taking place in an interview room under caution, legal representation present at the very least. But he'd said he wanted to speak to Warren privately, that he wanted an opportunity to set the record straight before he cooperated fully.

Sutton disagreed, but Warren overruled him.

'I thought I could finish them off.' The man's voice was bitter.

'Who, the BAP?'

He nodded. 'I thought I had what I needed. Everything necessary to take the bastards down. To rip them apart.' His tone was clipped, and for the first time since they'd started speaking, he made eye contact with Warren.

'Why? What was so special about the BAP that you had to take such a risk?'

'They were different.' His eyes searched Warren's. 'Tommy Meegan was different.'

'How?'

'He was clever. Old school racism won't get you supporters beyond the usual idiots and inbreds; they're a dying breed, they're marginalised. The battle isn't won, but these guys will just disappear eventually.

'Meegan understood this. That's why he was shifting their focus, following the trend. He knew that Islamophobia struck a chord with a broader swathe of the public and that he could use it as a smokescreen for other, more violent, activities. The party faithful largely accepted that – you've heard them speak, if you didn't know better you'd think it was all about Islam. But scratch the surface and they haven't changed. They're as dangerous as before. More so in fact.'

'So you decided to take him out.'

'No! That was never the plan.' His tone turned imploring. 'You have to believe me.'

'Convince me.' Warren's tone was flat; no hint of a compromise.

'The BAP was already straining at the seams. Tommy was their leader, but many didn't agree with the path he was following and felt that they were being sold out. They didn't have the patience to play the long game. Lots of their supporters had defected from other organisations precisely because they were getting too political and many felt that Tommy Meegan was starting to go down that route. Openly sharing Facebook posts from non-white anti-Muslim groups because they advanced the cause was a betrayal to some. Tommy believed in the old saying "the enemy of my enemy is my friend". Not everyone in the BAP was that nuanced.'

'Including Jimmy?'

'Yeah. Apparently Tommy had tried to make him see sense; to persuade him that to survive they had to look to the future. But he was definitely old school. It all got pretty nasty. Besides, Jimmy had always been a bit of a nutter, and the Colombian marching powder was making him even worse.'

'So why not just let them tear themselves apart?'

'It wasn't enough. If we'd left them to it, the BAP might have split, but there was no guarantee. We've seen it before, loads of times. These groups are always fragmenting and merging; it's why there are hardly any good acronyms left.'

Warren ignored the weak attempt at levity.

'What was needed was a way to destroy their credibility in the eyes of their followers, otherwise they'd just go and form a new party and we'd be back to square one. If Tommy's flirtation with Sikhs Against Jihadis became public knowledge it would have left him high and dry, but then Jimmy would be in the driving seat, and nobody wanted that.'

'So what did you do?' Warren wanted his version of events.

'I came across some incriminating photos of Jimmy.'

'Where from? What was the source?'

'An anonymous email.'

'What were the photographs?'

'You've seen them.'

'Jimmy's gay.'

'Yeah, you know the sort, "the man he doth protest too much". The BAP might not be campaigning overtly against homosexuals at the moment, but they still hate them. I figured that if Tommy knew Jimmy was gay, he'd use it to discredit him, then both factions of the BAP would collapse.'

Warren was incredulous.

'Or they could come to some sort of détente; they both know each other's dirty little secrets and it binds them together and makes them even stronger.'

The man looked down at his feet, his cheeks colouring. 'I misjudged them. I thought they hated each other too much for that to happen.'

'No, you misjudged one of them. You were right about Jimmy's hatred but you underestimated Tommy. Tommy proposed a truce. He blackmailed Jimmy into keeping quiet about Tommy's conspiracy with Sikhs Against Jihadis, by promising not to say anything about the photographs. But that just gave Jimmy two reasons to hate his brother.' Warren locked eyes with him. 'You signed Tommy Meegan's death warrant the moment that you sent him those photos and, in the process, you almost started a bloody race war. If word had got out about that Kirpan being the murder weapon, every gurdwara in the country could have been at risk.'

The man opposite said nothing. What could he say?

'And you signed Gary Hastings' death warrant at the same time.'

It was the first time Warren had said it out loud.

For the first time there was fire in the voice of the man opposite him. 'No, that's not fair. There was the no way I could have seen that coming.'

'That's the whole fucking point!' Suddenly Warren was yelling. 'You threw a bloody hand grenade into a crowded room and now you're claiming all the unintended consequences were just collateral damage? It doesn't work that way. You don't get to sidestep your responsibility for what happened the way you've been sidestepping all the other rules.'

'Oh, get off your fucking high horse, Warren. What rules were you following when you raced around to Mary Meegan's flat without back up? Her son, a known killer and coke-head, is on the loose with nowhere else to go and you don't think for one second that he might be waiting for you? Why didn't you call the Family Liaison Officer that's been posted there all week?' He mimicked picking up a telephone handset. 'Hello? Is that the FLO? You haven't seen that fucking psycho Jimmy, have you? Do you reckon I should bring an armed unit around?' His lip curled. 'The death of that lad is at least as much your responsibility as mine.'

It was as if the man had clambered inside Warren's head and taken the voice that hadn't stopped whispering since yesterday and run it through a loudspeaker. Warren felt himself recoil physically, he leant back against the wall, not trusting his legs to bear his weight.

'I'm sorry. That was a low blow. I didn't mean it.'

Whether he'd meant it or not, it didn't matter. The sentiment was out there and could never be taken back.

Warren had heard enough. He no longer trusted himself to speak. He no longer trusted himself not to hit the man. And keep on hitting him.

'Inspector Theodore Garfield, you are under arrest…'

Monday 11th August

Chapter 85

The day of Gary Hastings' funeral was, Warren felt, inappropriately warm and sunny. When an older person dies, after a long and fulfilling life, a nice, sunny send-off seems appropriate. The weather today should be grey, miserable and overcast. There was nothing to celebrate.

It had been ten days since the cataclysmic events on the Chequers estate – nine since the fall of Theo Garfield – and Warren hadn't stopped. It was his own choice of course, everyone from the Chief Constable down to Tony Sutton had told him to take time off, to deal with his grief properly. But he hadn't dared to, for fear that if he stopped, or even slowed, he'd lose the momentum necessary to finish the job. And he owed Gary that much.

Warren had worked hand-in-hand with the CPS and Professional Standards to ensure that Garfield would get everything that he deserved. The lawyers were still arguing over whether they could push for manslaughter, but misconduct in a public office and perverting the course of justice were all but guaranteed. Whether the recording Tony Sutton had made of Warren's confrontation with Garfield would be admissible in court was still a point of debate, but the Home Secretary's signature on the warrant authorising it would carry a lot of weight. It didn't really matter, Garfield had largely confessed to everything during a formal interview with Professional Standards, including eventually admitting to blackmailing Davenport to take the photographs.

Pete Robertson had uncovered evidence that the email containing the incriminating photos of Jimmy Meegan had been deleted from Tommy Meegan's phone around the time that Warren and Garfield had retrieved it from his flat. Garfield had yet to admit to tampering with the phone, but Warren could think of no other explanation.

In his halting, rambling attempt to justify his actions, Garfield had admitted to living a lie. He'd described how he'd down-played the extent of the racial abuse that he'd been forced to endure every day of his childhood; experiences that left a burning, visceral hatred for the far-right thugs who'd made his childhood so miserable. He'd been telling the truth when he told Warren of the talk he'd attended by the force's race relations representative. But he'd left out the bit where he'd found himself pouring out his heart to an increasingly concerned Greater Manchester Police recruitment officer, who had eventually suggested that joining the GMP might not be the best way to work out those demons.

'I guess they were worried that I was unstable; that the first time I came up against a bit of racial abuse I'd whip out my baton and handcuffs and mete out some justice. So I went away and reinvented myself, hiding my anger behind the famous Scouse wit. I applied to Merseyside to ensure that I didn't meet the same recruitment officer – and here I am.'

Warren couldn't care less. The lawyers were confident that Garfield would see the inside of a jail cell for at least a short period and of course his career was over. It wasn't enough, but it would have to do.

In related events, Goldie Davenport was facing a slew of charges relating to his unprovoked bottle attack on the Asian youth in Romford, whilst Bellies Brandon had done exactly as Warren and Hastings had feared and marched around to his estranged wife's house. He, too, was now facing assault charges. The CPS was deciding whether to charge Paige Brandon and Annabel Creasy over their lies.

The funeral of Jimmy Meegan had been held a few days before. He had no more family left to attend and the fatal body blow he'd dealt to the British Allegiance Party had ensured that none of his former friends had turned up to pay their respects. He'd been cremated in a private ceremony, attended only by the undertaker and the council officials leading the ceremony; his ashes would doubtless end up on a shelf, unclaimed, until they were quietly disposed of in a few decades' time. A fitting end, Warren felt.

His mother, Mary Meegan had fared a little better, with a few friends from her social club in attendance. As she'd not expressed any wishes to the contrary, she was buried in the same plot as her late husband. PC Lederer, the Family Liaison Officer who'd spent so much time with her said it was a shame that she'd be spending eternity with him.

* * *

Warren had arrived at the small Methodist chapel that the Hastings family had worshipped at for generations just a few minutes before the service was due to start. His plan had been to slip in at the back, to stay as short a time as was polite, then leave Karen and Gary's family to their private grief. As their senior officer it was unthinkable that he wouldn't attend, but he knew that he had no right to be there.

An internal investigation into the events of that night would almost certainly exonerate him and his decisions, but he knew that he had screwed up. What had he been thinking, racing around to the mother of a violent murderer without back up? Then parking in the only available space, directly below the Meegans' balcony. How stupid had he been? Garfield's accusation still rang in his ears and had haunted his dreams since.

And why had he let Gary stay in the car to take that call? He should have told him to save his personal business for when he was off-duty and forced him to get out at the same time. Then perhaps Warren would simply be awaiting the repair of the car's windscreen, not trying to work out what to do with the vehicle once his friend's blood and brain matter had been cleaned out of the upholstery. He couldn't imagine ever driving it again, yet simply scrapping it seemed disrespectful somehow, given that Gary had died in it.

Unfortunately, Warren's plan to maintain a low profile was scuppered. The funeral cortege had yet to arrive and the congregation was still standing outside the main entrance in small groups, a sea of black clothing interspersed with flashes of silver from the rank insignia on dress uniforms. Several minibuses worth of colleagues had driven the 100 miles to Gary's home town to show their support. In amongst the mourners he also spied Imam Mehmud, in muted conversation with an older, Sikh man and ACC Naseem.

Over the past few days, Susan had been his rock, even as she fought her own battles. Two days previously she had called her mother. Her voice firm but not raised, she'd told her that if nothing else, the last few days had demonstrated that life was too short for such silliness and that if she wanted to be a part of her future grandchild's life the door would remain unlocked and that Bernice could decide whether or not to walk through it. And then, dry-eyed, she'd hung up. Warren couldn't find the words he needed, but his hug had said everything he felt.

Taking a deep breath, Warren retrieved his cap and stepped out of the passenger seat, tugging his uniform into shape. His polished shoes scrunched on the gravel driveway. Immediately the conversations dried up. Warren swallowed hard; a wave of nausea passed over him and he felt a little light-headed.

First to approach him was Tony Sutton and his wife Marie; Sutton shook his hand firmly, whilst Marie gave him a big hug. After Marie had moved onto Susan, Sutton lowered his voice.

'How are you?'

Warren didn't trust himself to speak.

'It wasn't your fault. You must believe that. The inquest will show that you acted in good faith and couldn't have foreseen what would happen.'

Before Warren could reply, his hand was grabbed by both the Chief Constable and the Assistant Chief Constable in quick succession; and so it continued. Handshake after handshake, he slowly made his way to the main entrance, every step making him feel more and more like an intruder, an imposter. It was as if he was the one who had been bereaved, as if his part in the whole affair was that of the victim, rather than the man making the decisions that led to Gary's death.

The torturous procession was cut short by the announcement from the police officers holding back the press at the front gate that the hearse was due any moment. Susan's hand felt warm against Warren's clammy skin.

The gleaming car was covered in wreaths, the wooden coffin inside barely visible. The priest stepped forward to greet the undertakers. Another grind of gravel signalled the arrival of the rest of the cortege. Warren took a deep breath; this was the bit he'd dreaded most.

Warren and Sutton had visited Karen at her and Gary's flat the day after she had been discharged from hospital. It wasn't either man's first visit to the family of a dead colleague, but it was certainly the hardest. Karen had been so spaced out that the two men had spent less than twenty minutes with her before withdrawing and leaving her with her parents and Gary's, who weren't doing much better.

The passing of the past few days had aged Hardwick, but the glassy stare had gone. Warren braced himself; the denial phase had passed, what came next? Anger? It was impossible to tell behind her dark glasses. The slim, black dress was obviously pre-pregnancy, but even if Karen had started to fill out at this early stage, the weight she had lost over the past days had more than compensated for it; at least she hadn't been forced to go dress shopping for her fiancé's funeral because their unborn baby was making its presence obvious. As she stepped out of the car her mother took her elbow protectively. Again, Susan squeezed Warren's hand, as if lending him some of her strength. He felt sick.

'Karen…' he started, the sudden dryness of his mouth making his tongue feel swollen and clumsy.

'DCI Jones?' The question came from the other side of the limousine – Hastings' parents. He remembered them from the home visit and again he was struck by the similarity of Gary to his father. The men were almost precisely the same height and build; take away the grey and the laughter lines and Gary could have been standing in front of him. But, the question hadn't come from the father. Warren turned to Hastings' mother. He braced himself for the onslaught. It was nothing less than he deserved, and if it would make them feel just a little bit better he'd stand there and let them scream at him until they were hoarse.

'Thank you.'

Had he misheard?

'Thank you. My boy didn't die alone.' Her voice trembled. 'You were with him.' She looked over at DSI Grayson. 'John told me that you wouldn't let go of his hand until they made you get to safety.'

Warren couldn't say anything.

'Can we ask you to do something for us – for Gary? He always spoke so highly of you, it's what he would have wanted.' Now Gary's father had found his own voice, the exact same voice that Gary had. Warren nodded numbly, how could he say no?

And so, minutes later, Warren found himself lock-step with Tony Sutton, behind Hastings' father and the school friend Detective Sergeant Gary Hastings had asked to be his best man less than twelve hours before he died, walking deliberately slowly so not to disturb the coffin balanced upon his shoulder.

Acknowledgements

Writing a book is never a solo endeavour and it is always a great pleasure to give credit to those who have helped me. In the first instance, my ever patient beta readers Dad and Cheryl, whose eagle eyes and thoughtful suggestions immeasurably improve the first draft of anything that I hand them.

Legal process is at the heart of any police procedural, and as always my favourite lawyers Caroline and Dan are never more than a Facebook message away to advise me – any mistakes are of course all mine!

Lee, my friendly crime scene investigator, remains a fascinating source of war stories, many of which are too fantastic to commit to paper. You quite literally couldn't make up some of the stuff he's seen!

One of the things I find difficult (as my beta readers will attest!) is choosing character names; therefore I am very grateful to Jeff Tufnail for his generous donation to the Clic Sargent Get in Character charity auction – we got there in the end and I hope Laura likes her cameo!

Useful feedback from Juliet on the first draft changed the tone of the story dramatically and improved it immensely; again my heartfelt thanks.

My thanks also go out to Professor Niamh Nic Daéid, Professor of Forensic Science at the University of Dundee. A fascinating conversation at Theakston Old Peculier Crime Writing Festival in Harrogate left me with some very interesting story ideas…

Racism and Islamophobia are at the heart of this story. Researching these subjects as I wrote this story was an eye-opening experience to say the least; unpleasant, anger-inducing and (very occasionally) darkly humorous. Yet it is a topic that I have wanted to explore for a long time, and I hope I have done it justice. Many thanks therefore to my friend Charlie, for his invaluable personal insights into far-right extremism in Britain today.

Editing can make or break a novel, and as always my thanks go out to Clio Cornish and the team at HQ digital for all of their hard work. Thanks guys!

And finally to my readers. Your kind support and feedback over the past few years has given me the confidence to continue writing; so many kind people have told me that they were looking forward to reading more about Warren and his team, and so I hope it doesn't disappoint.

Best wishes,

Paul Gitsham July2018

Hello, and as always thank you for taking the time to read *The Common Enemy*.

Some years have elapsed since the last full-length outing for DCI Warren Jones, and so things have moved on a little. Warren has grown into a more seasoned investigator in that time, as have his team. His relationship with his wife Susan remains central to the story, and I hope you enjoy the new direction it has taken.

Far-right extremism and Islamophobia are the central themes of this book. It's a difficult topic to write about for many reasons, particularly for a writer who has never experienced it directly. Nevertheless, this ugly undercurrent exists within our society and to ignore its existence is naive. I hope that I have dealt with it realistically and sensitively and apologise for any offence that my characters' frank use of language may cause.

If this is your first taste of DCI Warren Jones, and you want more, then you'll be pleased to know that are several more entries in the series, and there are plenty more in the pipeline.

You can follow me on Twitter @dcijoneswriter

Visit my facebook page: www.facebook.com/dcijones or my website www.paulgitsham.com

Or email me on dcijones@outlook.com

Best wishes, Paul.

If you enjoyed The Common Enemy, *keep reading for a sneak peek at* The Last Straw, *the first book in the DCI Warren Jones series, available to download now.*

Prologue

Blood.

Everywhere. Across the walls, over the desk, even splattered on the glowing laptop computer. The human heart is a powerful, muscular pump and a cut artery bleeds out in seconds, spraying red, freshly oxygenated blood across the room like a fire hose.

Tom Spencer removes his gloved hands from the dead man's throat and rubs them down the front of his lab coat, leaving bloody trails across his chest. Hands shaking, he picks up the blood-covered telephone and presses 9 for an outside line, followed by another three 9s.

"You are through to the emergency services. Which service do you require?"

Spencer's voice is shaky, his breathing rapid. "Police. There's been a murder."

Friday

Chapter 1

Detective Chief Inspector Warren Jones slid to a halt with a faint squeak of tyres outside the main entrance to the University of Middle England's Department for Biological Sciences. Fifteen minutes had elapsed since he'd received the call and he doubted he could have done it much faster with blue lights and sirens. He switched off the engine and the sat nav on the dashboard beeped then went silent.

Two weeks into this new posting and the freshly promoted DCI was still reliant on the little device to get him around his new patch: the small Hertfordshire market town of Middlesbury. By driving everywhere with the device in map mode and where possible leaving for appointments early to take the most circuitous route, he was slowly building up a mental map of the local area. Although it was costing him a fortune in petrol — he felt guilty about passing on that cost to the force — it was the best way he knew to learn his way around.

The call could have been better timed, he supposed. He'd just finished pouring a bottle of Chilean red and was in the process of toasting his mother-in-law's upcoming birthday when his mobile had rung. The temperature in the freshly decorated lounge had dropped precipitously. Bernice had never been impressed

that her eldest daughter, Susan, had married a police officer —
feeling that she and her monosyllabic, hen-pecked husband,
Dennis, had raised their children to aspire to greater things.
Private education and all the accoutrements of a wealthy middle-
class upbringing in the leafiest part of Warwickshire had led
Bernice to expect her daughters to marry well. That being said,
she grudgingly acknowledged that Warren was a nice enough
man and at least he was a Catholic.

Mumbling his apologies, he'd slipped on a jacket and left the
house as quickly as possible.

Now that he was here, the familiar singing in the blood had
started, mixed with a tightness in his gut. He took a few deep
breaths to steady himself, whilst rummaging around for a breath
mint. He'd only had a sip of the wine, and had abstained
completely at the restaurant so that he could drive, but the last
thing he wanted was for somebody to smell alcohol on his breath.
Not on his first big case. A murder. This was what he'd joined
the force for; even more importantly what he'd trained as a detective for. For the past fortnight, he'd overseen his small team as
they dealt with the endless tide of robberies, burglaries and low-
level violence that plagued any society — a job that he was proud
to do and that he knew was important to the public. But a murder
was different. A murder was what got you known. A murder
could make your career. It could also ruin your career before it
really started...

Clambering out of the car into the hot, breathless, summer
night, he scanned the largely deserted car park. Adjacent to the
entrance an ambulance was parked up next to two police cars.
At the other end of the car park a silver BMW sports car sat
alone in the dark The ambulance's blue lights were off, but the
rear doors were open, light spilling out into the night, throwing
shadows across the thick black tarmac. The paramedics stood by,
chatting and smoking, relaxed, not expecting to have to do
anything for a while. According to the call that Warren had

received, the victim was beyond their help and they were now little more than a glorified taxi service to the morgue.

The front of the building was mostly glass, with two large, sliding doors leading into a well-lit reception area. As Jones strode briskly towards the building a young, uniformed police constable with a clipboard stepped out of the dark shadows to the side of the entrance.

"I'm sorry, sir, I'm afraid I can't let anybody enter the building at the moment."

Jones reached inside his jacket for his warrant card. "DCI Jones." Where the hell was his wallet? Bugger! He'd been in such a rush to leave, he'd grabbed the nearest suit jacket to hand. Unfortunately, it wasn't the one he'd been wearing to the office during the week and so the pockets were empty.

The young constable clearly didn't recognise either him or his name. Not for the first time, Jones regretted his forgettable surname. The PC flushed a little, clearly realising there was no way out of this awkward impasse without loss of dignity for one or both of the two men.

Fortunately, or unfortunately, the day was saved by a booming Essex voice.

"Don't you recognise the new boss, lad?" Jones suppressed a sigh. Great, his first big case and the DI first on the scene had to be Tony Sutton, the man who many believed should be the one wearing three Bath Stars on the epaulettes of his dress uniform, rather than this outsider, parachuted in from the West Midlands Police to clean up their mess.

Turning, he saw Sutton walking towards them, a barely concealed smirk on his face. Like Jones, he was dressed in a smart suit, although he wasn't wearing a tie. But there the similarities ended. Where Jones was a slim six feet one inch, Sutton was a short, squat bear of a man, his pugnacious features and crooked nose a reminder of his days on the force's rugby team. He was six years older than Jones, and most observers had expected him to be promoted when the previous DCI, Gavin Sheehy, retired. Unfortunately, Sheehy hadn't made it to retirement and although Sutton had been fully cleared of any involvement in Sheehy's disgrace he was nevertheless seen — rumour had it — to be too close to the shamed detective to be given such an important role. At least not yet. Hence Warren's sudden and unexpected appointment.

"Sorry, sir." The young lad was blushing now.

Jones patted him on the shoulder encouragingly. "Never apologise for doing your job, son."

Son? Bloody hell, when did I get so old that I call twenty-year-old constables "son"? thought Warren.

Putting aside his discomfort, Jones walked to join Sutton, who led them through the front doors into the lobby. Inside was a large reception desk with a computer and a bank of telephones, behind a reinforced glass screen, rather like a bank teller. To the right of the desk two large double doors were held open by another uniformed PC. A swipe-card lock flashed red and an angry-sounding electronic alarm buzzed insistently, no doubt triggered by the door being held open so long.

"What have we got, Tony?"

"Nasty one, guv. White middle-aged man, identified as a Professor Alan Tunbridge, throat slit right open and head bashed in, sitting in his office."

Sutton led Jones up a flight of stairs to the right of the entrance, before proceeding along a wide open corridor deeper into the building.

"Who found the body?"

"A young man named Tom Spencer, apparently one of the late professor's students. Claims he was working late, came back to the lab and noticed the prof's office door was open and the lights on. Figured he'd pop his head round and say 'Hi'. Found him in his chair, blood everywhere. Reckons he took his pulse but couldn't find anything, then phoned 999 on the office phone."

"What state is the crime scene in?"

"Untouched, except by Spencer. Two uniforms were first to respond and were let in by campus Security. They took one look and figured there was nothing they could do for him. Paramedics arrived a few minutes later and agreed, pronounced him dead at the scene, probably from loss of blood. Yours truly arrived just after the paramedics. Scenes of crime are on their way."

At the end of the corridor, Jones and Sutton turned a corner. "Here it is," said Sutton somewhat unnecessarily.

The corridor was crowded; two pale-looking uniformed constables were standing guard either side of an open office door. A couple of middle-aged men wearing blue woollen jumpers with 'Security' stitched in white writing on the left of the chest leant against the opposite wall, looking decidedly shaken. Standing awkwardly, answering questions to a uniformed sergeant, and looking like the demon barber of Fleet Street, stood a young man in a blood-stained white lab coat. His hands were covered in white latex gloves, also smeared with blood. A surgical face mask, rather like the ones worn by carpenters or DIY enthusiasts, hung on an elastic band around his chin. His shoes were blood spattered and crimson footprints led from the open office door to him.

Slipping his hands into his pockets and moving as close to the door as he could without stepping in any blood, Jones peered into the office and almost wished he hadn't.

As a detective with many years of experience, Jones was used to the sight of blood, of course. But this broke new ground. It looked as if every last millilitre of the life-giving red liquid had been forcibly ejected from the man's body. The pasty, greyish-blue tint of the corpse's skin confirmed the observation. He could see why the responding officers hadn't felt the need to contaminate the scene by checking his pulse. The Scenes of Crime team would have to check with the paramedics to see if they had touched the body.

The late professor had been a man in his fifties, with a shock of grey, unruly hair. About average height and weight for a man of his age, he was clad in brown corduroy trousers and a white polo shirt. That was about all that Jones could make out amidst the blood. The man was slumped to one side in a comfortable-looking padded leather office chair, pointed halfway towards the office's only door. The seat was a swivel chair, positioned so that the occupant could easily operate the laptop, answer the phone and reach the various pieces of paper that were piled carelessly on the remaining surface of the desk. A selection of different-coloured ballpoint pens was scattered across the work-space. A clear area to the right of the laptop suggested a space for a mouse.

The professor's throat had been slit, clearly by something very sharp. Whoever had wielded the blade had done so efficiently. It looked to Jones' eye as if the blade had managed to sever both carotid arteries. If that was the case, it put a different complexion on the attack. Contrary to Hollywood movies, cutting the throat of a surprised man wasn't a simple affair. The victim would almost certainly have struggled. Looking closer, Jones could see that, aside from the cut throat, the back of the professor's head — facing away from the doorway — looked to be a bloody mess. On the floor next to the chair sat what appeared to be a large lump of granite rock on a pedestal, blood and matted hair covering a particularly prominent edge. Jones could just make out the words "Boulder, Colorado" stencilled on the base. A souvenir perhaps? Significant or not?

Jones turned to Sutton.

"First impressions, Inspector?" he asked quietly. Jones was already formulating a theory himself, but he liked to see what others had to say first.

"I reckon he was sitting at the desk, probably working on his laptop by the looks of it. Whoever did it came up behind him and whacked him over the back of the head with that bloody great lump of rock. That probably stunned him enough for his attacker to slit his throat."

Jones nodded. "The question is, why didn't he turn around? It looks as though he was facing away from the doorway when he was hit. And then, did his chair turn around after he was hit or whilst his throat was being slit?"

"Well, either the attacker sneaked up on him, or he knew his attacker was around and wasn't surprised by their approach."

Jones nodded his agreement.

"And what about the angle of his chair?"

"Too early to speculate."

"I agree, let's not second-guess Scenes of Crime." Jones was pleased with Sutton's response. He was always a little wary of officers who jumped to conclusions without all of the facts. Good detectives, he felt, tempered their deductive reasoning with caution and were honest enough to admit ignorance, rather than stretching the evidence beyond breaking point.

With nothing else to be gained from the bloody office, Jones turned away from the carnage. He glanced at his watch: eleven p.m.

You were complaining how bored you were, Warren. Well, you know what they say: 'be careful what you wish for'.

It looked as though Susan and the in-laws would have to finish the wine without him.

If you enjoyed *The Common Enemy*, why not try another twisty crime novel from HQ Digital?

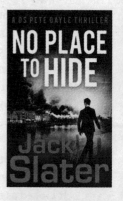

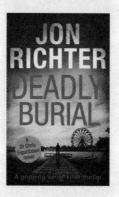